Xylene

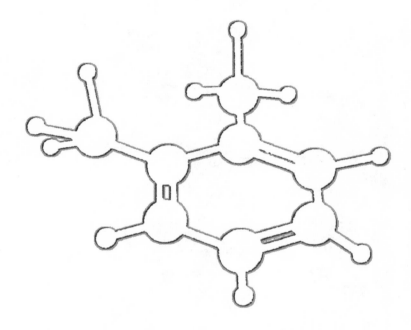

X Band

A fictionalized chapter in the history of X Band
by Charles Harvey

book #40

Cover art by Jasper Harvey

"I don't feel like I'm reading a book. I feel like someone's telling me a story."

— Sienna Volpe

X

"I literally laughed out loud more times reading this book than all the books I've read till now. When I got to the end of the book, I cried. And when I read it a second time, even knowing what would happen, I cried again. This would be one of my favorite books even if I didn't know my dad wrote it."

— Jasper Harvey

X

"Perhaps you should try a different plot and employ a different method of writing."

— [Name redacted]

X

"As the book progressed, and I got deeper into it, I couldn't stop reading it! I felt for Angie and Joe, and I really hated Stu. Characters that evoke feeling (good or bad) are interesting; I felt like they were real people. Altogether a good job."

— Robert "The Smart Guy" Hilton

Suddenly serious, he asked, "What is Angie to you, Joe?"

"Oh, I'm crazy in love with her. I've been with her almost constantly for months now, and I still feel like I'm gettin to know her. An with every little discovery, I lover even more. You know, a couple a weeks ago, she started calling me 'Mike'."

"So?"

"She doesn't just see me as a crazy Joe. She sees me as a different person."

Ed stroked his goatee and wondered if *he* saw New Joe as a different person. He knew he was different, but it was hard to see it, because he was Joe. He was in Joe's body. "And this is important why?"

"I need her to see the distinction, because I want to win her over. I want her to love *me*."

Ed was about to exclaim, "Of course she loves you! She married you!" But he saw that she had not. Not Mike. He asked Joe, "So you want to steal her away from Joe?"

"Yes."

"You realize she's married, right? Married to Joe?" Ed couldn't believe he was having this discussion with Joe. It was getting unreal.

"Yes," declared Joe. "But really, she belongs with me. She'd be happier, I think."

"Happier with you than with Joe?" Ed asked. "Do you think she would actually consider divorcing Joe to be with you?"

"No, I dunno," Joe admitted. "She's been with Joe for a long time." Ed started to speak, but Joe said, "Wait. She wouldn't have to. Hey!"

"Yeah," said Ed drily. "Maybe you've got a shot."

Dedication

For everyone who discovers that they're stuck doing what they hate because they're good at it.

Table of Contents

Chapter 1

Joe

Sam Foley, the sound engineer, actually didn't lose his temper; he decided to express his anger, and his decision turned out to be, literally, life-changing.

By Sam's experience, the sound engineer secludes himself with the raw recordings and polishes them into music. Occasionally, a member of the band drops by. Sam should have known better, though; he had been given this assignment because his predecessors had self-destructed.

Joe Ecks had been over his shoulder the whole time pulling his strings. And pulling. And pulling. And tweaking and twisting and pushing and on and on and on. Sam figured (correctly) that he had been patient longer than any mortal could be. He rose and stared Joe in the eyes and shouted, "What is *wrong* with you? We've been working over this same song for six days, and it's as good as it's gonna get! Besides, you've got some good songs on this album, so what are you worried about? You're all set for the rest of your life!"

The others in the room, Angie, Bill, and Patty, stiffened. It had been a long seven weeks in the tiny mixing room, and the clouds had been glooming. Lightning had struck, and now the storm would hit.

Joe Ecks stopped his pacing and stared at Sam, not with the fury that Sam had expected, but with an expression half despair, half terror and half desperation. Normally, Joe had a presence that filled any room he was in. Twenty-five years old, he stood at a lean 6'1", 190 lbs. Today he wore a black T-shirt over his sculpted torso. His black hair was tied back to a ponytail, and his dark eyes, the eyes that normally drilled holes through Sam's soul, begged Sam to put him out of his misery. And then, Joe doubled forward as if he'd taken a sucker-punch to the gut. Then he was jerked upright by an unseen hand. He staggered back for balance, stumbled over a chair, and both went down. He didn't move.

Angie flew to Joe's side and held up his inert head. His face was gray, his lips blue. She thought he was dead. Then Joe inhaled heartily, and life returned. "Joe, are you all right?"

"What happened?" Sam asked. He had grown to truly hate Joe, but he was concerned nonetheless. A true capital C Christian, forgiveness was Sam's superpower.

Bill Myers knelt beside Joe. He asked Angie, "Is he okay?"

Joe opened his eyes, focused on Angie and on Bill, and then back on Angie.

"Are you okay, Joe?"

"I'm okay." Joe struggled and sat up on the floor. Wincing, he put both hands on his head. "Swate Jasus."

"Does your head hurt?" Angie asked.

"Lack hail," Joe answered. His hands explored the surface of his head and his ponytail. He looked at Angie in confusion. Then he looked at Bill. "Hey," he said.

"What?" Bill asked.

"Huh? Oh, just 'hey'." Weakly, Joe tried to stand. Patty righted the chair, and Bill and Angie helped him into it. He looked around the small room and sniffed disapprovingly. Nodding to Sam and Patty, he said, "Hey."

They didn't answer. They stared.

Joe looked at the console with its hundreds of rows of knobs with large cassettes thrown around on top. Several water bottles perched on the edge of the console. The room had no windows.

Sam said, "Patty, call an ambulance."

"Fer what? A headache?" Joe said crossly. "I'm fine."

Patty didn't move.

Sam ventured, "Well, okay. Do you want to hear it again?" He was stunned that his outburst had been forgotten.

"Uh, okay," Joe agreed.

Sam sat back down and pulled himself to the console. He flipped a few switches and waited a minute. Joe rubbed his temples. And his face.

Angie rummaged in her purse. She withdrew several prescription bottles, opened one and tapped out two pills. "Take these," she said, holding them out to Joe.

Joe put them in his mouth. "What are they?"

"Codeine. For your head."

Joe swallowed them.

"Do you want to wash them down?" Angie asked. Everyone was watching Joe.

Joe looked around the room again, eyeing the water bottles. "No, thank you."

"All right, ready?" Sam asked.

Joe shrugged. "Sure."

Sam flipped a switch and turned a knob. After a second, music filled the room. A hammering keyboard solo led into a matching drum beat with distinct bass undertones. "You laugh but you don't get the joke," a voice belted out. "You'd like another line of coke." Joe listened to the song, nodding his head. Bill leaned against the console. The song thundered to its conclusion, and Sam flipped another switch. No one spoke. They looked at Joe.

"Yeah, I like it," Joe finally said.

Sam asked, "The way it is?"

Joe nodded. "Sure." He opened his mouth to say something, thought the better of it, and just said, "Yep. I like it."

No one stirred. They waited for the 'but'. Finally, Bill said, "I guess that's a wrap. Print it, Sam."

Sam turned back to the console. "Sounds good."

"Well, okay," Bill said, "I guess that's it for today." To Patty, he said, "Have our car brought around."

Angie said, "We'll see you tomorrow, Sam. Good night."

Angie and Bill left the room. Joe followed uncertainly. They walked down a hallway. The rooms on either side were empty and dark. Joe looked into several of them curiously. Angie and Bill reached the elevator doors. Bill pushed the button. Presently, the door opened. They held the door until Joe got on.

The elevator descended and opened into a rather expansive—and empty—lobby. They crossed the lobby, and went through the revolving door. Outside, Joe looked around. It wasn't just night. It was Advanced Night. The vast parking lot accommodated just two cars, not including a white limousine idling in front. A uniformed man stood beside the limo. "Here's our ride," Joe joked.

The man opened the back door. Angie got in. Then Bill. Joe stood by with a half-grin on his face, speechless. "Get in," Bill said. Joe got in. Angie sat on one side facing the front, and Bill sat on the other, facing the back. Joe slid in beside Angie. The man closed the door. Soon, the limo pulled away.

"How's your head?" Angie asked. She was concerned about Joe. He seemed disoriented. Unsure.

"It's feelin better," Joe answered. He looked out the window.

The limo passed several tall buildings then headed up the entrance ramp to the highway. The streets were vacant.

Joe looked at his bare wrist. "What time is it?" he asked Bill.

"About 2:40," Bill answered, studying him.

Joe blinked in surprise and looked back out the window. After a few minutes, he said, "It looks like we're in California."

Bill leaned forward. "Joe, do you know what day it is?"

"Um. Yeah, May 3rd. 1985."

Bill nodded. "Well, actually it's May 4th now, but you're essentially correct. Do you know your name?"

"Joe?" Joe guessed.

"You don't really know, do you?"

"I thought I did," Joe admitted, "but I dunno. Seems like I'm out-voted."

"What's my name?"

Joe frowned as he studied Bill. Bill was older than Angie, maybe in his 40s. He wore tortoise-shell glasses and an LA Dodgers cap. Then Joe smiled. "I know! You're Bill Myers! From X Band! You're the keyboardist." He turned and studied Angie. Then he turned back to Bill. "Am I right?"

"And how do you know that?" Bill asked.

"You're on the cover of 'Xenon'. And I saw you in concert, twice! Geez! Bill Myers!"

Angie asked, "Do you recognize me?"

Joe frowned again in concentration. Angie was young, maybe 22 or 3. She had brilliant red hair pulled back and sharp green eyes over a tiny nose and thin lips. Joe gave up and shook his head. "I'll bet I should, though, right?"

Angie looked at Bill. "He has amnesia!" she blurted. "From that fall?"

Bill shook his head slowly. "No, amnesia doesn't usually come from a blow to the head. Usually, it's caused by personal trauma. And the person who has it can remember facts, but nothing of their personal life. There was a guy who deduced he was Catholic from the fact that he knew all the Catholic mass responses. Joe, what do you know about X Band?"

"Their first album was 'Xylophone'. It was a good album. The big hit there was 'Tina', but 'See Me', 'Free Radical' and some others were good songs. Next was 'Xenon' with the hit single 'Let's Move'. Let's see, Joe Ecks does guitar and vocals. Bill Myers—you—plays keyboards, Ed Brettington plays drums, and Roger Novak plays bass. They—well, you, I guess—have a new album coming out soon, I hear."

The three rode in silence for a long minute. The only sound was the limo thumping over the lines on the highway.

Then Joe said, "Oh, hell, I'm Joe Ecks, aren't I?"

No one answered.

Joe held out his hand to Angie and said, "Hello. I'm Joe Ecks, apparently."

Instinctively, Angie took his hand, and they shook. "Uh," she said, "I'm Angela Brettington Ecks. You call me 'Angie'." To Angie, Joe's hand felt cool and dry. The way he held her hand was different.

Joe's eyebrows lifted. "'Angela Brettington Ecks'. Are we brother n sister?"

"No, Joe," answered Angie. "I'm Ed's sister. And your wife."

Joe made a motion to push up his glasses, although he wasn't wearing any and never had. He blinked. "My wife! Swate Jasus." He cleared his throat and fidgeted, and then he seemed to compose himself. "Okay. Where're we goin now?"

"Back to the hotel," Bill answered. "So—"

Angie interrupted. "We should take him to the hospital. He's had a seizure or something, and now he's acting strange. Someone should check him out."

Bill asked, "You want to take *Joe Ecks* to an emergency room?"

"I feel fine," mentioned Joe. His words were lost.

Indignant, Angie answered, "He could be having a stroke! Yes! I don't care if it causes a fuss, he needs medical care!"

"I'm not having a stroke," Joe told Angie. "Strokes have specific symptoms, and I'm not presenting any of them. If I had a seizure, then I may be in a post-seizure fugue state, in which case I will recover soon. The only thing we have to worry about is the occurrence of a subsequent seizure." Joe looked from Angie to Bill. "Do I have a history of seizures?"

Bill shook his head while Angie answered, "No. You've never had one." She noticed that Joe was being unusually analytical. And calm. Especially for someone in a post-seizure fugue state, whatever that was.

"Then I'd say that risk is minimal," Joe concluded. "But I should probably mention it to my doctor at my next check-up."

The limo thumped along. Bill asked, "You don't want to see a doctor?"

Joe said, "I don't think it's necessary." He added, "If anything changes, then, yeah, maybe."

Bill asked, "You really feel all right?"

Joe answered, "Probably what I need most is a good night's sleep."

Bill prodded, "But you really feel all right."

Joe said, "Except for my headache, yeah, and that big problem with my identity."

Bill nodded in thought. "So you know about X Band. What do you know about Joe Ecks's personal life?"

"Not much," Joe admitted. "I didn't know he was married. No offense, Mrs. Ecks," he said to Angie. "That's big. I mean, that's a big thing to not know about. I don't know where Joe's from. Or anything, really." Joe again tried to push up his glasses, then tried to make it look like what he meant to do was rub his eyebrows. His fingers touched and explored a scar that crossed his left eyebrow. "I'm Joe Ecks," he mused. "I don't *feel* like Joe Ecks. Is this an elaborate gag? No, the inside of my mouth feels weird!" He touched his front teeth with his fingers.

Bill said, "Let's hope it's temporary. If you get some rest, maybe your memory will return." He looked at Angie. "I wouldn't panic yet."

"But Bill," Angie objected, "we have to get back to the studio tomorrow and start mixing 'Xylene'."

Bill replied, "We have to bring Joe. Sam won't do anything without him, because he knows he'll have to do it over." Bill shrugged as he said, "Maybe working will bring back his memory. It can't hurt. If Sam asks any questions about Joe, we can say he was up sick all night and is really tired."

"Yes, that sounds good, I guess," Angie agreed.

The limo took an exit from the freeway. Joe was absorbed with looking out the window.

"Joe," Angie said, her voice slightly louder than normal, "We're going to be mixing another song…"

"Yeah," Joe said, not removing his gaze from the window. Then, without inflection, he said, "But Bill, we have to get back to the studio tomorrow and start mixing 'Xylene'. We have to bring Joe. Sam won't do anything without him, because he knows he'll have to do it over. Maybe working will bring back his memory. It—"

"I'm sorry, Joe, I didn't know you were listening," Angie interrupted.

"There's nothing wrong with your short-term memory," Bill observed.

The limo slowed for a stop sign then proceeded ahead.

"Are we keeping my amnesia a secret?" Joe asked.

Bill and Angie exchanged glances. "For right now, it's probably a good idea," Bill suggested. "We really don't need Michael to hear about this."

Angie nodded.

The limo pulled into a hotel parking lot and swung over to the main entrance. The hotel was enormous, and it would fill a city block, if there were city blocks out here in the pseudo-suburbs. The building was modern and clean, as if the outside of it was routinely washed, all twenty stories of it. The landscaping was meticulous, even though it was obvious that if it weren't carefully maintained, it would die in seconds. In nearby areas *not* maintained, the local natural flora was dirt. But around the hotel, it was lush.

A uniformed man stepped to the limo and opened the door, standing at attention beside it. Joe hopped out. Angie and Bill followed. Another man opened the hotel lobby doors for the three of them as the limo door closed, and the limo pulled away. They walked in. The lobby was decorated with expensive southwestern Native-American artifacts made in China. It was utterly empty except for one man behind the ostentatiously long front desk.

They approached the man, who was in his 40s with leather-colored skin and short dark hair plastered to his head. "You have messages," he told them. He handed Angie a wad of notes and letters, saying simply, "Mr. and Mrs. Ecks." He handed a somewhat smaller stack to Bill, saying, "Mr. Myers."

The trio headed for the elevators. Joe stopped and turned to the man. "Thank you, Miguel. Good night."

The man didn't answer, and the two of them stood looking at each other awkwardly. Then Joe turned to join Angie and Bill, and as he turned, the man answered, "Good night to you, Mr. Ecks! Good night, sir!"

The elevator door opened, and everyone got on it. "What floor are you on, Mr. Myers?" Joe asked.

Then the door closed. Bill and Angie smiled at each other. Joe looked at them with puzzled amusement. He asked, "Is something funny?"

"Joe," Angie explained, "you've never spoken to Miguel. That's why he was so surprised."

"Yeah, I was wonderin why he just stood there. I thought maybe he didn't hear me."

"I'm on the 4th floor, Joe," Bill said.

Joe pushed the button. The elevator started to go up. "Uh, what floor are we on?" he asked Angie.

"Twenty-one," she answered and started digging in her purse.

Joe looked at the buttons. They only went up to twenty. He turned to Angie. "Are we on the roof?"

Angie produced a keycard and put it in an unlabeled slot under the elevator buttons. At the ding, she withdrew the card and put it back in her purse.

Joe raised his eyebrows in understanding.

"Let's meet at the limo at 11:00," Bill said to Angie.

She agreed as Bill got off the elevator on his floor. The door closed, and the elevator resumed its upward journey.

Angie broke the awkward silence. "How's your head?"

"Good. Perfect. I actually feel very good. Real tired, though."

Angie nodded.

"What happened to me?" Joe asked. "I was on the floor. Was I drunk?"

"No," Angie answered. "Uh, Sam asked you a question, and you had a seizure, it looked like. You fell over the chair. For a second, I thought you had died."

"Really," Joe mused. "Huh."

"How did you know Miguel's name, Joe?" Angie asked.

"Huh? Oh, I read it off his name tag."

The elevator door opened to the sunken foyer of a penthouse suite. The foyer had a pink marble floor and big potted plants. Three very wide steps led up to an expansive living room. The living room was populated with unused furniture. Tall windows opened over a great expanse of southern California, mostly dark. Joe wandered off the elevator into the foyer, dumbfounded. He drifted up the stairs to the living room and took in its expansiveness, pausing to touch a table or chair as if to assure himself of its reality.

On the left wall was a large, ornately framed mirror flanked by sconces. Joe drifted toward it, mesmerized by his reflection. Joe's dark eyes were set in a face all smooth planes and angles. He had a strong jaw-line and masculine chin. He opened his mouth and closed it. He touched his stubbled face and the vertical scar that ran through his left eyebrow. "Swate Jasus," he muttered.

He went into the kitchen and returned shortly with his mouth still open. He went through another door into the lounge. Then he returned. He was speechless.

"The bedroom is upstairs," Angie told him, indicating a stair-way to a mezzanine. "Actually, there are three bedrooms upstairs."

"How many square feet is this place?"

Angie smiled. "I don't know that."

"Is it expensive?"

"Yes."

Joe nodded slowly. He asked, "Can we afford it?"

"Yes."

Joe nodded again and murmured, "Wow."

Angie took a step toward the stairs then stopped. "Do you want to go upstairs? We normally go to bed now. It's late."

"Actually, I was gonna go out on the patio and have a smoke, but I don't seem to have any. Do you know where the cigarettes are?"

Angie didn't move. She explained, "Joe, you don't smoke. You never have."

Joe looked at Angie with disbelief. Then he just said, "Oh. Huh." Shrugging, he said, "Yeah, I'm tired."

Joe followed Angie up the stairs. The mezzanine had a coffee table, a cabinet and a couple of chairs. Off the mezzanine were the bedrooms. Angie headed into the master bedroom and turned on the light. Joe hung back. Angie looked at him.

"Um," Joe stammered. "Uh."

"Is something wrong?" Angie inquired. Joe seemed troubled.

Finally, Joe seemed to sort through something, and he said, "Okay. Which room is mine?"

"This room," Angie told him, "is *our* room."

"Yeah," Joe said. He entered the room.

"There's the bathroom," Angie pointed out. "You have the blue toothbrush."

Gratefully, Joe retreated into the bathroom. Angie could hear him opening and closing the medicine cabinets and sliding the shower stall door. She flipped through the messages from Miguel. She sorted the messages according to subject and left the piles on the dresser just so. She took off her shoes and socks and lined them up as Joe had specified to her weeks before. As Joe was brushing his teeth, she took off her blouse and wriggled out of her tight khaki shorts. At 5'2", Angie weighed a compact 95 lbs, and she never dared allow it to stray a pound higher. She put her clothes in the hamper. She removed her barrettes and fluffed her hair, and allowed it to fall casually past her shoulders. After ten minutes, about twenty minutes earlier than Angie had expected, Joe came out of the bathroom. He'd removed his shirt and boots, but not his pants.

"Um," Joe said. "Where're my jammies?" Seeing Angie in her undergarments, he abruptly studied the bedside table. "Uh, Mrs. Ecks..." he stammered to the table. "Uh."

Angie instinctively felt self-conscious about her state of undress, which was of course ridiculous, since she'd been married to Joe for over three years. And then she found his reaction endearing. Boyish and innocent and unnecessarily... respectful? And with a dash of terror. Angie smiled. "Your 'jammies'? You don't have jammies. You sleep in your underwear."

"Get out," Joe declared to the table. "I don't even have underwear on. Just these shorts." Joe looked down. "Well," he explained, "they're under my pants." He forced his eyes up to meet Angie's eyes, and this lasted for almost a second before they dropped down to behold Angie's intimate apparel.

Coyly, Angie shifted her stance.

Joe quickly diverted his gaze to the dresser behind Angie. "Oh, are those the messages Miguel gave you?" he asked.

Angie turned. "Yes, I set them out for you," she explained. "Of course, without your memory, they may not mean much to you. But you can look at them."

Joe picked up a stack and flipped through them. "Do we hafta answer all of these?"

"No, that pile, we forward to Stu, and he handles it. Stu is our agent. This other pile is junk. You know, ads and stuff. This pile is business. You have a message from Stu, and you can call him in the morning."

"Why didn't he call me at the other place? The studio?"

Angie smiled. "He knows better than to interrupt your work. Anyway, this other pile is personal stuff. Invitations, for example, and here you got a call from Douglas. Douglas is our estate manager back home. I usually handle all the personal things after you look at them."

"Wow, this is a lot," Joe commented. "But all I hafta do is call Stu? And the other stuff is taken care of by other people?"

Angie hesitated. "Bill wants to keep your amnesia a secret, so maybe it's better if you don't call Stu tomorrow. I'll call him so it doesn't arouse suspicion."

Joe shrugged. "You know what's best."

"Are you done in the bathroom already?"

"Yeah."

Angie picked up her silk nightshirt and disappeared in the bathroom. Normally she would have changed in front of Joe, but he'd been so embarrassed just now. She didn't want to make his head explode. When she came out of the bathroom, Joe was in the bed. He was at the extreme far edge of the king-size bed, facing away. Normally, Joe didn't like casual personal contact, but he seemed somehow different and vulnerable. Angie decided to risk rebuke. She slipped under the covers and snuggled up to Joe. He didn't move. His breathing didn't change. Angie held him for a moment, wondering what had happened to her husband and what was going to happen tomorrow. Then she thought about what was happening now. She was holding her husband in their bed. Safe. She fell asleep.

Angie awoke, and her arms were empty. Joe was not in the bed. Early morning light shot through a gap in the curtains. Angie got out of bed. She found Joe downstairs in the lounge. He was sitting in an overstuffed easy chair, examining his hand. He stared at the palm of his left hand, slowly opening and closing it. He looked up when Angie came in the room.

"Good morning," he said.

Perplexed, Angie asked, "What are you doing up?"

"I can't ever sleep much past 8:00 anyway, and that's Eastern Time. But here on the west coast... Well, I'm surprised I slept as late as I did."

Angie sat on the loveseat. "What are you talking about?"

Joe moved to push up glasses, then dropped his hand in frustration. "Mrs. Ecks," he said, "I have to tell you this. I don't have any memories of myself as Joe Ecks, but I have memories of myself as someone else. I remember myself as being Mike Smith. I just graduated from the Harvard School of Business, and soon I'll be in the GE Management Training Program. I... feel like I'm someone else. Look at my hand." Joe said, holding out his left hand, palm up. "I thought I was missin a piece of my ring finger. I cut it on a piece of glass when I was little. But now it's perfect, 'cept I've got these really thick calluses. But how can this be? How can I remember so many things that can't possibly be? I thought I wore glasses, and now I don't. I thought I was shorter than this. I don't sound right to myself." He looked right into Angie's deep green eyes. "I must be losing my mind. But I *feel* sane. But that doesn't mean much, really; doesn't every insane person think they're sane?"

Angie crossed her arms, aware that the outlines of her nipples were visible through the thin material of her nightshirt. This was the most agitated Angie had seen Joe since he lost his memory, and yet he still seemed more in control of himself than he had in a long time. And yet, these alternate memories... "What *are* these other memories?"

"A whole life," Joe answered. "It's like I was a whole 'nother person. If you'd a asked me who I was, I woulda said Mike Smith. I have so *many* memories. And they're so *vivid*." Joe spread his hands. "Okay, so I'm obviously *not* Mike Smith. But I *feel* like I am. That's not amnesia; that's Multiple Personality Disorder. My existence—me—is, I guess, a construction of Joe's mind in response to some tragedy. And to support the false personality, Joe's mind musta fabricated a whole history to substantiate it."

Angie leaned back and reconsidered Joe. Split personality made sense. Joe's behavior was different. Not like he'd only lost his memory. A Joe without memories would still be Joe. But then, Joe hadn't been himself in the last three years. Except, there were times—the break after 'Xenon', the cruise they'd taken, their honeymoon—when Joe would clamp down on his anxieties and force himself to relax. That Joe was not like this Joe.

Joe sighed. "I don't know what to do. My gut says to fake it until something happens. I don't want to do anything irreversible." Joe glanced around the penthouse suite until his eyes returned to Angie. He asked, "What do *you* wanna do?"

"Whatever you want to do," Angie replied automatically.

Chapter 2

Xylene

Angie went back to bed, alone. She dozed fitfully for an hour and then decided she'd better get the day started.

She guessed Joe was sleeping downstairs. She decided to let him sleep while she showered, so the bathroom would be all his when he woke. The risk was she might still be in the shower when Joe wanted it. But she didn't want to wake him to ask what to do. Her decision proved correct; she was out of the bathroom, dressed, and applying make-up when, at the ajar bedroom door, Joe knocked lightly.

Angie wore a form-fitting white Hard Rock Café T-shirt from Praha, and dark blue jeans, also snug. Her rich, red hair draped over her shoulders limp with water. She wore small, wire-framed glasses. "Good morning, Joe," she greeted warmly. "Did you manage to get any more sleep?"

"No," he answered, drifting into the room. "Did you?"

"I did, yes," Angie admitted. "I think I know why you couldn't sleep. You didn't take any of your pills last night. I should have checked. I'm sorry."

"What pills?"

"Your sleeping pill, blood pressure, stomach acid, and anti-depressant," Angie answered. "I put your morning pills on the counter in the bathroom."

"I don't need those pills," Joe told Angie. "Do I?"

Angie hesitated and said, "The doctors say you do..."

"Swate Jasus," Joe remarked. "I'm a mess. But, yeah, okay, thanks. Thank you." Joe hesitated. "Angie, uh, pardon me for asking, but, uh, do you have freckles on one side of your face?"

"I'm covering them," she told Joe, "with make-up." Joe didn't like freckles.

"Oh," said Joe.

Angie said, "I'm done in the bathroom if you want to take your shower now."

"I don't think I'll shower today, if that's okay."

Angie thought (hopefully) maybe Joe was kidding. "Well, I don't know," she said carefully. "We have to spend a long day in a little room with other people. But it's up to you."

"Yeah, good point," Joe conceded. "Where are my clothes?"

"I'll lay them out. They'll be ready for you."

"That's nice of you. Thanks." Joe went in the bathroom and shut the door.

Angie stared at the closed door for a long time. Putting out Joe's clothes was one of those things, like keeping track of Joe's medications, that started out being her favor. But with repetition, Joe had come to expect it, then demand it, until Angie was afraid to *not* put out his clothes. The transition from favor to obligation was imperceptible. And insidious.

The starting shower shook her from her musings. She went to his dresser and got out dress pants and a print shirt. She had tried many, many combinations before understanding Joe's eccentric taste in clothes, and even now, she still didn't always get it right. She got out the rest of his clothes and laid them out. Then she called room service for breakfast.

While Angie blow-dried her hair, she pondered this change in Joe. If the business pressure stopped crushing him, Angie assumed he would return to his old self. But Joe had *always* been meticulous and driven with a strong need to excel at everything. This memoryless Joe was none of these. He was quiet and compliant. Unassuming. Almost the opposite of Joe, even Young Joe. Or was there something in Joe's amnesia-obstructed past that made him driven to excel? Angie considered the alternate personality angle, but was doubtful. Memory loss was weird enough, but split personality? Did that even happen, really?

Angie switched off the blow dryer. Minutes later, Joe came out of the bathroom and started putting his clothes on. This was easily half an hour before Angie expected him. Joe usually spent well over an hour in the bathroom showering, shaving, brushing, trimming and who knows what else. Admiring, maybe. Angie still had to put in her contacts.

"Are you going to shave before breakfast?" she asked. Joe had a sparse beard that made him look like a wino if he didn't keep it shaved. So Joe shaved every day without fail. He would sometimes shave a second time in a day if something public was happening that evening. So his face was always baby-smooth.

"I thought I'd skip it today," Joe said. "Besides, I can't find the razor. Unless I use a Lady Remington."

Angie smiled. "No, you use a straight razor. It's on the counter, I think."

Joe didn't move. "No way. I ain't usin a straight razor. I'd use the leg shaver first."

"Well, what would you like to use?"

"A Norelco electric razor. The one with three heads."

"Okay, I'll call the front desk," Angie said as she went to the phone.

"But I'm okay for now," Joe said as Angie picked up the phone. "You don't need to bother."

"I'm fine, thank you," Angie said into the phone as Joe looked on. "I'd like a Norelco electric razor, with the three heads, sent up immediately." She listened to the reply. "If you don't, in an hour is fine. Thank you." She hung up.

Joe said slowly, "Or we could get an electric razor right away. Thank you. I guess I'd better dry my hair now." He slid back into the bathroom.

Angie waited for the blow dryer to start up before putting in her contacts. Then she pulled back her hair. The blow dryer shut off. Joe came out of the bathroom, his hair an ugly mess.

"Joe, what did you do?"

"Well, I tried to blow dry my hair, but I must a done it wrong. I got this side dry, and by the time I got this part dry, the first part was all frizzy like this."

A little smile softened Angie's face. "Well," she suggested, "we can put it in a pony-tail. Don't you remember how to use a blow dryer?"

"No, I don't even have one. I used to have short, curly hair."

Deliberately changing the subject, Angie asked, "Are you ready for breakfast?"

The hotel staff had set up breakfast in the dining room so silently, it seemed to have just magically appeared. Joe was delighted with the spread, and he ate an obscene number of waffles saturated in syrup. Angie nibbled on about four strawberries.

When Joe started to fill up, he asked about their plans for the day.

"Well," answered Angie, "we meet Bill at the limo at 11:00. Then we go to the studio and begin working on 'Xylene'. We usually quit around 1:00 or 2:00. I'll be in and out making calls and so forth."

Joe moved to push up his glasses, then fingered the scar through his eyebrow. "Oh. Well, I suppose you gotta do those things." He checked his bare wrist. "What time is it?"

Angie checked her watch. "It's 10:41. We ought to get ready to leave." She rose from the table.

A knock at the service door. "That must be the razor." Angie opened the door and picked up a small box containing the electric razor. She gave it to Joe, and he went upstairs and shaved. Shortly, he returned.

They got in the elevator. Angie pushed LL. "This time of day," she explained, "we can't go through the lobby."

The elevator descended five floors and stopped to let on a woman with two teenage sons of differing ganglinesses. Angie tensed. The woman pushed L. Angie saw one of the boys nudge the other, and they both looked conspicuously at Joe. Joe met their glances. "Hey," he said to them. The taller of them answered in kind. The woman looked over her shoulder to make sure Joe wasn't being dangerous.

Angie relaxed when she saw how Joe handled the kids. He wasn't acting like Mr. Big Time as in, "Hey, even though I'm a big rock star, I can still condescend to talk to nobodies like you." It generally turned admiring fans into disenchanted ex-fans. Angie and the other band members worked to insulate Joe from the public. Stu had even hired a public relations coach (who quit after two weeks). The elevator stopped at L. The woman hurried off the elevator with her sons loping behind. The taller one turned and said, "See ya, Joe!"

"Not if ya go blind," Joe quipped as the doors closed.

A moment passed, and Angie remarked, "That was cool."

Not understanding, Joe replied, "Yeah, did you see that? They recognized me!"

The elevator dropped to LL, and the doors opened. Angie and Joe walked the five feet to the open door of their limo. Bill was already inside, doing nothing but waiting. He wore a white dress shirt and the same Los Angeles Dodgers baseball hat. "Good morning, Joe," he greeted.

"Good morning, Mr. Myers," Joe replied.

Bill and Angie exchanged glances. Angie said, "No change from last night."

"That's obvious," Bill answered.

The limo pulled away. It left the parking garage and went into the bright sunlight.

"Well, I changed my shirt," Joe said to Bill.

Bill looked at Joe.

Joe gestured to his shirt.

Bill blinked. "It's probably best if you say as little as possible today. Do *not* reveal that you have lost your memory."

"Sure," Joe answered. "But I can talk as much as I want, right?"

Bill glowered at Joe. "No. I just said—" He stopped when he saw Joe smiling. Confusion turned to irritation.

"Sorry," Joe said, "it reminds me of a joke." Before Bill could stop him, he continued: "A doctor says to a patient, 'I've got some bad news and some more bad news. You've got cancer, and you've got Alzheimer's.' And the patient sez, 'Well, at least I don't have cancer.'"

Bill laughed despite himself. "That's a terrible joke," he chuckled and then sighed. "Don't mind me; I'm just wound up a little tight."

"How come?"

"The band is in a delicate situation right now," Bill explained. "We're wrapping up the third album of our three-album contract. Theremin Records hasn't been making any moves to sign us up again, and if *they* don't, nobody else will, and then we're has-beens." The words tumbled out. Bill actually felt better, having verbalized his tension.

Instead of chastising Bill for his lack of confidence, Joe only nodded. Then he said, "Geez, it seems premature to be putting us out to pasture. Nobody's even heard our third album. Hail, it ain't even *done*. What if it does well?"

In his teacher-voice, Bill explained, "Joe, third albums are typically buried. Many times, a minimum lot size is cut, and those go straight to the cut-out bins, if the producer bothers to ship them at all."

"Yer kiddin! Why would a record company go to all the expense of producin a record and then bury it? Unless," Joe's eyes rolled upward as he thought out loud, "The third album is more of an option than a product. If the band's good, then the record company has rights on three albums. If the third album is good, then they promote it." Joe tilted his head. "What are the production costs compared to the promotion costs?"

"Well, that would depend on many different factors," Bill hedged, because he had no idea.

"Of course," Joe said, absently bypassing Bill's bullshit answer, "if the promotion costs are way higher than the production costs, then a record company would have no problem handin out contracts and makin records. But then they hafta decide which ones are good, and then they promote those and hope they're right. Still, we got brand loyalty goin for us. The record company doesn't need to promote our records, because people who enjoyed our earlier albums are likely to buy our third one just because it's on the shelf. So if they don't promote it, they may recoup the production costs anyway."

Bill was astonished. "Where'd you hear all this? Have you talked to Michael?"

"No, it just makes sense. Right?"

Reassessing Joe, Bill answered slowly, "Yyyyyyes."

The limo was cruising along the highway. Bright sunlight streamed in. Angie got a big pair of sunglasses from her purse and put them on.

Bill asked Joe, "What do you know about Sam?" Then he asked Angie, "Did you tell him anything?"

"Not a thing," Joe answered for both of them.

"Okay," Bill said, dropping into his familiar Teaching Mode. "Sam is the recording engineer. He takes all the tracks we've recorded and puts them together. A *good* engineer can make art out of garbage. Sam's not that good."

"Because we don't need one that good?" Joe guessed. "Or kin we not afford one that good?"

Bill chose his words carefully. "Well, neither, exactly. Sam's strength is that he can work under demanding conditions. He's extremely patient. And a good team player."

The limo thumped along the highway as Joe regarded Bill. He said, "Mr. Myers, are you saying we have to settle for Sam because I'm such a jerk?"

"No, not at all!" Bill back-pedaled. "I mean, we—those of us who are close to you—know that you're not, as you say, a jerk. We know that you're under a lot of pressure, and sometimes you come across a little strong, and that can be misinterpreted."

"Oh, so I *am* a jerk, but you-all forgive me."

"No!" Bill denied.

"Do you think I should be a jerk to allay suspicion?"

Confused, Bill answered, "Well, we don't want suspicion..."

"What was your point, Mr. Myers?"

Angie watched the exchange between Bill and Joe. Bill had thought he stood on solid ground, but Joe kept shifting the ground on which Bill stood. Bill didn't really know to whom he was talking. Literally.

For a moment, Bill was speechless as he mentally backed up to where he'd had a point. Then he said, "Oh, I wanted you to know that Sam may be defensive at times. So just keep in mind where he's coming from."

"What's our planning horizon?" Joe asked. "I know we want to keep my amnesia a secret, but how long is that possible? Or desirable? I mean, I can fake my way along, but we can't do that forever, can we?"

The limo pulled off the highway. Bill removed his Dodgers hat and rubbed the bald area of his head. "I don't know. No, we can't do it forever. But we shouldn't have to. You're in familiar surroundings doing familiar things. I'm surprised your memory hasn't come back yet." He replaced his hat. "Have you had any return of your memory at all?"

Angie wondered if Joe was going to confess about the other memories and the multiple personality theory. But he just said, "Not a bit."

Angie certainly wasn't going to spill it; it wasn't her place.

Bill sighed. "Well, if you don't say *anything*, we'll just be wasting time," he said miserably. "And we are very much behind schedule. Just try to do your best, and we'll get through it."

Joe said, "Actually, I'm lookin forward to it. I've never done anything like this before. It oughta be fun."

Bill just looked at Joe as the limo pulled into the studio parking lot. Fun! This was the first time in years he'd ever heard Joe mention fun. It was refreshing, but at the same time, spooky.

The limo pulled up to a door behind the studio. Bill, Angie and Joe left the limo and scurried in the door. They walked down a narrow corridor to an elevator. They took the elevator to the 6th floor, walked down a hall to a door with "6F Mixing" lettered on the door. It was the same room in which they had been the day before and the months before that. Bill muttered, "Home sweet home," as they went in. Inside, Sam sat on a stool, talking to Patty, who was standing.

Sam Foley was slightly tall and overweight, but just pudgy. He had shortish blond hair that hung in disorganized curls around a cherubic face. Sam was 34 years old and had been in the music biz his whole professional life. He sort of slid into sound engineering sideways, having started out as the studio's electrician. After he'd wired enough boards, he found he could run the boards, and so he started mixing. And when the digital technology took over, Sam found himself on the leading edge. Mostly, he did local radio commercials and TV sound bites. But he had a talent for tolerating Joe Ecks, and this was his big break. So he wasn't going to jeopardize it. At least, not until his explosion last night.

Sam's intern was Patty Clark. Patty was black and shy of medium height. Her build was compact in a way that comes natural to athletic 23-year-olds. She pulled her long hair back into a monster afro-bun and was pretty, in an unassuming way. Unlike Sam, Patty was taking a traditional route to sound engineering. She had earned a BA in Broadcast Communications at UCLA, and this was why her résumé got picked out of the pile at the studio's personnel department. Her job was to learn the job and be the gopher. Not exactly what she had gone to college for, but she was smart enough to know that if she survived her internship, she'd be earning big money. When would that be? She didn't know, but Sam had taught her more than all the other engineers put together.

"Good morning," Sam greeted uneasily. Any fall-out from yesterday's outburst would come now. "Ready to get started? You need anything?"

Bill and Angie shook their heads. Joe said, "Yeah, I'd like a really big diet Coke."

Wordlessly, Patty left the room. "Thank you," called Joe after her.

As the door closed, Patty muttered some words that didn't sound very pleasant. Patty was less adept than Sam at staying pleasant, but, fortunately for Patty, no one listened to her.

Turning to the mixing board, Sam said, "Okay, I've gotten started on 'Xylene', but it's just a rough starting point." Without further comment, he flipped a switch and turned a knob.

The room was alive with sound. An electric guitar dominated over a background of bass and piano. The music settled, and then Joe's voice rang out:

> You're needed to manufacture drugs
> And with your aromatic smell
> You can easily get rid of bugs
> But life with you would just be hell.

Joe smiled through the stanza and laughed outright after the last line. Despite himself, Bill chuckled, though he recalled how Joe had fought with Ed over the lyrics. "You're making a joke out of X Band!" he accused. But Ed had held fast. Finally, at the end of the day, Ed had spoken with Joe alone, and the next day Joe sang the lyrics.

Then Dawn's voice rang out for the chorus. X Band had rented the talents of Dawn Barlas for a few other songs. Her voice was pure and clear, and she nailed those notes with confidence, if not swagger.

> They call me Xylene
> Dimethylbenzene
> I'm explosive (Beware!)
> And heavier than air.

Joe laughed again in delight. He looked from Angie to Bill. "This is great!" he beamed. Then his recorded voice returned and sang:

> When we're together, I feel dizzy
> Waves of pain assault my head
> Now I'm clumsy and in a tizzy
> It won't be long before I'm dead.

Even on this run, Sam was honing the song. He beefed up the background brass instruments and softened the guitar slightly.

> I'm needed by men
> At C_8H_{10}
> I'm hardly gigantic
> Though fully organic.

And then Joe launched into a solo with the band backing him. He wound around and then seemed to resonate with the others and jammed into that rhythm. Finally, worn-out, he twisted away into the last verse:

> You're so bad for me, but I need you.
> Can you understand what I mean?
> You are into paint and resins, too
> So I've got to have you, Xylene!

As the song faded away, Joe was already praising it. "That was outstanding! Fabulous!" He turned to Bill and said, "That was great! Brettington did a good job with the lyrics!"

Sam looked on in astonishment. Joe didn't compliment anything, unless it was perfect or better. Plus, most of the stress with mixing was the conflict between Joe and Bill. And this was why Sam had judiciously scheduled 'Xylene' last, even though it was the title song. So Sam expected Joe and Bill to be like rams bashing their heads together. Not like this. Not like this at all.

Bill smiled, but then his eyes narrowed. "How did you know these were Ed's lyrics?" he asked suspiciously.

Unaffected by Bill's suspicion, Joe answered easily, "Come on. Brettington wrote 'Free Body Diagram' and 'Delta Kronecker' on 'Xylophone', didn't he? And 'Free Radical'? Those songs are such genius, and on such a hidden level! And he has such a devious sense of humor and a technical viewpoint."

Still smiling, Bill said, "True, but Joe, we're not sticking to the plan."

Sobering, Joe acknowledged, "Oh. You're right," and he added, "you dick." He turned to Patty, who held his giant Coke. "Gimme that, you Hokie."

Confused, she offered the Coke to Joe, who took it and drank deeply.

Then he said to Sam, "Okay, Mr. Foley, that was a good start. Whaddaya think we oughta do next?"

Sam asked, "Is that the only coke you've had today?"

Joe stopped. "Why do you ask?"

"No reason." Mortified, Sam turned back to the board. He was aware that no one else in the room was moving. Damn! He could feel Joe's piercing eyes on the back of his head.

Rescuing Sam, Angie told Joe, "I think Sam is looking for an explanation for your good mood, and at the same time making a joke of his own." Angie thought (hoped) she could diffuse the tension with an explanation. "Sam, last night after we left, Joe came to the realization that he's been stifling the creative process. So he decided to loosen up a bit. Does that explain it okay, Joe?"

"Well, yeah, thank you. I didn't wanna just come out and tell everybody, though."

Sam turned back around and looked at Joe uncertainly. "Okay. I'm sorry if I insulted you." He really was.

Joe held Sam's eyes. "Mr. Foley, I'm truly sorry for all the times I insulted you. I hope you will forgive me."

Joe's sincerity took him off-guard. Sam answered with equal sincerity, "I hope I do, someday."

Joe replied, "Fair enough. Mr. Myers: What do you think? About the song, that is."

"Bring up the instruments a bit during the verses. Let's try to bury the lyrics a little."

Sam looked at Joe.

Joe at first didn't do anything. Then he said, "Oh, yeah, sure. Go ahead."

Sam pushed up some slide bars to different degrees and replayed the song. Bill offered some refinements, which Joe approved, before Sam replayed the song. Then Bill suggested some changes to the introduction.

Joe asked, "Kin we rein in the guitar fer the whole song? I mean, it just dominates. And it's fuzzed a lot so it has the subtlety of a fist. 'Sides, there's a lot a interestin stuff goin on that you can barely hear. Like in the introduction, I'd start out with just the bass and piano with guitar in the background. Then I'd bring in drums just before the first part with the lyrics." Joe looked from Sam to Bill. "Well, at least that's what *I'd* do," he concluded. He moved to push up his glasses and stopped himself. He finished his diet Coke instead.

Angie excused herself to return some phone calls.

Sam turned to the board and adjusted many of the controls. "Okay, let's see if I'm close," he said and started the song. As the song played, he jockeyed the relative volumes. When the song was over, he turned to Joe.

Joe observed, "Well, that was different. It sorta changes it from a regular hard rock song to something more X-Bandish. More, uh, complex," Joe judged. "But not really any better."

"Try this, Sam," Bill injected, and he gave Sam about a dozen instructions. Sam listened, checked with Joe, then moved some slide bars and flipped switches. Then Sam restarted the song. As it played, Joe seemed to be listening to the song as a whole, where before he picked at details. Of course, then, after picking at a dozen details in a section, he might have the whole section cut. When the song ended, Sam shut it off and turned for further instructions.

"Do you wanna try speedin it up?" Joe asked.

Joe had to be kidding. Even digitally, changing the beat was impossible without also changing the pitch. Duh. No one could be in the music business for a day without knowing this. And yet, Joe seemed sincere. Sam replied, "No, we're stuck in the twentieth century, with *this* technology."

"No, Joe," Bill stepped in. "they don't have that equipment here."

"Oh," Joe said. "Okay."

Sam wanted to know who would have equipment to do that. NASA?

Bill said, "Sam, I'd like to hear that again."

Sam turned to the board and started the tape rewinding.

Joe said, "You musta heard that joke about 'Play it again, Sam' a hundred times."

"Uh, huh," Sam answered, not looking up. He had.

Sam replayed the song. Bill suggested a few minor changes, which Joe approved and Sam effected. And this process repeated itself for several iterations. Joe tended to stand behind Sam and watch his manipulation of the board, but he refrained from comment. Joe contributed little to the song's mixing. This suited Bill fine, because every time Joe opened his mouth, he betrayed his ignorance. Sam, he figured, definitely knew that something was strange with Joe, but he wisely kept quiet.

Bill was correct in this. Sam had recognized the change in Joe almost immediately. In fact, if he hadn't, he would have been about the most socially oblivious person in the Southwest United States, because Sam had been working in the same tiny room with Joe for the last two months for twelve hours per day. Sam knew Joe's every physical habit, gesture, and expression. And today, suddenly, he didn't.

Sam's guess was that the previous evening, Joe had suffered a mental breakdown. Sam wasn't sure, though, because he thought after a breakdown, it took months for a person to resume proper functioning. And yet today, Joe was back at work and behaving more or less rationally, a whole new person.

A few minutes later, Angie peeked in the narrow mixing room. "Joe," she said in a low voice, "Michael called for you. I told him you'd call him back right away." She couldn't keep the dread out of her voice.

"Uh, okay," Joe answered. To Sam and Bill, he said, "Don't wait for me, okay?" He followed Angie out into the hallway.

Before the door closed, Angie heard Sam say to Bill, "Dead man walking."

"Michael's the producer?" he asked Angie when the door closed.

Angie waited for Joe to walk ahead down the hall, but Joe held back. He gestured for her to go ahead. "Ladies first," he remarked.

"Okay," Angie agreed. In the hallway, Angie explained quietly, "Yes, he's responsible for payments, production, promotion, and so on." She wondered if she should warn Joe that he and Michael hated each other.

"He sounds like an important person to have on your side," Joe remarked, saving Angie from further explanation. "What does he wanna talk about?"

Angie replied, "I don't know. He doesn't talk to *me*."

By the elevator at the end of the hall was a small lounge. It had a coffee machine, a water cooler, a cigarette machine, a table with a telephone and several chairs. Angie had pulled one of the chairs to face the loveseat and spread out an organizer on the loveseat. She picked up the telephone and punched in Michael's number. She handed the receiver to Joe. "Um, he yells a lot."

"Okay." Joe listened to the ringing with calmness. Then he said, "Hey, this doesn't sound like Michael. Is he around?" Pause. "This is Joe Ecks. I'm returning his call." Pause. "Yeah, okay." To Angie, he said, "What's Michael's last name?" Then his attention was yanked back to the phone. "Hello? Is this Michael? Hi, this is J—" Pause. "Well, we're on the last song now, mixing it." Pause. "I don't know, to be honest. We just started, really." Pause. "I'm not sure. Everything seems to be takin longer than we expect." Pause. "Well, I would guess about a day or so." Pause. "I don't know." Pause.

Bill trotted up the hall to join Angie in watching Joe. Beads of sweat were actually forming on Joe's forehead. Absently, he reached for his shirt pocket.

"I'm sorry we're so late. We'll get this last song mixed as fast as we can." Pause. "I'm sorry we're so late." Pause. "I didn't realize that." Pause. "I guess I hadn't thought about it. I've just been focusing on mixing the songs. We all want them to be as goo—" Pause. "I'm sorry we're so late." Pause. "No, I'm not blaming Mr. Foley. He's doin a good job." Pause.

The conversation lasted for another twenty minutes. Most of Joe's end of the conversation was apologies and I-don't-knows. Throughout, he stood still and stared into space. Angie was impressed with his ability to keep calm and to keep addressing Michael respectfully even though she could hear Michael's voice growing progressively louder. Finally, the call crawled to its conclusion, which was Joe saying, "Take it easy." Advice Angie was sure Michael would ignore. Joe replaced the receiver and looked up wearily.

"Our producer has scheduling concerns," Joe summarized to Angie and Bill.

"That's an understatement," Angie observed.

Bill nodded. "What did Michael actually say?"

Joe answered, "Let's see. He expressed his disappointment at our lateness, and he was curious as to *why* we were so late. And he wanted to know exactly when we would be done with 'Xylene'. He alluded to several personality characteristics of mine that he believed were the root cause of our tardiness."

Sympathetically, Bill said, "Tough call, then?"

"It's just words," Joe halfway shrugged. "Besides, Michael was just blowin off steam, and, from what I understand, he was justified. At least he was blowin off steam to the right person."

Bill shook his head. "It's just that normally, you and Michael would have been on the phone for well over an hour, arguing and debating everything. How long was your call today? Fifteen minutes?" Bill frowned. "Michael must be wondering why you were so mellow. Did he seem suspicious about your amnesia?" Bill asked.

"Ya know, I think I had im completely bamboozled," Joe stated wryly. "It was pretty easy, though, since he wasn't listening to me. Well, we'd better get back to work. I promised Michael we'd finish this last song quickly."

They left. Angie stayed behind to make more phone calls. When Joe and Bill returned to the mixing room, Sam was giving instructions to Patty. He looked up suddenly when Joe returned.

Joe walked in easily and propped himself on a stool. He said, "Sorry for the interruption, Mr. Foley. What've ya done since we left?"

Sam uneasily answered, "Um, not much. Not anything, really. I didn't see any point in changing anything without you around to approve it. What do you want to do next?"

Joe leaned back and regarded Sam. "Mr. Foley, you've probably mixed about a billion songs, haven't you?"

Guardedly, Sam answered, "A lot, yes," and awaited the fury. He recalled the last time Joe had talked with Michael during a mixing session. Joe had thrown the stools around until one broke, which took longer than Sam had expected. The stools proved stronger than they looked. While Joe had raged, no one had dared move until the storm had passed. To Joe's credit, he hadn't taken his anger out on any people. Still, it was scary. Today, his reaction was scary, too, but in a different way. Suspenseful.

"Do you ever sit there and think about how you'd do things differently? I mean, you run the board. You gotta have a good feel for what works. And for what works for us. What we like. Do you ever wanna just take a song and do it your way?"

Sam sat up a little straighter. "That's how it works, most of the time," he told Joe.

"Really?" Joe asked in surprise. He looked at Bill, who rolled his eyes and nodded. Joe turned back to Sam. "Well, what would you do with this song if you had carte blanche?"

Sam leaned forward and repeated the question. "What would *I* do? You want to know what *I'd* do?" When Joe nodded, Sam said, "Okay, you asked for it. For one thing, the raw material for a great song is here. But it's way overpowered by *you*." Sam paused, expecting argument.

"So what would *you* do?" was all Joe had to say.

"I'd make it less you. Tone down the guitar. You said it yourself, there's interesting stuff behind the guitar, but you can't hear it. Oh, the guitar's not bad, but it has its place." Sam paused. To Bill, he looked like someone who had walked off the ledge and is still in the air and can't figure out why he isn't falling to his death. "Then on the instrumentals, I'd lengthen it even further. But I'd start it off with just drums for a measure or two. Then bring in the other instruments slowly. The contrast with the verse before it would make it absolutely jam."

"How long would it take to make those changes?" Joe asked.

Bill interrupted, "Joe, we don't have that kind of time if you promised Michael we'd be done soon."

Joe turned back to Sam. "How long?"

"Half a day?" Sam guessed.

"Can you finish it tonight?" Joe prodded.

"I think so," Sam shrugged, and he added strongly, "*If* you let me do it my way, and I don't think you can do that." Sam didn't want to spend all night crafting a masterpiece that Joe would end up tearing apart. He said, "I don't want to spend all night crafting a masterpiece that you're going to end up tearing apart."

Bill interrupted. "Joe..."

Joe stayed focused on Sam, ignoring Bill. "I'll let you try, if you let me try."

Sam believed in his soul that reformed people seeking redemption should be encouraged. And Joe was trying. Sam said, "Seriously? Okay, you're on."

"Excellent," Joe said.

Bill clenched his teeth and said, "Joe, could I talk to you in the hall?" When they got in the hall, Bill barely contained his frustration. "What in the hell are you doing? You're acting like you haven't ever done this before!"

Joe raised his eyebrows.

"Yeah, okay," Bill conceded. "But that's my point. You're giving yourself away. Sam's bound to know something is wrong with you."

"Really?" Joe replied dryly. "Mr. Foley knew something was *different* with me five minutes after I came in the room. And you know? That's good. Mr. Foley's not gonna do anything unless he has the confidence to do it without my approval on every detail. So the only way I can extricate myself from the process is to shatter the paradigm. Now he believes he has the liberty to work independently. Well, independently of *me*. You can still consult."

"That's another thing," Bill seethed. "We don't have time for this little detour."

"We can't afford to *not* take this detour. I'm not contributing anything. You go in and work with Mr. Foley. That's how it would be anyway, just you and him. So what's the diff?" Before Bill could answer, Joe added, "But I'm concerned that we're not talkin about what's really buggin you. Is there something else on your mind right now?"

Bill bit back his retort. Joe was right; he was overreacting. As much as he hated to admit it. What was bothering him, besides the obvious? He shook his head and said, "I don't know. I guess I ought to go back and work with Sam. You coming?"

"No I'm gonna stay out for a while. I'll go sit with Angie."

Bill went back in the mixing room, and Joe wandered down the hall to the little office Angie had set up. Angie sat in the chair with the organizer in the loveseat before her. She had just gotten off the phone with Stu and was jotting notes on a sticky pad and putting them in the appropriate squares of the calendar-at-a-glance. Depending on feedback from Stu, then, she would assess the firmness of the engagements and literally pencil in the appointments, or she would skip the pencil step and go directly for ink. The ink's color (black, green, or red) designated the nature of the engagement, such as business, personal, or "performance". Priority was established by the color of the highlighter.

Joe sat down in the remaining unoccupied chair.

Angie looked up, unaware of Joe's approach. "What is it, Joe?"

"Oh, nothing. I'm letting Sam and Bill work on their own. What're you doin?"

Angie looked down at her organizer. "I'm postponing your obligations for the next couple of weeks. Or at least trying to. Not too many people are accessible on Saturdays. And I was wondering if maybe you should see Dr. Vrakas?"

"Who's he?"

"Dr. *Nastassia* Vrakas is a clinical psychologist. She worked with you, oh, up to about two months ago, on anger management. I thought you might want to get a professional opinion on your, uh, amnesia." She waited.

"Did she do a good job?"

Angie answered, "I think so. She was the one who diagnosed you as clinically depressed and prescribed your antidepressants. It's made a difference. And you seemed to like her."

"Were there other psychologists before her?"

Angie leaned forward. "Yes, are you remembering?"

"No, you just said, 'She was the one...', so I thought there were others."

"Oh." Angie leaned back. "Yes, you saw one psychologist and one psychiatrist before we found Dr. Vrakas. But they didn't do you any good. In fact, they just made you mad."

Joe chuckled. "I guess that's a bad thing when you're workin on anger management."

"So should I call Dr. Vrakas?"

"Sure, go ahead."

Angie made a note in her organizer.

"Angie, did I ever hurt you?" Joe asked directly.

Angie remembered stepping on a piece of broken champagne bottle and needing eleven stitches. A grip on her upper arm so fierce it left a bruise. She's seen the business end of Joe's clenched fist more than a few times, but she'd never felt it. She'd never known Joe to willingly hurt anyone, physically. That was a territory that Joe would not invade no matter how furious, or drunk, or both, he was. "No," she answered, looking down. She could feel Joe looking at her. He had a look that was a silent soul search. Angie knew she could never lie to Joe, because she would have to hide that lie from The Look, and Angie knew she couldn't do that forever.

"Well, I'm sorry," Joe said. "I don't know what happened, but that doesn't matter. You deserve affection and devotion. I, uh, I, uh, I'm really sorry."

And Angie knew that he was sincere. This sudden openness was almost embarrassing. She felt her face growing warm.

"What're we doin tomorrow?" Joe asked, mercifully changing the subject from the profoundly personal to the profoundly ordinary.

Angie gratefully consulted the organizer. "Tomorrow is more mixing. Monday is the album production meeting up at Theremin's main office. At Airline Park."

"Cool," Joe said. "How long's that meeting?"

"All day," Angie answered, "and more."

"Well, maybe we could see Dr. Vrakas tomorrow, if she'd see me on a Sunday. I don't hafta be here all the time."

"Are you really going to let Sam and Bill do the mixing themselves?"

"Yeah. Why?"

Angie said, "I'm just surprised that you would hand over control that easily."

"Why not?" Joe asked. "I like the direction they're going in, and I trust them to do a good job. I've liked Bill's other solo songs. Plus, I'll listen to it when they're done. It's delegation."

Not convinced, Angie replied, "Okay."

Joe asked, "Why is Bill mixing Ed's song?"

"Ed will join us starting tomorrow. He's meeting with a Zildjian representative today."

Joe nodded. "Well, I didn't mean to interrupt your work."

"Yes, I have to call Stu back." Angie went back to work, albeit self-consciously. Although Joe was apparently staring into space, Angie was aware that he could hear everything she said. She called Stu and made a few scheduling changes. She argued about the timing of a magazine interview. Stu said he hadn't gotten any news regarding another contract. He wanted to wait until the production meeting. He thought they would find out then how much commitment Theremin Records was going to have in promoting 'Xylene'. This simple conversation took 45 minutes, due to Stu's habit of carefully explaining every detail that Angie already knew.

Angie had never liked Stu much, ever. Joe agreed that Stu was annoying, but argued that he was harmless, and he got results.

Then Angie put a call into Dr. Vrakas' office and left a message with her service. She requested an appointment for early the next day. It was short notice, and for a Sunday, so Angie thought it was a real long shot.

A couple of times, people passed them to or from the elevator. One time, two women in their early twenties walked by, and Angie heard one of them whisper 'Joe Ecks' to the other. Joe's eyes met Angie's, and Joe smiled slightly.

Over an hour passed. At times, Angie almost forgot Joe was there, or at least she would have, except he was sniffing periodically. Angie wondered if he were catching a cold. Or maybe it was another nervous habit he'd developed.

Eventually, Bill and Patty showed up at Angie's 'office'. Bill had his hat off and was rubbing his head. "Are you ready for dinner?" Bill asked.

"Now that's a good idea," Joe stated. "Let's go." He stood.

Bill held out his palm. "You're not going anywhere."

"Huh?"

"Tell Patty what you want, and she gets it from the cafeteria," Bill said.

Joe opened his mouth but didn't say anything.

Angie said, "Patty, I'll have a tuna sandwich and a bottle of Evian."

Joe's eyes flashed. "Yeah, I'll have the same, Patty, and a big bag a chips and another big diet Coke."

Bill ordered, and Patty got in the elevator.

When the elevator doors closed, Joe said to Angie, "Thanks for ordering first. I didn't know if they had hot dogs or pizza or what. Course, I had to be told Patty would get our food, so that was a goof."

Bill asked, "Do you think she suspects anything?"

"Why are you so nervous about people finding out?"

"Joe, we don't need—If Michael finds out, he's almost sure to not offer us another contract."

"Yeah, assuming he even decides to produce 'Xylene'. And there's no possibility that we could sign with another company?"

Bill smiled. "Remember—sorry. Way back before we signed with Theremin, we knew the record companies were looking at us. Finally, we got a contract offer from PTI. Geez, you wanted to grab it with the ink still wet! But Stu told us to wait, and sure enough, the other companies gave us offers within a week. They watch what each other's doing. Stu says if we fail to get a contract offer from Theremin, no one else will touch us."

"Oh, yeah, you mentioned this on the way over. So that's interesting, the record companies have a herd mentality." Joe tilted his head. "I wonder if you could get them to actually start bidding against each other?"

Bill shrugged and said, "Theoretically, but I've never heard of it happening. Once a company offers a contract, it won't take it back and improve the offer."

"How close together are the offers, usually?"

"Oh, there's a range, which depends on the circumstances under which the offers are made," Bill generalized, exhausting the totality of his knowledge. "Why?"

"Because if the offers were all about the same, that might indicate collusion. Or that the companies formulate their offers in similar ways from common information. Interesting."

The elevator door opened. It was Patty with the food. She handed it out and took hers and Sam's to the mixing room.

When the door closed behind Patty, Angie said, "Bill, I'm trying to make an appointment with Joe's doctor for tomorrow."

"So you guys can do the mixin on your own, then," Joe finished. He took a big bite of his sandwich.

"Absolutely not," Bill declared. "You have to be here."

"Even if I'm not doin anything?"

Joe and Bill debated for a few minutes. Against any argument, Bill insisted that Joe's presence was necessary. Bill felt it important to have Joe's vision accessible.

"My 'vision'?" Joe repeated. "Mr. Myers, do you mean my approval? Because I obviously don't have my vision."

"Yes you do. Your suggestions for the most part have been spot-on. You don't have your memory, but you're still the same person."

Joe started to say something then changed his mind. Finally, he said, "Well, I won't argue that point. Angie, could you reschedule

Dr. Vrakas for Tuesday? Bill, do you think we can finish the mixin by the end of tomorrow? It would be a good statement to make at our meeting with Theremin Records on Monday, ya know? It might pacify Michael somewhat."

Bill smiled. "Okay, that gives us something to aim for. Let's get busy." He got up.

"Mind if I watch?" Joe asked. "I promise not to interfere."

Joe and Bill went into the mixing room. Sam was concerned that Joe's return meant he would be directing the mixing again. *Well, he lasted a couple of hours,* Sam thought, *that's longer than I would have guessed.* Bill sat on a stool, and Joe took a position behind Sam.

Bill said, "Joe has promised not to interfere."

"Yeah," Joe added. "Do you mind if I look over your shoulder?"

"Well, I haven't minded before," Sam replied, "but thanks for asking now."

Sam and Bill went back to work on the mix. Joe's presence distracted Sam for a while, but Joe kept his word, and he didn't say anything. Except once, a few seconds of the song sounded strange, and Sam commented on it. Joe pointed out a control that hadn't been turned on.

"Are you learning my job now, Joe?" Sam asked.

"Oh, no," Joe answered. "I just like watching you work. You play that board like it's an instrument."

Sam said, "You ever see Louis run a board? I think he could do it blind."

Bill said to Joe, "Yes, remember Louis? He was good, wasn't he?"

"One of the best I've seen," Joe agreed.

They went back to work. They would change the settings and relisten to the song. Sam would call out settings and times, and Patty would jot them down. Then they would listen again to the song while Sam and Patty changed settings at the noted cues. Each iteration took fifteen minutes or more. Or a *lot* more if sections were to be moved. Cutting and splicing was an exacting process even with the digital technology. Sam would splice in a measure and then listen to the transitions and then, half the time, repeat the process. 'Xylene' had started out long at five minutes and fifteen seconds. But as the night progressed, it grew out to over seven and a half minutes. In fact, one version stretched out to over ten minutes. No one was really keeping track of the time, and it flew.

Angie joined them awhile later. She sat out of the way. She saw that Joe was dragging. His nose wouldn't stop dripping, and his head hurt. Angie gave him codeine, and he washed it down with buckets of diet Coke.

This was the stretch that Angie disliked. There was just them in the room, tired and frustrated and exasperated with no place to go. Usually. Today, it felt different. Sure the room still stank of sweat, but not a desperate sweat. Sam and Bill and Patty worked together over the board with Joe standing over them like an angel. Or a gargoyle.

Once, when they had finished a run-through, Sam looked over his shoulder at Joe and asked, "Did that sound right to you?"

Surprised, Joe answered, "Since you asked, I'd say the end of the splice hitches. And the lyrics of the last verse are hard to understand. The relative volumes are okay, but the voice sounds fuzzy, indistinct, I mean. But otherwise, it's real good."

Sam hesitated. "Yeah, okay," he said. He fixed the splice and removed some distortion from the vocal track. It worked.

Instead of tense, everyone was cordial. Bill and Sam and Patty worked together cooperatively. As 3:00 approached, Bill called it quits. The collaborative process was engrossing, but they were losing steam. "We're not going to finish this tonight," he admitted. "We might as well get on it tomorrow."

Everyone collected their belongings. Angie, Joe and Bill left first. As before, they passed through the empty lobby to the waiting white limousine. When they got in and the limo started, Bill exhaled heartily. The session had gone better than he'd hoped. They'd made great progress on 'Xylene', and it looked like they might even have it done by the production meeting on Monday. He looked forward to *that* meeting with dread, but at least the whole album would be on masters. Still, Joe and Michael would be at each other's throats. Except they wouldn't be; Michael would just be at Joe's throat, and Joe wouldn't know what was happening. He had to prepare Joe for the meeting, in case his memory hadn't returned by then.

He looked across at Joe, rapt at the passing vacant California cityscape. He seemed like such a child to Bill, full of innocence and wonder. And ignorance and vulnerability. He was a fundamentally different Joe.

Angie asked, "How's your head, Joe?"

"Oh, fine, thank you for askin," Joe answered.

His answer reminded Bill of something he'd been meaning to ask. "Joe, is that a southern accent?"

Joe smiled. "Hail, no! Ah'm the only one heah *without* an accent!"

Bill smiled back. "How would you have a southern accent? Have you ever lived in the south? Like, did you ever live in the South, and maybe your memory loss reverts you back to that time?"

"Okay," Joe replied with a shrug.

Bill waited for him to explain, but he didn't. Bill thought of something else. "You know we've got the production meeting on Monday, right? I think it would be wise to brief you on some things you ought to know going in. And you'd better meet Ed and Roger."

Angie spoke up. "Ed's already planning to be at tomorrow's session. I can call Roger."

Joe tilted his head. "Shane Skinner isn't with the band any more is he? He left before 'Xenon' came out, right?"

Bill laughed. "Yeah, Joe, he 'left'. Right after you kicked his ass out of the band. You and Shane didn't really get along. It was Shane's fault, really."

"It was?"

"He had a talent-to-ego imbalance. And he didn't know when to shut up."

"Whatever happened to him?" Joe inquired.

"He put out a solo album, 'Skinner Alive'."

Joe searched his memory. "I don't think I've heard that one."

"Not many people have. But he's still hustling. To be honest, X Band is better without him." Bill paused to think as the limo thumped along the empty freeway. Then he asked, "How is it that you know *of* Skinner, but you don't know anything about him?"

Again, Angie tensed. She could tell Bill was detecting something strange about Joe's amnesia.

"That's a good question, Mr. Myers," Joe replied. "I hope when I see the doctor, she's able to explain it."

Bill regarded Joe for a moment. "Joe, what are you not telling me?"

Joe considered this as the limo drifted into the exit lane. "Okay, you're right," he said finally. "But this is not the time. Let's all meet at Angie's, uh, and mine, my, apartment tomorrow after the mixing is done, and we'll have a good visit. That's the best place to meet, don't you think?"

Bill nodded and said, "Yes. We need to meet someplace secure." Bill mulled for a minute. "In your current state, I wouldn't make any big decisions," he told Joe.

"Don't worry," Joe said as the limo pulled into the hotel parking lot.

"Too late," Bill sighed as the limo came to a stop.

The driver opened the door for them, and a doorman opened the hotel door. At the front desk, Joe and Miguel exchanged pleasantries as Miguel handed out messages to Angie and Bill. Then Bill, Joe and Angie got on the elevator.

"Why are you so chummy with Miguel, Joe?" Bill asked.

"Why not?" Joe answered. "It doesn't cost me anything, and maybe it makes his day a little better. Besides, it's just good manners."

The elevator opened on Bill's floor, and Bill stepped off the elevator. "Well, Joe, I have to admit, I actually had fun today. Thanks."

"That's when people do their best work, Mr. Myers. Good night," Joe said.

The elevator took Joe and Angie to their suite. They went upstairs. But instead of going into their bedroom, Joe went into the adjacent bedroom and turned on the light. It was a second bedroom, but it had become Joe's music room. Seven guitars sat in stands along one wall. There was a variety, including an acoustic, a red and white electric, a bass guitar, a 12-string electric, a silver flying V2, a brown electric, and a banjo. A small amplifier sat on the floor behind the bed. Picks and packages of strings cluttered the bed-side table. Also on stands against a second wall were a trombone, a French horn, and a ukulele. Sheet music was in three stacks on the dresser and one stack in a chair.

Joe heard Angie behind him. "Joe plays all these?" he asked.

Angie answered, "You play everything. If someone *invented* an instrument, you'd master it in an afternoon."

"Really? Hmmm." Joe lifted the brown electric guitar off its stand. He seemed to expect it to be lighter. He handled it awkwardly, tentatively, as he examined it. "Is Joe right- or left-handed?"

"Right-handed," Angie answered guardedly.

"That would explain the calluses on Joe's left fingertips," Joe commented, lightly touching his fingertips with his thumb. He sat on the bed and propped the guitar on his leg. And stared at the guitar neck. Then he stood and replaced the guitar in its stand. "Well, really, I can't play guitar. I didn't think I could, but I had to check. Actually, I never had any musical talent."

"Sure you do," Angie encouraged, "you just don't know it. Try it again and just relax. Try it."

Joe shrugged. "There's no point. I know I can't. I tried to play the trumpet in the fourth grade, but that only lasted for about a month. And I took a music theory class in college."

This was going too far. Joe without his memory was an impaired Joe, but Joe without his music wasn't even Joe. Joe *was* music. And here he stood, casually casting it aside, and without a second thought! "Joe, you *have* to play guitar! Bill said people lost their memories and still retained their skills, so you have to know how to play guitar."

Joe just spread his hands. "I don't have amnesia, and I can't play guitar."

"Joe, what are we going to do if you can't play guitar? It's the end of X Band! Don't you care? Don't you even care about anything?" Angie knew she was getting irrational, but she couldn't stop herself. Tears came to her eyes. "You let Sam and Bill mix your song, and you let Michael yell at you, and you don't care!" A sob escaped. Angie turned her back to Joe and fought to control her breathing. Joe hated it when Angie cried. She had disciplined herself to maintain control in front of Joe and then let it out in private. As she contained her emotions, she expected Joe to start the criticizing. (Unless he was pre-occupied, in which case he would simply do something else.) She braced herself and turned around. Joe still stood where he had been, with a look of concerned confusion. For a moment, they just looked at each other. Finally, Angie asked shakily, "What are we going to do?"

Joe brushed his eyebrow scar and replied objectively, "It's been just over a day. Plan A has been to maintain secrecy. But we don't have a longer-term, strategic Plan B. I woulda hoped to meet Dr. Vrakas and get some information. Then develop a strategy and sell it to the band. But we're meetin with the band and *then* Michael and *then* Dr. Vrakas. So your question is a good one at a good time." He stroked his stubbly face. Suddenly, to Angie, he seemed literally to be a different person, but then the illusion passed. "Because if we meet with the band empty-handed, then *they* will decide our strategy." Joe picked up a small pile of sheet music off a chair, dropped it on the floor and sat in the chair. "I can't fake it in front of people who know Joe well. Like you and the band. And probably Sam and Janet. But maybe I can fake it front of people who don't know Joe well.

"I could drop out of the game entirely by bustin my hand or even goin public on my mental illness. But I really don't want to wreck up X Band or Joe's position in it." Joe considered this and shook his head. He was looking at Angie while he spoke, but, to Angie, it looked

like he was talking to himself. The thoughtful tone to his voice re-
assured and calmed her. Abruptly, Joe reached for his shirt pocket,
stopped, and stood. "Yeah," he concluded, "I definitely need a Plan B.
But this early in the morning ain't the time to figger it out. Let's go to
bed."

The bedtime routine was a bit smoother than it was the night
before. Joe had to ask which toothbrush was his, but when Angie laid
out his nighttime pills, he took them. Joe seemed less flustered when
he saw Angie in her intimate apparel. Nevertheless, when Angie came
out of the bathroom, Joe was again curled up on his side of the bed,
facing away. Angie slid into bed and snuggled up to him. Joe didn't
respond, and his breathing stayed slow and steady.

Angie's thoughts drifted over the events of the day: Joe
burning his hair in the hair dryer, Joe staying calm as Michael shouted
at him. Joe hovering over Sam as he manipulated the sound board.
Not one tirade. It was a good day.

Angie heard Joe swallow, and she knew he was still awake,
faking his sleep. Keeping his distance.

What is he really like?

Chapter 3

X Band Converges

Angie found herself in the limousine with Bill Myers and her brother Ed. She looked around and saw that Joe was absent. "Where's Joe?" she asked. No one seemed to hear her. "Did Joe get in the limousine with us?" she asked. Finally, Ed turned to her and said, "Joe isn't with us now, as you can see." In a panic, Angie opened the door to the limousine and then she was in the den of her childhood house. Ed and Bill were still with her. "All I want to do," she told them, "is find Joe. He's confused, and he needs my help." Ed exclaimed, "Hey, look! Joe finally got on TV!" Atop the old black-and-white TV was Joe's disembodied head. "But Ed," the head said, "I'm not Joe." Angie grabbed Joe's head with both hands and yelled into it, "You ARE Joe! You HAVE to be Joe! BE Joe! Listen to me!" Suddenly, the consistency of Joe's head changed from that of a normal disembodied head to that of a week-old pumpkin. At the same time, Joe's face melted and dripped.

Angie's eyes snapped open, and she came to realize she was in her bedroom, alone. She slid out of bed and headed down the stairs. That's when she heard a guitar from the second bedroom. She reversed course and flew into the room. Joe sat on the edge of a chair picking strings on the 12-string electric. Angie hurled herself at Joe and wrapped herself around him. "Oh, Joe, you're here, you're here." She held him fiercely. A tentative arm placed itself across her back.

She inhaled deeply his scent, only it didn't seem wholly familiar. Plus, his hair was damp. And the way he held her was awkward.

"Well," Joe finally said, his face buried in Angie's shoulder, "it depends on how you mean that."

Angie let him go and stepped back, disappointed that Joe really wasn't here, just the imposter Joe. She saw her disappointment reflected in his expression. She had to leave the room. "I'm taking a shower now," she said as she fled. As she showered and toweled dry, she mulled over her dream. She had been lost without Joe, and his melting face hit her like a slap in the face. As if she was losing Joe permanently. She had to get Joe's memory back. Maybe Bill was right, and familiar things triggered recovery. But maybe the Greater Los Angeles Area wasn't familiar enough... She had an idea.

She got out of the bathroom and put on her clothes. Presently, Joe edged in the room and asked if the bathroom was free. When Joe disappeared in the bathroom, Angie considered that living with this memory-impaired Joe was like living with a stranger. All the morning routines, which used to happen with graceful coordination, were suddenly confused and had to be re-choreographed. Before she dried her hair, she selected Joe's clothes and laid them out. Then she stood looking at the clothes, black pleated pants and a polo shirt. What if she let Joe pick out his own clothes? Maybe there was a certain freedom here; maybe this was an opportunity to redefine a *lot* of old routines. Angie replaced the clothes in the dresser.

After a while, Joe came out of the bathroom again visibly perturbed. The fried hair had recovered from the day before, but the hair on his right side stuck out like a giant wing. "I'm perplexed!" he declared. "The more I try to get this side to flatten out, the more it flies out. If the other side did this, I'd look like the Flying Nun, but at least I'd be symmetric."

Angie smiled. "I don't think that will fit under a hat. You may have to soak it down and start over."

Joe huffed in frustration and returned to the bathroom. A moment later, the tub faucet came on. Then the blow dryer started back up. Angie, executing her idea, called Douglas and then ordered breakfast. She was applying make-up when Joe came out of the bathroom. His hair looked closer to normal but still had a strange flip on the right side. Angie refrained from comment.

Joe looked at the clothes-free bed. "Which dresser is mine?" he asked.

Angie pointed it out.

Joe went to the dresser and opened and closed each drawer. Then he pulled out the black pleated pants and polo shirt.

"Is that what you're going to wear?" Angie asked, surprised that Joe had selected the same clothes that she had.

Joe shrugged. "Uh, yeah. It looks like something Joe would wear. And they were on top. Is it all right?"

"That's what I would have picked," Angie answered, truthfully.

Joe put them on.

"It would look better if you tucked in the shirt tail," Angie advised.

Joe looked at her.

"More like how Joe would wear it," Angie clarified.

"Yeah," Joe agreed, and he tucked in the shirt tail.

"Your electric shaver is in the bathroom," Angie said. It had become her habit to offer suggestions obliquely, so it didn't appear as though she were offering suggestions. Or criticism.

"Yeah, I saw it, but I don't think I need to shave today, either," Joe replied as he rubbed his face. "My face doesn't grow in too quickly."

"Yes it does," Angie asserted, surprising herself. "And you do."

Joe went back in the bathroom. Angie was impressed with her bravery. But Joe wouldn't have wanted to appear in public looking disheveled. When Joe was done shaving, his face still had some stubble. Angie figured the electric razor probably just didn't shave as closely as the straight razor. As Joe walked by, Angie reached to brush his face. Joe flinched so suddenly that he almost fell.

"I'm sorry," Angie smiled.

Vexed, Joe asked, "What were you doin?"

"I just wanted to see if I could feel the difference between the straight razor and the electric one," Angie replied.

"Oh. Okay."

Angie reached up and ran her fingers down Joe's jaw and under his chin. She brushed his cheek with the back of her fingers. Joe held himself unnaturally rigid, as if Angie's hand were a hornet buzzing around his face.

"Does it feel any different?" he asked.

Angie withdrew her hand. "Um, yes, rougher, I'd say."

"Let's eat breakfast. Is it here? I think I can smell it." Joe hurried from the room.

Over breakfast, Angie asked Joe if he'd decided what to tell the band.

"Well, I'm gonna come clean. I wanna be able to be honest with you and the band. I don't know what my plan B is gonna be, but I know I gotta be honest and be myself. At least to the band. And to you, of course. To everyone else, I can lie and be Joe."

"That's commendable," Angie commented, thinking that it was not at all commendable.

"Not really. I figure I can't work closely with the band without them figurin me out. I've only seen Bill for 24 hours, and he's already gettin wise. So since I'm gonna get busted, I might as well fess up right away and save some credibility points."

Angie blinked. "Is honesty your back-up plan to deception?"

Joe dropped his eyes and seemed to study his plate. Finally, he looked up and admitted, "Yeah. I guess that's right. I suppose I should think about my motives."

"Well, that will have to be later, because now we should go," Angie said, standing.

A few minutes later, they rode the elevator down to the parking level. As before, Bill was waiting for them in the limousine. He wore a black tee shirt and a baseball hat that said "Security".

"Hey, Bill," Joe greeted as he climbed into the limo. "Where'd you get that hat?"

"A guy gave it to me on our 'Xenon' tour," Bill answered. "Good morning, Angie. Ed is running typically late." It was obvious to Bill that Joe had not regained his memory.

The three of them sat in the car, not speaking for five minutes or so.

Joe asked, "Are you married, Bill?"

"Yes. Cassie and I have been married for almost fourteen months."

"Newlyweds!" exclaimed Joe. "What's she doin while yer workin on the mixin?"

"House hunting," Bill replied. "In Denver."

"Denver? How come? Are either of you from there?"

"I don't know. No, Cassie went skiing once and liked it, so she wants to live in the mountains."

Joe nodded. Angie noted his diplomacy in not questioning Cassie's logic, which often defied logic. Joe inquired, "How did you and Cassie meet?"

Bill, poker-faced, replied, "High school."

Angie grinned to herself.

Joe noticed.

"I'm sorry, Bill," Angie said, and she explained, "Joe, Cassie and Bill met in high school when Bill was teaching music. And Cassie was, um, his student." Angie withheld many of the crass euphemisms she'd heard, mostly from Joe. Well, maybe mostly from Ed.

"Bill, you dog," Joe said. "But can't you get in trouble for that?"

Bill looked positively sheepish. He knew what his marriage looked like, but he knew that it wasn't what it looked like. His attraction to Cassie and their marital relationship was too complex for him to fully understand, and certainly too complex to explain to conclusion-jumpers. Most of the time, he capitulated and tried to roll with the misunderstandings, because what most people thought just didn't matter.

Angie nudged Bill. "You might as well explain it to him."

Bill sighed and began his defense. "Yes, Cassie and I met as student and teacher. We liked each other, but we were never romantic. We sort of 're-met' about three years later. She was working at a vet's office, and I brought my cat in for her shots. We talked in the lobby for almost an hour before the vet, uh, intervened, and so I asked her out. I didn't think she'd say yes, and I didn't think anything would come of it."

Every time Bill told the story, he was brought back to the veterinary office smelling of cat urine and alcohol. Cassie standing there with her big brown eyes and barely-contained energy, and all Bill wanted to do was keep talking with her. He must have looked damned goofy, but he didn't care. And that wasn't the last time he ever looked damned goofy around Cassie, either. He didn't care then, and he still didn't care. He loved Cassie.

Joe's reaction surprised Bill, but it shouldn't have, not from this new Joe. He said, "What a cool story! And you lived happily ever after. That's great." He turned to Angie and asked, "How did we meet?"

"I don't remember exactly when. You and Ed were good friends in the seventh grade, and you used to come over all the ti—" Angie was interrupted by the limo door opening. A gangly, red-headed man climbed in and sat next to Bill across from Joe and Angie. His hair was short and scraggly. A goatee poorly hid the scar of his cleft palate. "Sorry I'm late," Ed apologized. The limo pulled away.

Bill nodded a greeting, and Joe said, "Hey. Good morning."

Ed turned to Bill and asked, "What's up with Joe? Possession by evil and malevolent spirits?" With a hint of a smile, he looked from Bill to Angie and then to Joe. "Am I close? What?"

Bill spoke up. "Ed, Joe has lost his memory. He lost it Friday night when we were mixing 'You'."

Smiling, Ed replied, "Heh. Are you fooling?"

"No," Joe answered. "Apparently, I had some kind of seizure. So I don't remember anything before that."

"Really? You don't remember that you owe me $100?"

Bill said, "Knock it off, Ed, this is serious." He outlined the plan to keep it quiet and mentioned the band meeting that evening to plan for the next day's production meeting. Bill also described how he was mixing the song with Sam. Ed listened carefully, occasionally looking at Joe, who sat passively through the narration.

After Bill finished, he said, "Well, if you two aren't fighting, then I could have slept in today."

"Knock it off, Ed," said Bill like he'd said it a million times.

Joe looked at Bill and asked, "We argue a lot?"

Ed answered, "Only when you're together. Well, mostly."

Joe fell silent and gazed out the window of the limo. Then he asked Ed, "What about you and me? Do we fight a lot?"

"Not really."

"'Not really'? As in 'Yeah, but I can stand it.'?"

Ed started to answer, but Angie interrupted. "Joe, you've been under a tremendous pressure lately, and you're doing your best. We understand." She placed her hand on Joe's forearm. "Right?"

Bill and Ed nodded.

Joe looked at Angie's hand on his arm and then stared out the window at the passing California landscape. No one spoke as the limo thumped down the highway. The atmosphere was strained, but not with the undercurrent of fear. Fear that Joe would lash out. Joe now seemed miffed, but Bill didn't know at what. Himself? After a few minutes, Angie withdrew her hand. The limo pulled off at the exit and cruised down the streets to the studio. The foursome slipped from the limo to the studio back door and up the elevator.

Ed broke the silence with his usual brazen precision: "Okay, Joe, what's wrong? Are you angry at us for telling you that you have a temper, or are you angry at yourself for having a temper? The logic of which is a bit circular, you know."

Joe looked up at Ed and said, "You're tall."

"Everything is relative," Ed answered casually. Ed, at 6'7", was indeed taller than almost everyone. "But that doesn't answer the question."

"Yeah. No, I guess I'm not really mad. I just don't think of myself as a real jerk. What I'm hearing about myself doesn't coincide with my self-image."

"How much of a self-image could you have after a day and a half?" Ed asked as they left the elevator and headed for the mixing room. "I mean, how ingrained could it be?"

Joe regarded Ed. "Do you think one's self-image is dependent on memories? Or on the opinions of others?"

Ed was about to answer when they reached the mixing room and went inside. Sam was at the board with his shirt collar already unbuttoned. He looked like he'd been at work for hours already. "All right," he said with no introduction, "it's still not finished, but tell me what you think." Without waiting, he pushed the big PLAY button. The drums were dominant with a guitar melody weaving through the thunderous beats. The bass joined in, reinforcing the guitar. After several measures the guitar took the front. Bill listened carefully to the new mix. Some changes from last night were so subtle, Bill wasn't sure they were really changes. Others were obvious. He listened also for opportunities for further improvements. There were a few points, Bill decided, that he would've done differently, but not necessarily better.

Angie watched Joe carefully. He perched on a stool and stared into nothing. He didn't tap his feet. He didn't nod his head to the beat. The song ended. The others looked at Joe.

"What's your opinion, Bill?" Joe asked.

Instinctively, Bill balked. But he realized Joe had been so different lately, so he decided to risk committing himself. "I like it. I like it a lot. I honestly couldn't find a flaw."

"What do you think, Ed? You're listening to it with new ears, I'd like to hear your opinion."

"I like it more than Bill does," Ed stated bravely.

"I think you're done, Sam," Joe said. "Good job."

Sam smiled uncertainly. "What? That's it? No changes what-soever?" Instantly, he regretted the question.

But Joe just answered, "No, it's good the way it is. Stop fiddling with it."

Sam grinned. "You really have changed, Joe. I can't believe those words came out of your mouth. But there's a splice in the third stanza that chops, and a few other details I'd like to clean up." Sam paused and then added, "Y'know, the mixing part would be a lot smoother if you spent more time recording."

"Sam," Joe declared, "I hope we get a chance to take your advice." Several people laughed in relief. "Seriously, though, how 'bout we hang around while you finish up, and I'll take everybody out to lunch."

Sam answered, "Well, I can't make it. I've got some personal stuff to catch up on."

"What about you, Patty? Are you free?"

Patty had been standing at the back of the narrow room, ineffectively blending into the wall. "Me? Sure, okay."

Sam said, "We could order some take-out and it would be here by the time I'm finished. And we wouldn't have the hassle of a public appearance."

"Yeah, like pizza?" Joe asked, looking around.

They agreed and decided on five small pizzas of various toppings to be delivered to the lobby. Angie thumbed through her wallet and gave Patty two $50 bills, and she went down to accept delivery. Sam went back to touching up the song, and while he did it, Joe assumed his position over Sam's shoulder. Angie left to make some phone calls. Ed and Bill left the room.

Sam deliberately concentrated on his work. Finally, he asked, "Why are you watching me so closely?"

"I just like to watch you work," Joe said. "It's like watching a pro golfer or a pianist. You really know your instrument. Did you ever play an instrument?"

Sam worked as he talked. "No, I did geeky electronics things. At least guys like you thought they were geeky."

"Things like what?"

Sam explained how he had broken the HBO scrambler so he could watch it on his oscilloscope. He talked about the TVs and stereos he had salvaged and repaired and sold. He recalled the heap of circuit boards by his little desk in his room. And the time he had turned on a radio while it was sitting on a length of solder, abruptly frying the radio. He had a workbench at home, but he hadn't used it in years, and it was covered with bike parts and other clutter. Joe encouraged him to get back at it, if that's what he enjoyed doing. Sam said he was too busy, and he refocused on his work. He finished right when Patty arrived with the pizzas.

They all took the pizzas to an empty recording room and spread them out on the floor. The room fell silent, because everyone had pizza in their mouths. After a few minutes, Joe asked, "What's the typical celebration for an album completion?" He looked at Patty.

"I wouldn't know," she answered quietly.

Sam said, "Usually no one notices when the mixing is done. No one's around. Finishing the recording is sometimes a big deal, but only for the band members. It depends."

Bill said, "Sometimes the label makes a big deal over an album's release. A black-tie party, with distribution reps and re-viewers. It could be a real fancy affair. Like when Theremin released 'Xylophone', remember?" Bill hoped that Joe could keep up with the "everything's-normal" pretense, though this whole conversation was like Jack Nicklaus asking about golf etiquette.

"I remember it like it was yesterday," Joe answered. "Well, maybe the day before yesterday."

Ed decided to test Joe's improvisation skills. "Yeah, you were pretty trashed that night, but throwing up on that woman seemed to help a lot. What was her name?"

Bill shot a warning glare at Ed, who deliberately didn't notice.

Joe held up his hand. "Okay, I threw up because I had the stomach flu and not because of what I'd had to drink. And those weird seaweed rolls or whatever they were. Anyway, I didn't exactly throw up on the woman, just some of it splashed on her shoe. She was, uh, Carol Something from Rolling Stone, I think? But thanks for bringing that up while everyone was still eating."

"Yeah, sorry," Ed mumbled. "But you know, this story gets better every time I hear it."

"I don't know why you say that, Ed. I haven't ever told you anything different."

Bill broke in nervously. "Am I going to have to separate you two?"

Ed answered, "No, we were separated at birth."

Everyone laughed. The mood was light.

Conversation bounced around. Angie asked Sam and Patty about their families. She had seen them nearly every day for the past six weeks, and they had traded a lot of information about themselves. Joe asked Sam if he was happy to be moving on to another project.

Sam surprised everyone in the room (except Joe, but including himself) by not answering "God, yes!!" right away. But he did admit that it would be a nice change to be doing something else. Eventually, everyone filled up on pizza. They cleaned up and left the studio.

Joe stopped to shake Sam's hand. "Thanks for your patience, Sam. I learned a lot from you."

Sam looked up at Joe. "Maybe our paths will cross again," he said. He was growing convinced that Joe had been Born Again.

Joe shook Patty's hand. "Thank you for the million things you did that I didn't thank you for but should have."

"Um," Patty stammered. "You're welcome?"

Angie, Joe, Ed and Bill went down the back elevator to the waiting limo. When they were all inside, Ed pointed to Joe and declared, "I am *never* playing cards with you, okay? You're just too smooth."

The limo picked up speed and wound through the studio's back lot. "Are you talking about our conversation about me getting sick at the party?"

Bill said, "*I* was convinced. You were so sincere about it that I started to think maybe it had really happened, and I'd forgotten it."

The limo pulled up to a stoplight. Joe said to Ed, "When you first got in the limo, it took you about two seconds to realize something was different about me. What tipped you off?"

Ed answered, "I was late, but you didn't yell at me, and no one else seemed especially tense. Also, you're trying to cover up a southern accent, and your hair is a mess, and you looked like you haven't shaved since last night."

Joe rolled his eyes. "Okay, those are all good reasons."

Ed commented, "It's like you're a different person."

By this time, the limo was thumping down the highway. Angie looked out the window at the setting sun. She hadn't seen the sunset in a long time. She hadn't seen the sunrise for a lot longer than that. They were just about on schedule to meet Roger. She looked back at Joe and Ed discussing the mixing of 'Xylene'. Ed never said anything without meaning it, and Joe had always respected that. That, and the fact that Ed never had a hidden agenda. Ed kept Joe grounded. Many times, Joe had teed off about something and stormed out. Someone would say, "Ed, you gotta talk to Joe." And Ed would talk to Joe. Or else he would calmly explain Joe's position and then wouldn't need to talk to Joe. No matter how serious Ed was, though, you would never know it, because it always sounded like he was joking. Bill got in the habit of saying, "Knock it off, Ed," but Joe hadn't needed to. He had seen through the screen.

Angie observed this new Joe and how he interacted with Ed. They traded information and opinions easily. The new Joe treated Ed with a bit more respect, and he was easier for Ed to talk to. Ed was more like Ed than he had been with Joe for a long time.

The limo pulled into the hotel parking lot and drove around back to the parking level. The limo door opened, and the foursome darted to the elevator. Angie inserted her card to send the elevator up to the penthouse, but she got off at the 14th floor to pick up Roger, and the others went ahead to the penthouse. When the doors opened, they went to the lounge and, appropriately, lounged. Joe sat in the big armchair facing away from the TV. It was the same chair in which he had sat two nights before when Angie caught him examining his hand. Ed took one end of the couch and propped his feet on the coffee table. Bill busied himself fixing drinks for himself and Ed, Joe having declined one for himself.

Abruptly, Ed asked, "What's your favorite album, Joe?"

Joe replied, "'The Yes Album'."

"Yes is your favorite group?"

"Yes."

"What's your favorite joke?"

Joe thought and answered, "A truck driver driving a huge 18-wheeler comes into a truck stop diner. He gets a hamburger, fries and a Coke. Just then, three motorcycle thugs swagger into the diner and approach the trucker. They insult him and poke at him, but they can't get the trucker to react. One of them takes the fries and dumps them all over the guy. Another guy opens the hamburger and smears it on his shirt, and the third guy dumps the Coke on his head. The trucker doesn't flinch. He gets up and walks out of the diner. One of the motorcycle thugs says, 'That guy ain't much of a man.' Another customer in the diner says, 'He ain't much of a truck driver neither. He just backed over three motorcycles.'"

Bill and Ed laughed. Then Ed leaned back, stretching his long legs and regarded Joe. "Where'd you hear that joke, Joe?"

"I don't remember."

"Really?" Ed leaned forward, fixing Joe with his eyes.

Joe looked away and sighed. "Ed, I'm not ever playing poker with you, either. Actually, I heard that joke from my friend Jack O'Boyle in about the seventh grade."

Bill's eyes lit up. "You remember that?"

But Ed knew Joe in the seventh grade and just about all the people that Joe had known. He asked, "Who?"

"Yeah," Joe answered as Angie and another man joined them. "I remember that Jack lived around the corner and was the oldest of about five or six kids. He was a good guy. I lost track of him when I went to high school, though. Maybe he went to Catholic school." Joe paused, then went ahead. "Okay, I haven't been completely honest with either of you. I don't have *no* memories; I have someone *else's* memories. Like I'm actually someone else. So my guess is I don't have amnesia; I have a split personality."

"Are you serious?" Bill demanded.

"Yep," Joe answered straight up.

"So you really think you're someone else completely?"

Ed muttered, "Thanks for the recap, Bill."

"Yep," Joe answered. "I feel like a whole new man."

Ed asked, "So who are we speaking to now?"

Joe hesitated. "Mike Smith. Michael Koop Smith."

A silence dragged until it got awkward. Then Joe stepped toward the man accompanying Angie and held out his hand. "You must be Roger Novak. It's a privilege to meet you."

Roger smiled uncertainly and shook his hand. Roger sported long dirty blond hair and about four days of beard stubble. His eyes were a very light blue that gave him a mystic look, like he was actually looking at you from another plane of existence.

"In fact," Joe continued, "it's a real pleasure to have met all y'all. I've been a real fan of X Band since 'Xylophone', and I went to two concerts, but I never thought I'd meet you all in person. This is really cool."

Watching Joe move and talk, Bill realized that he believed Joe's explanation. It explained the southern accent and his new mannerisms. It also explained the different demeanor and attitude. Would a Joe with no memory allow him and Sam to take control of the mixing process?

"Well, this day is turning out way different than I thought it was going to," Ed commented. "But you definitely owe me $100."

Joe smiled and replied, "You lent that to Joe. You'll have to get it back from him. But you know, Ed, you figured it out as soon as you saw me. It's just taken this long for you to be sure, right? What were those questions about my favorite song and joke about?"

"Two things that are unique to people are their taste in music and their sense of humor," Ed explained.

Bill asked, "Angie, did you know about this?"

"I knew," she answered. "I kept it to myself, because Joe wanted to tell everyone at the same time."

"Do you believe him?"

Angie had to think about the question. She hadn't wanted to believe it; it was a lot easier to believe he had just forgotten everything and would remember it soon. She had just been playing along to this point, watching. Waiting for it to be over. To believe him was to admit a serious mental illness, but to not believe him was contrary to everything she had seen. Dammit, she couldn't think of anything that would indicate there was any remnant of Joe left in Joe. So, grudgingly, she conceded, "Yes. I believe him."

Bill nodded and rubbed his chin. "Has your Mike personality lived in the South?"

"Yeah, Davenport, Virginia. It's right in that panhandle under West Virginia," Joe confirmed. He added, "Oh, I have a whole personal history in my memories. Growin up in Davenport, goin to University of Virginia, and then on to Harvard Business School. I remember my family, friends, classes, teachers, girlfriends, room-mates, you name it. But I don't remember anything, anything at all, about bein Joe Ecks. Except for what I read off my album covers. So as Bill noticed, I know *of* Joe Ecks from an impersonal, distant viewpoint, but I don't know about *being* Joe Ecks."

Angie muttered, "Tell them about the guitar."

"Huh?" asked Joe.

"What about the guitar?" Bill prompted.

"Oh. I can't play it," answered Joe. "But I know I can read music."

There was a stunned silence. Joe reached for his shirt pocket and put his hand in his pants pocket. Roger sat down.

Ed noted, "That's a big part of your job description, you know."

Bill said, "But Joe doesn't have to play guitar for a while, now that the recording is done."

"Well, no," Ed agreed. "But there might be music videos or something. Eventually, we're going on tour. I hope."

"Yes," Bill said to himself. To Joe, he said, "We have to get Joe back as soon as possible. When you meet with the psychologist on Tuesday, find out how to do that. Hey can you get Joe back on purpose? Maybe it's just a matter of allowing him to return. Have you tried that?" Suddenly, to Bill, the whole mess seemed easily solvable.

Joe could just come back, and then everything would be back to normal.

Joe answered, "I've tried, believe me, but nothin's happened. To be honest, I don't feel like anybody else is in my head. I feel normal; sane. I know that having Joe back solves everything. But I don't know how to make that happen."

Bill slumped. "Well, maybe the psychologist can help you figure it out."

"Yeah," Joe agreed, "but between now and then is the production meeting. What're we gonna do for that? I don't even know what it's about."

Ed explained, "Basically, it's about what Theremin is going to do with 'Xylene'. If they decide to release it, then we need to approve the packaging. Some people show us cover lay-outs, and we work out the order of the songs, and Michael tells us which songs he's going to release as singles. And we talk about release dates and tour dates and some appearances and events and which songs will get videos. Stuff like that."

"Cool!" Joe exclaimed. "That's gotta be really interesting. Who's gonna be at that meeting?"

Ed replied, "Well, all of us and Stu and Michael. And Michael has a bunch of label people trooping through who all have their own thing to talk about. Maybe there will be an executive or two. I hope so, because they keep Michael subdued. It's funny to see the hierarchy in action. The execs intimidate Michael, he pushes us around, including Stu, and the others look at us like we're famous."

"Yeah, okay," Joe said. "Tell me about Michael. He seems like the central figure."

"Well, that's Michael's perspective," Ed allowed. "But from your perspective, *you* are the central figure." Ed continued his explanation of Michael. He described Michael's job function, which Joe had already heard. Then he talked about how authoritative Michael was and how he and Joe argued all the time. Ed warned that Michael ran the meeting, and he could shut down X Band at that meeting if he chose.

Joe nodded in understanding, but didn't seem particularly worried. He summarized, "Okay, so Michael's power over us is absolute, and he hates us. Why have this meeting at all? Why not just bury 'Xylene' and move on?"

Ed shrugged.

Bill said, "You tell us."

Joe replied, "Okay, I don't know anything except what you've told me. But I would guess that Michael's power over us may be absolute, but we do have a use to him. If 'Xylene' does well, that would be a good thing for Michael. But if 'Xylene' does well, and we move to another label, that would be bad. Maybe the safest thing for him is for us to do badly. For 'Xylene' to tank. Or for him to bury it and tell everyone it would have tanked. But he can't afford to be completely safe, because I'm sure he only gets rewarded for successes." Joe fingered his eyebrow scar, thinking. "There are too many permutations for us to anticipate Michael's strategy, assuming of course that he acts by reason and not emotion. If he hates me that much, then we're doomed. But if he is in the least persuadable, then we have to convince Michael that 'Xylene' is worth the risk of promotion." Joe stopped and looked at each person in the room. "By the way *is* it any good?"

No one spoke right away. Ed thought each song was pretty good in some way. Bill thought some songs were dogs, but one or two might do well. Roger hadn't heard any of the songs in their completed state. Angie had heard all of them, and she thought that, of the three X Band albums, it was the third best.

Joe prompted, "It's *not* that good?"

"Well," Ed hedged, "I wouldn't say it's not good..."

"What is this?" Joe demanded. "Nobody wants to tell me what they think? C'mon! Remember who you're *not* talkin to! I didn't write any of these songs, and I didn't play any of them, and I didn't mix any of them. Okay? So you can talk to me. But besides that, if we're gonna work together from now on, we *hafta* communicate. Maybe we didn't do that before, but we're gonna start doin it now. Right now. Starting with you, Ed."

"Me? Why me?"

"Because you are the most outspoken to me."

Ed sighed. "Okay. I think it's better than the average rock album. Each song has something going for it." Ed hesitated and added, "'Xylene' is very good. I think it's possible that this one song could sell enough albums on its own."

Bill said, "You're saying the song you wrote is going to save the album? Did you forget to take your modesty pills this morning?"

Fortified by morality, Ed answered, "Joe wants us to be honest."

Joe cut in. "What do you think, Bill? About 'Xylene'?"

"Yeah, okay, I admit 'Xylene' is pretty good. But 'Cincinnati Fan' is a great song. Way better than 'Xylene', and I helped mix 'Xylene'."

"No, what do you think of the 'Xylene' *album*?" Joe demanded. "Geez."

"Oh." Bill settled down. "It's about as good as 'Xenon'. Maybe a little better."

Ed and Angie half-heartedly agreed. Roger shrugged.

Joe asked, "Could I actually listen to the album? I'll bet not."

Bill answered, "You'd win that bet. Right now, the album is a collection of masters somewhere. I suppose Sam has his own copies stashed away, though."

Joe thought about this. "I'd hate to drag him back out here to play them for me, though. Can you guys at least tell me about the album? I just want to have a feel for what it's like."

So, for over an hour, the band told Joe about 'Xylene', about the songs and who wrote them and what their concept was. Joe heard writing anecdotes and stories about recording.

Bill and Ed refilled their glasses several times, and this loosened them up. Roger had a drink or two, but he was unusually subdued, even for Roger. Angie made herself a martini that she sipped all night, and its level didn't noticeably change. Joe continued his abstinence, and this attracted no attention. He regularly refused alcohol under the pretense that it interacted with his various medications.

Angie knew that this was true, though not the real reason. In reality, Joe just never drank, because it would loosen his grip on himself. But when it was safe, he would drink a ton real fast, go off on some bizarre emotional jag, throw up and pass out. He was always very careful to never be seen in this state by anyone other than Angie, though, on occasion, Angie had enlisted help in handling him.

Angie could never predict into which extreme emotion the binge would launch Joe. More than once, he tried to call Michael and tell him off (but failed because Angie gave him the wrong number). A few times, he actually turned congenial and wanted to be everybody's friend. Or he would beg Angie for her forgiveness for his recent behavior (whatever it had been). Or he would fall into an abyss of despair. At these times, a suicide attempt was possible. Once, for example, he filled the bathtub and attempted to drown himself in it. Another time, he tried to throw himself off an 8th story balcony. Angie believed that these attempts were genuine. It was, she thought, an indication of the extent to which Joe tortured himself.

But she saw no trace of this tonight. It seemed as if the upcoming meeting with Michael was intriguing Joe. She could see him collecting facts, drawing conclusions, developing strategies. And she also saw that his energy was infecting the others. She had hoped that when Joe announced his split personality theory that the rest of the band would debunk his delusion. But instead, they were working around it, even using it. Even embracing it.

So after the band had reviewed the album, Joe asked them about Stu.

"Well, I'll tell you what you always said," Ed answered, "'He's an idiot, but he's a harmless idiot.'"

Bill defended Stu. "He's not that much of an idiot."

Joe asked what an agent actually does. Bill and Ed explained to him that, foremost, an agent negotiates recording contracts with record producers. The agent also books appearances on TV, radio, music stores, bowling alleys, birthday parties or anything he can. But the agent has to balance this with the needs of the label for publicity and promotion.

Then they told him the history of the band's agents. Their first was Rob Caminiti. He took them on when X Band was a semi-polished garage band and got them playing at parties and bars around Connecticut (especially at the University of Connecticut) and up into Massachusetts. But X Band got too big for Rob to handle, and he had the wisdom to recognize it. Essentially, he sold out the franchise to Caputo & Associates, which was really Mark Caputo and his answering service. But Mark, distracted by a messy divorce, left X Band adrift. Stuart Cress showed up at the right time with some big promises, so the band fired Caputo & Associates and went with Stu. To everyone's surprise, Stu made good on his promises, and it wasn't long before labels were eyeing them. Stuart deftly piloted X Band through the courting, negotiating and signing process, and, in the end, X Band had their three-record contract.

"Sounds like he knows what he's doin," Joe commented.

"Yeah," Ed conceded, shaking his head. He added. "Hard to believe, though. He's *such* a doofus."

By this time, dinner had been set up in the dining room, a spread of different dinner foods: Roast beef, ham, potatoes, green beans, broccoli, and so on. Everyone filled their plates and sat, leaving the chair at the head of the table. Angie was seated at the other end. Joe put a stack of ham slices on his plate and sat down. He said, "I gotta ask you guys something. I'd always thought big famous rock bands were into decadence and debauchery with women and drugs and stuff. But I haven't seen anything like that. I mean, not that I'm complaining, but is this just a big stereotype?"

Bill gestured with his fork like it was a blackboard pointer. "Some bands are like that, Joe, but some aren't. You've always encouraged us to stay straight and put our full minds on the task at hand. *Then* party. Personally, I'm too old for that lifestyle."

Ed quipped, "And besides, you got Cassie to keep you young."

"Yes," Bill groaned, "But I don't know if she makes me young or old." He smiled sheepishly.

Joe cut off a big piece of ham. "What about you, Ed? Are you married?" He squeezed the ham into his mouth.

Ed answered, "Uh, Joe? How is that ham? Is that the best ham you've ever had?"

Joe stopped chewing. "Why? Is there somethin wrong with it?"

"Joe, you know what your name was before you changed it to Joe Ecks?" Ed replied.

Fully confused, Joe answered, "No, I never thought about it."

"It was Joshua Eckstein."

Then the pieces fit together. "I'm Jewish." He turned to Angie and asked, "I'm Jewish?"

"To quote *you*, you're not a Jew; you're Jew-*ish*," Angie explained. "Your father was. Your mother's Catholic. Your religious background is kind of a hybrid."

Joe leaned back and swallowed his mouthful of ham. "Swate Jasus," he commented.

"Now, that's an irony," Ed pointed out.

"Is that a problem, Joe?" Bill asked.

"Well, no," Joe answered, "and yes. It's another area in which I'm totally ignorant." Joe pondered this and then asked Angie, "How religious am I? Are *you* Jewish?"

Angie laughed and flipped her red hair. "No, I'm Irish Catholic. Actually, you're probably more Catholic than you are Jewish, although you never converted officially. You have always not eaten pork, but that's more out of respect for your father than for religious reasons. When he passed away, your mother took up your religious up-bringing."

Joe's face fell. "My father died? When did that happen? What happened?"

"It was a heart failure, Joe. You were fourteen at the time," Angie told him. "Susan was nineteen. She's your sister."

Joe leaned back, stunned. He looked vacantly around the room then back at Angie. "Is there anything else important that I oughta know? Do we have kids? Do I have any degenerative diseases? Do I have a police record? Have I made any deals with the Mafia? Or the devil?"

The others at the table instinctively shrank back. But Ed answered, "No kids. No degenerative health conditions, unless you count high blood pressure or an ulcer. No police record of convictions. No deals."

"Thank you," Joe said. "Well, in the last five minutes, I learned I'm Jewish, my father is dead, and I have only one sister." He hesitated. "A course, you guys learned that I'm literally insane, functionally ignorant and occupationally incompetent. An that's just today. Who knows what tomorrow might bring?" That left everyone silent as they pondered the sharp turns in their paths.

Bill stood up. "I ought to go. The morning comes pretty early around here." The band set a time to meet at the limo, and then Bill left. Ed left soon after.

Roger hung back, apparently unable to commit to leaving. His gaze was unfocused.

Joe stood by Roger for a minute, sharing his silence. Angie wondered who was the one acting weird. Usually it was Roger, but lately Joe had been outpacing him. Finally, Joe said, "It was nice to have met you, Roger. I look forward to working with you in the future."

Roger looked up at Joe with those white-blue eyes. "You're here for a reason, man. That's the key," he said.

Joe met his gaze. "I wish I knew what that was."

Roger stood still. Then he pushed the elevator button and said, "It was nice meeting you, Mike."

"Thank you. See you tomorrow."

The elevator door opened, and Roger left.

Joe turned to Angie. "He's a strange guy, isn't he?"

Angie replied, "He's high on something all the time."

"Oh," Joe answered. "What do we do with all this leftover food and stuff?"

"I call room service, and they take it away. Are you still hungry? All you ate was a bite of ham."

"No, I'm not hungry," Joe said. "I'm just tired. And tomorrow's a big day."

Angie had to agree. She excused herself to go down to the lobby to collect the messages. Joe brushed his teeth and examined his face. He stripped down to his boxer shorts and managed to get in the bed before Angie returned with the messages. She flipped through them quickly. "Looks like Stu wants to ride with you in the limo to the meeting," she told Joe.

"Yeah, okay. But aren't you coming with us?"

Angie set the messages down in their places on the dresser and answered, "The meeting is for band members, reps and production guys. Spouses aren't invited." She kicked the shoes off her tiny feet.

Joe frowned. "Angie, you're more than a spouse. You do all the scheduling and keep my personal life in order. I'd really be swamped if it weren't for you."

"You really know how to work a room," Angie snapped. "And now you're working me. You never really stop, do you?"

Joe opened his mouth and closed it.

Angie continued, "And you had the band eating out of your hands."

Joe said slowly, "It sounds like you don't think I'm sincere."

"No, I guess I don't," Angie stated.

"Well," Joe said, "do you think I fooled the rest of them? Be honest."

Angie turned. She noticed an imperceptible grin. She had to smile. "Yes. Yes, I think you completely fooled them." She chuckled to herself and then asked, "*Are* you being sincere?"

"Angie, I've always thought if you think something good about a person, then you should tell it to them. Why keep compliments to yourself?"

Angie pondered this as she went into the bathroom. It occurred to her that Joe hadn't answered her question about his sincerity. She resolved to nail him down when she went back to the bedroom. But, of course, Joe was pretending to be asleep by then.

Chapter 4

Production Meeting

Joe slept. It was early morning, and the room was dark. And quiet. Except for a humming from the digital clock on the bedside table. Joe's breathing was slow and regular. Angie was no longer draped over him; she lay beside him curled up with only the top of her red hair visible out of the covers. Joe pulled in a deep breath and shuddered. His eyes snapped open. Moving only his eyes, he scanned the room. After a few minutes, he closed them and fell back asleep.

Hours later, the telephone rang. Angie slid across the bed to the phone and put it to her ear. "Okay, thank you," she said and replaced the receiver. "Joe," she said. "Joe, it's time to wake up."

"Yeah," Joe groaned. He pulled himself to a sitting position. "What time is it?"

"6:30," Angie answered. "You've got to be in the limo so it can leave at 8:00."

Joe sniffed. "Ah guess Ah'm gettin over the jet lag." He stood.

"Why don't you get the bathroom first; I'll shower after you leave," Angie recommended.

"Okay," Joe agreed as he went into the bathroom.

As he showered, Angie ordered breakfast. Then she brushed her hair out and touched up her eyes, doing what she could for her appearance in the little time before Joe got out of the shower.

She heard something from the shower that made her stop and listen. It was Joe, singing. Angie listened carefully and determined that he was singing 'Ice Age' from the Xylophone album. That was like Joe, to sing his own songs in the shower.

Angie hesitated about laying out Joe's clothes, but she did it, because she wanted him to look good for the meeting, and lately, he didn't seem to have a good eye for looking good. She got out Joe's pills for the day as the shower shut off. She put on the hotel-provided bathrobe. As standard-issue as it was, it still looked good on her. She stood sideways to the mirror and pulled in her already flat stomach.

Just then, Joe came out of the bathroom, wearing just his boxer shorts. His black hair hung wet over his shoulders. Joe looked at the laid-out clothes. He opened his mouth to talk when Angie interrupted. "How long have you worn those boxers?" she asked.

Joe looked down, like he could tell from their appearance. "Longer than I can remember," he answered.

Angie winced.

"Yeah, I should probably change." Joe went to his dresser and pulled out a fresh pair. Then he said, "Shouldn't I wear a suit to the meeting? It's pretty professional, right?"

"You wear underwear for three days, and you want to wear a *suit* to the meeting?"

"Okay, when you put it that way, it sounds inconsistent," Joe allowed as he cleaned his ear with his finger and wiped it on his boxers. "But if I dress like a drop-out rock star, then I probably won't get much respect. If I dress like a businessman, then Michael may respond to me a little better."

Angie answered thoughtfully, "It's not what's on the inside that counts, it's what's on the outside?"

Joe shook his head. "No, they're both important, but what's on the outside is people's first impressions. *You* make an effort to look nice. Why? Because if you look nice, people will react to you better. You'll get more respect." He smiled.

The smile chilled Angie. She said, "I like to look nice. I'm not trying to manipulate people." She didn't really know the stranger in her husband's body at all. He manipulated everyone within his reach and with such a skill that they didn't know he was using them.

Angie went to the closet and opened it. "Here are Joe's suits."

Joe looked. "Joe has all these suits? Does he wear them often? These here still have tags on them."

Angie said, "You don't get to wear suits often, but you like to look professional." She pulled out a dark blue suit, Joe's favorite. "Try this on."

Joe inspected the suit. Then he inspected Angie. "What's wrong?" he asked.

"Nothing."

Concern in his voice, Joe said, "It's not nothin."

"Just try on the suit."

Hesitantly, Joe said, "I want to shave first." He picked up his clean boxers and went back into the bathroom.

Angie heard the electric razor turn on. She missed the old Joe. At least she knew what to do for him and where she stood. This new Joe, she'd accidentally antagonized. She didn't want that.

She got out a white dress shirt for Joe, and a tie. The razor shut off. Joe came out of the bathroom wearing the new boxers. He picked up the pants.

Angie asked, "Would you like me to blow dry your hair?"

"Yes!" Joe declared.

"Okay," Angie said. She looked up at Joe. About eleven inches separated them in height. "Why don't you sit on the bed?"

"Good idea," Joe agreed as Angie retrieved Joe's blow dryer and brush. He put on the pants and sat down.

Angie plugged in the blow dryer and went to work on Joe's hair. He held still while Angie brushed and dried his hair. Angie liked touching Joe's hair. It was thick and full and well-behaved, if cared for competently. Angie's own hair was not quite so well-behaved, but she beat the rogue curls into submission with lots of hairspray. Joe could usually go without it, but he always used it anyway, or at least he had until recently.

The bathrobe kept restricting her movements, so she shrugged herself out of it. Now she was dressed only in her sleepwear (camisole and loose shorts). Immediately, she could sense Joe tense. She continued to brush and dry his hair. Joe's extreme shyness was irksome, and it made Angie self-conscious. Why did her body make him nervous? Maybe it was him. What if he didn't like women? Then she caught him staring down her neckline. No, he liked women. Angie smiled to herself.

When Angie finished the blow-dry, Joe put on the shirt. Angie handed him his tie. With exaggerated care, Joe tied the tie. The knot was tiny, and the thin part of the tie hung down to his zipper. Joe untied it and retied it, again, with great care. The knot was still tiny, but the thin part was at least above his belt buckle.

Removing his tie for the next attempt, Joe commented, "I heard the story that, when Dad was gettin married, he was so nervous, he couldn't tie his tie. Uncle Gary tried to help, but he couldn't get it right, either, until Dad lay down." Joe explained, "Uncle Gary is a mortician." Joe's tie still wasn't right. He sighed. And started over.

Angie was anxious to help, to head off a tirade, but she knew not to help without being asked.

On the next try, though, Joe got it more or less right. Relieved, Angie centered it and straightened his collar.

They went to breakfast, down in the dining room. Joe picked up a bagel.

"What're ya gonna do while I'm away?" he asked Angie.

Angie nibbled on a piece of dry toast. "Go shopping, I suppose."

"What for? Whaddaya need?"

Angie smiled. "You men. You see shopping as something you have to do to get something. Women savor the experience of shopping."

Joe considered this as he finished his bagel. "Interesting. I wonder what insight that provides on other perspectives in which men and women are different." He stood and put on his suit coat, pulling his long, black hair out from under the collar.

Angie noticed that the suit didn't fit Joe very well, especially for one that was tailored to him. The suit looked wrong. She wondered why, until she realized it wasn't the suit, it was Joe. Somehow, he no longer fit the suit.

"Well, I'd better get goin," Joe said. He put another bagel in his coat's side pocket. "Wish me luck." He went down to the foyer and pushed the elevator button.

Angie stepped down into the foyer behind him. "Good luck, Joe." She was aware of an awkward hesitation between them. Do they kiss goodbye? Or hug? Shake hands? Wave? She watched for any motion toward her from Joe, but he stood rigidly, perhaps feeling the same awkwardness.

Joe said, "I like your freckles, Angie. I'm glad you didn't cover them today."

The elevator door opened, and Joe got on.

"I'll miss you today," Joe said. "It's been really nice, um, bein, y'know, when we're together." He pushed the button, and the doors closed.

Angie stared at the elevator doors for a long moment after they closed.

Joe rode down the elevator to the Lower Level uninterrupted. The doors opened, and he strode to the waiting limo. The driver, who stood by the door, opened it for him, and Joe climbed in and sat beside Bill. Bill Myers sat facing the rear. Roger Novak and Stu Cress sat facing the front. Bill and Roger wore short sleeve shirts. Stu was packaged in a full three-piece pin-stripe suit. The limo smelled of cologne.

Stu was in his mid-thirties with short blond hair, combed to the side. He maintained a perfect weight for his 5'8" height. He sported a thin blond mustache. "Good morning, Mr. Ecks. How are you this morning?" he greeted, holding out his hand.

"I'm fine," Joe replied, shaking Stu's hand. "How is Stuart Cress today?"

"Good, thanks. I called Michael this morning, and he's got everything lined up for the meeting."

"Good, Stu. Way to stay on top of things," Joe commended.

Bill remarked, "I should have known you'd wear your favorite suit today, Joe."

"I'm so predictable," Joe answered easily.

An uneasy silence filled the limo for about ten seconds before it was broken by Stu. "How did you sleep last night, Joe?"

"I woke up," Joe answered. "I had a bad dream. I went right back to sleep, though. I've been sleepin like the dead lately. I get in bed and just conk out. How'd you sleep, Stu?"

"You've been working very hard," Stu told Joe. "It's good that you can sleep well and get your rest." More uneasy silence. Stu made a point to check his watch. Then he pulled a telephone receiver from a compartment in the limo door and punched in a number. The phone on the other end rang and rang. On about the 15th ring, it was answered. "Good morning, Ed," Stu said pleasantly. "We're all waiting for you in the limousine." He listened to Ed's brief response. "Good. Then we'll see you soon." Stu put the phone away and told Joe unnecessarily, "Ed will be down soon. He's very sorry for the delay."

"Thank you, Stu," Joe answered.

A few uneasy minutes passed. Stu shifted position five or six times. He was reaching for the phone again when the door opened, and Ed climbed in. "Hiya, friends," he greeted in a goofy voice. Ed wore a lime green T-shirt with the phrase "The X-Band Cometh!" in big, red letters. Ed squirmed a little and said to Stu, "Can you scoot over a little?"

"Certainly," Stu answered, scooting over about a nanometer.

"That's only about a nanometer," Ed told Stu. "Move over a little more, please."

Stu this time moved over a measurable amount.

"Ed, I'm glad you could make it today. I know what a busy schedule you have," Stu said.

"I wouldn't miss this for the world," Ed stated. "Hey, Joe, your hair looks pretty good today. Nice suit."

"Thanks, Ed. I see you're as tall as usual."

Stu flashed a confused glance and said, "Well, you're right, Ed, this is an important meeting. Of course, it's always good when we can meet with Michael face-to-face. You know, then we see each other as people and not opponents or enemies." Stu was mostly talking to Joe, who listened carefully. Occasionally, Stu would address the other band members to keep their attention. Stu reviewed the agenda that had been discussed the night before. Nobody else had anything to add to what Stu was saying. "The important thing," Stu told Joe, "is for us to stay on the subject and not digress into irrelevant areas. This is a critical stage for us. It wouldn't hurt the cause for all of us to show Michael some respect. He's been working hard for you."

Bill asked bluntly, "Is he ready to offer us a contract?"

"Well, you know I've told you about the nature of the beast, and you've seen it for yourselves when we were fishing for the first contract. If one label succeeds at something, then all the others will follow. For a year or so, it was female soloists. The labels were all signing female soloists and promoting the hell out of them. Today, they're almost all forgotten. Now it's rap music. Rap is in, and hard rock is out. All the labels are searching out rap talent and pushing. Five years from now, the phase will be over, like it was with New Wave before, and Disco before that. But without a contract, where will you be in five years? So with rap coming on strong now, this is a really bad time for a rock band to expect a contract. And you don't have the luxury of being a new sound."

Joe said, "No, but we have a proven record, uh history, of sellin records. We're established. We don't need to be introduced."

Stu smiled benignly. "A new band has a new sound, and people want to hear it. Then they want to hear a different sound. For a band to sustain an audience over time, they have to have incredible depth, and a band like that comes along very rarely." He let the implication hang.

Joe stared at Stu, frowning. Uncharacteristically, he did not debate the depth of X Band.

Stu cleared his throat and said, "Hey, I don't make the rules; I'm just telling you what they are."

Joe turned his gaze out the window, deep in thought. The limo had turned onto the San Diego Freeway and was passing the Santa Monica Mountains. The landscape was bleak with scrubby trees clutching the sides of barren hills. Traffic was light. The limo passed an Exxon tractor trailer down-shifting noisily on an incline. The limo changed lanes and crested the ridge and started a long descent. Joe turned to Stu and said, "So it's pretty hopeless then. It was a good ride, but it's over. We had our moment in the sun."

"Well, I didn't exactly say *that*. We have some options."

Joe stared at Stu, not asking the obvious question. Finally, Bill asked it. "What *are* those options?"

"We could offer our own contract with terms we can live with," Stu answered. "If Theremin took it, we'd still be in business, and if 'Xylene' does well, then they're more likely to tap you to record album four."

Bill said, "That makes sense."

Joe mulled it over. He reached into his coat pocket for no reason. "It makes sense," he admitted. "But let's not do anything yet. I want to see how this meeting goes."

Stu smiled indulgently. "Well, the meeting isn't going to *change* anything, you know."

"Humor me," Joe said with finality.

"Well, I need you to give me the word, so I'll know right away what to do if Michael closes the door on us."

"Right now I'm telling you to not do anything," Joe said. "Except contact me."

"Michael will want an immediate response," Stu insisted.

"You don't work for Michael," Joe countered.

"No, I work for you, Joe, and for X Band, and I want to work for you for a long time, and I won't if I don't keep you in the business. You, all of you, have worked very hard to do what you've done, and it would be a shame if at this point, you sabotaged your success for no reason. Or do you have a reason?"

Joe thought this over. "Okay," he said, "send me the contract you want to propose. And send me the contract we have now. I want to compare them."

Stu hesitated, then said, "All right. I'll have my office send them over today. I'll call tomorrow for your approval."

Joe thought. "Better call the day after tomorrow," he advised, "for my *decision*."

"Don't delay this, Joe. I know how you can be. Better leave the details to me," Stu cautioned.

"You can spare a day," Joe told him.

"I'd rather not," Stu said, and the limo was quiet for a minute. Then he said, "You know, one thing you could do to help your case would be to have a definite completion date for 'Xylene'. I know you just started mixing the song, but it's the last one, and the album release is waiting for it. Committing to a completion date would show Michael that you're sensitive to his time constraints."

"I can give you a definite date," Joe said. "Yesterday."

"Yesterday? What do you mean?"

"Well, Michael called Saturday and expressed his dissatisfaction with our pace, so we changed our strategy and did it in 24 hours."

Stu just looked bewildered. "Did you really do it? What did you have to sacrifice?"

"I got out of the way," Joe answered. "I handed the reins over to Bill and Sam, and they did a great job. Of course, the song was pretty good to begin with."

Ed chimed in, "Yeah, it's actually pretty good. This one song will save the album."

Bill interjected, "Along with 'Cincinnati Fan'."

Stu settled back and smoothed his skimpy mustache. "Well, that's good. Michael will like that."

Joe returned his gaze to the window. The limo had descended into the San Fernando Valley and continued along I-405. Traffic thickened in the beginning heat of early morning, but still moved smartly. The smoked windows of the limo filtered the reflected glare of the rising sun.

Stu asked suddenly, "How is your wife Angie, Joe? Is she doing okay?"

"Yeah, she's fine," Joe responded. "She's gonna go shoppin. I think she's glad somebody else's gonna baby-sit me for the day. She could use the day off." He smiled.

Stu frowned. "You seem unusually relaxed today considering the importance of the upcoming meeting. Is everything okay?"

"Everything is fine," Joe answered.

Stu hesitated, and then he asked Ed, "And how has Vicky been? Is she enjoying southern California?"

"Oh, yeah. She couldn't stand that long Connecticut spring any more. She's been here working on her tan for about the past month."

Stu and Ed discussed the climatic differences between southern California and Connecticut. Bill asked Stu if he'd spent much time in Denver. He hadn't, but they talked about the weather there as well. And Cassie's house-hunting trip. Stu made several observations about real estate nationwide. The whole time, Joe looked on disinterestedly or fished in his coat pocket, finding nothing. Roger dozed.

The limo took an exit off I-405 onto Rosco Boulevard, a wide, five-lane avenue. Stu picked up the phone and notified someone of their location. The limo pulled off onto a smaller street and then into a parking lot. A small crowd of people milled around the front door of the building, and this is where the limo stopped. Two large men with thick necks bulled out the front door of the building, and ordered the crowd aside. The limo driver opened the door. Roger dragged himself out and stood.

"It's Roger Novak!" someone yelled. "Hey, Roger!"

Oblivious to the call, Roger hurried in the front door.

Ed bounced out, followed closely by Joe.

"Hey, Joe!" a voice called. "When're ya goin on tour?"

Joe slowed and studied the crowd. Bill urged him forward, saying under his breath, "Let's go, Joe. Keep moving." He hurried Joe in the front doors while Stu held back, announcing, "A press release on X Band's future..." The front door closed off the rest of his address. The big necks took up positions inside the lobby doors.

A tall, gaunt and severe woman addressed the band. "Good morning."

"Good morning, Ms. Deborah Bonisch, Michael Rost's administrative assistant," Ed piped up. He nudged Joe.

"Smooth," Joe whispered.

"I'll take you to your meeting with Mr. Rost," Ms. Bonisch told the band primly. "This way, please,"

X Band was led into an elevator, which took them to the third floor. Ms. Bonisch ushered the band off the elevator and led them down the hall and into a room. It was a large room with three windows facing the front of the building and another on the side. A giant conference table dominated the room. Framed photographs of rock stars hung on the walls opposite the windows. "Please wait here," Ms. Bonisch directed. "Mr. Rost will be with you shortly. Coffee, juice and water are here at the bar, and pastries and bagels are right here." She gestured to a side table.

She departed just as Stu came in. She ignored him, and he didn't seem to notice her, either.

Stu scanned the room. "Okay, good. We're in." He poured himself a cup of coffee. It was steaming. Bill and Roger sat at the table. Ed sat on the table. Joe examined the framed photos. The subjects were celebrities, but the shots were candid. In one, Mike Rutherford and a woman were talking to an older man at what was apparently a formal occasion. In another, Rick Wakeman was getting out of the back of an antique limousine. And another showed a man with a strange guitar scratching his nose with huge amplifiers forming the entire backdrop. Stu sided up to Joe and asked, "Do you find these pictures interesting?"

"It's an interesting choice of décor," Joe answered. "I would have expected something polished, professional, you know, publicity shots. This is an interesting choice."

Stu assessed Joe, and then asked, "Do you recognize this shot of Mike Oldfield? It was taken in San Francisco when you opened for him on his Airborne Tour."

Joe was about to answer when the door opened, and Michael Rost plowed through, followed by two men and two women. At 47, Michael had the build and demeanor of a football defensive lineman in a tailored pin-stripe suit. His big, white head was completely shaved. Piercing blue eyes looked over a strong nose, and his mouth was set in a permanent scowl. Michael stopped at the head of the huge conference table. "I'm not late," he said. "You're early, and it took me by surprise." The two men took positions at the table while the two women hovered near the door. Gesturing to one man and then the other, Michael said, "This is Wasielewski. This is DeLisa." He sat and dropped a thick organizer on the table in front of him. Everyone else also sat. Stu opened a spiral notebook.

The two women stood by the door uncertainly. Michael noticed them and said, "Wait outside. Close the door." They hastily complied.

"Okay," Michael said to the others at the table, "I've decided to release 'Xylene'."

Stu immediately lit up and nudged Joe happily. Bill beamed, and Ed smiled. Even Roger looked happy to hear the news. Michael didn't seem to notice anyone's reaction. "It's past late, and people are tired of waiting for it. And what I've heard is so-so. But I pushed Larry, and I even hit up Sandi. On my advice, they agreed to go ahead with the release. Wasielewski, tell us the schedule."

Wasielewski was a skinny young guy and obviously nervous. As he spoke, he stared at the single sheet of paper before him. "Um, I had to issue a release date, so I gave them July 12th for the North American markets. We're already behind schedule, though. Backing up from that date, you would have to have all your masters in by yesterday at the latest." He paused, unsure of how to continue.

Joe interrupted the pause. "We can do that," he assured.

Michael pounced on this. "Your promises mean nothing to me. You've promised a lot of dates to me, and you have met not *one*. And now you're telling me you can have something done yesterday. At least *try* to be credible."

"He's right, Michael," Stu said gently. "They finished mixing 'Xylene' yesterday and sent it on. It's done."

Michael stared at Stu and then at Joe. Then he nodded to Wasielewski and said, "Continue."

Wasielewski listed off the album's release dates in other markets. Stu copied the dates down studiously. Everyone else just nodded. "For singles, we're planning to pre-release 'Cincinnati Fan' July 4th, if that's okay. Then when that drops off the radar, we'll release 'Xylene'. Probably early September. Then 'Contents Under Pressure'."

Michael interrupted. "'Xylene' had better be good. I don't know why I allowed you to mix the title track last."

Stu piped up, "We appreciate the trust you've placed in us, Michael."

"Okay," Michael said, ignoring Stu's comment, "then we can move onto the song 'Shut Up and Suck'. The lyrics are indecent and totally unacceptable. Rerecord the vocal track with new lyrics. And," Michael pointed his finger at Joe and jabbed it on every word, "I want you to know that I don't appreciate this kind of stunt." He glowered at Joe to drive home his point.

"It won't happen again," Joe replied easily.

"Do you think this is funny?" Michael growled.

"No, I think this is *business*," Joe answered. They locked eyes for a minute.

Finally, Michael looked down and checked something off in his organizer. "Okay. I'll have it scheduled and notify Stu. Be ready. Don't get there and start composing. Studio time is expensive." He looked again at Joe. This time, Joe sat still, conspicuously quiet.

Michael asked Wasielewski if he was done. He wasn't, and he read off the release dates of the singles in different markets. Then he fled the room.

DeLisa was slightly older and more confident than Wasielewski. He said, "I'm responsible for the material product. The vinyl, tape or other medium. I need to establish the sequence you want for the tracks."

"What is there besides records and tapes?" asked Joe.

"Compact disks are just catching on," DeLisa answered. "And we still sell the odd reel-to-reel."

Joe nodded. "Any 8-tracks?"

DeLisa shook his head, but before he could answer, Michael demanded, "What does this have to do with anything? Stay focused!"

"Yeah, sorry," Joe said. To DeLisa, he answered, "I don't have a sequence ready to give you. Do you have any recommendations?"

"Me? No."

The band members looked at each other and then at Joe. Joe suggested, "Why don't we try to alternate paces? Do a faster, higher-energy song and then a slower one? I think the contrast makes each song more striking." No one said anything, but there was a general agreement. "Also, I like it when the two sides are about the same length. Y'know, so on a cassette, ya don't have a lotta dead tape at the end of one of the sides. I hate that." Joe hesitated. "Do you have the recording times of the songs, Mr. DeLisa?"

DeLisa flipped through some sheets of paper as Joe went to stand by the easel. "Yeah, right here." He read them off, and Joe jotted them down. DeLisa didn't have a time for 'Xylene', but Bill remembered what it was.

Joe said, "The total album time, then, is forty minutes and nineteen seconds, so we want each side to be close to twenty minutes and ten seconds." He stepped back from the easel. "You go first, Roger, what do you think?"

Roger appeared to pull out of a daydream. "What? Me?"

"Sure. Ya gotta do some actual work today besides showin up."

Roger looked blankly at the words on the easel. "I don't know. For Side 1, 'You', 'Sacramento', 'Xylene', 'Anesthesia', and 'I Wish'." Roger shrugged.

Joe jotted down the sequence and the total time. Then he called on Ed. Ed had a slightly different version: He switched 'Xylene' with 'You'. Joe nodded and asked Ed why he thought it would be better than Roger's idea. At first, Ed was reluctant to say. Joe asked Roger if he would be offended by Ed's differing opinion. Of course, Roger wasn't. So Ed admitted that he thought it was common for the title track to go first, or sometimes last, on a side.

Bill watched Joe engage everyone in the room, admiring his skill at drawing people out, including DeLisa and Stu and even Michael. He always gave people time to answer. Once, while Ed was describing the intro to 'Xylene', Stu interrupted, and Joe shushed him. Throughout, Bill saw Michael and Stu trading glances of astonishment. This was a major contrast with the old Joe. Old Joe would have had the sequence already worked out, and then everyone else would agree with it, because it would be perfect. But in a short time, New Joe had the room consensus on display, and he presented it to DeLisa, who dutifully copied it.

Michael dismissed DeLisa and told him to send in the graphics women.

"Okay," Michael said. "We have to pick out an album jacket."

The women, who had been standing in the hallway for the last hour or so, mobilized. The younger of the two arranged material on the table, while the other stepped forward and introduced herself. "Good morning. I am Donna Scanlon, President of Cherry Point Graphic Arts, and this is Debra Darley, your Sales Account Manager. I want to thank you all for your time." Despite her polish, her voice trembled slightly, and she tended to brush non-existent hair out of her face. "Mr. Ecks, when I spoke with you March 5th, you suggested two approaches. The first was a simple view of a xylene molecule. So we put together several choices." Debra handed a stack of album covers to Donna. Donna would hold up the cover for all to see and then hand it to Joe. Each of the covers showed a diagram of a xylene molecule in a different style: C's and H's joined by lines, a two dimensional diagram, spheres connected by tubes, etc. On each cover, "Xylene" and "X Band" were lettered in a different location and font.

Joe turned over the covers and found them to be blank. "What about the back?" he inquired.

"Um, well, what we put on the back will depend on our approach with the front, Mr. Ecks," Donna explained. "Once you decide on a front, then we'll do several variations for the back related to the same theme." She looked at Joe curiously.

Joe just said okay and passed the covers down to Stu. When Joe had looked at the last of the molecular covers, Donna said, "The second approach, of course, was the group shots at the Exxon plant."

To Joe, Ed complained, "I can't believe you wouldn't give up the molecule idea after all the trouble we went through on the pictures."

Joe turned to Ed and replied, "I don't know what I was thinkin."

Donna continued: "Out of the shots that were taken, we selected the best of each pose." She held up the first example, which showed the band members arranged around several large parallel pipes. The background was a maze of piping and a distant distillation tower. In the picture, Joe stood up front, dominating the view. Ed stood behind a pipe, looking at the camera. Bill (wearing a ten gallon hat) was to the side leaning on a valve handle, and Roger sat on a pipe, almost not noticeable.

Joe studied the cover carefully and passed it on. The next one was taken in the same area, but the band was lined up in front of a five-foot diameter pipe. Joe stood with his arms crossed. Ed faced the side as if he were talking to someone out of the picture. Bill was caught looking down, so the hat obscured his face. Roger just stood sullenly, looking through the camera.

The third cover showed the band around a giant valve wheel. Bill kneeled, and Roger squatted, and Ed and Joe stood behind them. Bill was now wearing a scuffed, yellow hard-hat. The next one was a grainy black-and-white of the band lined up by the valve wheel so it looked like the valve wheel was a member of the band. Joe stood a half step ahead with this forearms crossed over his chest and his hands in fists. Joe studied this cover for about twice as long as the others. Then without comment, he passed it on. The next shot was taken from just above the ground, so the band members looked like giants. There was a shot apparently taken from a nearby tower that encompassed the entire photo shoot: Lights, photographers, and various other assistants and technicians, and a substantial crowd of yellow hard-hatted Exxon employees. In the next one, the band all wore hard-hats and safety glasses. Holding a clipboard and pointing to something distant, Joe seemed to be giving the others orders. Bill and Ed stood looking at Joe dumbly. Roger stood behind them, studying his wrench. Joe held up the cover to the others and stifled a question. He handed it on. The last sample showed Joe standing under a huge Exxon sign. The front of the plant could be seen in the background. Joe stood directly under the double x's. He crossed his forearms over his head. He wore a tight T-shirt that showed his muscular chest in relief. Joe studied himself in the album cover, and he looked at his own chest. Shrugging, he passed the sample along.

"What do you think, Mr. Ecks?" Donna asked after Joe had passed along the last cover. "Do you want to see them all at once?" When Joe agreed, she signaled Debra, and Debra produced a 3' x 4' poster for each scheme. Each poster showed the options in reduced size with identifying numbers beneath them. Debra smoothly placed each poster on an easel that faced the table.

Joe settled back and studied the covers. Nobody said anything. Finally, Joe moved. He looked over his shoulder and asked, "What do you think, Stu? You sell our image every day. What do you think suits us best?"

"The fourth one of the group shots?" Stu guessed. It was the grainy black-and-white.

"Is that what you think?" Joe asked, surprised.

"I don't know," Stu answered.

Michael slammed his hand on the table. "Just pick one, dammit!" he barked.

For a moment, Joe didn't move. Then he said, "Michael, a lot of people went to a lotta trouble to give us these choices, and you spent a lotta money on 'em. Given the resources that have been expended already, I'd hate to make a decision without even any thought." Michael subsided, and Joe went back to extracting ideas and opinions from the room. They finally agreed on a simple xylene molecule (version #3) for the cover. A montage of the group shots would be all over the album sleeve.

"Okay, Ms. Scanlon, can you do that?" Joe asked.

"Yes, sir, Mr. Ecks!" she exclaimed. "Good choice!" She nodded to Debra, who quickly gathered the various samples. "If you have any questions or you have any further work for us, we'd be happy to serve you." With that, she handed her business card to Joe and another to Michael. Then she and Debra left the room.

On that cue, Ms. Bonisch entered and announced that lunch was ready. Everyone rose and went to the next room, where about twenty feet of table held a wide variety of foods. Several servers stood behind the table for the purpose of picking up the food and putting it on a plate. The room also had a wet bar with a bartender. Stu had the bartender pour everyone a glass of champagne. Michael excused himself brusquely and disappeared. Stu, with a flourish, raised his glass. "To the success of 'Xylene' and X Band!" The wait staff clapped enthusiastically.

Joe waited until it was polite to sit. Stu stopped him and said, "Joe, your seat is at the head of the table."

Joe moved to the head of the table and sat.

"So, Stu," Bill asked, "how do you think it's going so far?"

"Well, they're releasing the album, though Michael doesn't seem to be 100% behind it. I'll have to see what kind of promotions budget he's preparing. Still, at least that's not bad news." He turned to Joe. "This would be a good time for us to pitch our own contract proposal."

"I want a chance to review the proposal," Joe said simply.

"Joe, this is a unique window of opportunity for us to meet with Michael in person as a united front—" Stu began.

Joe cut him off. "No."

"I don't understand why you won't let me move this band forward into another three-record contract."

"I think I've been clear," Joe said. "I want to review this contract before committing to it. I think that's a reasonable position to take. Do you not understand that?"

Bill said, "Joe, we've got to have a contract if we're going to stay viable. Stu wouldn't advise us to do anything that he didn't feel was in our best interest."

Joe studied his fork sullenly. Then he looked up at everyone at the table. "I want to review the contract," he told them.

Stu's face darkened as he scowled. "Joe, this is not the—"

"I want to review the contract," Joe stated.

"Just consider what—"

"I want to review the contract," Joe stated.

Stu's nostrils flared. "As you wish," he growled. "Someday you will realize how foolish you're being, and I hope that's someday soon, otherwise you're going to blow the best opportunity you've ever had."

"You could be right," Joe conceded easily, "but I still want to see the contract."

"Yes, you've made that abundantly clear," Stu grumped.

"Splendid! Then we can finally talk about something else. How 'bout this weather, huh? Is this warm for May or what?"

No one moved.

Stu's expression softened. "How's your head, Joe?"

"Functional and unusually attractive," Joe stated. "Thank you for askin. How's *your* head?"

"Well, I guess I'm feeling some stress, Joe," Stu admitted. "I'm very sorry I snapped at you just now, and I'm sorry if I dampened what should be a celebration for us all."

Joe relaxed, and so did the rest of the room. "Forget about it," he said. "It's good to be passionate about your work."

Stu nodded. "You know, though, Joe, you are behaving awfully calm today, almost serene. You've been tolerant of Michael, and just generally easy-going. Is there a reason for this?"

Joe sighed in thought and reached into his coat pocket, where he found nothing. "Well, I've started takin a wider view of everything. I'm breaking all my old paradigms. It's like I'm seein everything anew."

Stu said slowly, "Well, I can see it's making a difference."

"Yes," Bill agreed. "He's throwing us all off."

Ed lowered his voice and said, "It makes you wonder what he's up to."

Bill and Joe chuckled.

"Hey," Joe said. "Whatta we got goin on this afternoon? I mean, we already went over the production and the album cover and the order of songs. What's left?"

Stu answered. "Well, like I explained in the limousine, there's the text. And your upcoming schedule. Which is possibly video production or tour dates. It's essentially the same agenda as our production meeting for 'Xenon'."

Joe nodded.

Nobody said anything while they ate. But Stu's tolerance for silence was less than anyone else's.

"So what have you got planned for tomorrow?" he asked Joe.

Joe swallowed his bite. "I have to take care of some personal business," he answered.

Stu chuckled. "That sounds ominously vague. Nothing serious, I hope."

"I hope not," Joe sighed. "I'm getting my head examined." (Ed and Bill stiffened.) "It's the headaches. I'm getting an MRI."

"Didn't they do one recently? A week ago?" Stu inquired.

"Yeah," Joe acknowledged. "This is a follow-up, like a comparative thing." He shrugged. "Maybe they want to do a time-lapse photography thing. 'This is Joe's brain in action, sped up one hundred times.'" He smiled.

Ed laughed. "Well, I hope they find something. Like your brain. Can they do magnification?"

"Har har," Joe answered. "At least my brain has a part that controls social function."

"Hey, that's good!" Ed laughed. "With the MRI, do you think they can activate it?"

Stu held out his hands and said, "All right, that's enough. We don't need you to start a brawl." Although he said it lightly, Stu was serious. He had seen several such exchanges explode into furious confrontations. If X Band were ever to come apart, it would be from an internal fracturing. So Stu did what he could to keep the band together. But he knew, too, if the band broke up, he could keep Joe, and Joe was good for at least one solo album and maybe more. And before Joe lost his steam, Stu could leverage Joe's fame to hook into some other rising talent. But on this occasion, he saw that there was no tension between Joe and Ed, to his amazement. And Joe and Bill had been downright cordial all day.

The room fell silent as the band resumed eating. After a few minutes, Stu checked his watch and excused himself to use the phone. Still the band was quiet, since there were still a bunch of food servers and others in the room. Bill watched Joe in this uniquely awkward situation. The food served up by Theremin was outstanding in its quality. The roast beef was tender and had been flavored with something good. But if you didn't like that, there was shrimp cocktail, lobster, tuna salad, etc. Despite the hanging silence, Joe seemed at ease, though he only moved food around on his plate. Then he pulled a bagel out of his coat's side pocket, and without any preparation, he bit a huge chunk out of it.

Eventually, Ms. Deborah Bonisch collected the band members and returned them to the empty conference room, then left. The band milled around. Joe went to the window and gazed out, where some serious solar radiation pounded southern California. Waves of heat boiled off the cars and parking lot. A Mineral Springs water truck drove through the gate and passed along the side of the building, out of sight.

Meanwhile, Bill was watching Joe staring out the window. What is happening in his head? Bill wondered. He decided to find out. He walked up and stood beside Joe, joining him in gazing out the window. "What are you thinking about, Joe?"

Joe looked at Bill and seemed to take a second to recognize him. "Oh, uh, I saw a water cooler truck pull in, and I was thinking about the costs of the product versus the cost of delivery. The delivery costs are probably way more than the cost of the water. So really, the company isn't selling water; they're selling the *delivery* of water. Like they're a water distribution company."

"You sound like the president of the economics club," Bill observed.

Joe went back to staring out the window. "I was never much of a joiner," he replied.

Just then the door opened, and a man entered. Although he was white, he had dark curly hair frizzed into an afro. "Good afternoon, X Band, I'm Ken Welch. I want to find out what you want for text."

The band members sat in their previous seats. Ken sat in the seat previously occupied by Stu and opened a notebook. "Okay," he began, "we want to say who plays what. Mr. Ecks, what instruments do you want to take credit for playing?"

"Vocals," Joe answered. "And guitar."

Ken jotted these down and looked back up at Joe, expecting more.

Bill added, "Banjo. Clarinet. Clavichord. French horn. Mandolin. Saxophone. Trombone. Trumpet. Tuba. Ukulele. Viola. Did I miss anything, Joe?"

Joe had been gaping at Bill. "No," he conceded. "I can't think of anything else. Nice job putting everything alphabetical, by the way."

Ken finished writing in his notebook and looked up. "Mr. Ecks, do you want to clarify some of these instruments? Like, do you want to specify acoustic guitar, electric guitar, twelve-string guitar and so on?"

"No," Joe answered. "I think that looks too much like padding, you know? It looks like I'm just trying to bulk out the list." He looked at Bill. "In fact, do you think we should add all these others? I mean, vocals and guitar is really what my big contribution is."

Bill shrugged and said, "That's up to you, I suppose."

Joe thought about this. "Naw, okay, leave the other instruments, but don't embellish the guitar types and stuff, okay?"

Ken nodded. "And what about you, Mr. Myers?"

"Keyboards. Back-up vocals."

"That's all?" Ken asked.

Bill nodded.

"Okay, Mr. Novak?"

"Bass guitar," Roger said without stirring. "And back-up vocals."

"Mr. Brettington?"

"Drums and percussion. And the anvil. No, leave off the anvil; that counts as percussion."

"Were there any other performers?"

"Yes," Bill said. "Dawn Barlas does vocals in 'Xylene'. And we should give credit to, uh, Nile Ekvall. He's the announcer in the intro of 'Cincinnati Fan'. Actually, it's Nile Ekvall, Jr." Bill spelled it for Ken.

"And Rhonda Cushman played the harp in 'Anesthesia'," Ed added.

"Yes. Are we forgetting anybody?" Bill asked Ed.

Ken obtained the names of the mixers and engineers and the recording locations for the different songs. Then he asked, "So who wrote which songs?"

It was not an easy question, nor an insignificant one. Every song began with an idea from one person. But then the song was fleshed out with contributions from everyone. X Band's tradition was the song's originator had the option to name others as co-writers. 'Anesthesia' was undeniably Bill's vision, and he saw it to completion. 'Xylene' was Ed's, but Bill contributed a lot, so Ed named him as co-writer. 'You' started out as Joe's, but everyone pitched in something, so credit was shared among them all.

The significance was much more than whose name was on the album. All songs were copyrighted by X Band, but the writer(s) got two extra shares of any money earned by that particular song. So, for example, when the video for 'Free Radical' was released, Ed got a share, because he was a member of the band, but he also got two shares as the song's writer.

So Bill and Ed, pretending to consult Joe, detailed the writing credits for Ken.

Ken asked, "Any special thanks?"

Bill spoke up. "I'd like to thank the Cincinnati Bengals for their generosity and hospitality."

Just then Michael Rost entered the room, surveying all with a dark glower. Seconds later, Stu bustled in.

Not distracted, Joe said, "I'd like to thank Sam Foley and Patty Clark for their tolerance and endurance. And Angie, for always bein there."

Bill shook his head.

Ed said, "We don't want to start thanking our wives. Then we gotta thank our girlfriends and our moms, and it's a slippery slope. Plus, we're down-playing the fact that you're married."

Joe looked from Ed to Bill. Bill shrugged.

"Yeah, okay, I guess that makes sense," Joe said uneasily. "Well, I would like to thank Michael Rost for being the Voice of Reason, which is never popular, but very necessary."

"Huh?" said an astonished Michael, leaning forward. "What did you say?"

"It's true. You keep us on track. You keep our ultimate objectives in mind and urge us to meet them."

Michael stared at Joe, then turned to Stu. "Did you put him up to this?"

Stu put his hands up as if to deflect the accusation. "No! But don't you like the idea?"

"No, I don't," Michael growled. "It's fake. For another thing, it's my job. *I* don't get mobs of people cheering me when *I* do *my* job. Now move on."

Ken looked down. "Um, okay, I have your lyrics for the songs. Except of course for when you rerecord the vocal track of 'Shut Up and Suck'. When that's done, can you send me the lyrics you end up using?"

Joe seemed not to hear that Ken had spoken. He said to Michael in a smooth and comforting voice, "You have a lot of anger. Today, I and the band and everyone here have been working to be as cooperative as possible, and I think we've gotten a lot accomplished without very much wasted time. Yet I don't see that having any effect on your mood, so I'm thinking maybe that's not what's bothering you. So if you can tell us what we can do better, we can work on that. Or if whatever's bothering you is unrelated to us, then we'd like to know that, too. But there's nothing we can do until we know what you want us to do. What can we do to help you?"

Everyone in the room stiffened except for Joe, who seemed blanketed in serenity.

Michael scowled, but when he spoke, his tone was more even than it had been at any other time that day. He almost sounded cordial. The effect was sinister. "That's a nice speech, Joe. It sounds like something Stu would say, except he wouldn't have the balls to say it, or even tell you to say it. But, no, I don't think I'll open up to you today, Joe, so let's move on. Shall we?"

"That's too bad, Michael, because if you did, everyone would win. You'd get something off your chest, and we might even be able to solve your problem. Then everyone else might be able to work more effectively in a more relaxed atmosphere."

Michael answered testily, "I said, 'Let's move on.'"

Joe waited for Michael to say something else, which he refused to do.

Finally, Ken said, "Uh, okay, don't forget the lyrics when you have them. I'll be reminding Stu." Stu made a note in his organizer. "I'll forward the lyrics to Morin in the sheet music department," he added to Stu, "to make sure he gets it this time. And there's the boring, 'recorded and mixed at Sunbeam Studios, Culver City, California, produced, manufactured, distributed by blah blah blah'. Is there anything else?"

Joe looked around at the others and answered, "No, I don't think so."

Ken thanked the band members and fled. "Send in O'Reilly," Michael barked after him.

Moments later, a man entered the room, and this was, of course, O'Reilly. He wore a T-shirt which featured a guy with a cigarette in his mouth, a big mug of bear in one hand and a bowling bag in the other with the caption, "Bowling Is Exercise." O'Reilly himself looked like he had exercised quite a bit in his time. He had a pug nose and uncontrolled, wiry hair. He carried nothing in his hands, and he carried himself with the confidence that he knew what he was doing. First, he shook hands with Joe. "Nice to meet you, Mr. Ecks." O'Reilly told him.

"Mr. O'Reilly, it's a pleasure," Joe answered.

O'Reilly snorted. "Nobody calls me 'Mr. O'Reilly' but the police. Call me Bruce."

"Not unless you call me Joe," Joe replied.

"Fair enough." O'Reilly nodded to the others in the room and sat down. "Okay, video schedule," he said, wiping his big hands together. "We're going to do videos for 'Contents Under Pressure' and 'Xylene' and one other. You have any preference for the other?"

Joe shook his head slowly. "Not me, what about you, Ed?"

"Well, I'd like to see a video of 'Cincinnati Fan'. You could probably do half of it from old Bengals footage. Football is a real visual, dynamic game."

Joe looked from Ed to Bill. Bill said, "A minute ago, I'd've said 'Anesthesia', but Ed's right. 'Cincinnati Fan' would be a lot more visually impacting than 'Anesthesia'."

Joe looked from Bill to Roger, who blinked and said, "Sounds good to me."

"Okay, so you want to go with the football theme. We can show the Bengals getting ready for a game, then playing, then walking off the field. We could probably show X Band playing at halftime maybe."

"Or in the middle of an empty stadium," Ed offered.

O'Reilly nodded. "Yeah, that would look cool. Okay, I'll get to work on it. What about 'Xylene'? Any thoughts about that?"

"Well, I was thinkin we could be playin at several sites around the Exxon plant those photos were taken at," Joe suggested.

"I don't know," Ed said with a mischievous grin. "The xylene in the song was represented by a dangerous yet attractive woman, like a Siren. You know, 'You're bad for me, but I need you.' You know? So I'd like to see some sultry biker chick climbing all over Joe."

"That's not necessary, Ed," Joe began.

Bill cut in, "Actually, you'd have to have some sultry dangerous woman being a tease. So she leads him on and then slaps him or cuts off his necktie or something. It looks like he wants to leave her, but he can't."

"Hey, that might work," O'Reilly agreed. "We could have some fun with it. Don't you think, Joe?"

Joe looked pretty miserable, looking around for help and finding none. He said, "Okay, let's give it a shot."

"Good. Now what do you have in mind for 'Contents Under Pressure'?"

"Maybe we could have a working guy in a high-pressure job under a lot of pressure," Joe said.

O'Reilly added, "Then we have him flip out and bust up stuff. Destruction is popular in videos, especially in slow motion."

"I don't know," Joe said. "That might not go over too good in light of the recent workplace violence headlines. I was thinkin he has a high-pressure job, and he has to work late, and then he has a frantic drive home, and then he has a high-pressure home life, and then he gets to bed late, and then he wakes up and starts it over. Maybe it's a high-paying, high-pressure job, and though the guy is surrounded by expensive things, he doesn't have the luxury of enjoying them. So even though he's rich and successful by some standards, he's really in a living hell that he can't escape, and he has to push his way through it day after day for eternity."

The table was quiet. Then Ed and Bill both said, "Nah, we like stuff getting busted up. Let's go with that."

Resignedly, Joe agreed.

O'Reilly spread his big hands. "Okay, is there anything else?" When no one had anything to add, O'Reilly left the room.

He was replaced by a man in his forties with slicked-back black hair who introduced himself as Roger Smyth. Smyth was prim. He sat stiffly and opened a loose leaf notebook to a page in which tightly-written print formed columns. "Good afternoon, Mr. Ecks, it's a pleasure to be working with you again. Only this time, you'll be the tour headline."

Stu nudged Joe significantly and beamed. "That's great news, Smyth," Stu bubbled.

"Yes," Smyth acknowledged. "To date, I have the tour beginning October 26th, but it's open-ended either way. And with a July 12th release date, it would be better to get the tour underway earlier than late October. I'm accepting engagements from August and into the spring next year, but of course we won't get a lot of takers until at least the prerelease. Plus, I haven't booked an opening act yet, which is important."

Stu cut in. "Who are you looking at for an opener?"

Smyth pursed his lips and said, "I shouldn't say anything until the contracts are signed, but we could get Thomas Dolby. Failing that, we could get Mike + the Mechanics or Metro Gnome."

Joe looked at Stu, questioningly. Stu shrugged.

"Metro Gnome is due to release their debut album not long after yours," Smyth supplied.

Joe commented, "A rock and roll band getting a three-record contract? Now?"

Stu countered, "With a new sound."

Bill asked, "Do you have any bookings for us yet?"

"Yes. The first engagement is Majestic Theatre in Dallas on the 26th. And I've got half a dozen others." Joe nodded, and Smyth continued. "So I'm your tour manager throughout. Anna Williams is your tour director, and David Burrill is your performance director." Stu jotted the names in his organizer. Smyth added to Stu, "Contact Burrill ASAP. He'll want to begin practice immediately. Any questions?"

For a moment, no one said anything. Then Ed asked, "What about Cody? Why don't we have her again this time?"

Smyth answered prickily, "Cody is on another assignment. Anything else?" When no one stirred, Smyth left the room.

As Smyth left, Michael was writing in his notebook. He kept writing after Smyth left, and no one said anything until he finished. Then Michael looked up and regarded Joe. "Stu tells me he has a contract to propose, but you're holding him back, is that right?"

Joe hesitated. "Yeah, I guess that's right. I wanted—"

Michael threw down his monogrammed pen, which bounced off the table, over Roger's head. Michael leaned forward, poised to leap over the table and strangle Joe. "What's the matter? Have you gotten a better offer? Or *any* offer?"

"Well, no," Joe admitted. "I just—"

"Then I'm taking the contract, and we can move forward," Michael stated as he rose from the table.

Joe didn't budge. "Stu isn't authorized to submit a contract proposal. If he did submit a contract, it would constitute a breach of confidentiality." Joe leveled a stare at Stu. "I'm sure you know what that would do to the status of your representation." He looked back at Michael, who now stood. "And of course that would render the contract null and void. I just—"

Michael slammed his notebook down. He stormed over to Joe and loomed over him like a thunderhead. "You worthless turd, who do you think you are? You're nothing without us. Submit the contract or you won't be worth shit. Now."

Joe rose slowly and stood, his chin level with Michael's shaven head. By standing, only an inch separated him from Michael, but though Joe pressed into his personal space, Michael held his ground. "I want to read the contract, as is my right. It will take two days. Can you wait two days? There's not some reason why you need to close a deal today, is there?"

"You're really blowing it, Ecks," Michael growled and turned. "Meeting's over. Good day." He slammed open the door and strode out and away, leaving the door ajar.

Joe rubbed his chin and reached into his coat pocket, finding nothing. "Now he's mad," Joe observed out loud.

"No duh!" exploded Ed, throwing his long arms out wide. "And I thought you weren't the sensitive type!"

"You're right, Joe," Stu confirmed. "I might be able to calm him down if I could—"

Joe whirled on Stu. "If you suggest one more time that we submit that contract to Michael, then you are fired!"

Stu froze with his mouth open. Then he held his palms outward. "Okay, Joe, I hear you, I hear you. Michael came on a little strong, and the tension level is high. It's better that we discuss this at another time. But you know, Joe, you did an outstanding job of holding your temper and working with Michael, and today's meeting went very smoothly. I think Michael appreciates how smoothly the meeting went."

Joe cried, "Are you kidding?! He's furious! He was pissed off all day! I couldn't reach him. He was impenetrable."

"Still," Stu began, "he's releasing 'Xylene', and—"

Ms. Deborah Bonisch appeared in the doorway. "Your ride is ready for whenever you'd like to leave," she said formally. Everyone moved to the door.

Ed said, "Yeah, I guess we've done all the damage we can do here. Let's go someplace else."

Ms. Bonisch led the band to the elevator and down to the first floor lobby. Outside, a larger bunch of people were standing around, held back from the front door by the same guys with the suits and thick necks.

Stu touched Joe's shoulder as they approached the door. "Just keep going to the limo, Joe. I'll handle the questions. Okay?"

"Sure, Stu," Joe answered, and he added, "Y'know, I've done this before."

"Yes, of course. I have to stay here and clear up some minor items with Michael, so I won't be joining you in the limousine. Let's go."

The band darted from the lobby to the limo while Stu walked toward the people, confident as a lion tamer. The band climbed into the car and closed the door just as Stu began speechifying. The limousine smoothly accelerated away to the parking lot exit.

Chapter 5

Post Meeting

Joe flopped into the limo's seat with a monster sigh. He loosened his necktie and unbuttoned the top button of his shirt. And he smiled. "Man, that was fun!" he exclaimed. "Did you have fun today, Roger?"

Roger managed a smile. "Yeah."

"Hey, Bill, what was your favorite part?"

Bill just looked weary, like his favorite part of the meeting was leaving it. Ignoring Joe's question, he said, "Joe, we have a lot of stuff to talk about. Like the contract." He expected Joe to jump down his throat like he had with Stu, only with more zeal. Bill didn't agree with Joe's stance, but he admired the way he handled Stu and Michael on the issue. Despite the fact that Stu and Michael sensed weakness and dove in for the kill. Despite the fact that Joe frustrated the both of them by absorbing their attacks with no reaction. The old Joe would have been more adversarial. But not on this, because he would have allowed the contract proposal. Joe's nature was to pry into and fiddle with everything concerning the band, but he had trusted Stu and left Stu's business to Stu. So his involvement was unexpected to Stu and Michael.

"Yes, let's talk about the contract," Joe agreeably agreed. "Let me ask you something. Do you think Stu had a copy of the contract ready to give to Michael today?"

"Yes, that's what I thought," Bill answered cautiously. "I don't think he ever said so, but he seemed ready to act."

Joe nodded. "Yeah, you'd think he'd a had a contract with him if he was so hot to give it to Michael. So why do you think he wouldn't let me see it? Why didn't he offer to let me take it home tonight? He said he'd have someone deliver it, in fact, as if he *didn't* have it."

"Okay, so maybe he didn't have it with him. So what?"

"I don't know," Joe admitted. "It just seems weird. Somethin's not right. Why didn't he want me to see the contract?"

"Well, Joe, you have to understand your history with Michael and Stu. For as long as you've known them, you've driven them crazy, especially Michael. He lives and dies on a schedule, and you are absolutely oblivious to schedule. The thing is, your drive for excellence makes the extra time worth it. But it still drives Michael crazy, and then Stu has to run interference. I'm surprised the two of them don't have ulcers bigger than yours. But you've always let Stu handle the business so it gets done. So you can see why he's resisting your little invasion. Right?"

Joe said, "Yeah, I guess Stu's shakin with fear right now." He added, "But I still wanna see the contract."

Bill threw up his hands in exasperation.

"Bill, I'm not like Joe! I can take a look at something and not take all week. Trust me on this. And besides, something doesn't feel right. What's the deadline? Why are Stu and Michael so hot for us to submit a contract? If Michael wants a contract so bad, why doesn't he offer us one like the way it's usually done?"

"Who cares?" Bill exploded. "We've got a shot at another three albums right now! Let's get it!" He turned to Ed in desperation, "Ed, talk to Joe. Please."

Ed had more influence over Joe than anyone, possibly because he had the longest history with him. Ed and Joe met in the 7th grade, and they filled their days as teenagers do. They bicycled all over Wallingford, they watched TV, they threw Frisbees, and they pretended to be famous movie stars. Joe already played the guitar pretty well. One day, he said to Ed, "Hey, you wanna learn to play the drums and start a band?" And Ed replied, "Okay." It seemed like a good idea at the time. (Turns out, it was a *great* idea.)

So Ed bought a used drum set and learned to play the drums. He was as uncoordinated with drumsticks as he was with hockey sticks, but he worked at it and got better. As the band developed, Ed followed Joe's lead. Not out of blind faith; because Joe repeatedly proved himself. And because Joe drove the band forward, Ed trusted him completely, and it had become a habit.

And Joe trusted Ed. Ed didn't "talk to Joe" unless there was a solid reason for Joe to change his mind. This was not one of those times.

Ed said, "Bill, Joe wants to read the contract." His tone was conversational, as if Bill was not aware of this simple fact. Bill looked at Ed and leaned back with a sigh. The limo thumped along in silence. The sun by now was setting behind the Simi Hills, casting long shadows.

Joe said, "You know, I could really use a beer. Is there any beer hidden in this road yacht?"

Ed answered, "Your drink of choice is vodka martinis, and we've got lots of that." He opened a compartment and withdrew a small thermos.

Joe wrinkled his nose and said, "No, I'll pass." He huffed and crossed his arms across his chest. After a moment, he asked, "Well, would you mind if we stopped at an ABC store?"

"A what?"

"An ABC store. Or a package store. What do they call liquor stores out here?" Ed started to answer, but Joe added, "Oh, never mind. I don't have my wallet with me anyway. You know, I haven't seen my wallet since, uh, since Saturday night."

Bill said, "Think about it, Joe. What do you need a wallet for? Identification? Money? A library card, maybe?"

"Yeah," Joe agreed, thinking. "I'd just thought Angie carried all the money and stuff. Anyway, didn't ya think it was a cool meeting? Pickin album covers and the order of songs? I always wondered how that stuff got decided. I figured it was by a room full of marketing people with focus groups."

Ed said, "I have to admit your enthusiasm was contagious. The best part was how buffaloed you had Stu and Michael. They weren't expecting you like this at all. They were totally blindsided."

Joe looked sheepish and said to Bill, "I did a lousy job of pretending to be Joe, didn't I?"

"Yes," Bill answered. "But it looked like you were intentionally being super cooperative and doing a good job at it. And with no sarcasm."

"I couldn't help it," Joe explained. "I just... I dunno." He let the sentence hang.

Ed said, "What I thought was funny was Donna from the graphics company. If you had snapped your fingers, she would have kissed your feet, and you pretended all the time not to notice. And so all of us there went along! It was a scream!" Ed laughed.

Joe actually blushed. "Wail, she was noss, but I didn't wanna date her or anything. B'sods, I'm married, you know, to Angie." Joe looked from Bill to Ed. "Rot?"

Ed laughed harder. "Joe, for one thing, you wouldn't have had to buy Donna dinner to get to the romance, if ya know what I mean."

Joe looked a little embarrassed. "Yer exaggeratin."

"Hey, it's not like I haven't seen it a million times, but the funny thing was how oblivious you were to it. You used to practically glow when women hit on you."

Joe sighed and leaned back. He looked out the window at the darkening barren landscape.

Ed turned to Bill and said, "I liked O'Reilly. It'll be cool working with him on the videos..." Bill and Ed discussed the videos they had done in the past.

"What about the tour?" Joe asked suddenly. "I'm worried about how we're gonna manage that."

Bill answered, "Well, let's see what your doctor has to say about it. I have a feeling this whole thing may be resolved tomorrow." Bill was feeling expansive. All things were lining up: The tracks were mixed, the album was being released, tour dates locked in, video shoots planned. And once Joe returned to normal, he'd get the contract signed, and X Band would be in business for years. Then he and Cassie would have the money to get a big house (somewhere) and then start a family. The financial security was worth hanging with Joe for another couple of years.

Joe asked, "Who wrote the lyrics for 'Shut Up and Suck'?"

Ed answered, "Uh, that would be you."

"Of course," Joe responded. "I suppose I should write the new lyrics since I caused the problem to begin with."

Bill rolled his eyes. "Joe, I appreciate the thought, but you haven't even heard the song. I'll rewrite the lyrics. Don't worry about it."

Joe frowned. "Okay, the nobility thing is part of it, but not all. I'd just really like to write lyrics. It would be so cool to write words down and then hear 'em on the radio. Or hearin your own voice. Or you hear other people singin your lyrics. Wouldn't that be cool? Swate Jasus!"

Ed smiled. He remembered the first time he'd heard an X Band song on the radio. It was one of those defining moments that could never be forgotten. It was back in the summer of '82, and 'Xylophone' had just been released. The band was about to go to Prague to film the 'Free Radical' video, so there was an odd lapse in the schedule, which happened to fall around July 4th. It was an early afternoon, and Ed was driving his girlfriend Kitty to his parents' house for barbecue and hanging around. Ed had the radio on, and he recognized the intro to 'Tina' immediately. "This is it!" he screamed. "This is it!" At first, Kitty didn't know what Ed was going berserk about, and he cranked the car radio and rolled down the windows.

"I've always liked the lyrics in X Band songs," Joe concluded. "They make the songs *about* something. Oh, hey, I gotta ask: Did I really play all those instruments on 'Xylene'?"

Bill confirmed that he had.

"That must have been a lot of work," Joe figured.

Bill replied, "Well, you *are* Joe Ecks."

"So it would appear," Joe allowed.

Roger turned on the limo's radio, and they listened to Motley Crüe and Led Zeppelin. Then the station played "Tina". Joe's eyes lit up. "Hey!" he exclaimed, "that's one of ours!"

"Okay," Bill instructed, "Now listen to what *follows* the song."

As the song's last note stretched out, the disc jockey said, "That was 'Tina' from X Band. This just in: they've finished recording their third album 'Xylene', and it's due in the racks July 12th. You heard it here first, at KCL 106 in the shade." A commercial for Stri-Dex brand medicated pads replaced the DJ.

"Stu's been working hard today," Bill commented.

"Wow," said Joe. "News about us is on the radio. Hundreds of thousands of people heard this one message, and radio stations all over the country are broadcastin the news. Millions, *tens* of millions, of people will know about the new album. It's staggerin." Joe seemed lost in the vastness. "Wow," he added.

Bill cautioned, "Don't let it go to your head. When you're surrounded by screaming fans and toadies and sycophants, you lose track of who you really are, and what you can really do. You start thinking you're more than you really are. The best advice I ever got was, 'Don't start believing your own press releases.'"

Joe nodded. "Yeah, I can see how that might happen. But so far, I haven't seen that we're surrounded by suck-ups. And Michael really brings down the average. I mean, we worked with Sam and Janet, and they didn't treat us like we were special, I didn't think. Stu's a shameless butt-kisser all around except for when he wants a contract approved, and then he tells us how worthless we are. So far, it seems like we keep getting reminded how easily we can be replaced."

"Well, this is a weird time," Bill told him.

Joe looked back out the window. About this time, the limo pulled into the exit lane to leave the San Diego Freeway and get on the Santa Monica Freeway. Rush hour had passed, and traffic had eased. The playing radio discouraged conversation, but Joe didn't seem especially approachable anyway. Bill let it slide. It had been a big day for everyone, and he didn't feel talkative, either. Bill thought about what he would do when he got back to the hotel. He was still full from that big lunch so dinner was out. Cassie was still in Denver. Then his mind picked over different details of the day's meeting. He thought about Joe going straight at Michael's aggression: "Somethin seems to be botherin you..." That was an approach more like what Ed would take. Or Joe answering, "No, I think this is *business*." And Joe's insistence that he read the contract before allowing Stu to submit it to Michael. Joe, this alternate Joe, looked like a softie, but he had the spine of a steel rod.

Meanwhile, Ed had been thinking of his little sister. He had forever felt a responsibility to protect her, but he couldn't protect her from herself. Angie, he thought, responded to aggression with submission. When their father berated her for the way she did the dishes, she tried to do the dishes more in the way he wanted. She was pliable, but too much so for her own good. And Ed saw that the more pressure Joe put himself under, the more he increased his control over Angie. And Angie responded by trying to be a better wife. Ed knew that Joe loved Angie, and when the pressure was released, things went back to normal (Ed hoped). But this new Joe, how did he treat Angie? Ed cleared his throat. "Uh, Joe, how's Angie doing?"

"She's holdin up great, I think," Joe answered. "I mean, she's concerned and everything, but that's to be expected. She does a great job at keeping the wheels movin, if ya know what I mean." Joe saw that Ed did not know what he meant. "She does all the little things that would take me forever to figure out. Y'know, orderin breakfast and all the organizational things it takes to get me where I need to be."

Ed nodded. "What do you think of her?"

Without hesitation, Joe answered, "Oh, she's great! She seems a little quiet and nervous, but I figure that comes from bein in close quarters with a psychotic. I mean, that would put somebody off, wouldn't it? But sometimes it seems like she forgets, y'know, everything, and she's so..." Joe searched for a word. "well, refreshing. Uplifting. An her laugh, it just makes ya feel great."

Ed nodded, satisfied.

Joe removed his tie. He muttered, "I actually hate wearing a suit. I can't believe I worked so hard to get a job where I would have to wear one every day."

Bill realized Joe was talking about his fabricated life. "How do you think the suit worked today?"

"You tell me. Have you ever seen Joe and Michael together when Joe was wearing a T shirt?"

Bill thought back. "Maybe it *did* work."

Joe shook his head. "Michael must be an asshole to the core. You see how nervous people were when they came in?"

Bill said, "Maybe they're nervous because of you."

"Wow," Joe said. "Joe's a *giant* asshole!"

Bill said, "No, truthfully, he's not. It's that the stress is killing him." Bill looked at Joe. "You, I mean. You can tell there's a good guy in there, deep down screaming to get out."

Joe rubbed his stubbly jaw and mused, "I wonder what would happen if he did get out?"

Roger said, "This." as the phone rang. Roger turned down the radio as Ed answered it. "Well, let me see if he's here," Ed said to the phone. He handed it to Joe.

"Hello?" he asked. "Oh, yeah, hi, Stu. You've apparently been workin very hard; we already heard the announcement on KCL." Joe paused, listening. Occasionally, he was able to utter a "Yeh" or a "N—". Finally, Stu let him answer. "No, I don't mind, Stu, but I'm not sure what my schedule is tomorrow." He waited for Stu to shut up. "No, not at the hospital, I guess I can meet her in the hotel lobby maybe, but I don't know when." Joe listened to Stu. "No, I don't know. Why don't you call Angie? She's probably at the hotel, and she can set up the details." Pause. "She'll be with me tomorrow." Pause. "Okay, thanks for lookin out for us. Good job." Pause. "Okay, yeah, good." Finally, Joe got off the phone. He said to the others, "Looks like I have an interview with Hot Rocks Magazine."

Ed responded, "And so it begins."

Eventually, the limo reached the hotel exit and pulled up to the front door. The door was opened for the band, and they walked through it. In the lobby, Joe came to a quick stop and told the others that he had forgotten his elevator card. Ed, Bill and Roger went ahead to the elevators. Joe went to the front desk and explained the problem to the front desk clerk, who fooled around on his computer for several minutes and then picked up a phone. He spoke into it quietly and then set it down.

A few minutes later, Angie appeared. She wore tight denim jeans and a fitted striped cotton shirt. "Did you forget your keycard again?" she greeted warmly.

They started walking back to the elevators. The other band members had already gone up. "No, I don't think I ever had it. I must've left it in the room," Joe guessed.

"How did the meeting go?" Angie asked with not a trace of expectation in her voice.

They stood at the elevators. "Well, Theremin is releasing 'Xylene'," Joe offered. "I guess that's the big thing. It sounds like they're linin up some videos, and they're even gettin started bookin a tour."

Angie didn't reply to Joe, because several people collected around them, waiting for the elevators. Angie feared Joe would be recognized, which would be especially likely if they were talking about releasing an album.

An elevator door opened, and Joe and Angie got on, along with everyone else. A man in his 40s parked himself at the buttons and asked people for their floor. When he asked Joe, Angie spoke up and said, "Twenty." The man pushed 20 for Angie. Joe held back his answer. Everyone was quiet on the elevator. At the 18th floor, the last guy got off, and the door closed. Angie then removed her card and inserted it in the slot. Joe looked at her and asked, "Why did you do that?"

"I didn't want to explain to everyone we're in the penthouse. It just attracts attention. And I didn't want to have to push my way through the elevator to use my card." What Angie didn't say was that it was actually a habit to isolate Joe from his fans.

"That's good thinkin," Joe commended.

"Thank you," Angie said. "Stu called about the Hot Rocks interview. He told me you wouldn't let him submit a contract to Theremin Records."

"Yeah, he just wouldn't back off. Did he start in on you, too?"

The elevator rose to the 20th floor, and the doors opened. Angie and Joe mutely stood, looking at the 20th floor lobby. Then the doors closed.

"He's Stu," Angie answered. "Of course he did."

The elevator stopped, and the doors opened to their suite. They stepped off.

Joe asked, "So, what did you do today?"

"I went to the mall," Angie said. "I bought this shirt." Angie struck a pose.

Studying the shirt, Joe appraised, "Very nice."

"I bought some other shirts, too, and I bought some books."

"Books?" Joe asked. "What're you readin?"

"Um, romance books. Well, I also found a book on amnesia, and also one on multiple personality disorder." Angie had been worried all day that Joe would take offense at her intrusion.

"Hey, that's a good idea!" Joe exclaimed. "Can I read them when you're done? Or, better yet, can I read the one you're not reading? Then we can switch off."

"You really don't mind?"

"No. It's a good idea. Let's find out what we're dealin with."

All that worry for nothing. "But first, tell me how the meeting went! Give me all the details."

Joe sat in the big chair in the recessed rec room. Angie perched on the loveseat. Joe told the whole story from beginning to end. He included what Ed had said about Donna from the graphic arts company, and concluded that he still thought Ed was kidding him. And Joe talked about the pressure Stu and Michael put on him to allow the contract proposal.

Angie shifted her position on the loveseat. "Why *didn't* you allow Stu to propose the contract?" Angie knew that another three-record contract with Theremin was Joe's primary objective. Writing, recording, performing, they were all done with that ultimate objective in view: A second three record contract. With three records behind them, the band had the established name, and with three records to go, they could pave the way for everlasting stardom. At the end of six successful records, they could not be stopped. But the crucial step was getting from the first contract to the second. Joe would have made any sacrifice to get there. Angie knew, because she'd heard Joe speak endlessly on the subject. So it alarmed her that this new Joe would, without a solid reason, hold back Stu's contract proposal.

Joe hesitated, then started to answer, then stopped. Finally, he answered, "I guess it just doesn't feel right. All the information that we're given tells us we have to grab this chance. But all the information we're given comes from Stu. And Michael. If production guys typically offer contracts, then why are we offering a contract to Theremin? By doing that, we're actually shutting out Theremin's competition. If we offer them a contract, then they can take it, and the game is over." Joe frowned. "If we're in a staring contest with Theremin, then we blinked. They know we want a contract bad. But now I'm going to make them wait. And see what happens."

Angie tucked her foot under her seat, shifting her position as she considered her next statement. "Joe, do you think this is wise in your present mental state? After all, you aren't familiar with the business or your relationship with Michael."

Joe nodded. "Yeah. I'm in a position to see everything a lot more objectively than anyone else. I took 'Negotiation Mastery', and this has red flags all over it! For example, I wanna know why Stu won't show me the contract. I think he had it with him the whole day. Why did he pretend to not have it? Because if I'd a known he had it, then I'd a wanted to see it! And he wouldn't a had any reason to not give it to me. The more he stalls, the more I wanna know why.

"And also I'm a little curious as to why nobody else does. Is Stu really worthy of that much trust? Or is everyone that blindly desperate for a contract?

"And why is there such a rush all of a sudden? What's *their* deadline?"

Angie saw that she wasn't going to move Joe on this subject. She stood and stretched, noticing that Joe was eyeing her little 5'2" frame. "Are you ready for bed?" she inquired.

"Uh, no. I think I'm gonna stay up a bit. I'm still wired from the meeting," Joe said.

Angie nodded and padded up the stairs. Joe rested in the overstuffed chair until he fell asleep, six minutes later.

Chapter 6

Dr. Vrakas

He woke up. Early sun shone through the den window. A blanket had been placed over him. He could hear the shower running. Joe stood and stretched. Then he went upstairs to the guitar room. He picked out the red-and-white guitar, apparently the oldest of the set. The finish was worn; the back of it was worn to a matte, but still smooth, finish. Several dents decorated the bottom of it, and there was a dark stain at the base of the neck. Joe sat on the bed and picked out a few notes. He tried picking the notes that made up "Let's Move" and after much trial and error, he succeeded in reproducing the chorus. He started on the verse, when Angie said from behind him, "Even I can tell you're holding the neck wrong."

Joe jumped. "Geez, I didn't hear you. Sorry."

Angie smiled. "No, I'm sorry. I snuck up. I've always liked to see you play." Joe always immersed himself in his music, and floated in it with an undistracted bliss.

"Oh. How should I be holding it?"

"Put your hand under it," Angie told him, "and put your thumb on the back of the neck."

Joe complied. His knuckles lined up under the neck with his thumb bent and touching its tip against the neck. "Like this?" he asked.

Angie smiled. "Not at all." She came around the bed and knelt in front of Joe. "Put, cup your hand a little." She manipulated Joe's hand so his thumb pad touched the neck, and the thumb was parallel to the neck. "See, your fingers can reach all the strings. Here's a C-chord." She lifted each finger and placed it on a string. "When you strum it, you get a C-chord."

Joe ran his right thumb down the strings, half of which buzzed. "That sounds bad," Joe accurately judged. He adjusted his fingers and tried again, this time achieving a harmonious sound. Joe smiled a boyish smile. To Angie, it was a smile without concern or conditions. It was smile of appreciation.

"Thank you," he said. "I made my first chord! Angie, do you play guitar?"

"No, but you can't live with Joe and not learn about it." The absurdity of telling Joe about living with Joe reminded her of their appointment. "You're going to be late for Dr. Vrakas," Angie said, standing.

Joe took the bathroom. While Joe showered, Angie put on some light make-up (leaving her freckles visible, but not obvious) and phoned down for breakfast. She flipped through yesterday's messages. She hesitated. Should she pick out Joe's clothes? Then she had an idea. She pulled out what she had bought yesterday: A pack of fresh, white briefs. She laid them out on the bed, and nothing else. Then she sighed and called Stu.

When Angie talked to Stu, especially on the phone, time sped up by a big factor. Because with Stu, information flowed much slower than it would in a normal conversation. Today's conversation listed reasons why Joe shouldn't involve himself in negotiations between Stu and other parties. Angie agreed with Stu on every point, but he wouldn't stop making his point.

Joe came out of the bathroom dressed only in his boxer shorts and stood looking at the area of the bed on which his new underwear rested. "Is this mine?" he asked Angie.

"Hold on, please," Angie told Stu and covered the mouthpiece of the receiver. She was tempted to say something witty like, "No, it's the pool boy's" or "No, I've decided to take up cross-dressing," but she just answered, "Yes. I bought it yesterday. Enjoy."

Joe answered, "Good, cause it looked way too big to be yours." He snatched it up and headed for the bathroom, then pivoted and went to his dresser. He opened his drawers and picked through the clothes. Having assessed the inventory, he whipped out a pair of black pants and an orange and green polo shirt. Angie wondered if he was waiting for her to stop him as he reentered the bathroom. Apparently not. She went back to trying to complete the conversation with Stu. He picked up on his one-sided debate as if there had been no interruption. Eventually, Joe came out of the bathroom. Angie disengaged herself from Stu, figuring she would have to work out more details later. Joe headed down the stairs first with Angie following.

"Wait a minute, Joe," Angie said. "Your collar is flipped under back here."

He stopped on the stairs so Angie could fix his collar. "Thanks," he said and continued down.

They ate breakfast. "Tell me about Dr. Vrakas," Joe said. "How many sessions did Joe have with her?"

"About six or eight," Angie answered between nibbles. "She's very professional. Nothing but business. I never really liked her. Too cold." Angie was uneasy criticizing Dr. Vrakas in front of Joe, knowing that he liked her.

Joe swallowed his bagel. "Joe must have liked that about her."

"Yes," Angie admitted. "I never really understood it." But she thought she was beginning to. Changing the subject, Angie said, "I don't know how long you want to spend with Dr. Vrakas today. I can call in every few hours to see how it's going. Or I can just leave the car and you can drive yourself back when you're done."

Joe looked up in alarm. "Aren't you staying? Do you have to be someplace?"

Angie was surprised, because Joe had always been very private about his sessions. Maybe she misunderstood him. She asked, "Do you want me to wait for you in the lobby?" She would have, if he wanted, but she would have been bored, at least, after the first couple of hours.

Joe shook his head. "No, I want you to be in the room. Y'know, like part of the conversation. That is, if you want to."

"Okay," Angie agreed. "If that's what you want."

Breakfast ended. Angie packed up a book and her purse on the way to the elevator. Joe trailed. They got on the elevator and rode to the parking garage. For the first time, there was no limousine waiting. Angie led Joe across several aisles to a BMW coupe (dark blue). Angie headed for the passenger side.

"Would you drive?" Joe asked. "You already know where we're going."

Another surprise. Joe had always insisted on driving. This was fine with Angie, because he was such a terrible passenger. Mainly he just kept giving direction: "Get in this lane. Speed up to get by this guy," etc. Even in the limousine, he was tense, frequently commenting on the driver's tactics. But he hadn't been since the transformation. So she agreed.

She put on a pair of huge sunglasses and pulled out of the garage into the bright sunlight. She took a different street and got onto Interstate 10, going east. Joe's presence unnerved her; she kept expecting him to start "helping" her drive. So, though she reminded herself not to, she kept second-guessing her actions. Traffic was light. It was past rush hour, and they were traveling out of the city besides. Joe sat beside her, quietly watching the world go by. Finally, he asked, "What town is Dr. Vrakas in?"

"San Gabriel," Angie answered. "We'll be there soon."

Joe nodded and continued looking around. He looked like he was taking it all in, like his mind was absorbing everything, and completely without judgment. Then he said, "Are you nervous about seeing Dr. Vrakas?"

"No," Angie answered.

Joe considered this. "Well, you seem nervous about something. Are you?"

Angie glanced at him. "Yes, you're making me nervous. I don't like driving in front of you."

Joe smiled. "Why not? You're doin a great job."

"I'd rather not discuss it," Angie told him. She didn't want to have to justify her discomfort.

Joe accepted her rebuff. After a minute, he asked, "Whose car is this?"

"It's a rental."

Joe stayed quiet.

Eventually, Angie pulled off Interstate 10 onto San Gabriel Boulevard North. Then she turned off the boulevard and soon arrived at Dr. Vrakas' building and its clean, white parking lot. She eased into a space. The building was blocky and sprawling. Angie and Joe went in the front door and up the stairs one floor. Dr. Vrakas' office was across the hall. The corridor smelled of acrid carpet cleaner. The waiting room, though, was smell-free. Angie and Joe approached the receptionist, a young man with precise hair. Angie announced them. He ushered them directly into the office.

Dr. Nastassia Vrakas was a medium height with long black hair pulled tightly back into a thick braid. She had dark eyes and a strong nose and a jutting chin. When Joe and Angie entered, she sat behind her desk. She stood and came around to meet them. "It's nice to see you again, Angie, Joe." She said it as she shook their hands. She gestured to a trio of stuffed chairs. "Please sit down."

Dr. Vrakas' office was expansive, and it contained her large desk (At which she did no work; her real desk was in another room off of this one.), a cabinet against one wall, and several conversation areas, each apparently arranged for a specific function: a sofa facing two chairs, a circle of chairs, and the three chairs in which they sat now. Large windows faced over the back parking lot. And if they didn't provide enough light, track lighting lit the several conversation areas. The furniture was all dark wood and velvet, except for the desk chair which was dark wood and leather. Angie doubted that Dr. Vrakas' involvement in the décor was anything further than selecting an interior designer.

Joe and Angie sat. Dr. Vrakas sat facing them. She wore a loose silk blouse and a short skirt, and she held a spiral notebook. Her attire, Angie thought, was entirely professional and yet innocently provocative. Dr. Vrakas crossed her shapely legs. "Are you comfortable?" she asked. When they said yes, she responded, "What would you like to talk about today?"

Joe and Angie exchanged glances. Joe said, "Well, I have a problem. I have no memories of myself as Joe Ecks. Instead, I remember myself to be Mike Smith. I think that qualifies me as crazy."

Angie smiled behind her hand. Dr. Vrakas stiffened. "We don't like to use that term, you kn—"

Joe held up his hand. "I know. I'm sorry." He chuckled. "See, I'd think I had simple amnesia, if I didn't think I was someone else. So it sounds more like multiple personality disorder."

Dr. Vrakas tapped her pencil against her lips. "To whom am I speaking now? Mike?"

"Yeah, Mike. That's who I would swear I am, if the evidence wasn't overwhelmingly against me."

"Tell me about yourself, Mike," Dr. Vrakas suggested. "What's the first thing you remember?"

"Huh? Swate Jasus, the first thing I can remember is seein the ocean. Mom and Dad tell me I was two then."

"What do you remember about the ocean?"

Joe shrugged. "It was a lotta water. The waves were huge. They scared me."

"Did you go in the water?"

Joe chuckled. "I don't remember."

"Okay, what else can you tell me about yourself?"

"My name is Michael Koop Smith. I was born March 10th, 1960. I'm the third of five children. My father owns a garage in Davenport, Virginia. That's where I grew up. Davenport's a little blip on route 80 in the south corner of Buchanan County. Y'know that little upward bump on the west tail of Virginia?"

"I know where Virginia is," Dr. Vrakas allowed.

"Uh, okay," Joe said. "Well anyway, I didn't go to school there, though. I went to Clintwood in Dickenson County. We were right on the county border. My first grade teacher was Mrs. Cody. I was already readin pretty fluently, but that was because my older sister Denise was teachin me. She was a year ahead of me and liked to show me what she had just learned. When I caught up to her, Annette, my oldest sister, started teachin me. They liked showin off what I could do."

Dr. Vrakas interrupted. "So you're saying that you are intelligent."

Joe nodded. "Yes. I skipped the third and fifth grades, and then my dad put a stop to it. So I graduated in ten years magna cum laude. Course, we're talkin 'bout Clintwood High School, so it's not a real big deal. Dad had me doin the books and orderin at the garage, and that was okay. I did it for about a year and a half before I realized that's what he expected me to do forever. I was still livin at home savin my money. On a lark, I applied to UVA, business. See, I'd taken the SATs, and after that, I had colleges from all over writin to me. I got a night job in Charlottesville at a grodge, and I went to college. After the first year, I was broke and exhausted. I told my counselor I had to drop out for a while, and she set me up with a scholarship. It wasn't a full scholarship, but she set up loans to cover the difference." Joe looked at Dr. Vrakas. "Is this the stuff you want to hear?"

Angie's mouth was practically hanging open. Joe was utterly convincing in describing his history as Mike Smith. She could see him as a bright kid in a little school in the hills of Virginia, going home to work in his dad's garage. And maybe that was why he was so out of place in the air-conditioned southern California limousines and mixing rooms. She had thought so much about how he wasn't Joe that she never wondered about who he thought he was. Not that it mattered in the long run anyway. But he was so convincing.

And as he talked and relaxed, his southern accent became more apparent.

Dr. Vrakas answered, "Do your memories seem continuous? Any big gaps or unexplained periods of time? Amnesia?"

"No," Joe answered.

"What's the last thing you remember before you found yourself here?"

"Well, I was at Harvard, and I'd just successfully defended my thesis, my master's thesis. It was such a big relief. Like I'd taken a big-ol' C-clamp off a my head. I was packin up my apartment gettin drunk an sloppy. I was pacin and gripin, and my roommate goes, 'I don't see what your problem is, you're all set for the rest of your life.'" Joe stopped. He inhaled slowly and exhaled unevenly. His voice quavered when he spoke again. "An Ah realized he was rot, an the thot horrified me. Then Ah got dizzy, an it felt like mah brain exploded. The nex thing, I was lyin on the floor in the mixin room lookin up at Angie."

"What did the doctor say? Did he find any possible medical cause?" asked Dr. Vrakas.

"No," Joe said.

"We didn't see a doctor," Angie started to explain.

"You had a seizure and didn't see a doctor?" asked Dr. Vrakas. "You should see a doctor and get an MRI; you could have a tumor. Maybe also—"

"I had an MRI last week," Joe informed the doctor. He turned to Angie. "How many doctors have I seen in the past few weeks?"

Thinking, Angie replied, "Well, the neurologist, the derma-tologist, the gastro—"

"That's enough, I get your point," Dr. Vrakas said testily. "Most people would see a doctor regardless."

Joe crossed his arms. "I am."

Dr. Nastassia Vrakas regarded Joe Ecks. She said, "Indeed. Very well. Let's leave that topic. Joe, what do you know about multiple personality disorder?"

"I know this ain't it, exactly."

"No, not exactly. But it could be. MPD manifests itself in many different ways." She considered this. "J—Mike, are you aware of any other personalities?"

Joe shook his head. Angie concurred.

Dr. Vrakas pondered this for a few moments, and then she asked Angie to explain in detail what had happened prior to Joe's seizure and personality change. Angie described the pressure on Joe and the tension in the mixing room. She described Sam's outburst and quoted the last words he said before Joe's seizure. She described the seizure and how she thought Joe was dead, and then Joe had come back to life, but not as Joe.

"Interesting parallel," Dr. Vrakas observed.

Angie said, "What about reincarnation?"

Dr. Vrakas admitted with a smile, "It could be reincarnation. But I'm a psychologist, and I help people with situations involving psychology." She turned to Joe. "Have you tried to verify the existence of Mike Smith?"

Joe blinked and answered, "No."

"Why not?"

"Cause I'm Joe Ecks." Joe chuckled. "I mean, all the evidence points to that. It's kinda hard to dispute."

Dr. Vrakas asked, "And how do you feel about being Joe Ecks?"

"Well, I'm quite nervous about not bein able to play the guitar. Or anything else. I feel like a fraud, because eventually I'm gonna hafta do my job, and I won't be able to do that. There's a lotta people dependin on me to be Joe and have Joe's abilities and talent. But I can't satisfy 'em, cause I'm not Joe." Joe huffed in frustration.

"Okay," Dr. Vrakas said, smiling, "but what if you had Joe's abilities? Would you like that?"

Joe laughed. "Are you kidding? This is a dream! People recognize me everywhere, I'm hangin with X Band, 'cept for Joe a course. I'm tall and good lookin, and I've apparently got tons a money, and I'm married to a beautiful woman who's really nice to be around. People look to me to make important decisions. I mean, swate Jasus, I'm a rock star! What could be better than this?"

Dr. Vrakas nodded. "Yes. I want you to take some personality tests, if you would. It should take about an hour. Meanwhile, I'd like to talk to Angie alone." She went to a file cabinet and pulled out several booklets. She handed them to Joe with brief instructions and set him up in the adjacent conference room.

Joe went to work on the questionnaires. After about ten minutes, he looked up. The receptionist was in the doorway.

"Hey," said Joe. "Can I help you?"

The receptionist answered, "Um. How're you doing?"

"I'm fine. How are you?"

"Oh. Okay. I liked your album 'Xylophone'."

Joe smiled. "Thank you. We did another one since then. 'Xenon'."

The receptionist said, "Yeah. That one wasn't as good."

Joe nodded. "No, I don't think so, either. It's like we were trying too hard. I thought 'Xylophone' came off more spontaneous."

The receptionist agreed. He added, "That's pretty cool that you can listen to your own work so objectively. Do you think you'll get a replacement for Skinner in the band?"

Joe started to answer, but then he said, "You know, I could talk about me all morning, but I've got to fill out these surveys. About me. Otherwise, Dr. Vrakas will get real mad, at both of us, probably."

The receptionist jumped. "Yeah. Oh, could I have an autograph?" He handed Joe a pad of paper. "I'm Felix."

Joe accepted the pad. He wrote, "Please allow Felix to be in the halls between classes, Joe Ecks." He handed back the pad. Felix looked at it curiously. "It's like a hall pass," Joe explained.

"Oh, yeah," Felix said and left. Joe went back to his surveys. After 45 minutes, he looked up. He was done. He looked around the room. He stood and stretched. He looked out the window down at the back parking lot. He wandered into the hall and saw Felix.

Felix stood. "Hi, Joe. Do you need something?"

"No, I'm done, and I'm waiting for the ladies to stop talking."

Just then Dr. Vrakas opened her door. "Do you need some help?" she asked.

"No, I'm done," Joe answered.

"Fine," she said, a trifle surprised. "I'll be with you in a moment." She closed her door.

Joe watched the door for a few moments. The muffled sounds of Angie and Dr. Vrakas talking filtered through. Joe looked at Felix, who was looking at him, and said, "It would seem I'm a little ahead of schedule." Felix agreed, and Joe kept watch on the door.

Several minutes later, Dr. Vrakas opened it. "You may come in, Joe." She took Joe's paperwork as Joe entered the room. A box of tissues sat on the floor by Angie's chair, and Angie's eyes were bloodshot. Dr. Vrakas thumbed through the sheets to see that they were all filled out. Then she told Joe and Angie, "I'm going to need a while to score these. You might as well go out for an early lunch." With that, she diplomatically ushered them out of her office to the lobby.

Joe started to say something when Angie said, "I have to go to the bathroom," and she fled to the one off the lobby. Joe waited. He reached for his shirt pocket, then he went to push up his glasses. He settled for lightly touching the calluses on his left hand fingertips. Then he wandered into the men's bathroom. When he returned, Angie was still absent. A few minutes later, she returned.

She was looking better but still feeling wrung-out. There were times when Angie would realize there was no upcoming break to anticipate, that the sprint was really a marathon. Those times drove weariness to her core, and this was one of those times. She handed the keys to Joe. "You drive," she said, too tired to even brace for an argument. To her surprise (and irritation at being surprised by Joe yet *again*), Joe simply accepted the keys. They got in the BMW. Joe adjusted his seat.

"Do you have a preference?" he asked. When Angie shook her head, he pulled away. Angie knew she was treating Joe unfairly, but she couldn't help it. A part of her blamed Joe for this mess, and she was too tired to talk herself out of it. Joe drove back the way they had come until he pulled into a Taco Bell.

"Taco Bell?" Angie asked. "Are you kidding?" The cars at the drive-thru wrapped around the building. Joe pulled into a space beside the front door. "We're going in?" she asked.

"Yeah, they don't come to your car anymore," Joe replied.

They went inside and got in line. It was a short line. Shorter than the drive-thru, anyway. Most of the tables were vacant. Three young professional men at one table were pretending not to notice Angie and Joe. Angie tried to be inconspicuous by studying the overhead menu, but she worried that it wouldn't work. Joe seemed oblivious, though, Angie noted. Before, he would behave with such a flourish that he would have the attention of the room in seconds. The line didn't move.

"Angie, do you have the money?" Joe asked. "I haven't seen my wallet in days."

"Um, yes, I have your wallet here. I keep it in my purse."

"Most guys keep their wallets in their hip pockets," Joe commented.

Angie looked up at Joe. "You never liked sitting on it."

"Can I see it?" Joe asked. Angie handed it to him, and he looked through it. He pulled out business cards and examined them. He counted the money without pulling it out, which was good, because it was enough money to attract attention in a Taco Bell. He pulled out a few pieces of paper, unfolded them and read them. Everything he looked at, he carefully replaced in its original condition. He said a concluding "Hmmp," and handed it back to Angie. "I'll have to take a closer look at that stuff at a more appropriate time," he said. The line moved forward one step. Joe asked Angie if she were feeling any better.

Angie considered the question. "Yes. I guess so." Actually, her despair had been displaced by tension from their exposure at Taco Bell. But, she reflected, despair and tension are both bad, so, not a clear gain. Then they advanced to the counter. Joe ordered a taco salad. Angie got a burrito. Joe led her to the table across two aisles from the young professionals.

As he crammed salad ingredients into his mouth, he asked about Michael, things that Angie would know. What had their starting relationship been like? What had driven Michael to such aggression? Angie answered as best as she could, despite the frequent glances from the professionals. At any minute, she feared they would come over and draw everyone's attention to Joe. Meanwhile, she struggled to eat the burrito without getting any of it on her.

Then Angie realized Joe had stopped talking. He said, "Do you miss him, Angie?"

At first she thought Joe was talking about Michael. When she understood, she didn't know how to answer. To say yes would figuratively slap this Joe's face, but to say no would betray her husband Joe. She couldn't win either way. She hesitated. Joe waited. She answered truthfully, "Yes. I miss him."

Joe didn't seem at all hurt by this admission. With a deep understanding, he nodded. "Yeah, I'm sorry. Y'know, I've been thinkin so much about me that I forgot all about you and what you had lost. Um. Do you wanna talk about it?"

Angie sighed. "Not right now." Just then, the young profess-sionals got up from their table. Angie froze. With a few departing glances their way, they left the restaurant. Joe turned and watched them leave. Angie let out her breath.

Joe asked, "Were they botherin you? They sure were checkin you out, I'll say that."

Angie shook her head. "You don't know how dangerous it is for us to be out in public," she said in a low voice. "It's a good thing no one has recognized you yet, otherwise, this place would turn into a madhouse. I think those men recognized you, but it was so weird that you would be in a Taco Bell in San Gabriel that they didn't believe it."

"You don't give yourself enough credit. If *I* saw you in a Taco Bell, *I'd* be checkin you out."

Angie didn't know what to say. She didn't think anyone ever looked at her when she was with Joe. And she couldn't tell if he was even serious. So she changed the subject. "Let's go," she said.

They got up and headed out. Joe held the door open for her, as he had since the change.

Joe started to reach for Angie's breast area, and he pulled his hand away like he saw a tarantula there. "Uh," Joe said. Blushing, he pointed. "Uh, you have a crumb there. I'm sorry, I didn't mean to get in your space," he stammered.

Angie looked down. A flake of bread was on her blouse near her collarbone. She brushed it away delicately. "Thank you," she said.

They returned to Dr. Vrakas' office. Felix wasn't there, but Dr. Vrakas' door was open so they peeked in. She sat at her desk with papers spread out and two books lying open. She absently speared a melon piece from a Tupperware and ate it. When she saw Joe and Angie at the door, she waved them in. "You're much earlier than I expected," she greeted, "but I'm ready." She gestured for them to sit as she stowed her Tupperware into a desk drawer. "Okay. As an intern, I did a bit of career counseling, and that experience has been useful. So I had you fill out this survey." She held up one of the surveys. "This asks you random questions and compares your answers to those of people who have been successful in a wide variety of fields. You took this same test about three months ago when we were meeting. Do you remember the conclusion?"

Joe looked at Dr. Vrakas indignantly.

"Oh, no, of course not," she said. "At that time, the highest match was with entrepreneurs. The next highest was with business executives."

Joe raised his eyebrows. "Interesting."

"Yes," Dr. Vrakas agreed. "Today you took that same test. Your results this time were quite different. Your highest match was with entertainers. The next highest was with artists. Then salesmen."

"I can believe *that!*" Angie stated.

Joe said, "The implications are astounding. What about the other test I took?"

"This is what I was just finishing. It's called Predictive Index. It uses four indices to map your personality. Not just your personality, but what you believe is required of you by your job. Three months ago, I had you do this exercise. And here's your profile from then."

She laid a single piece of paper on the desk. The paper showed three jagged lines. "This shows that, at that time, Joe's dominant personality trait was his drive to prove himself."

Angie shifted in her seat.

Dr. Vrakas continued. "He had a considerable ego, which he had to sustain by continually logging successes. A close second to his ego was his attention to detail. High attention to detail also implies maintaining a fastidiously neat appearance and environment with a rigid system of organization. The high ego and high attention to detail drove Joe to succeed through control of detail. At the same time, he was fairly reclusive and energetic. So Joe would spend a lot of time alone, energetically manipulating details to assure success." Dr. Vrakas looked up from the paper. "Does this sound like the Joe from before?"

Angie said, "Yes."

Dr. Vrakas nodded. "Exactly. Now here's the mold that Joe felt his career was forcing him into. The dominant characteristic here is a high level of social adaptation, combined with an extremely casual attitude. Joe's job forced him to be far more social than was natural and to relax on details. And he had to be a good team player."

"He was not a good team player," Angie confirmed, poker-faced.

Dr. Vrakas nodded. "Not a good job match. In fact, the worst I've seen, ever. According to the publisher, these test results can't be faked, and they never change. People have been tested decades apart, and their results are the same, because people don't change their personalities." Dr. Vrakas looked at Joe. "That's one reason I was so eager to have you take this test, Joe. I mean Mike." Dr. Vrakas put another set of profiles beside the first. "Here are Mike's results." She hesitated.

Joe leaned forward. "They're the same!" he exclaimed. "No, wait. They're opposite. Sort of."

"Exactly. Your new personality matches exactly the demands of the job that Joe outlined. And look at this: Your old job, as a budding business manager, matches Joe's personality."

Joe studied the sheets with intensity for a moment. Several moments. Neither Angie nor Dr. Vrakas wanted to break his concentration. Finally, Joe leaned back in his chair and said, "This supports the results of the first test."

Dr. Vrakas answered, "Exactly. A bad job match induces tension, and a really bad job match like this induces an incredible amount of tension, as a person is forced to behave in a way that is not natural for them. The tension is manifested in different ways, but usually what you see is anger. Sometimes in explosive outbursts. Or there's anger turned inwards so you get depression or self-destructive behavior. Or the person could suffer psychosomatic physical maladies. Tell me, Joe, how have your headaches been since the change?"

"Well, bad at first, but they're gettin better. I didn't have one yesterday."

"What about your depression? Have you been taking your medication?"

"Uh, no problems there. I've been takin the pills Angie gives me to take."

"How are you sleeping?"

"Soundly. 'Cept, I have bad dreams and wake up. I go right back to sleep, though."

"What about your blood pressure? Do you know what it is?"

"No. I don't know."

"What about your skin rashes?"

"I don't have any."

"How's your stomach?"

"It burns sometimes, but it's not bad."

"How is your lower back pain?"

"No problem there."

"How's your impotence?"

Joe chuckled. "Well, I'm not impotent." Then his face fell and reddened to his collar.

Dr. Vrakas looked at Angie for confirmation. Indignant, Angie looked at Joe. "How would you know that, Joe?" she demanded. "*I* wouldn't know that!"

Joe sank into his chair like he wanted to sink through it to the floor, or possibly through the floor below that. "Uh," he said, covering his eyes. "I've, uh, y'know, tested the equipment." He continued to stare at the floor. "It's been a long time since I was uncircumcised."

Dr. Vrakas interrupted Joe's embarrassment. "Well, the point is, you've had a host of ailments that are all stress-induced. Now these have all subsided or are downright resolved. And you say if you could play guitar, then you'd love to have this job forever."

Joe nodded and looked up.

"Well, uh, Mike, what does this suggest to you?"

Joe said wearily, "Dr. Vrakas, I don't want to play therapy games. Just tell me what you think."

"Okay, this is what I think: Faced with an indefinite future in a job that opposes your personality, you, I mean Joe, fabricated a Mike personality who would fit the demands of the job perfectly."

"But the amazing part," Joe said excitedly, "is that the Mike personality came from a career that Joe would love! It's symmetric! And utterly seamless! But what about all the memories? Joe created all that in an instant?"

"No," Dr. Vrakas said. "I'll bet you really don't have those memories until you call for them. Joe is creating your memories on demand."

"Amazing!" Joe uttered.

Angie asked, "What do we have to do to get Joe back?"

"Generally, in the case of multiple personalities, it's impossible to retain one of the personalities and make it permanent. What we, uh, psychologists, try to do is integrate the personalities into a fusion personality. But from what I've read, the success rate is low. The subject's personality keeps splitting off more. But the actual number of documented, authentic cases is very low. Anyway, a fusion may never happen here. Joe has worked hard and has done a masterful job at creating a personality that is a perfect match for his job. We may never see Joe again. Or Joe may return when it's safe, like when Mike retires or changes jobs. On the other hand, Joe may return when being Mike is more stressful than being Joe."

Angie nodded. So, then, all they had to do would be to wait, and eventually Joe would return, and in time to handle whatever faced them.

"Dr. Vrakas," Joe said quietly, "if Joe should return, will I cease to exist? Would it, in effect, be the same as death?"

Angie gasped. The implications of Joe's questions were vast.

He seemed to anticipate Angie's thoughts, because his next question was, "And would my permanent existence essentially kill Joe? Who has more of a right to life? And who decides that?"

Dr. Vrakas was speechless, at least until she answered, "I think this is why integration of the personalities is preferred. We should work on that. And if you're not here, you should keep up the effort."

Joe spread his hands. "How? How do I do that? I don't sense another personality in me or anything. What do I do?"

Dr. Vrakas picked up a paperclip off her desk and held it up. "I want to try something. Joe, focus on the paperclip. This isn't hypnosis, but I want you to relax. Okay?"

Joe slouched in his seat, preparing to relax. "Okay."

Dr. Vrakas continued to hold up the paperclip. "Watch the paperclip. Relax." She continued to softly urge Joe to relax, let go, allow his mind to wander free. Joe sagged slowly. Even the muscles in his face seemed to loosen up. His breathing deepened and slowed. "Okay, Mike, do you sense Joe with you?"

"No."

"Would you step aside so I can talk to Joe?"

"Okay."

Dr. Vrakas paused. "Joe, can you answer me?" Joe was silent. Dr. Vrakas repeated the question. Joe didn't say anything. His eyelids were even sagging. Dr. Vrakas waited for a long minute. Then she asked, "Mike, are you there?"

"Yep," Joe answered.

Dr. Vrakas repeated the calming down mantra until it looked like Joe was nearly unconscious. But Joe refused to answer. Finally, Dr. Vrakas gave up and brought Joe back to life. "You may want to try this on your own," she suggested. "I would suspect, though, that your fears about losing control are preventing Joe from returning. Both of you have very strong egos." Dr. Vrakas stood, and Angie and Joe stood in response. "Angie, will you excuse us? I'd like to talk to Joe alone."

Throughout the session, Angie was troubled by the way Dr. Vrakas had been speaking to Joe, as if they had been a little more familiar than they should have been. She didn't want to leave Dr. Vrakas with her short skirt and her big, dark eyes alone with Joe. "Uh, okay. May I use your phone?" When Dr. Vrakas said yes, she left the room.

Dr. Vrakas sat, and so did Joe. She looked at Joe.

Joe asked, "Why did you ask Angie to leave?"

Dr. Vrakas started to answer, and then she changed her mind. "No therapist games. I asked her to leave, because I want to ask you some very personal questions that you may not answer truthfully if Angie were in the room. Then, if I asked you later, you would repeat your previous answers."

Joe nodded. "That makes sense." He grinned. "I don't hafta answer if I don't want to, do I?"

Dr. Vrakas smiled. "No, of course not. But I'm trying to help you, and you're paying the bill." She inhaled. "Joe, I gather that you haven't been intimate with Angie since you changed to Mike."

"You go right for the jugular, don't you?" Joe laughed nervously. "Well, yeah, that's true."

"Why not?"

Joe didn't answer. Dr. Vrakas didn't break the silence. Finally, Joe said, "Angie's married. I look like Joe, but I'm not. To me, Angie is another man's wife. And even if she were available, from my perspective, I've only known her for a few days. It feels too soon for, uh, for y'know."

"That's not really the reason, though, is it?" This was not a question.

Joe looked down. "No. Well, yeah, some. I mean, what I said was true." Joe took a breath and let it out. "Dr. Vrakas, I'm not an attractive guy. Every relationship I've had with a female ended when I touched her. In fact, if I *wanted* to end a relationship, all I'd hafta do is suggest, uh, physical, uh, romance." Joe sighed. "I'd do anything to not repel Angie."

"You don't repel Angie," Dr. Vrakas pointed out.

Joe frowned. "*Joe* doesn't repel Angie. But *I'm not Joe!*"

Dr. Vrakas side-stepped by asking, "Mike, are you a virgin?"

Joe grimaced. "Well, sorta."

Dr. Vrakas smiled and asked, "'Sorta'? What do you mean by that?"

Joe wiped his forehead. "Swate Jasus, this is *rilly* personal! Kin we talk about somethin else?"

Dr. Vrakas pressed on. "Mike, are you heterosexual?"

"Yes," Joe answered. "I am." He wiped his forehead again. "Why is this so important?"

"I suspect there is a sexual component to the formation of your new personality," Dr. Vrakas told Joe bluntly. "You and Joe seem very different in this area, and I wonder what that means."

Joe chuckled. "Joe and I are very different in a *lot* of areas."

Dr. Vrakas nodded absently. "Joe may be fixing more than a bad job match by creating you." Then she said, "All right, Joe, what do *you* want? Why are you in my office? What do you want from *me*?"

"I want..." Joe stopped. He wiped his forehead and eyes. He said, "Angie and the band want Joe back. So I came..." Joe didn't finish.

"You came to sacrifice your identity for their benefit."

Joe nodded.

"So what do *you* want, Mike?"

Joe pushed up his non-existent glasses. He wiped his eyes. "Joe's life."

"Excuse me?"

"I want Joe's life." Joe looked up and met Dr. Vrakas' dark eyes.

Dr. Vrakas smiled. "Yes. Excellent. Joe—Mike—this is a critical time for *you*. Focus on what *you* want and figure out how to get it. We can talk about this at your next appointment."

Dr. Vrakas walked Joe to the lobby. Angie, seeing them from the conference room, closed her notebook and came out.

Dr. Vrakas offered her delicate hand to Joe. "It was good seeing you again, Joe."

Joe smiled wryly and shook Dr. Vrakas' hand. "It was nice to meet you," he said in gentle correction.

"Of course," Dr. Vrakas acknowledged. She shook Angie's hand. "And you take care of yourself. Remember what we talked about." She told Felix to schedule them both again in a week. "But," she told them both, "if anything changes before then, call me immediately." Dr. Vrakas went back into her office.

Angie and Felix, each consulting appointment books, negotiated an appointment less than two weeks out. Then Joe and Angie left. They went down the stairs to the BMW. Joe got out the keys and said, "I'll drive." It was still early afternoon. Waves of heat wafted from the concrete parking lot. They got in the car. Joe didn't start the engine. "Where do you want to go?" he asked Angie.

"Back to the hotel, unless you want to go somewhere else," she answered. In truth, she hadn't expected the question. Where else would they go? Besides, she had to get back on the phone and work out some details in the schedule for the upcoming week. With the album release announced, the demand on Joe's time would soar. And Stu did a poor job managing the practicalities; he accepted just about everything and left it to Angie to sort out what was possible.

Joe shrugged and started the car. He drove through the parking lot and pulled into the street. Angie watched the way he drove. It was, for New Joe, predictably casual. He drove at a normal rate and kept an eye out for traffic. He didn't shout at other cars. If you didn't know he was driving, you'd think he was just sitting in a chair. He came up to the stop sign by the Taco Bell and pressed his left foot against the left wheel well before stopping. Then he pulled away and drove on. Angie leaned back and relaxed. Old Joe drove like it was a competition, and he angered everyone on the road, including himself. Angie felt like kissing the ground when they would get to their destination. Angie looked over at Joe. She remembered that he believed he was Mike from Virginia. Yet he still drove a BMW along the California highway with ease. Angie wondered what he and Dr. Vrakas talked about in her absence. Probably her. Why else would Dr. Vrakas have asked her to leave? Angie really wanted to know, but she wasn't going to ask. Not like Joe would answer, much less tell the truth.

Traffic started slowing down and eventually came to a dead stop on the highway. Again, Joe's foot pressed the wheel well. Angie was about to ask him about that when Joe commented, "It looks like there's trouble up ahead."

Angie looked but couldn't see anything.

"Oh, I just mean, y'know, because the traffic stopped. They must've closed the whole highway."

Angie nodded. "Do you want to listen to the radio or some tapes?" she asked.

Joe frowned. "No, I want to talk about you and me." Angie blanched. She feared that she was about to find out exactly what Joe and Dr. Vrakas had discussed. Joe plowed on. "See, to me, you're like someone I just met a couple of days ago. An it seems to me like you're married to Joe, not me." Joe hesitated. "Does that make sense?"

Angie frowned. She could follow the implications, and she didn't like the destination. "I suppose," she admitted guardedly. "Why?"

"Well, I don't think it's right that we have a physical relationship," Joe concluded. Angie just waited for him to finish. "Y'know, with each other. It would be like you were being unfaithful. To Joe. With me." Joe turned up the AC.

Angie nodded. Unfortunately, the conversation was going exactly where she thought it would, but Joe was actually putting the sin on her. "Then I suppose it would be okay if you had a physical relationship with someone besides me. It wouldn't be Joe being unfaithful to me, it would be you. But you wouldn't be being unfaithful, because we're not married, according to you." Suddenly, Angie was defenseless, utterly without claim. She was sunk. "Is that it? Is that what you and Dr. Vrakas worked out today?"

Joe faked surprise convincingly. "Is that what you think? No, Angie, I would never do that. It wouldn't be right. But that's not the point of what I'm tryin to say."

Angie looked up at Joe. Was there hope?

Joe forged on. "See, when I admitted, y'know, that I knew I wasn't impotent, you seemed sorta upset, like rejected maybe?" Joe sighed in frustration at his inability to express himself. "But I wanted to tell you that it's not you. I'm not rejecting you. I'm just, y'know, uncomfortable."

Angie was at a loss. She could only say, "You're not thinking of leaving me?"

"Oh, hell, no," Joe said easily. "I'm grateful we spend so much time together as it is. I love... being with you." Angie was restraining herself from asking about Joe's close relationship with Dr. Vrakas, when Joe asked, "What tapes have we got in here?" It was a welcome diversion.

They listened to 'Who's Next?' by The Who and Led Zeppelin's 'In Through the Out Door'. The Eckses did not converse. Joe sang along with a few songs off 'Who's Next?', and encouraged Angie to join him, which she did not. As 'In Through the Out Door' concluded, traffic was creeping forward.

"What kind of music do you like?" Joe asked.

"60s," Angie answered, "like the Beatles. The Lovin' Spoonful. Some early Stones. Simon and Garfunkel and the Carpenters and stuff like that."

"I don't see any of those tapes in the pile," Joe commented.

"No," Angie answered. She couldn't really imagine Joe listening to music that she chose. Whose music they listened to wasn't ever discussed; it was always Joe's. She probably could have pushed the point and gotten to choose the music, but it just wasn't worth it. It was easier to keep the peace.

Chapter 7

The Album

In good time, Joe brought the car back to the hotel parking lot. Angie noticed that not once did he ask for directions. Either he was more observant than she thought him to be on the way out, or he remembered taking the drive before. Angie hadn't quite given up hope that, somehow, memories would bubble up.

They got in the elevator. Angie carded it so it would go to the penthouse, but she got off at the first floor to pick up messages. Joe rode alone up to their suite. While he waited for Angie, he poked around the different rooms, looking in drawers and cabinets. Then Angie appeared. "Are you looking for something?" she asked. She was holding the usual stack of messages.

"Yeah, but I don't know what for. I'm just lookin around," Joe answered.

"I've got a surprise for you," Angie said. She led him to the foyer. A 2' cube box was sitting on a chair. Angie ripped it open, with Joe looking over her shoulder. She pulled out a really thick notebook from a stack of notebooks. "Look," she said, "I had our photo albums sent from home."

"No kiddin!" Joe exclaimed. "Lemme see that." Angie handed him the notebook. He flipped through some pages, looking at the photographs. "Can we go through these together sometime?"

Angie beamed. "That's why I had them sent. When I thought you just had amnesia, I had these sent from home. I thought if we looked through these together, maybe your memory would return."

"Yeah, that's a good idea," Joe agreed.

Angie was happy that Joe liked the idea, but she was confused. "But Joe, you don't have amnesia. So this won't do any good, will it?"

"No," Joe agreed. "But I want to know more about Joe's history anyway. I mean, it will help me fake my way through bein Joe, but also, I really just wanna know."

Angie wasn't especially happy that Joe wanted to use the album to promote his deception, but he'd also said he just wanted to know, and that was a good sign. So Angie called room service and had dinner sent up. While they were waiting, she and Joe took their seats in the lounge. Joe seemed more at home than before in his big chair.

Before Angie could say anything, Joe asked, "Angie, what do *you* like to do? So far, you've spent all your time on me, so I don't have any idea."

Angie tucked her foot under her, pleased that Joe took an interest. "Well, I like to shop," she admitted. "I like helping the band. I've been sort of keeping a history of it. I don't know why. Maybe to help me remember these times. I suppose someday, I could put it together in a book. If I thought anyone would want to read it. I like to read. Mostly gothic romances." Angie squirmed a little in embarrassment. She didn't have any reason to be embarrassed; Joe knew about this already. It was almost as if she were seeing herself through new eyes, though it was just Joe. Well, New Joe, and New Joe had new eyes.

Joe smiled. "So those albums, are they the raw material for your book?"

"Yes," she answered. She hadn't really thought of her albums that way.

Dinner was served. Joe had a great big T-bone with steak fries. Angie had boneless, skinless chicken with rice and broccoli.

Joe asked, "Angie, who are *your* friends?"

Angie had to think about it before she answered, "Well, I like Cassie."

Joe nodded.

"Well, I spend most of my time with you and Ed. But you're not really friends, you're family." Angie hid an awkward silence by eating.

Joe waited patiently. Finally, Angie added, "I don't see any of my friends from high school any more. It just got too uncomfortable to see them. Linda joked that I was showing off the money, so I tried to play it down, but I think it came off as false modesty. They think I look down my nose at them and flaunt our fame and money. I can't talk about anything."

With conviction, Joe answered, "I can't believe you would flaunt anything. It's not in you. They may be envious. Y'know, I think I might know what you mean, though. In Davenport, barely nobody went to college. I'd come back between semesters, and it was like if I said anything about college, people got all offended like I was braggin. But, y'know, what am I *supposed* to talk about? That's where I *am*. Or *was*, I guess. Like with you, are you supposed to *not* talk about your glamorous life with your friends? Can you not invite them over if you live in a half-million-dollar house?"

Angie felt better from what Joe was saying. Possibly the chasm that had grown between her and her friends hadn't been her fault. All her fault. "Yes, maybe you're right," Angie conceded. "For the record, though, our house in Connecticut didn't cost a half million dollars. It was $4.1 million."

Joe's eyes widened. "Really? I gotta see this house!"

"I put pictures of it in one of the photo albums," Angie replied.

"Can we look at em after dinner?"

"No, I have to catch up on the phone calls," Angie told Joe. "Stu called four times while we were out."

They finished dinner. Angie offered the albums to Joe for him to look over while she was on the phone, but he declined. Instead, he leafed through the amnesia book while Angie talked to Stu. At first, she thought Joe wasn't paying attention to either the book or her call, but Angie realized he was overhearing her conversation. Then she figured he was really reading the book. Then she figured maybe he was doing both.

This call to Stu was like all the others and was going to leave Angie vaguely dissatisfied and frustrated: With Stu, the band was always on the brink of great events, only it was being held back for reasons out of their control. Today, Stu mainly had to say he was pushing out tomorrow's magazine interview, because Tour Excellence was calling a special tour-planning meeting. Of course, this was a good sign, indicating that Theremin was strongly backing the tour, and therefore the release. Angie listened through Stu's assessment of

Theremin's mood, and then jotted down the details of the upcoming meeting.

Stu then asked about Joe, as he always did, only today, he seemed to be actually listening. Usually, a general response such as, "He's doing well" or "He's a little tense today" was sufficient, but Stu wanted to know the details. How did Joe feel about yesterday's meeting? Was Joe preoccupied by his health? Angie was flustered by the direct questioning, since Joe was right in the room, pretending to be not listening. Stu was too thick to detect her evasiveness. Then Stu talked about how peculiar Joe had behaved at yesterday's meeting. "He just didn't seem like himself," Stu concluded, which made Angie smile to herself, because it was the most accurate thing he had ever said, and he didn't know it. Angie gave a non-committal reply, because if she agreed, she was afraid that Stu would begin another interrogation.

Then Stu changed the subject to that of the contract. He reviewed the importance of a new contract (as if Angie hadn't lived every minute of this herself) and generalized on the opportunity it presented. Did Angie know why Joe was getting in the way? Angie suggested that Stu would have to determine Joe's motivations for himself. Stu cast out several speculations, possibly fishing for a response from Angie.

Then the phone was snatched out of Angie's hand by Joe. "Stu, knock it off," he barked. "You're buggin my wife, an yer buggin me. If you want to move on the contract, then get it to me, so I can look it over. Clear?"

Stu was cowed. He apologized, and then asked if Joe had had any additional thoughts on the contract.

"No, I don't have any *additional* thoughts, because I don't have any *original* thoughts! Because I don't have a contract to look at and formulate *any* thoughts! Now, if I were you, I'd get me a copy of the contract right away. Okay, do you understand what I'm asking you to do now?"

Stu began to recap the significance of the contract when Joe hung up. "Swate Jasus!" Joe exploded to no one in particular. "No one could be that stupid by accident!" Joe turned to Angie, his face suddenly softening. "I'm sorry. I shouldn't have done that. It was rude. I guess I'll leave the room so you can make your other calls."

Angie watched him leave. His outburst brought forth mixed feelings in her. She hated it when Joe lost his temper, because he generally stayed in a foul mood for the rest of the day if not longer.

And if he wasn't angry with her to begin with, he'd get angry with her inept mollification. On the other hand, Stu had been a bigger-than-usual jerk lately, and when that happened, he needed Joe to bring him down. And that gave Angie a guilty satisfaction.

And, it was remarkable that Joe seemed to cool down immediately. He was angry with Stu, he expressed his anger to Stu, he expressed his frustration to Angie, and then he calmed down. Still, Angie felt a residual tension that maybe it wasn't over with Joe.

She continued her calls. An hour later, she went to find Joe. She found him watching TV. Old Joe hated TV; it was too passive. And it was a huge waste of time, he felt. Angie knew he felt this way, because he'd told her so hundreds of times. But here was New Joe sitting in the loveseat. Silver, Joe's silver electric, sat in his lap. Joe was watching MTV.

Joe said, "Hey, I saw an X Band video just now."

Angie nodded. "Yes, before an album is released, MTV plays that band's prior releases to increase consumer recognition."

Joe was about to say something, and then he stopped. Angie watched his mind processing the new information. "Yeah," he said, "that would make sense. Does the production company pay them for that? I'm sure they don't want to goose our record sales just because they're good guys."

"They get compensated," Angie confirmed. "I don't know how, though. I think direct payment is against FCC rules."

"There's a lot more strategy to this business than I thought. Anyway, I saw the 'Tina' video. I'd seen it before, but I never really watched it. Were you in it? I thought I recognized you."

Angie was surprised, because she really was in the video, but as a background extra in a dramatic sequence. Once the filming had started, the director suddenly wanted a lot more people in the background, so Angie, along with some production crew, friends and bystanders got to get in the action. It generated a blip of publicity about the video. When the next video ('Xylophone') was filmed, thousands of people, including a horde of desperate actors, came to watch, even though it had a different director who didn't ever want any strangers at his shoots. "Yes, I was in that video," Angie acknowledged. "I'm surprised you would notice me in it, though, if you didn't know where to look."

"Yeah, the other thing I noticed was how good Joe really is. Wow." Simply recalling Joe's performance in the video seemed to stagger him. Joe looked at Angie. "How can I fake doin *that*?" Joe reflected for a moment on this Herculean task, and then he said, "Well, let's hope it doesn't come to that. Are you ready to show me Joe's life?" He set Silver on the loveseat behind him.

Angie hadn't realized how much she was looking forward to this. She'd been collecting the story of Joe for almost a decade, and no one else had seen her work. Quickly, she retrieved the box from the foyer and lugged it to the den. She pulled out several tomes and set them down. She selected one, the first one. "Okay," she began, "This book is all I could get from the years before we met. I've been calling them 'the early years'. It sounds a little dramatic, I suppose." Angie opened the cover.

The first page held four baby pictures: Joe as a newborn, looking as much like Joe as any newborn looks like the resulting adult. In one of the pictures, a woman held the newborn in a hallway. She wore a business suit and cradled the baby awkwardly. She had narrow, intense eyes and a narrow, straight nose. To Angie, the mother-and-son relationship could not be mistaken.

Joe leaned forward. "Is this Joe's mom?"

"Yes," Angie answered, surprised that he wouldn't recognize his own mother. She allowed time for Joe to study the photo before she turned the page. Photos of youngster Joe: Joe in kindergarten and Joe's kindergarten class. Three-year-old Joe with his mother and a preteen girl at the beach, a black-and-white posed shot. Joe on his knees shoveling mud into a rusty wagon.

Joe asked, "Is this Joe's sister here at the beach?"

"Yes, Susan," Angie answered. "You used to go to Cape Cod for vacations. This other shot was your backyard when you lived in Meriden."

Joe nodded. He turned the page. The evolution of Joe, grades 1-4. Joe went from prickly-headed to having hair that needed to be combed. In these photos, he went from having large front teeth to almost normal-sized teeth, though the size of the teeth obviously hadn't changed. "And then Joe grew up," Joe summarized. He turned a few more pages, studying photos of birthday parties and vacations. The vacation shots were almost always of Joe's mother, Susan and Joe standing unnaturally close, squinting into the sun. Behind them would be a vacation icon, such as the front of their Cape Cod beach cottage, or a sign or a scenic overlook. "Joe's father is quite the photographer, isn't he?"

Angie was discomforted by Joe's use of the present tense. "I never met your father," she told Joe.

Joe nodded, understanding. He flipped through a couple of pages, scanning each one. "How is it that you have these pictures?"

"About a year and a half ago, I went through some pictures your mother had in a box. I chose these, because they included you, and the photography was decent."

Joe looked at Angie. "Are you a photographer?"

Angie smiled modestly. She owned several cameras and had experimented with them, but found the results vaguely disappointing. She intended to take a photography class, but doubted she actually ever would. "I take pictures," she admitted. "But I don't photograph. There's a big difference. I'd like to learn, though."

Joe went back to the album. He turned a few more pages and then stopped. He studied a picture of Christmas morning. In it, Joe triumphantly held up a red-and-white guitar. Beside him was a small amp and the guitar case. In the photo, Joe had to have been about 13; acne was ravaging his face. Susan, cut off by the shot, was nearing adulthood. "Angie," Joe said, "is this the same guitar as upstairs?"

"That's Good," Angie replied. "Good Guitar. Your father gave it to you the Christmas before his heart attack." The subject of Joe's father's death was always a sensitive one, and Angie always approached it delicately. "Good Guitar has always been special to you," Angie said, and she noted that Joe missed her massive understatement.

"Well, then, this is an important picture, then," Joe pointed out. "A real formative moment: Joe Meets Good Guitar." He turned the page. There was only one picture on the page. Teenage Joe standing in a room full of dark suits, wearing a dark suit himself. Though the room was full, Joe stood alone. His expression was unreadable, but intense. Twin tear streaks marked his cheeks.

Joe studied the photo. Finally, he said, "Another formative moment." He looked at Angie. "I guess Joe's father didn't take this one."

Angie shook her head. She was thinking that Joe had always treasured the memory of his father, and now he no longer had even that.

"Y'know," Joe said, "I can't help but feel sorry for the kid in this picture."

"Your father was very important to you," Angie told Joe. She told him the stories that he had told her over the years. Joe's father had introduced him to various sports and encouraged him to succeed, coaching, prodding, drilling. With Susan, Mr. Eckstein was the same, only different. He coached her to succeed in schoolwork, and encouraged her to explore student government and drama. Joe was also near the top of his class for academic performance, but his father declined to push him in that direction. "You could be good at academics," Mr. Eckstein judged, "but you don't have what it takes to be the best." Joe was confident that the emphasis on sports was the first step of his father's program to turn him into a successful, competitive, conquering machine.

So as Joe entered his teens, Mr. Eckstein transitioned him from sports to music. He knew that Joe (Joshua, then) had an interest in music and recognized that he had some innate talent.

Then Mr. Eckstein died. He'd been having trouble with his shoulder, feeling an increasing discomfort and pain, until he suddenly dropped dead of a heart attack he'd been having for a week.

"Where's Susan now?" Joe asked.

"She lives in Florida now. She's an office manager in St. Petersburg," Angie replied. "Your mother lives there, too. She's retired, and a part of her retirement is money from you."

Joe raised his eyebrows. "Funny, I wouldn't have thought of Joe as havin strong family ties."

"Oh, yes. You also give money to Susan, but she works anyway."

Joe nodded. "How do the gift taxes get addressed? Or does Joe put them on the payroll?"

"Oh, I don't know. You always let George handle those details. He's our accountant."

Joe shrugged. "I'll check it out. At least Joe's doin good by his own. What about you? Do you send money to your parents?"

Angie shook her head. "No, Daddy is okay on his own."

Joe turned the page and was confronted by a family portrait. Mrs. Eckstein sat in the front. At about fifty, her dark brown hair was shot with grey. Her big brown eyes regarded the camera coolly. It was as if, without looking, she knew that her subordinates were all at their posts. Mr. Eckstein stood behind her, his hands resting on the back of the chair. A few grey hairs also adorned Mr. Eckstein's hair, but he looked like he had a youthful energy. To one side stood Susan. Susan had her mother's big eyes. To the other side stood Young Teen Joshua, ready to take on the world and fifth period. Already knowing everything that was worth knowing. Joe examined the page. "What a nice looking family," he commented. "Is Joe's mother Italian?"

"No, second generation Spanish. Why the interest in nationalities?"

"We don't really have that distinction in Davenport," Joe answered. "Everyone's roots are local. Except the D'Amatos. They're from Kingsport."

"Where's Kingsport?" Angie asked.

"Over in Tennessee," Joe replied. "Angie, you're a big world traveler. Your concept of local and distant is a whole lot different from mine. And my concept is different from just about everybody else's who grew up in Davenport. Y'know, because I've been around. I've even flown in an airplane."

Angie smiled. "Davenport has an airport?"

Joe laughed. "No, the nearest airport is Tri-Cities in Tennessee. But that's farther away than most people go in a year."

Joe was telling Angie this information like it was factual, not like it was fabricated memories in his head. But maybe the information was true. Maybe Joe had met someone from Davenport who told him about it, and Joe had incorporated what he had learned into his memories. Because Angie was pretty sure Joe had never been to Davenport, Virginia. If there even *was* a Davenport, Virginia.

Joe was turning pages. He asked, "When did Joe's father die?"

"Summer of 1972," Angie answered. "Between middle and high school."

"Hey, when's Joe's birthday?"

"October 29th," Angie answered, and added, "1960."

"That's odd," Joe said. "Mike Smith was born May 10th, 1960. It's interesting that we're just about the same age. But why not invent another personality with the same birthday?" Joe shrugged and then asked, "Hey, when's your birthday? It's not comin up, is it?"

"No, it's January 10th."

Joe turned back to the album. There were more vacation pictures, only they were just Joe and Susan.

Angie said, "January 1st was the cut-off for the grade in school, so I was always about the oldest in my class." Joe looked at her. She continued. "It's awkward for a girl, really. Because you end up dating guys in higher grades. Otherwise, you're dating guys younger than you. Plus, you mature faster. Fortunately, for me, it wasn't that noticeable."

Joe seemed to be hiding his confusion. "Why was it not noticeable? I don't understand."

Angie answered, "Well, I'm not tall now, so I didn't get taller than everyone else. And my, uh, bust didn't grow... much." She noticed that Joe's eyes verified her statement, thoroughly.

"That must have been awkward," Joe said to her face. "You're compelled to date boys in higher grades, and yet you didn't appear to have matured. Does this lead to how the two of us started dating?"

Angie opened her mouth. That was exactly what she was thinking. She said, "Well, we'll get to that in the next book."

Joe nodded. "I was the youngest in my grade by two years. So compared to my contemporaries, I was small and developed late. The girls in my own grade didn't take me seriously. They thought I was 'cute' and 'safe'. I didn't get my license until months after I had graduated. But I didn't want to date girls my own age. They were too young." Joe thought about this. "Does that make sense?"

"No," declared Angie.

Joe went back to turning pages. He came upon a photo of an older teenage Joe standing beside a display. Reflection obliterated much of the display, but he could see it showed drawings of vibrating strings. "What's this?" Joe inquired.

"The science fair," Angie answered. "You won third place in the regionals."

"Really?" Joe asked in surprise. "The science fair doesn't seem like the kind of thing a guitar player would get into."

"Well, you were into it with a lot of energy," Angie said. "You signed up out of the blue, and then you worked hard at it, and no one knew why. Then you won first place at the school and took third at the regionals in New Haven. You qualified for the state competition, but you didn't even go. And you didn't ever do anything like it again." Angie looked at Joe and added, "And you never even talked about it much."

"That's odd," Joe agreed, and turning back to the album, he said, "Joe's a complex guy."

Silently, Angie decided they were tied on massive understatements.

Joe turned a page and found he had reached the end of the album. "Some of these pictures apparently were taken after we knew each other," he said.

Angie explained that the pictures in the first album were obtained after she had started collecting the raw material for the others. She handed him another photo album.

Joe opened it. The first picture was that of a giant snowman flanked by three young teens. Joe carefully examined the picture.

Angie waited a second and supplied, "That's you, me and Ed, after we made the giant snowman. It's the first picture taken that contained the two of us."

"We weren't really 'together' in this picture, though, were we? I mean, how old were we?"

"In this picture, you and Ed were 13, and I was 11. You and Ed met in middle school. You had a lot of the same classes. You and I met when you would come over to see Ed. If I didn't have anything else to do, I'd go along with you guys."

Joe looked at Angie. "It's hard for me to believe you were ever a tagalong. Cause now you're so together and independent. You don't want for nothin."

"Thank you," Angie said graciously, because she couldn't think of anything else to say. Joe turned a page. "But I wasn't a tagalong. I was doing stuff *with* you guys. We were all together."

Joe looked up. "Isn't that unusual for that age group? Isn't that when boys and girls polarize? Then in high school, there's dating and courtship rituals, and much later do boys and girls learn to see each other as people and not as relationship raw material. If ever."

Angie shook her head. "Not all the time. Not with us. We were friends." Truth was, Angie had been attracted to Joe since he started hanging around with Ed. They were in the seventh grade, and she was in the fourth. But she was too shy to do anything but be around them. So she tagged along while the boys built a treehouse or rode their bicycles.

Joe shrugged. "I apologize. You're right; lots of times boys and girls can be friends through middle school, especially if conditions are right. I suppose. I didn't mean to imply that you were not wanted, uh, to be with." He turned back to the album. There were pictures of Joe and Ed at the beach. These pictures were spontaneous, action shots, not the police line-up shots of before. So there was Joe throwing a Frisbee, Joe digging a hole in the sand, Ed splashing through the waves. There followed other shots of Joe and Ed around the house or the neighborhood. Although they were still in middle school, Ed towered over Joe and everyone else.

Then there was Ed sitting behind a brand-new drum set. It was a basic starter set in an ugly orange flake. "Ah," Joe exclaimed, "Ed gets the drums! When was this?"

"You were freshmen. Ed practiced when he could, but he could only practice after school when our parents were at work."

Joe turned the pages of pictures showing Ed practicing in the basement and in the garage. Then a picture showed a band in the garage. Joe was playing Good Guitar, and Ed was drumming. "Who's this?" Joe asked, pointing at the third band member.

Angie leaned forward. "That's Matt Yeaman. He was the bassist in your band for about two weeks. Then he got on the basketball team." Joe turned a few more pages, mostly of him and Ed playing in the garage. Then there was a new bassist. This one was considerably older (maybe in his twenties) and grungier. "This is Jack Foran. You used to call him 'Jay', because he was a pothead. He knew a lot about showmanship, and he taught you a lot. Plus, he could really sing. In a way, he took you and Ed under his wing."

"What happened to him?" Joe asked.

Angie shrugged. "About at the end of your sophomore year, he disappeared. We never found out what happened."

Joe shrugged and went back to the album. He turned a few pages and came to a picture of a banner stretched over a high school entrance. "Battle of the Bands!!!" it announced. Joe, Ed and Jay stood under it. "Hey, what's this?" he asked.

"Oh, this was your first performance. Someone was setting up a battle of the bands at Cheshire, and you guys competed," Angie said simply.

Joe said, "Wow, that musta been a big deal. The first performance. Did you see it?"

"Oh, yes. I helped move equipment and set it up."

"Well, how did it go?" Joe turned a page in the album and shot a glance at it. "I don't see proud band members standing next to a trophy or anything."

"No, you came in second place. There were six bands. Actually, you did as well as you could have, but the odds were against you. The band that won was the local favorite, and the stands were packed with their fans. The winner was determined by how loud the audience cheered. It was disappointing to do so well and not win, but you did beat all the bands that weren't set up to win." Afterwards, Jay had been the essence of cool, reminding Joe that it was their first performance and that the band that won had a following that showed up and cheered for them. Angie had admired Jay's calm demeanor and positive outlook.

"Second out of six bands?" Joe echoed. "That's not bad, considering it was the first performance." Joe smiled. "Did the band have bad stage fright?"

Angie remembered Joe pacing furiously, reminding Jay and Ed (mostly Ed) of details they all knew. He was so pumped on adrenaline and so serious. He took it as seriously as he did their audition for Theremin Records, four years later. And when the spots came on, Joe channeled all that energy into a flawless performance. Angie smiled wistfully. "No, I don't think you've ever had stage fright in your life. You were never afraid of performing, but you were always anxious that you had to do your best."

"Yeah, I knew a guy at Virginia named Ron. For every test, paper, assignment, whatever, he was terrified of failing, so he would study his brains out. As a result, he aced everything. You'd think after a year or two, he'd start to realize he wasn't going to fail anything." Joe stopped when he saw Angie looking at him. "Does it bother you when I talk about my past? Or about what I think is my past?"

Angie was exasperated. "Joe," she said, "you're missing the point. We are trying to see if looking through these pictures will trigger a memory."

Joe was contrite. "I'm sorry. I guess you're right. I'm not even tryin. I'm just relivin my own past. I just thought it was fun, sittin here goin over these pictures with you, like we're just hangin out. I'm sorry."

Angie had to admit to herself that she enjoyed talking to Joe about himself. Then he would stain it by telling her about his made-up past. "Well, let's try to focus," she suggested.

Joe agreed and turned a page. "Who's this?" he asked. The photo was of the band playing at a school dance. The dance floor was dark, but the band was brilliantly lit. A girl sang into a microphone on a stand, and behind her stood a guy playing the bass. The neck of Good Guitar entered the edge of the picture.

"Now this is Robin Graves and Tom Hoagland. Robin was young, even for this band, but she had a clear, sweet voice. Tom, as you can see, played the bass. It wasn't long before he and Robin were an item, and they dated for a long time. You were always afraid they would break up and wreck the band, but it never happened. This was when the band really developed. So what happened was Tom and Robin hung out together and you and Ed stayed friends. They joined the band at the beginning of your junior year and stayed in it until Tom went to UConn."

Joe looked up. "*Yukon? Canada?*"

Angie laughed. "No, the University of Connecticut. He majored in animal science, and he and Robin formed their own band there. They're probably married now; they were such a happy couple."

Joe turned pages, seeing the evolution of the band from backyard parties to school dances to bars and auditoria. The equipment and the sophistication of their sets continually expanded. Then Joe turned to a picture of two people at a restaurant table. One had long dirty blond hair and half-open eyes. The other had a hawkish nose and wide blue eyes. Joe pointed to the first guy. "Wait. Is this Roger?"

"Yes. This is when we first met Roger and Shane Skinner. Robin and Tom had just left the band, and you got hooked up with Roger and Shane through Rob. That would be Rob Caminiti, the band's agent at the time. Roger played a solid bass, and Shane was very good with back-up vocals and guitar. The band really took off from there.

"In fact, this time was really critical in your life. You and Ed were out of high school, and it was time to get jobs or succeed with the band. You went to Rob for help and pulled Ed along, and the band came together. All of you had the same commitment and ambition that enabled you to play all over New England and the east coast."

"Wow," Joe said, appreciating the circumstances that initiated the band's success. He turned a page and reached the end of the album. Angie replaced it with another. Joe opened the cover and saw several photos of Angie in a long green dress. Joe, at probably 16 years old, stood nearby in a black suit. Some of the pictures included Ed with a towering Nordic blonde. Joe studied the pictures. "I'll bet this is Joe's homecoming dance," he said. Angie nodded. Joe added, "The green in your dress really sets off your eyes. You should wear green more often."

Angie inhaled. "That's exactly what you said that day!" she said.

Joe didn't attach any significance to his echo of the past. "Joe and I agree on something," he remarked. "It must be true." Joe turned the page and saw pictures of the inside of a school auditorium with streamers and balloons. "How did it go? I guess it wasn't *too* bad, because you went out again."

The dance marked a transition in the relationship between Angie and Joe. For years, Angie had had romantic notions about Joe. But he was way out of her league. He was always a school ahead. When she was in elementary school, he was in middle school and

Changed Classes. And when Angie got to middle school and got to know that, Joe was in high school. He didn't take 'science', he took 'geology' or 'biology'. And he didn't take 'math', he took 'algebra' or 'geometry', and there were all the teachers and kids she didn't know. But mostly, Joe was just cool. He had the self-assuredness that enabled him to be in command under any circumstances.

Despite being very cool, Joe never talked down to Angie or Ed or anybody else. He was just himself. He asked Angie to the dance like she might have turned him down. The dance was fun. Ed's date (Karin Something) drove them, because she was the only one of the four who could drive. Angie didn't know anyone at the dance (except for the older siblings of two of her friends), but she liked being seen with Joe, and Joe showed her off proudly. "Look at *my* date!" he said proudly about a hundred times. Angie cherished the night like it would be their last date ever.

Angie was most nervous about the after-dance agenda (Would they kiss?), but it was a needless worry. Karin drove straight from the dance to Joe's house and unceremoniously dropped him off. And she was pulling away as soon as Joe closed the door. Angie watched him through the back window standing in the street watching the car drive away.

Angie sighed as she returned to the present. "It was a perfect date. You were a perfect gentleman."

Joe nodded. "Lots of times I get complimented by my dates for not touching them."

Angie snapped, "That's not what I meant. You showed respect for me, like you valued my company."

Joe replied, "I'm sure he did, Angie, just like I do now." He went back to turning pages. There were pictures of Joe at the Indoor Miniature Golf Emporium on South Colony, and the two of them at a basketball game and several photos of rock concerts.

Looking back, Angie thought their dating was typical. Joe didn't get his driver's license until nearly his senior year, and even then he didn't have access to a car, so Ed would drive them around and then disappear at appropriate times. They went to a lot of concerts. Afterwards, Ed and Joe would compare notes on the performance and try to determine what elements they could work into their own shows. It influenced Angie so that she also started analyzing the performances instead of just enjoying them. And Angie took an increasingly active role in Joe's band, because it was an inseparable part of Joe.

Joe flipped through pictures of his junior prom without a trace of recognition, but it brought Angie back. Those were heady times for her; she didn't so much feel like she was in over her head but she knew she was in the deep end. Joe was a junior in high school now starting to play in college bars (not legally), and Angie was in the eighth grade. Trying to grow up fast enough to keep up.

Then Joe was a senior, and Angie a freshman. Angie was tasting high school for the first time from the inside. She had her share of friends, but not many suitors; Angie thought they were intimidated by Joe, who by this time, was a minor celebrity. Truth was, most boys took themselves out of the competition, because they weren't in Angie's league. Even as a freshman, she had the regal aura.

The next year, Joe had graduated, and Angie was a sophomore. X Band had begun, and Joe was away a lot. Angie missed him sorely, and she also missed being able to date like normal girls. Joe acknowledged this, once. He said, "If you want to date someone else, you can. Just respect me enough to give back my ring first." At that point, Angie and Joe had been going steady for over a year. Angie appreciated being given a choice, and it was a fair one. If she ended their commitment, then her dating wouldn't be cheating. On the other hand, then Joe would be free to date while he was away, and Angie was pretty sure those dates would be intense and short-lived. She was pretty sure Joe was faithful on the road. Although it was never said out loud, Angie knew Ed was safeguarding their relationship.

Joe flipped past pictures of dances and proms. Then he came to a picture of Angie in her wedding dress, and he stopped. "Angie," he whispered. "Wow." In the photo, Angie held her bouquet and looked to the side. It was a good angle, both showing off her perky nose and big green eyes. Joe reached for his shirt pocket and stopped. Then he looked at Angie and said, "You were so young here."

"I was eighteen," Angie answered. "I had just graduated from high school. I wanted to go with you on the road, but Daddy wanted me to go to college. I think this was kind of a compromise."

"It must a killed your pa to give you away so young," Joe supposed.

Angie sighed. Her father held Joe responsible for destroying the family, and, in a way, he was. Mr. Brettington had expected his children to get college degrees and then take positions in the lower upper class. Instead, his son was lured into a rock band and scraped a living inferior to anything he would have had as unskilled labor. Then his daughter, his jewel, wanted to follow him on the road. Two kids, both derailed by one Joe. And yet, Joe himself seemed to have his feet on the ground. He was reasonably intelligent and got good enough grades to go to college (if he had had the money). Joe always showed the proper respect to Mr. and Mrs. Brettington, and so when they were together, there was an uneasy truce. When Joe was absent, Mr. Brettington had no reservations about assailing him. "Yes, it did, Joe," Angie finally said. "But he had enough faith in you to let us go." That was a lie. Brettington was gambling on the failure of the band, and hedging his bets. If it crashed, he wanted to be the rescuer of his children. If it succeeded, he didn't want to be caught being wrong.

"He must have a lot of character," Joe said. He turned a page. There was the wedding party: Joe, Angie, Ed, Angie's best friend Linda, Susan Eckstein, Shane Skinner and some others. Joe asked about the others, and Angie, to her surprise, had to remember who they were. Other photos showed families with the wedding couple. Then there were the women and then the men, and then just the Ecksteins and the Brettingtons.

Then Joe got to pictures of the reception. It was a huge affair with apparently hundreds of people. Joe flipped through pictures of people at tables. Occasionally, he would ask, "Is there someone here I should know?", and Angie would usually shake her head. Angie did get to point out Rob Caminiti and some others.

Joe asked, "When did Joshua change his name to Joe Ecks? Was it before the wedding?"

"Oh, yes," Angela answered. "It was about six months after you graduated from high school. Actually, it could have been a shrewd maneuver. You and Shane had changed the name of the band to X Band. So then you changed your name to Joe Ecks. In fact, you'd originally wanted to change it to Joe X, but Ed started calling you 'Pope Joe the Tenth', so you decided to make it Joe E-C-K-S. I preferred that spelling, because it was more like a shortened version of Eckstein. But Shane was mad, because he saw it as a ploy to take ownership of the band."

Joe asked, "Was it?"

Angie hesitated. "I honestly don't know. I know for sure that you'd wanted to change your name for years. Maybe it was just a coincidence. Maybe you were taking advantage of an opportunity." Angie shrugged. "It set off a growing conflict between you and Shane.

Shane saw you and him as equals, and you saw yourself as the central figure of the band."

"Was I?".

"Yes," Angie answered. "Of course."

Joe nodded. "Okay. Who paid for this huge reception? It must have been thousands. Maybe tens of thousands."

Angie nodded. "Yes. Daddy paid for it. But he said I was on my own for college." Angie didn't completely believe him, though. But coming back for college money would have meant eating a lot of crow.

Joe regarded Angie. "Did you want to go to college? What would you have majored in?"

Angie sighed. "No, I suppose not," she said, answering the first question. "I never had my heart set on it. It never seemed like an option. I sometimes wonder what it would have been like."

"Yeah," Joe agreed. "What lies along the road not taken?" He locked eyes with Angie, and for a moment, she saw the man behind her husband's eyes.

Angie stood impulsively, not understanding the impulse, but compelled to explain her action. "I think I'll get a drink," she said and hurried to the kitchen. There, she mixed a gin & tonic that she didn't really want. She eyed the drink and silently sobbed, weeping quietly out of habit so Joe wouldn't hear. Everything that they had attained, and everything they had worked toward was on the verge of being lost. Her tears filled her eyes and streamed down her cheeks. Nearing panic, Angie had to act. What would Joe do if he found out she'd done nothing? Angie took several deep, shuddering breaths and gulped down her drink. Then she mixed another. She pressed the cool glass against her eyes to reduce the swelling.

When Angie went back out to Joe, he looked up, apparently oblivious to her long absence or disturbed visage. "Angie," he said, "I'm really enjoyin lookin at these albums, so I keep forgettin about tomorrow's meetin. What's this one about?"

Angie deliberately sat down. "Tomorrow is the tour meeting. The people who will be in charge of the tour and your performance are presented, and everyone will discuss the tour in general terms. From what Stu said today, there are still a lot of open spaces in the schedule, but it's encouraging that Theremin is backing a tour this early into production. Then they may talk about other tours, like European or Asian. But that depends on regional sales. There are some bands that only do so-so in the U.S., but they do very well someplace else."

"That's interesting," Joe commented.

Angie shrugged. She was suddenly feeling the effects of the long day and the strong drink. Left with nothing else to say, she sipped her drink.

"Well, Angie, I really like lookin over Joe's history here. You've done a very good job of compiling a photo history, but you're looking pretty tired. Do you want to finish this one and then save the rest?"

Angie nodded, and Joe went back to the album. He passed over pages of reception pictures, and then he came to beach pictures. There was Angie with the ocean behind her, and Joe and Angie standing with their arms around each other (and the ocean behind them). There was Joe digging a deep, narrow hole in the sand. There was a dark photo of a shoreline taken from the water (presumably from a boat). The terrain was craggy, but pastel houses crowded together.

Joe studied the picture. "Is this Key West?" he guessed.

"No, we went to Bermuda for our honeymoon," Angie answered. Their honeymoon had been their best time ever. Joe seemed to have taken the time off from all his continental worries. They went everywhere together, or nowhere, if they didn't feel like it. Their honeymoon was completely achievement-deficient. No goals, no schedules, no planning. Even their departure was open, or as open as the Bermudian authorities would allow. Eventually, they tired of paradise and returned home.

"I've always wanted to go to Bermuda," Joe commented. "Was it nice?"

Angie nodded.

Joe looked through several more pages of Bermuda. Then he came upon a picture of apartments in winter. The sky was slate, and Angie stood huddled in the alcove of an entrance.

"I don't think we're looking at Bermuda anymore," Joe quipped.

"No, this is our first apartment. We lived in Wallingford, not far from your mother," Angie explained.

"Where did we keep the band equipment?" Joe asked. "And where did we practice?"

Angie thought for a moment. "I guess by this time, the band was playing just about all the time. Well, you were playing or you were going somewhere to play. But when you weren't, you had a self-storage unit, and you sometimes played there." Angie laughed to herself and told Joe, "I think it was funny that people paid you to play all the time, but when you were practicing, everyone in the neighborhood would complain. Anyway, the warehouse was good, because you could get loud and not bother anyone. And you had an old white truck to move the equipment in. I have pictures of it in another book."

Joe smiled. "I look forward to seein it."

Angie regarded Joe. "This isn't helping at all, is it? Are you getting any of your old memories back? Does *any* of this look familiar?"

"Well, it's helping, Angie, but not because it looks familiar or brings back memories," Joe answered, looking her in the eye. "It helps me—"

"It helps you be a better Joe imposter," Angie snapped.

Joe spread his hands. "Angie, I think you have the wrong idea."

Angie huffed. "It looks like you want people to treat you like you haven't changed, and you want to do everything like you would have anyway, even though you're not the same person. Right?"

Joe looked away and admitted, "Well, yeah, but it's not the same."

Angie leaned forward and asked, "How is it not the same?"

Joe sat motionless as he thought it over. Angie waited him out. Finally, he reached for his shirt pocket and stopped himself and answered dully, "I guess it *is* the same. I'm sorry. But I really do like lookin at the albums with you. They're not just Joe's history; they're also your history."

Angie felt bad that she had put Joe on the spot. At times, he seemed so vulnerable that she wanted to protect him, like when he struggled with his blow dryer. But at other times, he seemed balefully manipulative. Or maybe not. He hadn't actually done any harm to anyone else since his change, at least not that Angie knew. But at times, he did seem capable of harm. And calculating with a cold logic.

When Angie didn't reply, Joe added, "And remember Plan A. I have to fill in as Joe and make things look normal until we can correct the situation." He eyed her hopefully.

Angie smiled. That was the original plan, she had to admit. Her drinks were beginning to relax her. She finished her second. Joe had gone back to the album, turning pages, studying pictures of apartment life and of the white Firebird he'd bought then. Angie noticed Joe's hair was parted crookedly. It was just a little thing, but meant so much. Joe groomed himself meticulously and then maintained his look throughout the day. His part would never have been crooked. It was the level of perfection and attention to detail that he demanded from himself and from everyone around him. But now, Joe was loose, un-focused, casual. Well, not casual. Angie found herself steering away from adjectives that might have a positive spin.

Joe reached the end of the album and set it down. "This has been really interesting," he told Angie. "You've really done a lot of work here."

"Thank you," Angie answered. Despite herself, she was pleased with Joe's praise.

A sort silence elapsed. Joe asked, "Do you wanna watch some more MTV?"

Angie shrugged and agreed. Joe turned on the TV. A commercial for The Monkees rerun was on. Joe turned to Angie. "They've really been promoting The Monkees lately. Do you think they're getting compensated for that, too?"

"I don't know," Angie replied. "Probably."

Joe turned back to the TV. A 'Leave It' video came on. Angie watched Joe as he watched the TV. The alcohol mellowed her thoughts. Into adulthood, Joe had become even more handsome than he had been as a teen. And more remote. Isn't it funny, she thought, that they could become distant even though they were married. And now this. It wasn't getting any better. So she was going to have to take action. But what? Could she somehow get Joe to like being Mike less than himself?

'Leave It' ended and was followed by Van Halen's 'Jump'. Joe turned to Angie, started to say something and saw that she was asleep. He turned off the TV, shifted position and watched her sleep. Later, he put a blanket on her and went to bed.

Chapter 8

Tour Meeting

The telephone rang in the Ecks's hotel bedroom. The room was dark, not because it was night, but because the heavy curtains had been drawn. Joe lay sprawled on his side of the bed, and Angie lay curled under the covers on her side. The telephone rang again.

Angie stirred and slid to the phone. She picked it up. "Hello," she croaked. "Yes, thank you." She hung up. "Joe?"

Joe answered, his voice surprisingly clear, as if he had already been awake. "Y'know, I don't like to have to talk to anyone the minute I wake up. I'm glad you're the one who answers the wake-up call."

"You're talking to me," Angie pointed out.

"True," Joe said. "I'll rationalize it later."

Angie considered that. Old Joe liked to get up early also. He never said why; maybe he felt the same way. As she pondered this, Joe slipped out of bed, crossed the room and occupied the bathroom. Angie stayed in bed, savoring the last few minutes before she would have to start the day. She heard the shower come on. She had to be faster than usual, since Joe was spending less than half his usual time in the bathroom, so she dragged herself out of bed.

She had awakened on the loveseat at about 3:00. Her contacts were still in, and her eyes were angry about it. By the time she'd prepared for bed, she didn't feel like sleeping. Alert, she lay in bed, listening to Joe's regular breathing. After a half hour, she took her book into the unused bedroom (not wanting the reading light to wake Joe), and read it until she started to feel drowsy. She got back in bed and fell asleep.

Angie's eyes still felt slightly sore. She wanted to wear her glasses, but Joe didn't like the way they made her look. So Angie gingerly put in her contacts, and looked forward to removing them soon. She dressed quickly, because she wanted to be ready for Joe when he was done with his shower. To save time, she left her face bare and fully freckled. She worked on her eyes, though, hoping to distract Joe from the fact that they looked like cherry tomatoes with pupils.

And she thought about her day ahead. There were the usual to-do tasks: Mail, phone calls, scheduling. But really, she could do whatever she wanted, read her book, watch TV, even go someplace.

Joe came out of the bathroom wearing only his new under-wear. He went to his dresser and rooted through the drawers and finally pulled out a polo shirt and khakis that matched as well as socks and gravy.

Angie said, "Joe, aren't you going to wear your suit to the tour meeting?"

Joe hesitated. "Um, I didn't think so. I was under the impression that the tour meeting would be more casual than the production meeting. Y'know, with lower-level guys."

Angie consulted her second-hand knowledge of the meetings. "I suppose, but not by much," she hedged.

Joe put on his suit coat over the polo shirt. "There," he said, "that's a lot better."

Angie stifled a snicker. "No, Joe, that looks terrible. Do you need someone to dress you?"

"What? Why? This is okay!" Joe protested.

"No, it's not," Angie informed Joe. She opened his closet, her nimble fingers flipping through his clothes. She deftly extracted a shirt. "Here, try this. It almost brings together the coat and trousers."

Joe took the shirt and put it on. "How's this?"

Angie assessed. It wasn't quite right, and she told him so. They tried another set of clothes, and then another. Exasperated, she asked, "How can you be so conscious of your image and yet be so ignorant about how to dress?"

Joe's admitted, "I'm not usually a fancy dresser. What I know about professional image comes from 'Dress for Success'. But aside from that, I guess I don't think too much about what people wear." He shrugged on his coat and asked, "How's this?"

"It wouldn't be bad if you tucked in your shirt," Angie appraised. "Do you want me to blow dry your hair now?"

Joe answered, "No, I gotta learn how to do this myself." He took a step toward the bathroom and reconsidered. "I oughta work on the blow drying when my image isn't as critical as it is today, I suppose. Y'know, like when I'm not going so public."

Angie doubted that would ever happen. In fact, she thought the previous day had been their first day in literally years that they had spent most of the day, together, alone. She dried his hair, scribing a straight part and brushing the wings back into the Joe Ecks style. When she snapped off the dryer, Joe commented, "It's nice of you to dry my hair. I appreciate it."

Another attempt at manipulation? "You're welcome," Angie answered.

Breakfast conversation was subdued. Angie and Joe talked, but only about minutia: "How's your toast?", "Pass the butter," and so on. But before breakfast was over, Joe asked Angie why she wasn't going to the tour meeting. She explained that she wasn't necessary, and Stu would fill her in later.

"I don't understand it," Joe griped. "You have as much influence over my management as Stu does. Why does Stu get to go to the meeting and not you? Do you need a title?" Joe leaned back, thinking. "What if I hired you?"

Angie shook her head. "No, I don't have influence. I keep track of your appointments. That's all." Even if she could go, Angie didn't want to today, because her eyes were stinging, and she didn't want to wear her glasses to the meeting in front of everyone and Joe.

"I think you're understating your contribution," Joe said.

Angie looked away. In spite of everything, she was glad Joe recognized her efforts, if it was authentic.

"Well, you can come if you want," Joe offered. "*I'd* appreciate it."

Angie declined. "I can't go. I'm not invited. I'd cause too much of a stir."

Joe looked like he would push the point, but he didn't. Instead, he rose from his chair. He hesitated. "I oughta go, but I don't want to," he said thoughtfully. "Something doesn't seem right between us. There's a tension."

Angie had felt it, too. "Yes," she agreed. "Maybe it's the tour looming."

"Maybe," Joe allowed. "But I don't think so. I hope I haven't done anything to bug you. Besides exist."

"No," Angie assured him. She wished he would go so she could take out her contacts.

Joe grudgingly moved to the elevator. "I don't know when I'll be back," he told her, "but I suppose you'll know when the meeting is over, because Stu will call."

Angie rose, but before she could approach Joe, the elevator arrived, and Joe disappeared inside. He rode down five floors. A young couple boarded the elevator. The husband looked at Joe with surprise. "I'm sorry for staring, but you look just like Joe Ecks," he told Joe.

"Yeah," Joe agreed. "A lotta people a been sayin that lately. Gotta say, it's been helpin me meet women."

The man laughed. "That's a trick! What do they do when you tell them you're *not* Joe Ecks?"

Joe snorted and shrugged. "They don't believe me!"

Everybody laughed. The elevator stopped at the lobby, and the couple got off. Joe's smile lingered as he descended to the parking garage. The doors opened, and Joe was greeted with a shrill "It's him!" Before he could get out of the elevator, four girls, possibly in the fifteen to sixteen range, rushed in with considerable enthusiasm. A notebook was thrust in his face. "Sign this! Sign this!" the owner squealed.

Joe was momentarily taken off guard, but he recovered. He slid gracefully out of the elevator, explaining (though no one was apparently listening), "Hey, let's let someone else use the elevator, okay?" Then he took the notebook and asked the owner's name and learned that it was Cindy, Cindy, Cindy!! He smiled and wrote a short note as he backed toward the limousine. Joe returned the notebook. "It was really nice meetin you. Stay cool, okay?"

A girl grabbed his arm. "Let me ride with you, please? Please?"

"No, I really gotta get goin," Joe explained.

"Can I? Can I?"

Joe had backed toward the limo. The chauffeur, then, deftly inserted his body between the girls and Joe. The limo door opened, and Joe slipped in, careful not to close it on anyone's limbs. The chauffeur returned to the limo and backed it out of its space. The girls followed by the back window until the vehicle outpaced them.

"Whew!" Joe said. "Does that happen often?"

The others had watched his retreat from the elevator to the limo with amused interest.

Bill answered, "More or less."

"Mostly more," Ed added. "It's been quiet lately, but with the new album coming out, it'll get worse."

"'Worse?' It sounds like you don't like teenaged girls begging for your attention," Joe observed.

Bill said, "For one thing, Joe, those girls back there will get you in legal trouble, and you—"

He was interrupted by Ed's laughing. "Bill solves this problem with marriage!"

As Ed laughed, Bill told him to knock it off. To Joe, Bill said, "So I take it there weren't any breakthroughs yesterday."

Joe sobered. "No, I'm still not Joe. Not fer lack a tryin. I had an interesting visit with doctor, though." Joe summarized the appointment and offered the conclusion that he would stop being Mike when that became more stressful than being Joe.

"Great," Bill griped. "When is *that* going to be? How deep into this do we have to get?"

Ed moved to intervene, but before he began, Joe was soothing Bill. "Bill, I realize the situation puts a lot of important plans of yours at risk, and that much uncertainty is bound to create tension. Try not to allow the tension to suspend your better judgment. We can get through this if we pull together. We're a—"

"Easy for you to say," Bill interrupted, "since the problem is all you. You're the problem, Joe, and you want us to rally around you."

Ed could see that Bill's acidity was affecting Joe, but Joe took it. "Yeah, you're right, Bill," he admitted. An uncomfortable silence followed. Ed was used to mediating between Joe and Bill. Recently, they couldn't hardly ever disagree and remain civil.

Bill looked up. "But?"

Joe shook his head. "No buts. I'm the whole problem. I'd fix it if I could, but I can't, at least not yet. So I'd recommend that we continue with Plan A."

Bill sighed. The limo thumped along the highway with KCL playing in the distant background. Traffic was heavy, but fast. The sky was clear, but the air was cooler, though the sun shone with the same intensity as it had Monday.

After a while, Joe asked where they were going.

Bill told him the meeting was in Anaheim.

Joe asked about the content of the meeting.

"It's a lot of fluff," Bill declared. "We talk about some stuff, and then they tell us what a great job they're going to do for us. Before they're done, we're going to think this tour is the very leading edge of entertainment. Because if we're dissatisfied with them and complain, Theremin might not pick them to manage their next tour. There's a lot of competition among the top three or so tour management companies." Bill's Teacher Mode displaced his Grumpy Mode.

Joe cocked his head. "Theremin doesn't manage the tour? They farm it out? I suppose that makes sense, otherwise you'd have a staff that was overworked some of the time and sittin around the rest. But then you'd lose some control."

"Oh, no," Bill assured. "Michael will have control, believe it." Bill explained in more detail the function of the different people involved in the tour. Smyth, whom they had met at the production meeting, was the tour manager and thus ultimately responsible for the financial success of the venture. He and his people negotiated tour locations, fees and facilities, and he answered to his own executives, but he was the point of contact with Michael. Anna Williams, the tour director, reported to Smyth. She and her staff handled smaller details, such as meals and lodgings, transportation, and incidentals. Williams controlled the details that would make the tour either a working vacation or a term in jail. Williams had been the director on their 'Xenon' tour, and she had made the long haul bearable. X Band was glad to get her again. On the other hand, nobody knew anything about the performance director for this tour, and that was probably beneficial, because the band worked closely with the tour p.d., and if they'd had their previous one, Denise Cody, she would have spotted the new Joe in a second.

Joe asked, "Should we tell the p.d. about my condition? Is he in a position to help compensate my, uh,—"

"No," Bill stated, and then he looked at Joe. "How long do you think you'll have this other personality? Into the tour? Damn, we'd all be doomed!"

"Forget about that," Ed told him. "What about promo gigs? If it's going to take stress to get us back Old Joe, then that ought to do it right there."

Bill objected, "Yes, but only if this Joe gives a damn. Otherwise, where's the stress? If he really believes he's someone else, what does he care if Joe fails? Or all the rest of us? This Joe hasn't worked his whole life to get a second three-record contract, either. What's *his* investment?" Bill was angry, but relieved, in a way. He had spoken his frustrations.

Before the occupants in the limo could freeze with tension, Ed answered Bill. He answered in the level tone that he used when he acted as Joe's mouthpiece, although he didn't realize he did it. "Bill, we all agreed on a course of action, and this is it. Do you want to propose an alternative?"

Bill could feel the tension tighten around him. Finally, he spat, "I think we're headed for disaster, but I don't know what to do about it."

Ed replied, "Then you're as frustrated as the rest of us. Or am I speaking for someone out of turn?" He looked at Joe and Roger, neither of whom denied it.

Bill settled back. Ed was right. They were taking the correct approach unless they could come up with a better plan. Still, if stress were the trigger, Bill doubted that Joe would ever change back, because this new Joe personality never seemed to feel any stress at all. And Joe's lack of stress was giving Bill stress.

The limo thumped along the highway. Traffic thinned a bit. The sun rose higher.

Joe cleared his throat and said to Bill, "Angie and I went through some old photo albums of hers last night. I learned a lot about Joe's past and the band's history, at least up until Roger and Shane joined the band. But I don't know about how you joined the band. You were in X Band from the first album, but X Band got the contract before you joined the band. How did that happen?"

Bill smiled a little, remembering. "I was teaching high school music, and I moonlighted as a studio musician. I'd finished a session, and you were early for yours, and we just meshed. You were just starting to record 'Xylophone', and, before I knew it, I had a cut on it, and you were working me into your tour." It was a whirlwind. Bill and Joe hit it off immediately. Bill admired in Joe his drive and skill. Joe valued Bill's creativity. Then he sought to control it. But that came later. Bill had to admit that it was years before he and Joe habitually locked horns. If it weren't for Ed, they would have split already, or killed each other. At least Bill hadn't made Shane's mistake. Shane believed he and Joe were X Band, when in reality, Joe was X Band. Bill was wise enough to see that there was no X Band without Joe Ecks.

Bill said, "People generally think I replaced Shane. Actually, Shane and I overlapped for a couple of months."

Joe said, "So you saw Shane's end."

"Hmm. Yes."

The limousine pulled into an exit lane and left the highway. "We're almost there," Ed commented for Joe's benefit. They passed the entrance to Disneyland and the Anaheim Convention Center. The limo rounded a corner and snaked into an underground parking garage. A dark man holding a walkie-talkie stood beside a door, and as the limo came into view, he spoke into it. The limo pulled up to him, and the man opened the back door.

"Gentlemen, come with me, please," he beckoned. The band emerged from the limo and followed him into the building. They hustled down a hallway and into a small elevator. The man pushed a button and smiled at the band. "Welcome to Tour Excellence Incorporated, gentlemen."

Ed, who almost had to duck to avoid rubbing his head on the elevator roof, said to Joe, "Did you hear what he called us? He must not know us very well."

"Hey, I've been a gentleman all day," Joe bragged. "Well, almost all day. Y'know for the last hour or so. He musta heard about it."

"Yes, Gentleman Joe, your friends call you," Ed pronounced.

"My friends are such suck-ups," Joe commented. "But I don't hafta worry that *you* guys are giving me insincere flattery."

"Because of our legendary integrity?" Ed guessed.

"No. You never say anything nice to me."

"Hey, I complimented your suit the other day, and it was really ugly," Ed argued.

"You're not making a case for your integrity," Joe observed. "Or your intelligence."

"Okay, but I am way taller than you," Ed pointed out. "And I have better fashion sense."

"Wait," smiled Joe. "Have you been talkin to Angie?"

The man chuckled at the exchange. The elevator door opened. "Right this way, sirs," he said.

"'Sirs'?" Ed repeated to Joe. "Did you hear what he called us?"

The elevator opened onto the side of an expansive lobby. The lobby seemed to primarily service a bank of elevators in front. There was a receptionist and several rows of clerical types in low-walled cubicles. A wide column displayed "Tour Excellence, Inc." in big chrome letters. And there was a sign on a pedestal that announced, in big, white letters, "Tour Excellence welcomes X Band!" The sign faced the bank of elevators, as though X Band was expected to walk in the front door like anybody else. Truth is, the sign was really more intended to brag on the company's image to regular people than it was to actually welcome X Band.

The lobby quieted as work (and other conversations) slowed down and stopped. As X Band paraded past, people would offer polite Good Mornings or How Are Yous. Tour Excellence handled a lot of different entertainers, many "bigger" than X Band. Regardless, it was always wise to be polite to the clients, especially if they expected it.

Roger, Bill and Ed walked through the lobby as if they were heading for a destination, which of course they were. Joe was looking around and almost tripped over a young man with green hair. Joe seized the man's hand. "Good to see ya, man!" Joe exclaimed, and, parting, he added, "Take it easy, okay?" The man was speechless as those nearby cracked up.

Bill turned as he continued walking. "What are you doing?" he asked.

"Just meetin with the constituents, Bill." Joe waved at a young lady. "How are ya?"

Bill shook his head, thinking this was almost as bad as having two Eds in the band. The band's guide showed them into a large, glass-walled conference room. Already in the room were over half a dozen people, including Stu, in business suits. As the band and the suits were introduced and shook hands, more suits joined them. The band was rapidly outnumbered, and then overwhelmed as the suits' reinforcements arrived.

Joe and the others were repeatedly asked how they were doing, how their trip was, and could anything be gotten for them. Ed kept an eye on Joe, in case he needed a rescue. But Joe seemed at ease in the crowd. He had a small audience, but he kept the others talking about themselves. He could do this to the end of the day, Ed thought, and by then, still no one would know anything about him.

But Ed couldn't watch Joe with any intensity, because he was surrounded by his own suck-ups. There were only so many times you could be patient with the same questions: How are you doing? How was your trip? How long will you be in California? Do you know Jack Celebrity? What's it like working with Joe Ecks? Ed found that his responses to many of these questions became automatic, and besides, you could answer anything with vague generalities, and that would satisfy the questioner. Ed detached himself and joined the circle with Joe.

"And what is your function here at TEI, Marcia?" Joe asked a young woman with straight, dark hair.

Taking herself seriously, Marcia answered, "I'm your account manager."

"And what does that do?" prompted Joe.

"Oh, I find tour sites," Marcia responded quickly.

Joe smiled and nodded. "Yes! You negotiate places for us to play! Like sales. You essentially sell X Band. Us. You must hafta co-ordinate with Smyth, then. You must work very closely with him."

"Well, yes," Marcia answered. "I report directly to Roger." It was clear that she was proud of this position in the hierarchy. "But my position is more than just sales, as you say."

Joe intently listened as Marcia condescendingly detailed the various complex tasks performed by Marcia. He prodded her to clarify several points, and Ed began to believe Joe was more than deflecting conversation from himself and pumping up the Tour people, he was delving into the workings of the company, understanding the business of tour management. And, Ed had to admit, it was at least different from answering the same questions.

Eventually, Stu and Smyth made the rounds, encouraging people to take their seats. Stu fairly pushed Joe and Ed into (what must have been) their assigned seats, near the middle of the long table, on opposite sides. Every seat at the table was filled with Tour Excellence people (and the band and Stu), and many of the seats around the wall were occupied as well.

Roger Smyth took the "stage" as the lights dimmed, standing in an area with additional track lighting. "Welcome to the 'Xylene' Tour inauguration," he expounded. The Tour Excellence people applauded. Ed forced himself to smile appreciatively, when, in fact, he hated the phony fanfare. Joe soaked it up, though, fairly beaming as he shook the hands of those around him.

Smyth went on to discuss the resources he was putting to work for X Band and the Xylene Tour, describing the various people and their credentials. A half hour into the monologue, it looked like the Xylene Tour would be the media event of the post-industrial age, and that X Band was the absolute pinnacle of the entertainment world. Bill had been right.

Bill sat three seats down the table from Joe. At the description of the tour, he felt himself swell with pride. It was hard to resist, even knowing Smyth's self-serving motivation for pumping up the band. Bill perceived that for stardom to sustain itself, there had to be an appropriate mix of confidence and fear. The confidence gave you the ability to face thousands and perform, and the fear kept you from getting lazy.

Bill looked around. Ed sat diagonally across the conference table with a slight smile of amusement on his face. Ed was immune to flattery, because he saw through it clearly. That was a strength of Ed's, Bill decided; he saw through the illusion. Joe's problem was he had too much fear. Oh, he had the confidence to perform, but the fear drove him relentlessly.

Roger, across the table, was also immune to the flattery. Motionless, he gazed across the room at a woman seated against the wall. Bill doubted that Roger even knew Smyth was saying anything. Roger seemed to survive on his absolute neutrality. He played the bass, for which he had a talent, and he stayed out of the fray.

But for the pride that developed in Bill on the tour production, there was an attendant fear, a fear that it would be sabotaged by Joe's inability to play. And X Band would collapse and dissolve, and everything would be lost, and none of it would be the fault of Bill's. Bill wasn't by nature a dominant personality, but he could not be passive while the X Band train derailed and crashed.

Smyth wrapped up his blab, and, on his signal, a projector came on showing the big words, "Xylene Tour". Smyth introduced Marcia Fenney, and she rose amid a polite applause. Fenney acknowledged the applause and then said to Joe (primarily), "We at Tour Excellence have only been working on the tour dates for just over a week, but I'm pleased with the results." At her signal, a map of North America was projected on the screen. Then points appeared, labeled by their locations: Oklahoma City, Atlanta, Jacksonville, etc. Fenney talked about her enthusiasm and that of her staff toward filling in the dates, and with the popularity of X Band and the success of 'Xylene', it would be easy to sell out an ambitious tour schedule.

"How long will we be on tour?" Joe interrupted to ask. When Joe departed from the script, the attention of the room shifted from daydreams to Joe, abruptly.

Fenney smiled down on Joe. "As you know, that depends on a lot of factors. If 'Xylene' were hugely successful and Theremin wanted to hold off on the next release, we could conceivably book you for over a year. And that would be North America alone. It really depends. And you factor into it as well."

"That's reassuring," Joe commented, eliciting polite chuckles. He looked about to say something, and then he turned to Stu and said, "I have to talk to you later."

"Right," Stu agreed, and he jotted a note in his notebook.

Fenney waited and then resumed her spiel. Gradually, the suits in the room returned to their daydreams. Eventually, she wrapped up with a re-affirmation that Tour Excellence was the best in the business, and they would do their best to satisfy X Band. And she introduced Anna Williams.

Williams, thankfully, was less polished than her associates. "Good morning," she began. "I just wanted to say that I, uh, don't need to introduce myself or what I do. You already know. It is nice to see you again in person, though, since we've spent so much time on the phone." Williams continued by expressing her true desire to make X Band comfortable during their tour. And she followed with some remarks about how X Band's happiness was good for everyone involved in the tour and the audiences and even themselves. It was droll, but Williams meant well, even though she was aware that she was filling time with platitudes. And then, with relief, she announced that it was time they break for lunch.

Smyth leaped to his feet and said they had reserved Teodosio's downstairs, if that was okay.

Joe started to get up when he realized everyone was looking at him. "Oh, yeah, that's fine with me, if you went to all that trouble." He rose. "Or maybe Anna did," he added quietly.

The room cracked up, more so than was warranted. Then there was a bustle of activity as the suits shifted their formation. Joe and the band were escorted out of the room and, protected by a wedge of TEI executive types, the contingent forged toward the elevators. The elevators were being held by interns, and the mob boarded like they were staging an invasion. Joe's elevator went down two floors and stopped. The doors opened to several impatient people waiting for the elevator.

"Elevator's full!" Smyth barked as he stabbed the Door Close button.

The doors closed on several disgruntled expressions.

The elevator descended to the lobby, and the suits trooped out, protecting Joe. They joined some others, and the mass charged across an atrium into a restaurant. They were then lead through the tables and into a back room. The back room was a banquet room, with two parallel tables set for lunch. Smyth directed Joe and the band to their seats, and then he sat beside Joe. Stu sat across the table. The TEI people all seemed to know where to position themselves.

Looking around, Joe commented to Smyth, "You seem to have prepared everything for us. What would have happened if I'd wanted to eat somewhere else?"

"We would have worked it out," Smyth assured. "I hope you enjoy the accommodations."

A waiter handed Joe a menu and stood by. Joe accepted the menu and looked back at the waiter.

"Are you ready to order, sir?"

Joe answered, "No, I just got the menu. I'm not ready to order yet."

Immobile, the waiter replied, "Yes, sir."

Concerned, Joe asked, "Are you waiting for me? 'Cause I'm probably going to take a couple of minutes here."

"I can return in a few minutes, if you prefer."

"Well, don't you have anything else you need to do?" Joe saw Roger ordering already with his waiter.

"No sir," the waiter replied.

Joe turned to his menu and flipped through it quickly and then looked at Smyth. "Why don't you go ahead and order while I decide?" he suggested.

Smyth looked concerned. "We ordered ahead of time," he explained.

"Oh," Joe answered. "I see. You're *really* prepared." Joe ordered the California cobb salad and a "really big" diet Coke. The waiter nodded and moved away.

On cue, Smyth leaned into Joe's personal space. "Joe, I want you to know what Tour Excellence can do to make your tour as successful as possible." He expanded on his personal commitment as well as that of the company. As he spoke, a salad was delivered, which Joe was forced to ignore. Smyth concluded with, "So, Joe, what can we do to make the Xylene tour more successful?"

Joe replied, "I appreciate your asking me my opinion, but *you're* in the best position of any of us to determine the factors for success. It's *your* business to know what makes a tour successful. *I'm* just a musician. You have to sell the most tickets for the most you can get. I'll do my part, with the others in X Band, to put on the best performance we can." Joe leaned back. "Deal?"

"You know, Joe, I'm glad to hear those sentiments, but you know selling tickets isn't simple." Smyth explained the complications of tour promotions and concluded, "We will need you, and your band, to participate in the promotions. Do you think you could do that?"

Joe smiled. "I'm certainly willing to cooperate for the benefit of the tour, but for specifics, you'd have to see Stu, and work it out with him."

Stu jumped into the conversation. First he complimented Joe on his cooperative attitude. Then he did some verbal dancing with Smyth as they traded ideas and sounded each other out. Joe appeared to stop listening as he attacked his salad.

To his right, sat April, a youngish girl who had joined the army for lunch. She had been silent to this point, and now she timidly asked, "Mr. Ecks, what do you see coming up for X Band?"

Joe chewed and swallowed. Then he smiled an easy smile. "You know, I'm lousy at predicting the future. But I'll tell you what I'd like it to be." Those around him stopped their conversations and listened, as if E.F. Hutton was about to give financial advice. Not noticing, Joe continued, "I'd like to see album after album, each one characteristic of X Band, but different from each other, and all of them perfect in their own way. In between, I'd like to see us touring and giving people great shows. And I'd like to see the band stay just like this, and for all of us to continue working together as a team."

There was light applause. Stu held up his glass, and the room toasted Joe's wishes. Joe sheepishly went along.

The lunch went on and on. After the entrée, there was dessert and coffee and drinks and drinks. Joe kept his drink diet Coke. He sustained small talk with April by asking her all about her job and her aspirations and her hobbies and pets.

At one point, Smyth got in his face again to ask about X Band's next album. "Blue sky," he said waving his arm, "when do you think you'll start working on it? It would be nice to put brackets on the tour dates." Smyth explained again the difficulty in arranging tours when the termination was unknown or frequently changed.

When Joe was allowed to answer, he offered, "The good news for you is the end of the tour is completely at your discretion. I have to say there are no commitments for further albums at this time."

Smyth said nothing. He looked at Stu for confirmation.

And Stu had a look on his face like he'd forgotten to put on pants. Then he recovered. He laughed. "Oh, right, Joe!" He turned to Smyth with a big smile. "What Joe says is *technically* correct, but I've been working out the details with Michael, and we're really close to sealing the deal for another three records. But I promise you, before the ink is dry, I'll advise you the new schedule."

Smyth looked uneasy. "Yes. Well. It would be good to know sooner rather than later. Stop fiddling with the details and put a bow on it."

Stu assured him that they would move forward, and the conversation continued. Joe excused himself and left the table. He walked to the kitchen and looked in. When he turned, he almost collided with April. "Oh, hello," he said.

April looked up at Joe and said, "Do you want to go somewhere?"

"Yeah," Joe told her. "I'm lookin for the bathroom, but I went the wrong way. It's over there." He stepped past her and hurried away.

Joe was relieving himself in the men's room (in the urinal, specifically) when he heard Bill's voice. "Well, Joe, what do you think?"

Joe exhaled. "Bill, I gotta tell ya, you nailed the agenda down perfectly."

Bill stood next to Joe. In a low voice, he said, "We'll talk more on the way back." Joe zipped up and moved to the sink. As he washed up, Bill added, "That was a good speech you made about the future of the band. I just wish you meant it."

Joe turned off the water and said to Bill, "Oh, I meant it. Don't you doubt that I meant that. Because I'll bet that's exactly what the trouble is."

"My doubt is the trouble?"

"No, my desire to see X Band succeed." Joe dried his hands and left.

He sucked in a deep breath as he approached the table. April was missing, so Joe listened in on Stu and Smyth trade business banter. The lunch, now in its fourth hour, was wrapping up. Everyone trooped back through the now-vacant restaurant and back to the elevators and back through the Tour Excellence lobby and back to the conference room. People settled into their seats. The lights dimmed, and Smyth took the stage. "I trust everyone had enough to eat." General laughter. "Okay, X Band, you have the talent and enthuse-asm, and we're shoveling coal in the engine room. The pilot of this ship is David Burrill." Smyth kicked off the applause.

Burrill rose and took his place beside Smyth. He was a little man, maybe 5'7", and compact almost to being wiry. There was an energy about him that he seemed to contain, with effort. His brown hair, with some grey, was immaculately groomed. His light yellow sport shirt was pressed with creases in all the appropriate places. His visage as a whole placed his age between 25 and 52.

He rubbed his hands together as he said, "I'm very exshited, er, excited to be working with you, members of X Band. Let me introduce myshelf, er, myself first." Burrill spoke with a slight lateral lisp that seemed to distract himself more than anyone else. As he talked about his experience, the lisp improved until it was barely noticeable. "Are there any questions?" he asked abruptly.

Ed loved to exploit such openings, and he was very bored. Without pause, he asked, "What happened to Cody?"

Burrill rubbed his nose as he answered, "Denise Cody is on another assignment."

Ed: "What's your first name, David?"

Burrill shot back, "Yes."

"Who's Reagan's vice president?"

"Bush."

"What color is purplish brown?"

"Puce."

Impressed, Ed leaned back, stroking his goatee. A few people chuckled nervously.

Joe leaned forward and asked, "What's the opposite of 'For'?"

Burrill shifted his attention to Joe. "Er, minus four."

"My man!" Joe blurted as he leaped to his feet. In two steps, he was in the spotlight pumping Burrill's hand. "That's it! You win!"

Burrill was bewildered. "I win?"

"Yeah, don't you see? You rolled with what Ed had to throw at you, and you were thinkin on your feet. And most people woulda said 'against' was the opposite of 'for', but you were thinkin along original lines, and you answered something original. Good job!" Joe turned to the others in the room. "Didn't he do a great job?" Joe clapped, and the others joined in the applause.

Burrill smiled uneasily as Joe took his seat. "Well, thank you, Joe. And Ed. I'll try not to lose your respect before I'm done." He rubbed his hands together as he continued with his semi-canned oral report. He talked about the importance of a good performance and his particular style. He explained that he'd seen the file footage of X Band from their previous tours, and he thought they were very good, but that he hoped he could shape a better show from the band. "That's not to say that Denise didn't do a great job, I want you to understand that," Burrill said, wrapping up. "Are there any q—q—, er, crackers on the table back there?" He grinned at Ed, acknowledging that he'd almost opened himself up to another round of brutal interrogation. Burrill took his seat.

Smyth took the stage again and introduced Pete McCann, the stage manager. McCann was middle-aged and all business. He pointed out that it was Burrill's job to create a good show, but it was his job to make it happen over and over. "I make sure you have what you need before you need it. I'll tell you a joke: How long does it take a stage manager, Done." A few people chuckled. McCann talked about how important his job was and how good he was at it. Bill was beginning to get grumpy. The whole exercise was pointless. It didn't require them to be there. Their input wasn't sought or considered. TEI was going to do what they needed to do to operate a profitable tour. So Bill sat and fumed.

While McCann was talking, Joe stood. With all eyes in the room following him, he snuck to the back of the room, picked up two pears and an apple and slipped obtrusively back to his seat. Only then did he seem to notice everyone noticing him. He said, "I'm sorry, I didn't mean to be a distraction. Go ahead." McCann picked back up on his monologue, and Joe crunched into his apple. Ed suppressed a laugh.

McCann finished his spiel, and Smyth again faced the room. He summed up what the others had said and concluded that Tour Excellence had good people and wanted to do an excellent job for X Band. And anyone who wanted to was welcome to join them for drinks at Fooz. Everyone rose stiffly in relief. Several people attached themselves to Joe and the band. The conference room thinned as employees ducked out. Smyth put a hand on Joe's back and guided him out the door to the elevator. They rode down to the atrium, where photographers were waiting.

The crowd, unrestrained, pressed. People shouted for Joe to look this way, and others grabbed his hand to shake. Joe seemed to expand in all directions. He smiled at the cameras and shook hands. He answered questions with real enthusiasm. Beside him, Smyth repeated that details of the X Band Xylene Tour would be released the next day.

Slowly, Joe worked his way out of the lobby and toward the idling limo and climbed in beside Ed, across from Bill. Stu, covering the rear, followed. When the door closed, it shut out most of the sound. The limo pulled away from the curb.

Joe said, "Hey, wait, Stu. Where's Roger?"

Stu smiled. "Roger has a date. He'll join us at Fooz later."

Joe sat back, apparently still confused, but not voicing it.

Stu announced, "That went well. I think they like you."

Joe let the comment hang. Ed and Bill didn't say anything. Then Joe said, "They sure spent a lot of time and money on us today. How much do you think that presentation cost per hour? It had to be in the thousands. Not to mention all the prep they did."

Stu replied, "That shows just how much they want to satisfy you. They really care about your satisfaction." Stu studied Joe. "How do *you* think it went, Joe?"

Joe shrugged. "It was good meetin Burrill and McCann, but we'll be getting to know them soon enough, I suppose."

"That's very true," Stu agreed. "You know, you handled yourself very well with the crowds just now. You've really been working up your public interface skills. It's good to see such notable improvement. I'll have to tell Lizzie her time wasn't really wasted." Stu withdrew his organizer and jotted a note. He turned a page and looked up at Bill. "You've got a meeting with Moog tomorrow. I'll pick you up at 10:00. Ed, you're appearing at Giant Music for the day, starting at noon. Any special requests?"

Ed stroked his goatee. "I assume they'll let me play their drums."

Stu laughed a boisterous, heavy laugh. "Without a doubt. Watching the great Ed Brettington play the drums up close is a real draw. People like to watch you, Ed. You're a crowd-pleaser. Remember to dress for photography."

"Joe, you've got an interview with Hot Rocks at 2:00. I'm trying to get your hotel to let us have a meeting room."

Joe shrugged. "Be sure to tell Angie," he suggested.

Stu nodded in emphatic agreement. "I will do that. I have left several messages at the desk, but she hasn't called back yet."

Joe shrugged. "I don't know what her schedule is today."

The limo pulled off the city street into a one-lane loop and eased to a stop in front of Fooz. Fooz' front was designed to look like a celebrity nightclub. Well-dressed patrons lined the ropes that protected a path to the front door.

"Okay, we're on," Ed smiled. "Let the entertainment begin."

The limo door was opened, and the band hustled to the club door, which was opened for them. Joe waved and greeted specific people in the crowd before being engulfed by the door. The band shot through the lobby and into a dimly-lit cavern. Immediately, they were swarmed with people. An expansive circular bar dominated the center of the room. Dance floors surrounded it; a stage behind it. On the stage, band equipment was arranged. Recorded music thundered.

Automatically, a vodka martini was put in his hand, and Joe found himself answering repeatedly the question of how he was doing. He shook hands. One young lady hugged him and wouldn't let go. She was deftly pried off by a man in a suit. Photos were shot with regularity.

Bill watched Joe as a stage hand sidled up and asked him a question. Joe and the hand exchanged some words, and then Joe broke away and approached Bill, with the hand trailing.

Practically shouting in his ear, Joe asked, "Bill, are we playing tonight?"

"It looks like it!" Bill shouted in answer.

Joe studied Bill's face. "You didn't mention this," Joe said.

Bill explained, "Promotions for the album! Sometimes promo performances come up without notice."

Joe stepped back, eyeing Bill. Joe's lips moved, though one would have had to be on his chin to hear him. But Bill could read his lips well enough to see that he said, "Okay." It seemed like Joe was listening closely. The stage hand waited patiently. "Okay." He nodded to himself. "Okay." Then Joe turned to the stage hand and shouted to him.

Joe turned back to Bill. "Bill, can you play the lead guitar track for 'Ice Age' on the keyboard?"

Bill started to answer yes, but instead replied, "No, that's the guitar track."

Joe huffed silently in the din. "When I give you the signal, I need you to take over the rhythm guitar chords."

Bill started to object when Joe spun and moved through packs of people. Bill sighed and turned back to the two guys to whom he had been talking.

Chapter 9

First Performance

Due to his height, Ed Brettington never felt confined by a crowd. He looked out over the tops of everyone, so even dense packing didn't bother him.

Most of the people in the bar were entertainment reporters. The rest were those people that seemed to get into exclusive events due to connections or gobs of money. Ed couldn't always tell them apart, and he didn't want to say something inappropriate to the press when he thought he was talking to a civilian, so he treated everyone as a potential snitch. You didn't want to say anything on the record that could be used against you. Fortunately, the music was so loud, an actual conversation was impossible.

Ed was deep into an impossible conversation when Stu appeared at his side. To be heard over the music, Stu shouted up to him, "You need to get ready to play!"

When Ed had first seen the band equipment set up, he'd assumed X Band would be expected to play a song or two. It was common enough to be unremarkable. Then he stiffened as he thought about Joe. He uttered an unheard swear. "Does Joe know yet?" he shouted to Stu.

"Don't worry!" Stu shouted. "He's already in! Follow me!"

Ed excused himself from the people with whom he had been not talking and followed Stu. Thoughts whirled in his head. He first thought that he could simply bolt. X Band couldn't play without him, and he could come up with a plausible reason later. Or, could he do something less extreme and believable and just as effective? Maybe fake a stomach virus? Stu led him through an unnoticed door into a narrow hallway lined with fans. The closed door muffled the dance music except for its pervasive, throbbing bass. Ed made his way through the gauntlet of fans, smiling appropriately in response to their cheers and greetings.

Ed was ushered through a narrow door into a large and yet still crowded room. Each of the other band members was surrounded by busy staff workers. One wall was mirrors. Uncharacteristically hatless, Bill stood looking in the mirror at the fit of his pants. "Do these fit?" he was asking no one in particular. Ed's eyes searched out Joe. He was holding up a T-shirt printed with a large xylene molecule. "I can't believe we have these already!" he exclaimed. "We just approved the design a couple of days ago!" Ed noticed the hands holding the shirt were shaking.

Two young women approached Ed. "Here are your clothes, Mr. Brettington," one of them said.

"Yeah, thanks," Ed said as he absently accepted the clothes. He pushed his way through to get close to Joe. "Joe," he said quietly. The throbbing muted him to anyone else nearby. "We gotta come up with something."

Joe met Ed's eyes, and Ed saw in them a deep fear. "No, I don't think we need to. I think I've worked it out with Bill. But can you tell Roger that when he needs to, he has to play the guitar riffs on the bass?" Joe squirmed his way into his xylene shirt.

"Tell Roger what?" Ed uttered.

Joe popped his head out the shirt collar and repeated the request. "I don't think you need to do anything different," he added.

Ed stood. "Okay. What are we playing?"

"Oh, right," Joe answered. He stood, and, above the noise, called out, "Does everyone know what we're playing?" The room silenced. "We're playing 'Ice Age' and 'Xylene'. Okay?" People nodded. Talking resumed at a lower volume.

Ed started, "Joe—"

Joe looked up into Ed's eyes and said, "Don't worry, Ed. Put on your clothes."

Ed still saw the fear in Joe's eyes and then he heard what Joe had said. "You know me, Joe," he said, "I worry about everything."

Joe turned away to submit to make-up. Ed wandered nearby and took off his pants. Years ago, Ed would have been aghast at changing in a crowd, but he'd been through so many performances, he didn't even think about it anymore. He pulled on his pants (black). They fit perfectly, even the length. Somewhere, someone that Ed didn't know had his measurements and was consulted every time he needed new clothes. Ed wondered if his size ever changed, would it be known instantly?

The music dimmed, and a DJ shouted over it for a minute. The crowd cheered. The first of the warm-up announcements, Ed figured.

Ed must have performed a thousand shows. He hadn't counted. But he still got nervous before each one. It wasn't until the performing was well underway that he would begin to relax. This was why Ed disliked short, little promo shows like this one. By the time he was in the groove, it was over. The result: A grooveless performance.

But today, Ed had a lot more to worry about than himself. He was petrified that Joe would stand before the crowds and utterly choke. What was Joe expecting? Was he hoping to bring out Old Joe with maximum stress? That possibility was looking increasingly remote, because he already looked terrified beyond reason. Joe was jumping off a cliff and hoping wings would grow, because he really needed them.

The noise level dropped again, and the DJ made an announcement that stirred the crowds. The music level came up again.

Ed sat and allowed his short curly hair to be combed and sprayed. His eyebrows were darkened. Oddly, nothing was done to hide his cleft palate scar. Nothing ever was.

Ed stood and saw the others were ready. "Joe," he said.

Bill headed for the door. "Let's go," he said. Joe turned to follow.

"Joe, wait," Ed called and caught up to Joe.

Joe turned. "Don't worry," he told Ed. "Everything will work out." And Joe turned back to the door.

Desperately, Ed seized the front of Joe's shirt and spun him around. "'Don't worry'? I'm worried! I am worried all the way up to fucking terrified! We need to come up with something, *now*!"

Everyone else in the room froze and gaped. No one but the band knew what Ed was raving about, but they all knew he was serious.

Joe stood calmly with his new xylene shirt bunched up in Ed's big fist. He looked up at Ed and said distinctly, "Ed. What we need now is for you to do your job."

Ed stared into Joe's terrified and determined eyes.

"Okay?" Joe asked.

Ed slowly released Joe's shirt.

Joe straightened his shirt and asked again, "Okay?"

Ed stared at Joe for an uncomfortable moment. Joe had a plan. He had worked it out with Bill and Roger. And he did see that Joe was determined to execute his plan, whatever that was. "Okay," Ed finally agreed.

The atmosphere relaxed, and people moved slowly through the door. The hallway had been cleared of fans, and so the band headed down the empty hall to the bar. Then, led by Bill Myers, the band exploded into the bar, to be blinded by harsh spotlights. Each person wanted to squint until his eyes adjusted. But, Ed remembered, you didn't want your squint to be the first thing the audience saw, so you had to look unaffected by the light. And the lights beamed heat directly into your body, as if you were a burger waiting to be served.

The bar was dense with people, and the cheering filled it with sound. The band members stepped the one foot up onto the stage, and each took his position. The standard layout of the band was a diamond. Joe took point at the microphone, backed by stands of guitars and other instruments he might be playing. Not tonight, though; he only had the one guitar for such a micro-show. Bill was to his left and behind, tucked into a V of keyboard stacks. Roger was to Joe's right. Ed's drums were behind. Ed liked to keep the drums low so he could see the other band members. And so the audience could see him.

Bill went to his keyboard corner and played some ominous chords. The crowd cheered in response. Ed sat at his drums and thumped each one. It was a habit of his to strike each drum and cymbal before playing, as if he were physically establishing their presence. Roger crossed the stage and, in one movement, hoisted his bass over his head and into position. No adjustment of the strap was necessary; it was always set perfectly. He ran a riff to check his sound, and smiled with satisfaction at the purity of his bass notes.

Joe loped to the front, holding up a hand to acknowledge the cheering. He lifted his guitar and donned it awkwardly, the action requiring his full attention. He shifted it several times as if it didn't hang right, moved to adjust the strap and then didn't. The enthusiasm of the crowd waned. Then Joe stood straight and addressed his audience. "Thank you," he said into the microphone. Ed could see already that sweat was soaking through the back of Joe's shirt. The front people in the crowd stood only five feet from the stage, separated by two floor amps and a half dozen thick cables.

"Thank you for coming," Joe continued. "It was nice to have met some of you…" As Joe spoke, Bill faded in with a chord progression. Ed backed it up with a light beat. A standard technique; it did not seem to distract Joe, and Ed was impressed with the ease with which Joe spoke. "…and now we have a couple of songs we'd like to play. But first, I'd like to thank, on behalf of X Band, the guys at Theremin Productions and Tour Excellence." Joe turned his back to the crowd and worked a knob on his guitar. He turned back to the mic. "We decided to play a familiar first song, 'Ice Age', off the 'Xylophone' album." More cheering as Joe turned and twisted the knob fiercely. Ed watched, wondering what Joe was doing.

Joe stood straight and said to Ed, "Okay, get us goin," and for some reason, Ed heard it clearly, as if the words dodged all the other noise on their way up-stage.

Ed shifted into the rocking beat of 'Ice Age'. It was, Ed thought, a vanilla rock and roll tune, its only distinguishing feature the audio impact of its lyrics. Joe wrote the nonsensical lyrics entirely for the phonics of the words and the sounds of their consonants. "And no one will ever remember them in order," Joe had predicted. But on this, he was wrong.

Bill and Roger joined the beat. Next, Joe would hammer down a few chords and begin singing. But Joe went back to twisting his guitar's knob. His entrance approached. Joe slammed the guitar with his fist and straightened with a measure between that instant and his guitar entrance. Joe looked at Bill and shrugged. Ed could only see Bill's profile, but he could see that Bill was looking down. The measure was played.

1

Joe didn't rip his first chord that would plunge the song onward. He stood planted, still shrugging to Bill.

2

Bill looked up and saw Joe standing alone, mid-shrug. Sweat matted hair to his forehead.

3

Bill looked away, off stage left, deliberately avoiding Joe's entreaty.

4

He looked back and regarded Joe grimly. Joe dropped the shrug and just stood.

and

Bill cranked the volume on his Korg.

1

And he hammered the first chord that Joe would have played on the guitar. He sustained the chord and then hit the next one. Joe smiled slightly in relief. Bill played the next chord, and as he sustained it, his eyes locked with Joe's, and Bill nodded almost imperceptibly as if to say, "Go ahead."

Joe turned to the microphone, where he stood unmoving until the first verse. And then he came alive.

> Ice age, road rage, paradigm shift
> Lock jaw, last straw, continental drift

Joe's singing voice hadn't changed, but its tone was altered, Ed detected. Maybe no one would notice, he thought, but he could. As Joe sang the first verse, his voice took on an edge, as if he were growing increasingly agitated.

> Batman, oat bran, Faraday cage
> Jet stream, ice cream, minimum wage

As the band continued, Joe turned and removed his guitar and unceremoniously dropped it in its stand. He nodded to each of the other band members. He turned back to the mic and grabbed it.

> Hey dude, you're screwed, now you're in a bind.
> Back drop, full stop, do you really mind?
> Snow cone, dog bone, Panama hat
> Rock slide, black pride, saturated fat!

By the end of the verse, Joe was leaning over the stage shouting at the audience, who was loving it. He turned and squeegeed his face with his hand. Ed had never seen Joe sing this song with such ferocity, and it riled the crowd. The band played through. Bill's chords mixed well in replacement of the guitar, and Roger ran a couple of riffs from up his bass neck to replace the absent guitar riffs. Bill looked across at Roger, and Roger actually smiled. When the guitar solo came up, it was all Roger. He played the solo an octave down but otherwise true to the recording. As Roger wound to a conclusion, Bill announced simply, "Roger Novak on bass!" And the crowd roared.

Joe took up the mic and shouted,

> Sad sack, hat rack, Caribou Maine!
> Dumb struck, tow truck, singin in the rain!
> Dog star, pace car, Reginald Dwight!
> Jock strap, rat trap, Michelob Lite!

The band finished the song to its sudden conclusion. The crowd cheered, and, as the applause faded, Joe gestured to Bill and announced, "Bill Myers on keys!" More cheers. Joe walked back to the front of the stage. His shirt was plastered to his body. "Okay, thank you! And now the title track of our new album, due for release July 12th." Joe paused for effect and then said in a low voice, "You heard it here first. 'Xylene'." He turned and nodded to Ed.

Ed started the 'Xylene' beat. He remembered it clearly from the recording session, but mostly from listening to the song over and over just a few days ago. But would Joe remember the lyrics? He sustained the beat.

Joe gestured to Roger to come in. Roger missed his cue, waited a measure, then put down a bass line. It was off from the song and awkward. Roger altered it and made it worse. He adjusted it again and hit it right. All the while, he gazed out impassively. Roger played the bass like a man waiting for a bus.

Bill eased in a background tone. Roger abruptly changed to play the introductory guitar riffs. Not the correct riffs, but appropriate nonetheless. Joe stepped up to the mic. Waited, and sang, "They call me Xylene, dimeth..." And trailed off, because he was singing the chorus, not the verse. The band kept playing, as Joe turned from the mic and covered his face. Then he looked up and saw Bill mouth exaggeratedly, "You're needed".

Joe froze, nodded and said to himself, "Okay." No one would hear that, though, because the atmosphere on the stage was solid sound. He re-engaged the mic just as the first verse was about to begin. "You're needed to manufacture drugs," he said quietly, and then with more force, sang, "And with your aromatic smell." The words didn't flow. It was as if they were coming to him just as he was singing them. "You handily get rid of bugs, but life with you would just be hell." He stepped away and took a deep breath, so deep, it was visible to everyone. Roger drifted off-beat and drifted back. The song sort of wandered to the chorus.

Joe was ready. The chorus, in the recording, was sung by a woman with a piercing soprano voice. But no one in today's audience knew that. Joe sang it out in his own range, loudly and off-key. He didn't hesitate over the lyrics this time, though.

The enthusiasm of the crowd had waned as X Band plodded through the song. Joe walked back to Ed and made a circling motion with his index finger. Pick up the pace? Ed wondered. Well, okay. Ed sped up a little. Joe went out to the edge of the stage and waved at people. For people at the back, he'd point at someone and wave. The second verse came up, and Joe sang the first verse with confidence. Bill looked across at Roger and caught his eye. Roger shrugged slightly.

Joe looked back and gave Ed the thumbs-up. He went back to engaging the audience. He sang the chorus—the same chorus as before—directly to a young woman in the front of the stage. She jumped up and down and screamed to her friend beside her. Roger diverted into a bass solo, completely unlike Joe's guitar solo in the recording. Ed and Bill fell into a holding pattern to support the rhythm as Roger worked his instrument. Joe urged him to take center stage with gestures, and Roger conceded by walking three steps away from his spot. Roger's solo was surprisingly good, employing lead guitar fingering techniques. When the solo wound up, Roger stepped back into his spot, and Joe took front stage. Without hesitation, he flew into the third verse, this time singing the correct verse, although with minor word changes. The cadences didn't exactly match the beat, which sounded weird, but could possibly be interpreted as intentional. Joe turned and rolled his eyes to Bill. Despite himself, Bill smiled.

The song started to conclude. Joe walked back to Ed and watched him over his tom-toms. Ed met his eye, and Joe gave him the thumbs-up. Ed smiled and nodded. Sweat was beginning to roll down his face. By contrast, Joe's Xylene shirt was soaked, and even his pants were getting damp.

Then Joe turned and strode to the stage front. "Ed Brettington on drums!" he shouted. On the last note, he raised his arms and crossed his forearms in an X. The crowd roared. Joe smiled and nodded, turning to beckon his band mates to come forward. They walked up to stand beside Joe just as the DJ ran onto the stage. He snatched the mic from Joe and shouted, "X Band!!!" The crowd cheered again, and the band was hustled off the stage. As they hurried back to the dressing room, they could hear, "Look for the new album 'Xylene' due out July 12th!!"

A big stage hand ran clearance, and the band was sucked into his wake, as they retreated back to the dressing room. There, Joe, circled by the masses, was handed a towel, and he mopped his face. At least a half-dozen people clamored for his attention, but he almost seemed oblivious to them, giving acknowledgements, but not inter-acting. Then someone near him repeated what a good job he had done, given the equipment failure, and this seemed to wake him up. Joe announced that the real good job had been done by the others, as they picked up what Joe couldn't do. Nobody seemed to notice what he said, only that he had said something, and they continued their adulation. Joe peeled off his sodden shirt to change back to his old clothes, only no one could find his old clothes. Unasked, a guy gave Joe his own shirt. Joe refused, and eventually put his Xylene shirt back on.

Then someone thrust a bar napkin in his face. "Sign this, Joe!"

"Oh, sure," Joe said as he accepted a pen and roughly signed it, using his damp leg as a backer.

Next, he was given a torn-out piece of spiral notebook paper. Joe pulled his make-up chair to a counter and signed the paper. Next, he signed the back of a liquor store receipt. Next, a guy wanted his picture taken with Joe.

By the door, Roger Smyth moved next to Stu, who was watching Joe with an unusual intensity. Smyth followed Stu's gaze and watched Joe curiously. Then he saw what Stu was seeing. "That public relations training really worked," he observed.

Stu didn't respond at first, except for a slight nod. "Not this well," he pondered.

Smyth considered this and nodded. He said, "How long are you going to let this go on? Joe looks like he's actually enjoying himself."

Stu nodded and mused, "Yes. About another half hour, I think. Then I'll get 'em in the limo."

"Good. These people paid extra for this; I wouldn't want them to be disappointed." When Stu didn't respond, Smyth added, "Don't lose control of him, Stu." He turned and walked away.

Stu scowled.

Joe sat with his face in his hands when Bill slid in the limo. The door thumped shut behind him. Slowly, Joe looked up.

Bill crossed his arms. "Well, that couldn't have gone much worse. Good thing no one knows what 'Xylene' is supposed to sound like."

Joe said, "Bill, thank you for bailing me out."

Bill humpfed. "It was obvious that stress wasn't going to bring you back. And it wouldn't do the rest of us any good for you to stand there looking stupid."

"Yeah," Joe said. "For a minute there, I thought you did a good thing. Out of kindness." He leaned back and looked away.

Bill studied Joe, realizing that he had indeed done a good thing out of kindness. He had originally intended to leave Joe hanging, naked in full view of everyone. If stress would bring Joe back, this would have been the best opportunity. But before Joe could really roast, Bill had rescued him. It *had* been an act of kindness.

Bill was frustrated with himself. He hadn't pushed Joe's stress to the limit, and so the theory was not completely disproved, though Joe *had* been subjected to a lot of stress. On the other hand, from the beginning, Joe had figured he could escape disaster, and as long as Joe thought he had a solution, he would not be under maximum stress. Bill would have to think of a way to beat this.

The limo door opened, and Roger and Ed climbed in. Ed exclaimed, "Well, Joe, I gotta give you credit. We got through it, but we don't get any points for style. Right, Bill?" The limo pulled away.

"It was an embarrassment," Bill declared. "We looked like a high school garage band. Joe, you stood on the stage like a manikin, that is, when you weren't singing the wrong lyrics. And that waving at the crowd? Nobody does that. You just looked like a dork."

As Bill tirade penetrated Joe, Ed spoke up. "The new shirts look good, though. Don't you think the new shirts look good?"

"Knock it off, Ed," Bill grouched.

Ed looked at Joe to see if he would defend himself.

"I guess I've got to work on my stage presence," Joe said.

No one added comment.

Joe filled a martini glass with the thermos in the refrigerator. He leaned back and sipped it. Then he held his breath and gulped it. His eyes watered. He filled another glass.

The band rode in silence. They were exhausted and relieved. Roger fell asleep. Joe filled a third martini glass.

Finally, the limo arrived at the hotel. It was late enough so the band could be let out at the front door. They walked in together and picked up their messages. Joe smiled a genuine smile and wished Miguel a good evening. Miguel beamed and returned the sentiment.

"Miguel," Joe added, "I forgot my elevator key card. Can you ring my room, please?"

Miguel flew around the counter. "Don't worry, sir, I'll card it for you."

The band boarded the elevator. Miguel quickly inserted his card and stepped out. "All done for you, sir," he said.

Joe thanked him warmly as the doors closed.

Bill remarked, "See, having Miguel as a buddy helps you out."

"It never hurts," Joe replied.

The doors opened, and Bill got off. The doors closed.

"Joe," Ed said seriously, "I think you did a really good job today. I don't know why Bill is being so harsh. That's usually *your* job."

Joe nodded. "Yeah, I did a good job for a complete novice, but a lousy job for a seasoned professional. Bill's right." Then he added, "Ed. Thank *you* for doing *your* job."

Ed smiled as the doors opened to his floor. He stepped halfway out and held the door. Ed looked like he was going to say something until finally, he said, "Bill's only half right, you know. You *have* changed. For the worse in some ways, but for the better in others." He stepped back and let the doors close.

The elevator rose to Roger's floor, and the doors opened. Roger stepped off, and Joe held the doors open. "Roger."

Roger stopped and turned. He regarded Joe with his bleached blue eyes.

"Roger," Joe said. "Teach me to play guitar."

Roger stared at Joe.

Joe added, "That is, if you're not busy teaching Rick Wakeman how to play the piano."

Roger nodded and said, "Okay, Mike. I will. Starting tomorrow morning."

Smiling, Joe released the door, and the elevator rose to the penthouse suite. Joe entered and saw the TV was on. He walked into the living room and turned it off. Then he noticed Angie curled up on the sofa, sleeping deeply. She wore a red negligee that inadequately covered anything.

Joe froze and stared. He swallowed noisily and stared again. He picked up the blanket, but before he draped it over Angie's small, perfect form, he appraised it again.

Then he hurried upstairs and locked himself in the bathroom.

Chapter 10

Roger Helps Joe

Sitting across the breakfast table from Joe, Angie was embarrassed. No, worse than embarrassed: Humiliated. Shamed. When she woke, she was covered with the blanket, and that meant two things: One was she had failed to stay awake long enough to seduce her husband. Another was he had seen her attempt, and covered her.

It had been a long time for Angie and Joe. Angie didn't know how long exactly, but she knew it had been months. And before that, making love had been worse than not, with the frustration and futility. No blame from Joe, though, not even unspoken. As with all things, Joe took responsibility for everything that happened to him. The frequency of attempts flagged, and neither discussed it. Now it was none.

Angie missed it. She missed the union, the connection. She missed the total submission of herself to Joe in every way.

And now he sat across from her, coating a bagel with cream cheese. Joe saw her looking at him. "Do you like these bagels? They're missin somethin, I think." Joe's hair was combed back, over his shoulders. It was still wet, and he was letting it air dry. His lack of concern for his hair annoyed Angie.

"I don't know," Angie answered crisply. "I don't eat them."

Joe nodded and resumed his bagel-coating. He had told Dr. Vrakas that he was potent. And yet he tensed when she held him, and he flinched when she touched him. And last night. Even though she had fallen asleep, she was obviously dressed for intimacy. And Joe had obviously seen her. And he had obviously rejected her.

Angie could count the number of times she had initiated love-making, so rare it was. Joe had always taken the lead on that, and that was good for both of them. Joe was never rejected, and Angie was never vulnerable to it. So when Angie made the opening move last night, she had exposed herself, figuratively. And was silently rejected. Angie wanted to cry, but the insult was so overwhelming, she hadn't gotten to that yet.

"What's on the schedule for us today?" Joe asked.

"In two hours, you have an interview with Joanna Day of Hot Rocks Magazine. I reserved a room downstairs."

"I thought Stu was gonna take care of that," Joe said.

Angie glowered. "Yes, he handled it by having me do it."

"Doesn't he have an assistant or something?"

"Yes and no. He has one, but he's having problems with her. She doesn't show up to work very often. So he gives me the overflow."

"What a putz," Joe muttered. "Hey, do you have his number? I want to ask him why I don't have the contract to look at yet."

"I'd better call him," Angie said without thinking. Lately, Stu had been annoying Joe, so she felt it wise to separate them.

Joe seemed disappointed. "Uh, okay. Well, I'm gonna go look at the guitars then."

"And I need to blow dry your hair," Angie added.

Joe smiled warmly. "Are you sure? I could just let it air dry."

Angie rose. "No, you couldn't."

Angie had changed from her negligee to a simple sleep shirt, and this morning, she covered herself in a thick bathrobe. Last night, she would have eagerly given her whole self to Joe, but this morning, she kept herself tightly wrapped, even though the robe got in her way while she dried Joe's hair. Joe sat obediently and stared into her middle.

She caught a sharp scent. It was familiar, but from her childhood. As she dried Joe's hair, the scent persisted. Then she had it: Chlorine. She snapped off the blow dryer. "Joe," she said, "what's in your hair? Chlorine?"

Joe chuckled. "Yeah, from the pool. I like to go swimming first thing when I get up." He looked up at Angie to see her step back to catch her balance.

"Joe," she said with a serious tone, "when did you learn to swim?"

"I don't remember. I was really young, so I've always known how..." Joe frowned. "No, Joe doesn't know how to swim, does he?"

"No," Angie leaned against the wall. "You really tried to learn, though. You took lessons almost every summer, but you never learned. You were too afraid of the water, and you never got over it. To this day."

"Well, until last week, anyway," Joe said. "Angie, this is actually easy to explain. See, Joe had the knowledge. He knew how to swim, but his fear got in the way. Remove the fear, and I can swim." Joe smiled convincingly.

Angie was unsure. "You should rinse out pool water. It's not good for your hair."

Later, Joe stood in the music room and looked at the guitars lined up. He lifted the old red-and-white and studied it closely, and then he replaced the guitar in its stand. He picked up the brown one. He strummed each string.

He sat on the bed. Placing his thumb behind the neck, he recreated the C-chord Angie had shown him.

From the doorway, Roger said, "Mike."

Joe turned around. "Hey, good morning, Roger. I didn't expect to see you so early. Don't you usually sleep late?"

Roger nodded. "I'll take the brown guitar, and you take Good. Good is your guitar."

Joe smiled. "You don't want to play that guitar? Would you rather play this one? Wait, you know the guitar's name? Is this common knowledge?"

"Yes," Roger answered. When Roger spoke, he didn't move. He had no mannerisms. Sometimes it was easy to not know he was talking. He spoke in a low voice, but he could easily be heard in the guitar room. "No one plays Good Guitar but Joe."

"I didn't know that." Joe cocked his head. "Can *I* play Good Guitar?"

Roger studied Joe. "You're not Joe."

"No," Joe agreed. "So maybe I shouldn't play Good, either."

Angie was at the door. "I left a message for Stu at his office."

"Thanks," Joe answered.

"You're welcome," Angie acknowledged, turning to go.

Roger turned back to look at Joe, but Joe was busy selecting another guitar. He stopped before picking one up. "Uh, is there anything else Joe has an exclusive claim to?"

Roger stared up with his unnaturally light blue eyes. "No. Nothing that you don't already know about."

Angie left the doorway.

Roger held up his guitar, the silver flying V2. Its shape was ridiculous in Roger's hands. "This is a guitar. This is the neck, these are the strings, these are the frets. Here are the pick-ups. Two sets." Roger explained the basics of guitar anatomy and function. Joe listened intently. "These are the strings: E, A, D, G, B, and E. This E is two octaves higher than this E. This fret with two dots is an octave higher than the open string." Roger never explained anything; he said facts. His tone and demeanor remained neutral. Roger never stopped for questions, and Joe didn't ask any.

Roger showed how to hold a guitar, how to sling it, and where it should hang. "Practice while standing up," Roger advised. "That's how you will be playing." He taught Joe a fingering exercise involving the index and ring fingers. And suggested that it could also be performed with the middle finger and pinky. "Learn to do these drills, perfectly, all the time, blindfolded. And distracted." Roger demonstrated, his left hand skipping up and down the neck as he picked notes with perfect clarity.

Joe's mouth dropped open. "Man, you're good!" he exclaimed.

Without expression, Roger replied, "Thank you. But I'm not even in Joe's league."

"Yeah, but wow! Hey, can you play the songs? X Band songs?"

"I will need to in order to teach them to you."

"Hey, why don't you take guitar, and I'll play bass? That's more feasible than my learning guitar, don't you think?"

Roger didn't pause to consider it. "No. I play bass."

Undeterred, Joe pressed. "What? Roger, c'mon. It would really help the band. The band needs this, Roger. At least temporarily."

"Why don't we get someone else to play guitar who already knows how to play it?"

Joe opened his mouth and stopped. Then he conceded, "Okay, I see your point."

Roger said, "Now I'll show you a song to practice. It's 'Twinkle Twinkle Little Star'." Roger fingered the notes slowly so Joe could follow.

Joe flawlessly repeated the sequence, only with buzzing and dampened notes. He tried again, with better results. Then he noticed Angie in the doorway. She announced that Joanna Day was waiting.

"Okay," Joe acknowledged. "Roger, ya wanna come?"

Roger didn't move. "No. You don't need any help."

"Ah, c'mon. I need ya to bail me out of tough questions, which oughta be almost all of them."

Roger still didn't move. "Okay."

So Joe borrowed Angie's elevator key, and they left. On the hotel second floor, there were a half dozen large rooms that could be used for conferences, training sessions or magazine interviews of famous rock stars. Joe, with Roger trailing, peeked into several rooms until there was only one left on the hall.

"This is the room here?" Joe asked as he blew through the doorway.

Joanna Day stood behind an industrial folding table, upon which various interviewing paraphernalia rested. Joanna herself was nearly as tall as Joe and sported short red hair spiked up. She breezed around the table and extended a hand. "Joanna Day from Hot Rocks Magazine. It's nice to meet you."

Joe shook her hand. "Yeah, I know," he agreed. "I mean, uh, for me it'll be nice to meet you." Joe winced.

Joanna noticed Roger standing behind Joe. "And you are... Roger Novak? How nice—and unexpected—of you to come." Joanna adjusted to Roger's unplanned attendance. She shook Roger's hand.

"Yeah, Roger plays the really *big* guitar," Joe quipped.

"Right," Joanna replied. "Have a seat anywhere." She gestured to the seat across the table from her seat.

"Anywhere?" Joe inquired.

Joanna frowned. "Sit here," she specified.

Roger and Joe sat in the thinly padded industrial folding chairs. Joanna sat and switched on her micro-recorder. She picked up a pad and pen and clicked the pen, in effect drawing her sword. "Joe," she said formally, "and Roger. I want to thank you for this interview."

"No problem," Joe assured her. "We only live upstairs."

Joanna's eyes shifted to Roger, who sat blankly not saying anything. "Yes. Well, thank you for your time," she amended. She waited for Joe to make a dumb comment, but, like Roger, he sat dumbly. "Hot Rocks Magazine readers are guitar players, mostly males from teens to early twenties. They want to learn guitar-playing tips and to learn about the techniques of those already established in the field. Okay, what do I know already? I know the core band members haven't changed since 'Xenon'..."

"Sure we have," Joe interrupted. "We're all changing, growing, evolving."

"That's not what I meant, but to follow that thought, how has your growing and evolving affected your music? How does the sound of 'Xylene' compare to that of 'Xenon'? Or 'Xylophone', for that matter?" Joanna pierced Joe with her green eyes.

"Uh, there's more guitar," Joe offered. And then he seemed to recover his wits. "Yes. Guitar is featured more prominently. The songs are more concisely mixed. We had a different mixer, uh, sound engineer than we had before, and he did a good job. He mixed almost the whole album."

When Joe stopped talking, Joanna waited. Finally, she asked, "How is there more guitar?"

"How? There's more of it. There are more guitar solos in the album. How many guitar solos are there, Roger?" Joe turned to Roger, who sat unmoving. Joe turned back to Joanna and answered, "A lot. Roger's still countin em."

Joanna waited.

Joe added, "Guitar runs throughout the album. Most of the songs are guitar-based. Not 'Xylene', though, that's a mix. And what about 'Anesthesia'?" he asked Roger.

The silence hung heavily. Roger answered, "Not 'Anesthesia'. Or 'Sacramento'."

Joanna waited. "What is your style in 'Xylene'? How has it evolved since 'Xylophone'?"

Joe considered this for a long time. "It's more controlled," he finally declared. "In 'Xylophone', there was some free-spirited fun. Look at the subtleties in 'Golfing Amoebas'. And look at the, uh, the little doodad things, the *licks* in 'See Me'. *That's* a guy havin fun. Then look at 'Xenon', and you see less of it. You see some hot guitar in 'Mrs. Kisses', but songs like 'Calculator' and 'Identity Crisis'—" Joe stopped suddenly and stared through Joanna. Recovering himself, he continued, "they're all business. And 'Xylene'... What would you say, Roger?"

Roger shrugged.

"Roger's not sure," Joe interpreted.

Joanna waited. "What kind of guitar did you favor when recording 'Xylene'?"

"Uh, electric. And acoustic. Some 12-string. But mostly 6-string. Roger played the 4-string."

"Fender, Les Paul, what?"

"Oh! Uh, I don't know. A mix, I guess."

"A mix of what?"

"Um, Fender and Les Paul." Joe reached for his shirt pocket, which he didn't have. He scratched his left shoulder instead.

Joanna waited. "What strings do you like to use?"

"Are you Canadian?" Joe asked. When Joanna shook her head in confusion, Joe asked, "Are you from North Dakota? Minnesota? You have a slight twang in your speech."

"Minnesota," Joanna stated, "about three hours north of Minneapolis. Where are you from? Arkansas?"

"Me? No, I'm from, uh, Connecticut," Joe answered.

Joanna waited.

"Okay, I pick up accents readily," Joe explained, "and I spent a lot of time with the recording engineer, who was from the hills of Virginia." (This was, of course, incorrect; Sam was from Seattle.) "Hey, that's an interesting ring," Joe said, indicating a diamond ring Joanna wore on her left middle finger.

"Joe!" Joanna snapped, "we're here talk about you. What strings do you like to use?"

Chastised, Joe answered, "Uh, you know, it depends."

"Of course. What do you like to use for what?"

Joe stared in disbelief at Joanna. "Do your readers really want to know about this?"

"This is *exactly* what our readers want to know."

Helplessly, Joe looked at Roger. Roger looked like he was about to fall asleep. Joe turned back to Joanna. He shook his head and confessed, "I don't know, Joanna. I don't keep track of things like that."

"Bullshit," Joanna declared. "Everyone knows you're *obsessed* with 'things like that'. So wwwwhat's going on here?" she asked, drawing out the w sound for emphasis. "You showed up for the interview, but you don't want to answer questions. Are you fishing for endorsements? Or have you switched? And now you can't be promoting your former brands?" Joanna smiled uncertainly.

"I'd rather not discuss the business side of what I do," Joe said.

Which widened Joanna's smile. "Okay." She pursed her lips and nodded. "What advice would you have for guitar players in their teens and early twenties?"

"Focus on the basics," Joe answered. "Keep your thumb behind the neck and proper hand position. You know, a lot of guitar players shown in videos and stuff actually have lousy technique. Just because they're doin it that way doesn't mean it's the best way." Joe went on to describe fingering exercises and drills. Joanna relaxed and prodded him on with questions. Joe eventually wound around to answering, in a way, the specific questions he had dodged earlier. It wasn't important what Joe Ecks used to play guitar. It was important for each guitar player to experiment and learn for himself what he liked, and what tended to produce what flavors of sound.

"'Flavors of sound'?" Joanna asked.

"You know, tonal qualities. The little barely audible nuances that can distinguish sounds."

Joanna nodded. "Okay, love, what about getting to the top? Any advice?"

Joe made a sound. "If I knew that, I suppose I'd be there," he said. "But here's what I'd say: You need talent, skill, and luck." Joe went on to define his terms and how they affected each other.

Joanna asked, "What about hard work?"

"Yeah, I forgot that. You need hard work to develop your skill and increase your exposure. But hard work alone won't get you there. Anyone who tells you they're famous because they worked hard is only partially right. They're also lucky. There are a lot of talented, skilled, hard-working guitar players who are nowhere simply because they haven't been lucky. I am where I am, because I'm luckier than all of them. If I think anything else, I'm giving myself too much credit."

Joanna leaned back. "That sounds artificial. Is that what you really think?"

Joe nodded slowly and answered, "Yeah. Unfortunately."

Joanne studied Joe. Joe flashed a smile. "Okay," she finally yielded. "What about the future? What are your plans?"

"There's a lot of pre-release stuff to do, videos and promotional gigs, you know." Joe expanded on the many different things that had to be done, in general terms. Joanna asked questions that could be answered vaguely. He concluded with the tour. "And then back to the recording studio for Album #4, I hope," he concluded.

"You hope?" Joanna asked.

Joe smiled wryly. "You never know what's going to happen."

Joanna regarded Joe with her pure, blue eyes. "What do *you* think is going to happen?"

Joe thought about it. "I couldn't even guess. I know that very quickly your life can change, and all your careful planning becomes obsolete."

"Yes," Joanna agreed. "Life can take some quick turns." Their eyes met, and there seemed to be a mutual understanding.

Joe checked his bare wrist. "Is that it? What time is it? Do you have enough material?"

"I'm done," Joanna answered. "Thank you for your time."

Everyone stood and shook hands.

"It was a pleasure," Joe said. "You're very good, Joanna."

Joanna narrowed her eyes. "That's why my editor chose me to interview you. But you're not nearly the jerk people say you are."

On his way out, Joe smiled. "Yeah, and Roger behaved himself, too."

Joe and Roger walked side-by-side down the ultra-wide conference room corridor. Joe had adopted a bouncy walk, and by contrast, Roger glided forward. Joe asked, "If I need your help in another interview, can I count on you?"

Roger replied, "I knew you wouldn't need any help."

Joe sighed heavily. The two reached the elevators.

They waited. Roger asked, "What are you going to do now?"

As if it were the only possible answer, Joe replied, "Practice."

Roger nodded and smiled imperceptibly. "Excellent."

Chapter 11

Bill Helps Joe

The elevator doors opened, and Bill stepped into the Ecks penthouse. Before he could do anything, he was halted by ragged electric guitar music from upstairs. What the sound lacked in harshness, it compensated for with dissonance. Bill wanted to recoil and wince, but instead, he stopped and listened. It was a skill-developing drill, he figured. Angie entered the foyer from the dining room.

"Damn," Bill said. "I was hoping it was you playing the guitar." Then he stopped as he saw Angie's red, swollen eyes. "Angie, what's wrong?"

Angie shook her head and in a low voice said, "It's like watching an Olympic runner learning to walk."

Bill saw that Angie was on the edge. He did the only thing he knew to do. He took Angie in his arms. Grateful for his understanding, she settled in. Bill reflected that he was stressed plenty with Joe not being Joe, but that only affected him professionally. Angie's world must be entirely turned over. Bill listened to the clumsy sounds coming from upstairs. After a long minute, Angie pulled away.

"Why is he playing the guitar?" Bill asked.

Angie sighed. "He wants to learn to play guitar. Roger gave him a lesson today."

Bill cleared his throat. "How long has he been at it?"

"Three hours. He came back from the magazine interview and went up there, and he's been at it ever since."

Bill frowned. "You'd think he'd be getting better by now."

"Oh, he is," Angie told him. "At first, he was very bad." Then she surprised herself by smiling.

Bill smiled back. It was funny, in a bizarrely tragic way. "Well, I guess I'd better go save Joe from himself." Bill headed up the stairs. "And *you* could probably use a break, too." Bill went to the music room. He opened the door and found Joe rigidly standing, wearing the brown guitar. His left hand walked up and down the neck, hitting alternate strings as it moved. Besides that, Joe was in a trance. His eyes were closed. The room stank of creative sweat, an odor that awakened memories.

There were times the band worked closely together for hours. Like when the band was working on 'Xylophone' in the studio, or, more recently, when they were mixing 'Xylene'. It seemed like their odors combined, just like their ideas. Bill came to associate that particular smell with the creative experience.

Joe opened his eyes. "Bill, how nice to see you." The way he said it, Bill believed he meant it.

"What are you doing?" Bill asked bluntly. More bluntly than he'd intended.

Joe deliberately set the guitar down in its stand. "Plan A is for us to move ahead as if nothing is wrong. I think I can do that more effectively if I learn to play the guitar."

"You're planning to learn to play guitar like you used to, all over again? Do you think you can do that?" Bill tried not to sound as incredulous as he felt.

"No," Joe answered honestly. "But I think our chances of succeeding on Plan A are better if I can play guitar *some*." Joe reached for his shirt pocket, then jammed his hand in his pants pocket in frustration. "Bill, the knowledge is in my head. I can coax it out and have the skill. I used to know how to play this, so I still do, some-where. Okay, look: Joe never learned to swim. He took lessons, but he was too afraid of the water. But I can swim, because I don't have the fear, but I do have Joe's knowledge of swimming. I also have Joe's knowledge of guitar. It's in there. I just need to find a way to it."

Bill understood Joe's logic. The analogy wasn't perfect, but it wasn't worth arguing the point. What did it hurt for Joe to work on the guitar, anyway? It might even do some good. Maybe in addition to drawing out the guitar knowledge, the practice would draw out the whole Joe personality.

Joe asked, "So what brings you here, Bill? Angie didn't ask you to intervene, did she?"

"No. I was working on the lyrics. Did you know you're going to rerecord 'Shut Up and Suck' tomorrow?"

Joe nodded. "Yeah, Angie told me."

"So I thought we could go over the lyrics and the song in general so you're not so totally ignorant when you're recording tomorrow."

"Bill, that's so thoughtful," Joe praised.

"I didn't really do it for you," Bill said grimly. "I thought it would help maintain the illusion."

"Well, yeah," Joe agreed. "Plan A."

Bill handed the sheets to Joe. He pointed out the original lyrics and the replacement lyrics. Joe read over the original lyrics and actually blushed. "Swate Jasus," he said. "Who wrote these? Joe?"

"Yes. You were trying to antagonize Michael, and it worked. But also, I think you were going for some notoriety and publicity. Censorship sometimes makes the news. At least the industry news. Here's my rewrite. I tried to keep the cadence exactly the same."

Joe read the rewrite. "'Stand Up and Shout'? I like it. It's very encouraging. The theme of the song, very up-beat. How does it go?"

Bill sang. His voice was deep and rich and strong. So he strained on the high notes.

> You're sitting there so full of thoughts
> We don't know what you're about
> Let out what is inside your head
> Go ahead, stand up and shout!
>
> Everything that you keep inside
> Now's the time to let it out
> Unexpressed they will do no good
> Unless you stand up and shout!
>
> Trust yourself or you will falter
> Dig down deep, destroy all doubt
> You'll never see what you can do
> Until you stand up and shout!

Bill cleared his throat. There's one chorus that goes between verses one and two. It's only two lines. It goes like this:

Why have you kept yourself all alone, hidden from the world?
Imagine the possibilities if like a flower you unfurled.

Joe said, "Your singing is very good. Have you had vocal training?"

"Actually, we all have. That was your idea. But I did before that, before joining the band. When I was teaching music."

"Yeah? And?"

Bill didn't want to digress, but he answered, "Well at that time, I wanted to be a piano man. Play in bars and restaurants. I already know how to play piano, but I wanted to sing well, too."

Joe thought. "You don't sing any X Band songs solo, do you?"

"Not so far, but I sing 'Sacramento' on 'Xylene'. I was going to sing 'Anesthesia', but you sang it instead. I intentionally wrote both of them in a key that I could sing."

"That's too bad," Joe said. "With your voice, you'd be good. And it would be a good contrast with Joe Ecks's. And mine." Joe changed the subject. "What does the music sound like in this song?"

Bill looked at Joe, then said, "Oh, yeah, you don't remember it. You know, it's very strange that you remember only the things about the band that an outsider would know. Sometimes I forget about... Well, you know. That's surprising, really, since you are so different, uh, this way." Bill was uncomfortable discussing Joe's mental condition with Joe.

Joe didn't seem to notice it. "Yeah, from what I've heard about Joe, he and I are polar opposites. I bet if Joe and I ever met, we'd drive each other crazy." Joe suddenly laughed. "Okay, crazi*er*. I'm not exactly a picture of mental health, *now*, am I?"

Bill relaxed. How could he not, given the ease with which Joe spoke of his insanity? He took off his cap and rubbed a hand over his bald head. "You know," he confessed, "if I didn't know who you really are, I would never question your mental health. Shoot, you're more balanced than anybody else in the band. It seems."

Joe smiled. "I'll take that as a compliment, Bill. You seem pretty sane to me, too."

Despite himself, Bill observed, "Except, everyone seems sane until you get to know them well. Then you find out how quirky they really are. And we in the band know each other *very* well."

"I guess that's true," Joe agreed, and he grinned. "Maybe you just don't know this personality very well, and I'm just as quirky as the rest of you."

"I guess that would follow." Bill found himself starting to like Joe this way. They'd been in the same room for a while now without even a disagreement. "Let's go to my room, and I can play you this song. You should at least know the general tune."

Joe agreed. Bill had a suite at the end of the hall on the 4th floor. The door opened into a living room/dining room combination. When they went in, Joe looked around, and Bill saw his residence of the past couple of months as Joe would see it. A heap of clothes was beside the loveseat. The desk was covered with piles of papers, spiral notebooks and magazines. The dining room table was a forest of Coke bottles.

Joe quickly appraised the room. "Now *this* is a bachelor pad!" he declared. "This is a place in which someone is obviously comfortable."

"Thanks, I guess. I'd better get it cleaned up before Cassie comes back." Bill took spiral notebooks out of a chair and added them to stack on the floor.

"When is Cassie coming?"

"A week or two." Bill chuckled. "With Cassie, plans are loose." He seated himself at a free-standing keyboard.

"Okay," Bill began, changing the subject. "Here are the melody and lyrics." Bill played the song and sang the new lyrics. He would sometimes back up and play the bass line or keyboard accents. Then he played through the song again.

"Now you try it," Bill said as he took off on another play.

Joe had the lyrics in front of him, and he started singing. "You're sitting there so full of—"

Bill stopped. "When you're recording, lift up your chin. It straightens your throat and gives your voice strength."

Joe complied. He held the notebook unnaturally high so he was singing up at the upper corner of the room.

Bill started playing. He stopped. "You have to over-enunciate to be understood. When you're singing it, it sounds forced, but on tape, it sounds natural."

Joe nodded, and they began again.

Bill stopped. "You have to lose the southern accent. Sing it like Joe would."

"Right," Joe said, and they began again.

Bill stopped. "You're never going to hit the high notes unless you place your voice in the roof of your mouth."

"What?" Joe asked.

"You're singing it like this," Bill said, and he demonstrated. "You need to put your voice up here like this." Bill demonstrated.

"They sound the same to me," Joe admitted.

Bill regarded Joe. "Are you tone deaf, too?"

"No," Joe answered testily, "just show me again."

Bill repeated the comparison. Joe attempted to imitate Bill. They went back and forth. Finally, Bill was satisfied. They started over.

Bill stopped. "Use your diaphragm," he told Joe. "You get more volume and control."

Joe sighed. "Use my what?"

"Use your diaphragm. Push the air out from here." Bill showed him using his hands.

"Okay," Joe said, shaking his head. "Swate Jasus, I thought singin would be the easy part."

"It is," Bill huffed in frustration. "You're *Joe*, and you can't even sing like Joe."

"Yeah, but I'm gettin closer," Joe pointed out. "I appreciate your help. I never woulda gotten it otherwise. You must like teachin."

Bill had been tensing up. But Joe, with this comment, eased the edginess. Bill thought about teaching. He was teaching Joe, and he was a good teacher. He wasn't a qualified singing instructor, but no one knew better how to sing like Joe than he did (besides Joe himself). "All right," Bill said. "Let's just run through the song. You can get the tune, and then we'll polish it."

They did. Joe was bad. To Bill, hearing Joe sing badly was worse than hearing him play guitar badly. It was more personal. It was Joe's voice. They completed the song.

"I'm sorry," Joe said.

Bill shook his head. "We'll get there. Okay, again."

They started it again. Joe was better, it seemed to Bill, or at least less bad. He was using his diaphragm more, but still not placing his voice correctly.

When the song was done, Bill asked, "Can I offer a suggestion?"

"Of course, Bill," Joe said. "Why so polite all of a sudden?"

Bill ignored the question and pressed on. "You need to breathe better. You're—"

Joe's mouth dropped open. "I'm not *breathing* right? Before, I wasn't *standing* right, and now I can't *breathe*? What about blinking? Am I blinking okay? And what about swallowing? Is *that* okay?" Joe stopped suddenly and smiled.

Bill was struck by how directly opposite New Joe was from Old Joe. He smiled, appreciating Joe's humor, though not participating in it. "There are certain breaks in the lyrics where it's best for you to inhale. When you know where they are, then you can plan for them." Bill took the lyrics from Joe and drew stars where he should inhale. "Try these," Bill said, handing back the sheet. "And for extra credit, inhale quietly. Your breathing should not be a part of the music."

Joe nodded. "Right."

They ran through the song again. Bill noted additional improvement. He had thrown a lot of instruction at Joe, but he seemed to be assimilating it. Maybe he was right that he would learn guitar quickly.

Joe said, "Once more, and I think I'll have the breathing down."

"Okay, then we can stop."

"Stop why?" Joe asked.

"Well, it's late for dinner, and then after that we can take it easy."

"Oh, do you have something else you have to do?"

Bill looked at Joe, recognizing this trait in common with Old Joe. The relentless, dogged Joe. Still, given the amount of criticism Joe had taken, he was surprisingly gung ho. There was no use resisting Joe, Old Joe, when he was like this. But Bill didn't really want to resist New Joe. He thought maybe they could nail the song, and then tomorrow it wouldn't be half bad. Maybe they really could pull it off. Joe seemed confident.

Joe called Angie and invited her to Bill's suite. They ordered room service dinner. Bill cautioned Joe to stay away from certain foods, particularly dairy, just before singing. ("Yeah, eating," Joe responded. "You haven't c'rected me on that yet.") While they waited, Joe made conversation. He got Bill to talk about his meeting at Moog. He asked Angie if she knew how to swim, and she did. Did she ever swim in the penthouse pool? Sometimes. Sometimes she used the big hotel pool in the basement. What about you, Bill? When was the last time you went swimming? Cassie and I went to the Disney water park... While they talked, Bill cleared the dining room table. Well, half of it.

The dinners arrived, and the three were awkwardly silent while the stewards set an elaborate table.

When they sat down, Joe asked Bill, "Are you an LA native? Do you live around here?"

Bill looked at Joe and replied, "We never talk about you."

"You're right. But everything I remember is fictitious"

"I guess," Bill said.

"Anyway, I was thinkin it would be pretty stupid if Ed and I live in Connecticut, and you live here in southern California. But maybe you're right, and we're wrong, because this seems to be where we work."

Bill answered, "We work all over the world. We can't live near where we work. We only go home on vacations."

"Wow, that's pretty depressing if you think about it."

Bill changed the subject, telling Angie about Joe's significant progress. But he added that the starting point was pretty dismal.

"Yeah, thanks," Joe said. "I'm goin for Most Improved."

"What do you mean?"

"As in Most Improved in a bowling league." Joe looked at their expressions of non-understanding. "Most Improved always went to the bowler who started out terrible and managed to climb up to bad. Usually it was someone who was just learning to bowl and joined the league."

Bill laughed. "That's so appropriate, I don't believe it!"

Angie stayed in the room to hear Joe train. Bill wanted to warn her how hard it was to hear, but he didn't want Joe to hear him say it and get discouraged.

As Bill played the intro, Joe said, "Listen to this:" and he sang,

> Steamin mad you rail at us
> As you wave your arms and clout
> But we don't know, man, what you want
> When you just sit there and shout.

Bill stopped. "What? What did you just sing?"

"I made up some lyrics," Joe smiled, "about Michael."

"Wow, that's good," Bill said. "Did you just make them up?"

"Yeah, while we were eating. Personally, I like the 'wave your arms and clout' zeugma."

"What's a zeugma?"

"It's two dependent clauses drawing different meanings from the same verb. Like, uh, 'I went crazy and bowling.' It's a literary device."

Bill pondered this. It had taken him three hours to work out his own lyrics, and Joe came up with a verse while he was chewing.

"Do you want to hear the second verse?" And Joe sang,

> You demandin, well-dressed man
> Please tell us what's the fuss about
> And we'll do the very best we can
> But don't just sit there and shout.

Bill was stunned. The lyrics were good. In terms of cadence, probably better than his. The content was a little esoteric, though. Although, even if no one knew the back story, the content had an appeal. Who didn't ever work hard only to get their efforts blasted by a loud, well-dressed man? At least figuratively.

Joe was saying, "It would be funny to record a version with these lyrics just to bug Michael. Wouldn't that be funny?"

"You're a genius," Bill concluded.

"Yeah," Joe answered casually. "Too bad I'm such a fool."

Without a pause, Joe got them back to practicing. To Angie, he sounded a bit forced and unsteady, but acceptably so. Bill heard every wrong thing, but he acknowledged that Joe was making progress.

They ran through the song twice more, and then Bill called it quits. Joe's progress was leveling off, and his voice was getting tired. Joe accepted this reasoning.

Before leaving, though, Joe said, "I was looking at this keyboard. I don't know what it is, but it looks complex."

It was Bill's pride, his latest acquisition. The keyboard produced sound digitally. It could simulate 99 instruments, including their attack and decay rates, furthering the simulation. Bill then lectured on the sonic structure of the different instrument groups.

"Wow, does this make other instruments obsolete? Like the sax or tuba?"

Bill shook his head. "No, there will always be techniques on an instrument that can't be built into a keyboard." Bill demonstrated different distortions and transition effects.

Joe thanked Bill for showing him the keyboard and suggested Bill play him the songs from 'Xylene'. "One of these days, I'm gonna hafta buy that album. When is it comin out? Oh, July 12th. How could I forget that?"

"Well, I could play the songs for you now. I've got all my notes here."

Joe looked around at the stack of notebooks and papers.

Bill pulled papers from piles as he said, "Okay, you already know 'Xylene', and you're somewhat familiar with 'Stand Up and Shout'." (Joe rolled his eyes.) "Do you remember 'You'?"

"Um, yes! That was that first day. 'You laugh but you don't get the joke'."

"Yeah, that's it," Bill confirmed. He sat down at the keyboard. "Here's 'Cincinnati Fan'. It starts out with crowd noises and a sports announcer. The crowd noise builds, and then you sweep in with guitar." Bill simulated it with his keyboard. "And Roger follows with bass." Bill guided Joe (and Angie) through the song. When he finished, he summarized it: "It's about being the underdog and trying your hardest every day anyway."

"You musta written this one," Joe said.

"Yes. I happen to really admire people who try hard even when the odds are heavily against them, and they're likely to get beaten and embarrassed. But they fight courageously anyway."

"Is that in sports or in everything?"

Bill looked at Joe. "You're talking about you now, aren't you? And the long odds you face."

"Actually, I was thinking about the Polish army standing up to the German blitzkrieg when they were way overmatched. But, yeah, I see your parallel."

Bill scowled. "You're so full of it."

"Yep." Then Joe said, "Your point is going to be missed, though, if the Bengals go to the Superbowl anytime soon."

Bill made a disparaging noise. "I'm not really worried about that. Okay, here's another one, 'Sacramento'." Bill switched the keyboard to 'grand piano', and he played an entrancing intro. "Bass and drums come in. Guitar comes in later. It's subdued and limited to background accents." Bill played an interesting piano piece. And then sang,

In Sacramento, we were happy, never asking why
We played all day and held each other through the night.
In Sacramento.

"Bass and drums build, and I do a strong piano thing."

We were young and so in love
We swore that we would last forever
In Sacramento

Bill continued to play. He no longer described the music. Joe and Angie exchanged glances. Bill finished the song, and he shuffled through some papers on the other side of the keyboard. Joe and Angie remained tactfully quiet. Finally, Bill said in a low voice, "Recording this was hard enough. I hope I don't have to do it in concert." He sighed. "Okay, here's 'Perihelion'. It's mostly instrumental, with only a few lines." Bill started to play it. "I can't do it justice. There's some excellent interplay between us, you and me, and some fine drumming from Ed."

"Who wrote 'Perihelion'?"

"You and I get credit, but it was really more you than me. Now here's 'Anesthesia'. I wrote this one." Bill played and sang. As he had said, the vocals were solidly in his range, and he sang with feeling and purpose.

When he was done, Joe struggled for words. "That's pretty creepy," he finally suggested. "Did Michael approve it? It undermines every religion but atheism."

Bill shook his head. "No. It just asks the questions, that's the thing."

Joe quoted, "'I can't stare at death without blinking / Is the afterlife just wishful thinking?' You don't think that's antagonistic?"

"No, I'm just asking questions. A person's faith should be able to withstand being questioned. Besides, I really want to know the answers. I want someone to give me the answers and reassure me that I have a soul. Maybe that means my faith is weak," Bill admitted, losing energy. "Maybe it should be."

Joe let Bill collect himself, and then he said, "Pretty profound thoughts for a rock 'n' roll album. But that's why I like this band so much. It's more than music that rocks. 'Xenon' was big, and I think you added a lot to it, with songs like 'Identity Crisis' and 'Isolation'. And your keyboard talent adds a lot of depth to the music. I liked 'Xylophone', too, with 'Tina' and 'Xylophone'. Okay, settle this for me, Bill. Is 'Xylophone' a metaphor for masturbation? 'When I'm home and all alone / I reach down and grab the bones / and then I play the xylophone'?" Joe spread his hands as Bill smiled. "What is that?"

Bill chuckled. "You'll have to ask Ed. He's answered that question a hundred times, and I still don't know for sure. You know how Ed can be."

Joe sighed. "Yeah, well, I'm starting to. I'm still gettin to know you and Roger, too. And you, Angie." Angie struggled to form an appropriate response as Joe reflected on his own words. "And Joe, I guess."

Bill nodded. "Okay, let me show you 'I Wish'. You wrote this one, and I think it's probably your best work. You don't think so, but it's exactly what I would be writing if I had your talent. It starts with an extended intro that builds." Bill played a winding melody that increased in intensity, and then, just before it reached its peak, it pulled back, and then the song started. "You can sense the potential for an extended concert version," Bill said, playing. After two verses, Bill took a detour, explaining he couldn't duplicate the intensity of the interlude. "You should hear it: Roger does this very simple A-E bass line, and you rock. Took you three weeks to work it out." Bill attempted to duplicate the song on the keyboard. It was close, but didn't contain the subtleties that separate great songs from passable ones. Bill finished out the song.

"Okay, 'Contents Under Pressure'. This is going to be released as a single. It's a good song," Bill admitted. "But I get the feeling it was picked for single release because it's 'typical X Band'. I don't want to be typified by a particular style. I mean, we have a style, but it's not always the same thing over and over. We've intentionally worked to broaden our music. Look at 'Sacramento' and 'Anesthesia'. They're nothing like 'You' or 'Calculator' or a lot of other ones. Or compare the tones of 'Anesthesia' to 'Xylene' or 'Delta Kronecker'."

Joe nodded. "I have, actually. Not with the third album songs, of course. But I was impressed that the same band could do 'Ice Age', 'Golfing Amoebas' and 'Tina'. On the same album. And that was before you came on."

"Actually," Bill said, "I came on during the recording of 'Xylophone'. I got partial credit for writing 'Xylophone' and 'Free Radical'. I wasn't considered part of the band then, though; not until we went on tour."

"No kiddin," Joe mused, studying Bill. "I stand c'rected."

Bill nodded. He said, "All right, so here's 'Contents Under Pressure'. It's yours, but all of us had a hand in this one." Bill played the song. When he finished, he commented, "This song has a complexity that will be difficult to recreate in concert. For example, there are at least three different significant guitar tracks. We *are* doing a video of it, though, if you'll remember."

"I remember," Joe answered. "Also 'Xylene' and 'Cincinnati Fan'. What's the schedule on those?"

Angie replied, "I don't know yet. Theremin will tell Stu, and then Stu will tell me. It should be soon, though."

Bill agreed. "For all I know, they've already started filming the story line." Bill saw Joe's confusion and explained, "You know in videos, there's a band playing, and there's also a story line. Sometimes the story line is simply images. In 'Contents Under Pressure', there's a guy in a high-pressure life. They've probably already picked the guy and started filming. Well, maybe they've picked the guy. I always underestimate how long it takes to do everything."

"They sure got us the 'Xylene' logo shirts quickly," Joe observed.

Bill agreed. "Sometimes it's hard to predict. There's a lot of hurry-up-and-wait. Sometimes things are pushed forward at great expense, and then nothing happens. The waste used to irritate you, even though it wasn't your money." Bill shook his head. "It's a funny business. Okay, here's the last song, 'I Can Be Your Friend'. This was you, me and Ed. I like it. It's simple and catchy. Here:" Bill played the song. He stopped at one point to describe a detail he liked. Then he finished out the song. "It's really a simple, unadorned melody. If you listened to the album a couple of times, this is the song you'd be humming later."

Bill and Joe discussed the songs in general, Joe asking questions, and Bill adding anecdotes and details.

"Well, thanks for playing all this for me, Bill. It really helps me know what we're doing. I had an interview this afternoon, and it was awkward answering questions about the album."

Bill smiled. "How did it go?"

Joe shrugged. "Passable, I think. I was very general. I don't know. I suppose the interviewer will take a guess at some reason why I'm a space cadet instead of an asshole, but it probably won't be that I have amnesia or multiple personality disorder." Joe shrugged again.

Angie firmed the next day's meeting times for the rerecording with Bill, and she and Joe left.

In the elevator, Angie searched for something to say to Joe. She liked hearing him sing and working with Bill so well. And, she admitted to herself, she even liked him learning to play guitar. He was terrible, but at least he wanted it, and he was working on it. He was working to be more like himself.

Joe stood with his hands in his pockets, looking up at the digital display of floor numbers. He seemed utterly contained. At peace. She admired the calm strength evident in his expression, and the mental power in his dark eyes. Especially since she was aware of how much pressure he was under.

Angie put her arm through Joe's arm. "What do you want to do when we get back? Do you want to watch TV?" For once, Joe didn't shy from the physical contact.

"That would be nice, but I suppose I should practice more."

"What were you thinking about just now?" Angie asked.

Joe looked down to her. "I was thinking about bands establishing a known style and then being confined by it. Angie, tell me something good about Joe. I'd like to know that he's not all bad."

The elevator doors opened to their foyer, giving Angie a chance to react to Joe's sudden, odd request. To buy time, as they entered the penthouse, she asked, "What do you mean?"

"I just keep hearing about what a jerk Joe is. I don't want to be a jerk," he told Angie. "I am not a jerk."

"No, of course not," Angie said. She released Joe to look in his face. "You're under a lot of pressure, and you demand the best from everyone around you, and especially you. You've kept X Band on course. The band needs you. Without y—"

Joe impatiently waved it all away. "None of this tells me Joe's not a jerk."

Angie mentally took a step back. Her voice softened. "Joe, I knew you before you even had Good Guitar, and I fell in love with you then. You've always been driven, and I've always admired that in you. And you make me be the best that I can be."

Joe stared at Angie, his face showing a tremendous sorrow. He took a deep breath. Doubtfully, he asked, "Is that what you want?"

Angie nodded.

"Thank you, Angie," he said quietly. "I guess I'll learn to play the guitar now." He turned and bounded up the stairs.

Angie wondered: *Is* that what I want? Really? If I had a choice?

Chapter 12

Stand Up and Shout

In the darkened bedroom, the phone rang. Angie's hand reached out and dislodged the receiver. "It's your ten o'clock wake up call, Mrs. Ecks."

"Thank you," Angie rumbled. She cleared her throat.

Joe was not there. It wasn't any more unusual than anything else he did lately. Even after adjusting to Pacific Time, Joe proved to be an early riser, and he would often get out of bed without waking Angie. But last night, Angie went to bed alone, and she fell asleep before Joe came in. She wasn't even sure Joe had slept in the bed.

She and Joe had always gone to bed together, when possible. It was convenient for when Joe wanted intimacy. Admittedly, that hadn't happened recently, but some habits persist long after they lose their purpose. Angie turned it over in her mind. And now, Joe was keeping his distance, but for a completely different reason (allegedly), out of loyalty to... Himself? The rejection was the same, but the reason made all the difference. Joe wasn't rejecting her now, not really. Not if he didn't think he was entitled to her. But the effect was the same.

Angie pulled herself into a sitting position and listened. No guitar. She padded out of the bedroom in only her short nightshirt and looked around. The brown guitar and an amp were missing. She put on a bathrobe and went downstairs. Not finding Joe, she stepped outside. The sun was already a quarter into the sky, and the temperature had just turned from morning chill to summer heat. She found Joe outside by the pool, guitar in hand. He stood stiffly before the amp, apparently unaware of anything, except that when Angie approached, he stopped and turned. And smiled. The smile was so open and genuine that Angie couldn't help smiling in return.

Angie said, "We should get ready to go."

Joe dutifully set down the guitar and unplugged it from the amp. Angie went back inside and ordered breakfast. Joe carried his equipment in and took it back up to the guitar room. Angie showered. She dressed while Joe showered.

She selected a snug blouse with strategic folds that she had recently bought. Joe came out of the bathroom, and the sight of Angie stopped him.

Angie turned and saw Joe looking at her. Smiling, she asked, "Do you like the blouse?"

"Oh!" Joe uttered looking away. "Sorry for starin."

"Joe, relax," Angie laughed. "You're allowed to *look* at me."

"Okay," said Joe, not looking at her. "Thanks." He moved toward the door.

"Wait. Do you think the blouse shows too much?" Angie had no reason to think that it might, but she wanted to get Joe to look at her.

Joe drove his vision over to Angie, and he studied her whole blouse. "No," he told the blouse. "it covers, uh, it's very modest, I mean."

Angie asked, "Did you want something?"

"Uh? Oh, yeah! I was hoping you'd blow-dry my hair again."

After Angie dried Joe's hair, he asked her to help him pick out clothes. She found that she didn't mind, not if Joe asked. She picked out a blue silk shirt and deep-blue jeans, and a gold chain necklace.

Joe dressed himself, and they went down for breakfast. Angie very delicately seated herself. Joe asked if Joe ever wore much jewelry. The chain was the first jewelry he'd worn since, uh, since he could remember. He didn't wear a watch or a wedding band. There was no mark or indentation where they would be.

Angie confirmed that Joe didn't often wear jewelry. The wedding band was out for image reasons. She explained that while their marriage wasn't denied to the public, it wasn't mentioned, either.

Joe was promoted as available, and, despite the facts, it was apparently accepted.

Joe put down his bacon. "How does that make you feel? Doesn't it make you feel, I dunno, excluded? Unwanted?"

Angie replied, "Image is very important in this industry. We all conform to the image. We have to look right in public. Bill wears hats all the time, you and Roger have long hair... Cassie is presented like she's a teenager to make Bill look hip, I guess. And Ed has— And Roger flaunts a different girl or two every night. It's all image."

Joe nodded. "What about Ed?"

"Never mind." Angie bit into her toast. She opened her organizer. "Today, you're recording the new vocal track for 'Shut Up and Suck' at 12:30. At 4:30, you're meeting with some promoters. At 9:00, there's a party at James and Sandra Flavell's house. Sandi's part owner of Theremin."

"Should I know anyone?"

Angie thought. "It's possible that you have met some of the promoters, but not enough that you would have to remember them. You have met Jim, but only professionally. You and Sandi have exchanged some letters, but you've never met in person. But she probably won't be there anyway. She earns the money, but Jim is the one who spends it like he's a big shot."

"Who else will be there?"

"The band will be, and Stu, and others."

"You?"

"No," Angie answered.

Joe frowned. "Well, can't you come to the recording session? Or is it that you don't want to?"

"I could come to the recording," she allowed.

"Why not the other things?"

"I'm not welcome," Angie said. "They're not for me." Angie hated that Joe had to circulate the way he did. She had come to accept it, though, or actually resigned herself to it and that there was nothing she could do about it. But she still hated it.

Joe examined a piece of bacon. "Well, what if you just came? You wouldn't get kicked out, would you?"

Angie thought being about dismissively ignored; the vaguely insulting treatment she had endured. "No. I don't want to go." And that was the truth. She'd had enough.

Joe looked away and said, "Okay." And then he added quietly, "But I wish you'd come."

Suddenly to Angie, he was exposed and vulnerable. He *did* want her to go with him, but he found it hard to ask. Instinctively, Angie wanted to obey, and she knew she would, but she held back long enough to ask gently, "Why?"

Joe maintained his gaze at nothing. Then the window closed, and he faced Angie. "I just think you would like it better than being here. You might like to get out and relax. Be social." He smiled almost convincingly.

In the limousine, Joe and Bill discussed the lyrics and the recording session. They didn't involve Angie, and that was okay, because she was thinking about Joe. The window had opened for such a brief moment, and Angie was wondering if what she thought she saw was real. She watched the way Joe and Bill interacted. After last night, Bill was much more relaxed with Joe, and Joe was more casual. But not less tactical. Joe was pulling information from Bill, encouraging Bill to teach him. Bill fell easily into this role.

The limousine arrived at the studio and cruised behind to its back door. They took the back elevator up to the 5th floor and met Patty in the studio control room. The room was similar to where the band had mixed the album. It was narrow and lined with stacks of electronic gear. Against one wall was the mixing board, and over that was a wide window to the studio. Beside the board and window, a sealed door (with a sign: "Authorized Access Only") connected the rooms. Patty explained that Sam was away for the morning, but could be called in an emergency. But, she assured them, it was simple track to record. She had already set up the board, and all that remained was the sound check. She looked at Joe expectantly. Joe stood looking back at her.

"Joe," Bill suggested, "why don't you go in the sound room and give Patty a sample of your singing?"

"Right, Bill, that's a great idea." Joe went to the door and tried unsuccessfully to push it open. Then he pulled it open and entered the studio. Bill sighed quietly and followed.

In the studio, a sturdy boom extended a big, bulbous microphone. A music stand, a chair and several bar stools were scattered nearby. Bill adjusted the boom so the mic was over Joe and pointed down. Joe raised the music stand and put the lyric sheets on it. Bill handed Joe the headphones, and he put them on.

An intercom clicked. "Okay, go ahead," Patty directed. The voice simultaneously spoke into the room and into Joe's 'phones.

Joe waited.

Click. "Joe?"

"Um, you're not— Can you play the music?"

Patty hesitated, then went to work on the board. Soon, the music, minus the vocal track, played over the headphones only. He reached and fingered the music sheets. He began softly, "You're sitting there so full..." It didn't match the music or anything, because he was singing in the complete wrong section of the song. His voice wavered.

Patty stared at Joe uncomprehendingly. Was this a joke? Bill was paralyzed, his worst fear realized. Joe stared at the lyrics, as he stumbled through another line, before he tapered to a whisper and then a stop. Then he took a breath as the song continued; Patty was too stunned to take any reasonable action.

Joe released his breath and said, "Okay." And he smiled a confident, tranquil smile.

In that instant, Bill's blood pressure dropped out of the red zone. He didn't know what was going to happen, but he knew it would work. Angie saw Joe smile from the other room. She wondered what she had just witnessed.

Strongly, Joe belted out, "I'm singin this song, don't know what I'm doin." It came from the diaphragm, placed correctly in the roof of the mouth. The words he sang and their rhythm didn't match anything in the music, but the volume was right. "But I'm here to fix this song that I did ruin," he continued, working down his accent. He shot a glance at Bill and winked.

Bill had to smile.

Joe sang out, "I'm singin this just for vol-*yoom*, so Patty can check it in the next room."

Patty jumped and started working the board. She hated setting the volume anyway. The objective was to set the highest gain without red-lining, but it was hard to estimate, because the needle was swinging all over the gauge. Patty tended to set the volume too low, and then the music sounded crummy after the volume compensation. She did her best, though, trying not to be distracted by Joe's silly lyrics. At the end of the room, the door opened. Patty assumed it was Sam, but discovered it wasn't when she heard someone say, "What the hell is he doing?"

Patty looked over and saw Michael Rost standing, feet apart, arms crossed. To the side and a half step behind was Stu. Stu turned to Patty. "You—" he began.

"Sound check," Patty snapped. She clicked the intercom and said, "That's enough, Joe. Thanks."

Joe looked over and waved. "Hey, Michael. Hey, Stu."

Michael didn't move. Stu shifted from one foot to the other.

Joe didn't wait for an answer before he said, "Patty, can you run through the song again as it was originally recorded? I want to refamiliarize myself with it." Then he added, "Don't listen to it, though, okay? I don't want you to be offended."

Patty shook her head and pushed the intercom. "Joe, I've heard it." She ran the tape.

The music played into the studio. Joe listened, nodding slightly to the beat. "You're not too bright, but it doesn't matter / You're into me so I'm in luck," the recorded Joe sang. Joe, in the studio, unsuccessfully hid his discomfiture. When the chorus passed, Joe told Patty to stop the tape and get ready to record.

Joe turned to Bill. "Go through it once for practice?"

Bill shrugged. "Why? Why not record the practice?"

"Yeah, I guess you're right. Okay, Patty, let's record this one."

Click. "Ready and set."

"Okay," Joe said.

Click. "Go?"

"Yes. Go."

The music played into the studio. Bill crossed his fingers. He hadn't counted on supervision from Michael and Stu. Joe could have been ignorant in front of Patty, and that would have been survivable, but Michael and Stu were the worst people to find out about Joe. The first word came in strong, and Bill hoped Joe would hit it. "Steaming mad, you rail at us as you wave your arms and clout," Joe sang. Bill blanched. Joe was singing the song about Michael! Was he crazy? Bill mentally braced himself as Joe sang the next lines. Inside the control room, Angie heard Michael begin to swear quietly.

The two-line chorus approached. Joe sang, "I think we could work together well, if you'd stop trying to give us hell."

Michael growled and burst into the studio just as the chorus ended. Patty, seeing the invasion, shut off the music. "You fucking moron!" Michael yelled. "What the fuck do you think you're doing here, idiot?" He barreled right at Joe. Joe didn't retreat an inch. Michael, expecting him to, collided with him, and this infuriated Michael even more. "Are these the goddamned lyrics you're singing? You know how much we have to pay for a minute of studio time, and you spend it fucking off?" Michael's face turned red, and a big vein pulsed beside his forehead. He ranted and shouted, his face an inch from Joe's. Stu hung back and tried to insert some explanation, but he couldn't get started.

Joe removed his headphones. "I can understand why you're angry, Michael, but these actually are not the lyrics we've written for the song."

Michael continued to assault Joe with insults and profanity and threats, blaming him for delays and cost overruns. Joe spoke in a normal tone, expressing understanding and a desire to continue recording with the correct lyrics. Michael didn't appear to hear a word, but he abruptly turned away. Stabbing a finger at Stu, he ordered him to watch Joe or he'd be in trouble, too. And then he stormed out.

Stu regarded Joe seriously and told him, "Joe, that was very foolish."

Joe leveled a stare at Stu. "Get out."

Stu held up his hands, deflecting Joe's ire. "Okay, Joe, I'm sorry I said that. Tempers are hot, Joe. Nerves are raw, I know. But I have to supervise the recording. Michael says."

"You work for *me*. And *I'm* telling you to get out."

Stu replied, "We all work for Michael. You have to realize—"

Joe took a step forward. "Listen," he began angrily.

Bill grabbed Joe's arm. "Don't, Joe," he urged. Joe twisted, but Bill got in front of him. "It's not worth it, Joe. Cool down."

"Get out of my way," Joe seethed.

Stu backed out the studio door. "Okay, Joe, I can see you're stressed, and I'm not helping any. We'll talk when tempers are a little cooler," he promised. Then he left.

Joe relaxed, and Bill let go. Joe smiled and said, "Thanks, Bill."

Bill smiled. "You were never mad at Stu, were you?"

"Not really. I just wanted him to leave." Joe chuckled.

Bill said, "You really are fucking crazy, Joe."

Joe grinned. "*Now* we're getting to know each other better." He took his position back at the mic and put on his headphones. "I'm sorry you ladies had to hear that bad language," he said. "Let's try it again, okay?"

Patty backed up the tape and reset it. Click. "Ready and set."

"Go."

Joe breathed in and nailed the starting note. He sang through the first verse.

Bill held up a hand. "Stop." The music stopped. "Don't forget to over-enunciate. And watch the accent."

Joe nodded. "Okay, right."

Click. "Set."

"Go."

The music played. Joe pounced on the starting note and sang through the first verse. He didn't acknowledge Bill as he sang; he focused on a point on the ceiling behind the mic. He kept his focus as the chorus approached. He sang through the chorus, but stumbled over the word 'unfurled'. The music stopped.

Click. "Do you want to start over at the chorus?"

"No, I wanna do the whole thing over," Joe answered. "I don't think I'm puttin enough feelin into it."

That surprised Bill, who thought Joe was expressing more feeling than usual.

"And there's somethin missin," Joe added. "The 'stand up and shout' line should have more force. Bill, when I get to that line, can you sing it, too?"

Bill opened his mouth to argue, but he found he didn't want to. He wanted to hear how it would sound. "Okay," he agreed. "Let me set up another mic." He efficiently set up another boom and connected a microphone.

While Bill was busy, Patty turned and said to Angie, "I think I'd rather hear the other version, the one about Michael."

Angie smiled and nodded.

Joe held up the plug to the window. Patty hit the intercom. "Plug it into Jack 5."

"Okay." Joe plugged it in.

Patty flipped a switch and pushed up a slide-bar. She commented, "He sure has changed, hasn't he?" Meanwhile, Bill adjusted the position of the mic so it was suspended similarly to Joe's. To Joe, he said, "You want me to come in low on 'stand up and' and then louder on 'shout'?"

"Yeah, that'd be good." Joe nodded to the control room. "Go."

Bill put on his headphones as the music started. Joe sang through the first verse, and Bill added his own voice on the stand-up-and-shout. Before, he had been listening to Joe sing without hearing the music, and he could pick out a myriad of flaws. But now, hearing it with the music, the subtleties were lost, and Joe sounded pretty good. Certainly light-years better than he had yesterday. Joe learned quickly.

Joe sang through the chorus and the second verse. He was working on the enunciation and the accent, but not perfecting either one. Still, it was a passable performance. The third verse came up, and Joe sang it with more intensity than before. When the last stand-up-and-shout was near, Joe locked eyes with Bill, and the two of them belted out the phrase.

A few second later, the music cut off. Click. "Okay, do you want to hear it back?"

"You bet," Joe stated.

Some time passed while Patty cued it up. Then the music played. Joe listened critically as the vocals played, but Bill couldn't determine what judgment he was forming. Joe had always done that. He would listen carefully, and then he would rule. When the song ended, Joe asked, "What do you think?"

Bill was caught by surprise. The way it usually went was someone asked Joe what *he* thought, and Joe would rendered judgment, and everyone would more or less agree. Not that Joe couldn't be swayed, but he was usually right. Or right enough. If you disagreed with Joe, you'd better be on solid ground. "What do I think?" Bill repeated. "It was okay, I guess," he hedged.

"A ringing endorsement," Joe commented. "What did you think, Patty?"

Click. "Don't get me involved in this."

Joe sighed. "C'mon, Patty, you've heard us so much, you're practically an authority on X Band. Plus, you'd be more objective than anyone."

No reply. Joe waited. Click. "Okay, I thought it could be better."

Bill realized that Joe was searching for an opinion that matched his before he leveraged it and got his way.

But Joe proved Bill wrong. "I think you're both right," Joe admitted. "I think it's okay, but it could be better. You know what it really needs? Even more oomph on the stand-up-and-shout. Angie, you wanna come in here?"

The request jolted Angie. She wanted to ask, "Me?" but they couldn't hear her. She went to the door and timidly opened it.

"Yeah, c'mon in," Joe urged, waving his hand, beckoning. Angie stepped into the studio.

Bill felt sympathy for Angie. He knew that she had terrible stage fright. "Here, we can share this mic," Bill said warmly.

Angie went to Bill's mic.

Joe said, "Okay, let's try this: Bill, you do it the way you did it before, and Angie, you just come in on 'shout'." He turned to the control room window. "Okay, Patty, let's do it again."

Click. "Go?"

"What is this, a special code word? Yeah, okay, ready? *Go-*pher!"

Pause. Click. "What?"

Joe smiled. "Sorry, Patty, I was just fooling. Ready? *Go*-mer Pyle!"

Patty didn't move. She wondered if Joe was taking his medications properly.

"You're good, Patty," Joe commended. "All right: Go."

Patty started the music. Bill could see Joe focusing his attention. He sang the first verse well. Not perfectly, but better than before. Bill sang his line, and Angie came in on her word. She was weak, but audible. Bill knew what effort it took her to make any sound at all.

Joe looked over and nodded encouragingly. "You gotta *shout*," he urged her.

Bill inwardly rolled his eyes. He expected the comment to cut the recording. The mic doesn't only record when you want it to. But Patty kept it running. Perhaps she thought she could excise it later.

Then the chorus came up. When Joe sang it, the timing was off, but he sang it with such feeling, the words affected Bill, even though he had written them. The verse came next, and Joe sang it with rising emotional power. Bill joined him to sing his line, and Angie shouted the last word. Joe smiled and gave them the thumbs-up.

They had to listen through the instrumental. Theoretically, Patty could have sped over it, but the interruption almost always messed people up. Joe returned his focus to a point behind the mic.

The music didn't especially build to the third verse, since it was written for a whole different set of lyrics. Joe adapted. His voice lowered, and he sounded of assurance. Then he quickly ramped up the energy for the final line. The energy infected Bill, and he charged in on his line, and Angie joined in when they all shouted, "Shout!" The music played a few seconds longer and shut off.

Joe clenched his fist and shook it. "Yes, that's it!" he exclaimed. "Ya got all that okay, Patty?"

Click. "Wait a second, and you can hear it for yourself."

Joe subsided. The music played back. It sounded good, Bill had to admit. The words didn't have the same inspiring effect on him that they had had when sung live, but they never did. Bill could still detect inflection flaws and breathing mistakes. The only serious mistake was Joe's off-mic comment to Angie. He wondered what Joe thought. As usual, Joe was unreadable as he listened to the music.

On the third verse, Sam came into the studio control room. He exchanged some words with Patty, gesturing to Angie in the studio.

The verse ended. Joe said, "Sam, you're like my old dentist! His assistant does all the work, and then he shows up at the last minute to just poke around. Are you getting paid for this?"

Sam and Patty said some things to each other, and then Sam leaned over and touched the microphone. Click. "Not much by your standards," he replied.

Joe chuckled. To Bill, he said, "I think that recording is about as good as it's gonna get. What do you think?"

"Whatever you say, Joe," Bill said, heading for the door.

Joe stopped him. "No, not 'whatever I say'. I asked you what you thought."

Normally, thought Bill, this would be Joe's way of picking a fight. But today it seemed like Joe really wanted to know. "Actually, I was thinking the same thing as you," Bill told him. "We may be able to do a little better, but it wouldn't be worth it. It's good the way it is. And by the way, I would leave in the part where you told Angie she had to shout. It fits."

Joe seemed pleased. "Really? Okay. Patty, can you leave that part in?"

Click. "Um, yeah."

"Well, I guess that's it," Joe announced. "Are we done? There's nothin else we need to do?" They crowded into the control room. Joe shook Sam's hand. "Good to see you again, Dr. Sam, even if it was for scant seconds. Patty did a good job in your place, though. Thanks, Patty."

Bill and Angie said their goodbyes to Sam and Patty, and the band left. Walking down the hallway, Bill asked Joe, "Is Angie going home after this? Are we taking her back?"

"No, she's coming with me to the other stuff," Joe replied.

Bill looked sidelong at Angie, who didn't respond.

"Bill, when you send the lyrics to Ken Welch, can you tell him to add Angie for back-up vocals credit?"

Bill looked at Angie and asked, "Do you want that?"

Angie had been terrified in the recording room, but she had done it anyway, and she had done a good job, too. Hadn't she really shouted her line? She was proud of that. And she wanted to be a part of Joe's product, the 'Xylene' album. Angie smiled slowly at both of them. "Yes. I'd like that a lot. Thank you."

They got in the back elevator. Joe thanked Bill sincerely for his help and coaching. Bill shrugged it off. "I'm just trying to keep us viable," he told Joe.

Joe asked, "Bill, do you know if Stu's office is around here? I oughta 'pologize to him."

They boarded the limo.

Bill answered, "It's on the way, actually. Do you want to call to see if he's in?"

"No, not if it's on the way. We'll just drop by."

"Sure, okay," Bill smiled. He picked up the phone, pushed a button and gave the driver some instructions. Bill put the phone down. "Are you going to apologize to Michael, too?"

"I would if I thought he would believe me," Joe stated. "But I think I would just make him angry. Is he angry all the time, or just at me?"

Bill thought. "He's not always mad, but he's always mad when he's with you."

"Hmmm. Wow," Joe said.

"Well, you have to understand what Michael's job is." Bill explained the demands on Michael and the pressures and pace of the music industry.

To Angie, Joe didn't seem very sympathetic.

The limo pulled to the side of the road. They were still on a busy thoroughfare, where street parking was not allowed. The limousine pulled halfway on the sidewalk and parked.

"I'll show you where it is," Bill offered. They climbed out. There were only a few pedestrians. Most turned and looked and walked on. Some looked longer than others. Bill and Joe crossed the sidewalk, opened an unmarked door and entered. They were faced with a bank of mail slots and a stairway up. At the second floor, there was a hall to more stairs and several doorways. Bill turned the knob on one of the doors. "Hello?" he called out.

They walked into a small waiting room with five steel folding chairs and a huge, stinking ashtray. As Bill headed for the reception window, Joe flared his nostrils and inhaled deeply.

"Hello?" a female voice called. The reception window opened to reveal a young, very attractive woman. She saw Bill and Joe, gasped and disappeared. "I gotta call you back, you won't believe who just came in." The office door flew open. "Bill Myers and Joe Ecks!"

she exclaimed, "I never thought I'd ever get to meet you! I'm Wendy, Mr. Cress's assistant. How are you?"

They exchanged pleasantries. Wendy had evidently never met them, or anyone else. Five seconds into the conversation, she admitted that she was new on the job. Mr. Cress wasn't in at the moment; hadn't been in all day. Bill started to wrap up the conversation, when Joe said, "Hey, you know, Stu has a contract he wants us to review, do you think he has it here?"

"Oh, I wouldn't know," Wendy said, "I don't think I'm supposed to look at the contracts. I'm really new here. It doesn't pay much, but I'm only doing it until I get some modelling assignments. Do you know anyone needing a model?"

"Now *that's* a business that would be hard to be in," Joe said with admiration. "You're really puttin yourself out there. Doesn't it get really personal if you get turned down?"

"It did when I was first getting started at home. I'm from Oklahoma City, and..." Wendy told Joe about her background and modelling career history. Joe nodded, encouraging her on.

Bill shifted from foot to foot. "Joe," he finally interrupted, "we don't have all day here."

Joe sighed. "You're right, Bill, we ought to go. It's really too bad we didn't get that contract." Joe turned.

"Well, hold on," Wendy said. "I might be able to find it. Just wait right here." She hurried into an adjacent room from which came the sound of file cabinet drawers opening and closing. "Here's one from January, is this it?"

Puzzled, Joe and Bill exchanged glances. Joe replied, "I don't think so. Is there one more recent?"

"Here it is," she announced. "May first!"

"Great!" Joe exclaimed. "Oh, can you get the existing contract, so I can compare them?"

"Um," Wendy said from the next room. Drawers closed and opened. "It should be here."

They waited. Bill checked his watch.

"Here it is, I found it."

"Fantastic!" Joe praised.

Wendy came to the door with three binders. Holding up the third binder, she asked, "Do you want to see your contract with Mr. Cress?"

Joe smiled. "Sure. Thank you very much, Wendy. It was great meetin you."

Bill shut the limo door, and it lumbered off the sidewalk back onto the street. Bill looked at Joe and saw he had the binders open, flipping through the contract pages. "That was what you had in mind all along, wasn't it?"

Joe looked up. "You give me too much credit. I was really looking for Stu. He had left us not too long ago, and I figured he'd be in his office."

"Right, and you would get him to give you the contract. Instead, you manipulated that girl into getting it."

"Wendy is her name," Joe said, "and she didn't do anything she didn't want to do."

Bill was silent.

"And Stu *did* say I could read the contract, didn't he? But wait, since this is a contract involving *us,* don't we have a right, a *legal* right, to read it over?"

Bill had to agree, but he felt uneasy, like he was getting involved in deceit without having done anything wrong.

Angie watched the exchange carefully. This was, she thought, Joe, New Joe, at his most calculating. It was impossible to know what he was doing or how far upstream he had been planning it. And yet, he was still new as Joe! She thought about what level of intelligence it would take to be planning so far ahead, and on so many levels. He had to learn about vocal recording techniques and at the same time, he had to get Stu to leave so he could come around and get the contracts. His intelligence was intimidating.

However, Angie saw no evidence that this New Joe was acting on malice. She didn't think he had even acted selfishly on anything. What *was* his objective? What was he ultimately after? Angie watched him flipping through the contract at about thirty seconds per page. And what was underneath? She thought.

The limousine thumped down the highway.

Bill also idly watched Joe thumb through the contract. He was relieved that Joe had finally gotten it, actually. Now Joe could read it over and approve its submission to Theremin. Or, he wouldn't read it, and Stu would submit it anyway. But, Bill observed, Joe was looking through it like a picture book. He certainly wasn't reading it very carefully. "You getting all that?" he asked Joe.

Joe owlishly looked up. "I understand it, but I don't know the relative values of the things contracted. For example, how much are non-North American residuals worth? Or merchandizing?" Joe smiled.

"I doubt if they will sell little Joe Ecks action figures, but, y'know, T-shirts might be big. Or ancillary related products. Has anyone done commercials? Or magazine ads?"

Bill looked blankly at Joe. He thought to himself, "Whoa." Out loud, he suggested, "You could probably get that from Stu. I'm sure he has an accurate accounting of your earnings."

"Maybe, but judging from his cooperation in getting me the contract, I'd rather not depend on him to provide me reliable figures. In a timely manner." Joe turned to Angie. "Don't we have an account-tant? Different income streams get taxed at different rates, so he must have a breakdown in earnings. I could back into the gross take."

Angie looked stricken. "Uh, I don't know. I'll ask him."

"No, I'd better talk to him myself. I gotta get my hands around what all the income sources are. I sure wish I had another band's contract as a benchmark. But I guess that's the game, isn't it?" Joe turned back to the contract, but then looked up again. "We have to keep these secure. I don't want to keep them on me, but I don't want to leave them here unguarded."

Angie spoke up. "I could take them back to the hotel," she offered.

Joe considered this soberly, then smiled. "That's a great idea," he commended. "Unless you have a better idea, Bill?"

Bill didn't want the contracts getting loose, because then he'd be implicated in their acquisition. He agreed with Joe.

"Okay," Joe said. "Angie, take 'em back to the hotel and put them in a safe place." Joe hesitated, eyeing Angie.

Angie swallowed. "Would you like me to return for the Flavell's party?"

Joe stared down between his knees. "I would like that, yes," he said.

"Okay," Angie replied.

Joe looked up smiling as the limo pulled up beside a large office building. "All right, I'll see you then."

Outside, the limo was swarmed with people. Bright lights held up on poles were ignited, turning the long-shadow evening into a shadowless noon. The people hovered around the limo. They cupped their hands on the windows to see inside. Bill appraised the crowd. "Something's wrong," he said. A few minutes passed slowly as the trio exchanged nervous glances. Then someone knocked on the door window with one knuckle and displayed a security badge.

"Let's go," Bill breathed as he opened the door into the masses. Immediately, the crowd volume rose. Joe followed close to Bill, and they struggled through the crowd, which did not yield. The security man was openly rude as he shoved people aside as Bill kept close behind. It was impossible to distinguish more than a few sequential words from anyone. Then Bill realized Joe was no longer behind him.

Joe was standing tall, a bunch of microphones in his face. "Is *that* what this is about?" he asked the angry woman in front of him. "Yeah, I'll answer that," he loudly stated. The mob quieted, poised to capture a sound bite. "First, though, I'm embarrassed that I did it to begin with, and I had no idea the lyrics would ever get circulated. No, it was me, my fault. I wrote 'em, and I sang 'em, and I had 'em sent to production. But I did it just to bug the producer; I really didn't want anyone else to hear them." The crowd had quieted to a low rumble. "Did you hear the lyrics?" he asked the angry woman. She shook her head. "Good," Joe said, "Don't listen to them. They're really degrading."

Bill watched Joe as he spoke. Joe locked eyes with individuals around him, speaking to them. Not like he was releasing a statement. In answer to another question, he said, "Well, you guys are the media, can ya tell everyone I'm sorry about my nasty lyrics? I did it, I shouldn't have done it, I'm sorry. Sometimes you do something you think is going to be funny, but later you look back and realize it was just really tasteless. The rest of the album is good, though, and your kids can listen to it." Joe heard a question and answered it. "No, it wasn't for publicity, but I guess if it was, it woulda worked." He smiled.

Joe saw Bill gesturing and said, "Okay, I gotta go now. Thank you for listening." He followed Bill and the guard into the building. People now moved out of their way. They got into an elevator held by another guard. The elevator rose to the 27th floor. Bill was impressed by how Joe had handled the media. Bill had believed it was futile to tell the press anything it didn't want to report, but Joe may have been successful at doing just that. The doors opened to a hall that led to an expansive room.

The promoter meeting was like a million others that Bill had lived through, but he saw it fresh through Joe's eyes. Why was that, he wondered. Joe didn't say anything or bring anything to Bill's attention that he wouldn't have noticed. Maybe it was a changed outlook. Instead of taking everything for granted, he noticed everything.

The observation room had mostly glass walls, and the panoramic view of the surrounding city was uncompromised except for that blocked by the neighboring 35-floor building. The serving staff, primarily young women, circulated with trays of drinks and hors devours. Knots of businessmen didn't quite fill the hall, so they clustered around the bar. Bill's eye found Ed right away, due to his towering height. He also spotted Michael and Stu.

Ed had immediately sensed when Joe appeared. It was as subtle as a change in air pressure; there was a shift in the focus of attention, an alteration in the tone of conversation. Joe immediately became the center of the room, and Ed was okay with that. Joe deserved it.

Instantly, Joe was surrounded. Bill figured, out of habit, that by default he had 'Joe duty'. But right away, Bill knew he didn't have to worry. Joe managed the conversations. Bill watched him work. If anything, he was more practiced than ever, as if he were sharpening his ability to schmooze. But he would never approximate Joe, because he had never seen Joe in a conversation. Old Joe didn't manage conversations, he ran them. There was a big difference, but what was it exactly?

Finally, as though no one wanted to be the one to do it, the subject of the lyrics was touched. Bill watched carefully as Joe explained his attempt to annoy Michael. Throughout the discussion, Joe apologized in four different ways. He was sincere and convincing. Someone asked about censorship. Joe replied that he didn't think it had gotten that far, thanks to Michael's thoroughness. Then the conversation lumbered on. Someone asked Bill a question and peeled him out of the conversation circle. He spent the next hour describing why he thought 'Xylene' was their best album yet, and he almost convinced himself.

Ed figured the way to handle these promoter meetings was to just drift. Everyone wanted something, and they would eventually get around to telling you what it was. Or not. In the end, they all had to go through Stu. Ed didn't envy Stu. Imagine having to deal with these guys, and guys like them, all day long!

As far as business receptions went, this one was better than most. The view was excellent, both outside and in. The hostesses or waitresses or whatever in their low-cut, second-skin tops caught his eye. There were two of them in particular, and they seemed to like that Ed was eyeing them.

Suddenly, Ed was disgusted. Women were attracted to his fame, not to him. It actually took a long time for a woman to see Ed as Ed and not as X Band's Drummer, and it took a long time for any woman to be herself around him. The process was long, and sometimes Ed doubted that he would ever find a good match, someone with whom he could hang out and be himself. Vicky was okay, but he could feel their connection unraveling. She was growing more distant, and Ed could sense it.

Maybe, Ed thought, he should admit that Vicky wasn't Miss Right and resume the search. He fantasized that he could corner one of the waitresses and ask her to the party that evening, and then they'd hang out till dawn or later. Then Ed was irritated with himself. What attracted him to the women, their bodies? Wasn't that as irrelevant as his fame? Didn't these women face the same difficulties as he in the search for a second half? It seemed so problematic. Did everyone eventually give up and then settle for whoever next fell in their path?

Throughout his musings, Ed would periodically return to the conversation to verify that it had stayed innocuously boring. Two guys were trading pompous observations about the private schools their kids attended. Then an official-looking guy approached Ed and told him he was wanted in the lounge. Ed shrugged and left the guys behind, who suddenly seemed to care that Ed had been in their conversation.

The guy led Ed to a door and ushered him through. Ed stepped into the room. Chairs were arranged in a deliberately random fashion. Joe sat in one, composed, but besieged. Stu sat in the chair that most faced Joe. Michael sat behind Stu, and two other men stood together in the periphery.

Stu stood, smiling widely. "Have a seat, Ed. We're glad you're here. Thank you for taking the time to sit with us."

Ed thought that what he was taking time out of was something else Stu wanted him to do. But Ed held back his reply. Something was not right. Ed wanted to say his spider sense was tingling, but he kept quiet. He lowered himself into a chair and sank down so deep it felt like his knees were higher than his shoulders. The room had a funny feel to it, funny and oddly familiar.

Early in his sophomore year, Ed was out late one night with Pat Murphy. Pat was a good guy, but he was always getting into trouble for doing stupid things. So if you were with Pat, it was a good bet you were going to do something stupid and get in trouble. This particular night, he and Pat found a shopping cart on William Street, and they took it over to Center Street, one of the main downtown streets in Wallingford. Center Street took a sharp plunge from William Street to the other of the main downtown streets, Colony Road. This night, no one was out, and it was so quiet, you could hear trucks on I-91. Pat and Ed let the shopping cart go at the top of the hill. Pat took off running, and Ed followed. He never knew if the shopping cart made it all the way down. (He doubted it.) The next day at school, he was summoned to the principal's office, where he was met by the principal, the assistant principal, and Pat. *This* is what it felt like right now. And what Stu said as an opening confirmed it.

Stu did not retake his seat in Joe's face. He paced and gestured with an affected air. "Ed, we all have one goal. Do you know what that is? To sell X Band records. There are a lot of separate people working together, there's Theremin Records, and Tour Excellence, and me and my company. There's the recording studio and the folks there, and the other musicians you've worked with and the leasing companies and financial backers and promoters, advertisers, and so many others, I couldn't even name them all without making a list. We all work together like a football team. You like football, don't you, Ed?" Stu didn't wait for Ed to respond, which was good for Stu, because Ed didn't care about football, and he was pretty sure Stu knew that. In fact, Ed didn't think Stu was much of a football fan, either. "In a football team, everyone has their positions, like their jobs. The center hikes the ball and blocks. The receivers catch the ball. Everyone does their jobs as well as they can, and they don't try to do each other's jobs. The center doesn't try to catch balls. If he did, then he wouldn't be blocking, and the play would be ruined. Do you see what I mean?"

Ed was bored and irked, but more nervous than anything else. What was Stu getting at? Ed pretended to be trying hard to understand. "Are you saying the Dolphins lost the Superbowl because the players were doing each other's jobs?"

Stu smiled and chuckled. "No, Ed, the football team is just an analogy. Bear with me here, and you'll see what I mean. See, the center blocks and protects the quarterback. That's his job. He has to trust that the quarterback will do *his* job and throw the ball, and the receiver will do *his* job and catch the ball. The center doesn't even have to make sure the others are doing their jobs; he just does his job the best he can, and he has to trust that the others are doing their jobs. We—" Stu gestured to everyone in the room and the universe

outside. "are like a football team. We do our jobs, and we trust the others to do their jobs. Michael isn't trying to book tours, and Sal isn't writing advertising copy, and I'm not playing the bass guitar. See? And if we all do our jobs right, we sell a lot of X Band records. How does that sound? Do you agree with me?"

"What if the center picks up a fumble and steps over the, uh, into the end zone? Shouldn't he do that if the opportunity is right in front of him?" Having fun with Stu wasn't even any fun at the moment, Ed discovered.

Stu smiled. "You're always thinking, Ed, that's what I like about you. Of course, something like that is very rare in football, so it's not even worth considering. What I'm saying is we should focus on doing our own jobs and to let the others do their jobs. Do you understand what I'm saying?"

"I understand," Ed allowed.

Stu smiled widely and put his hands together. "Fine! Then can you talk to Joe about this? He seems to think he's also an image consultant and press release agent." Stu gestured grandly to Joe, who only sat still.

Whenever Ed was asked to "talk to Joe", he had to make a quick decision, but this time, he couldn't, because he didn't really know what Stu was talking about. He said slowly, "I'm not sure I know what you're talking about."

Stu started to answer when Michael cut him off. "Joe is talking to the press and contradicting what we had planned to release. Now we've got to change our story or we look like fools. Make him stop it."

Ed didn't know what had been planned by whom. But the fact that he was being summoned to mediate indicated that Joe was being resistant. He had to get Joe out of the room, and he wasn't going to argue his way through these guys. Ed decided.

"Joe," Ed told Joe, "stop doing other people's jobs."

Joe thought on this. Finally, he answered, "Okay."

Ed pulled himself up out of the Venus fly-chair. Joe stood, too. Ed asked Stu, "Can we go now?"

Stu gestured to the door, and the two hurried out.

Before they re-engaged the promoters, Joe said to Ed, "Thanks. Thank you. I mean that."

Ed shrugged. "It's what I do. But, when you get a chance, will you let me know what's going on?"

Joe laughed. "Ed, if you need me to tell you what's going on, we got *big* problems!"

And then they were overrun with promotions people. Ed stayed with Joe, though they had been told to circulate. He wanted to be able to bail Joe out of sticky situations, but more than that, he wanted to stave off boredom. With Joe now, he could trade witticisms under the radar of the businessmen. It was more fun than fooling with Stu. Before he knew it, he and Joe and the band were being extracted from the party so they could make a timely appearance at the next party.

Ed had missed his chance to corner one of the waitresses. It didn't matter; he probably shouldn't be actively dating random women while living with someone else. He wondered where Vicky was tonight.

He learned that Joe had asked Angie to come to the party. Ed frowned; maybe he should have invited Vicky. He supposed that would have been good form, but he didn't think it would have made any practical difference, because he still wouldn't know where Vicky was.

The party was typical. It was in a huge house near the top of a huge hill overlooking a huge city. Ed wasn't sure which one. The surrounding property was extravagantly expansive by California standards. There was a unique, two-level pool with a waterfall between the levels that intrigued Ed. A local band was playing in a living room. Ed watched them for a while, particularly the drummer. It never hurt to see how others did things, and this drummer was pretty good, probably better than Ed himself, Ed estimated. That wasn't much of a stretch, though. Ed knew he wasn't very good, and he was very lucky to be tight with Joe, who had enough talent for everyone.

Ironically, the drummer, aware that he was being watched by Ed Brettington, forgot where he was in the song and messed up.

X Band attended the party as an attraction, but not as entertainment, because that would be expensive. They were for show, to give the party (and therefore host James Flavell) status. It wasn't enough to have just rich people at your party; you had to spice it with famous people also. Flavell circulated, constantly establishing himself as the host. He pulled Ed into a conversation with three others and introduced him, then buzzed away. Ed didn't have anything in common with the others, and he quickly excused himself and relocated to another room.

In it, Joe was holding court. There were four people listening attentively as Joe lectured on the barbarity of ancient Rome. Ed stood by and listened. He had read a book on Rome, and nothing Joe said disagreed with what he had read, but Joe seemed to have a more thorough understanding of the subject. Only instead of being arrogant, he was interesting, and he engaged the attentions of the others, and he involved them. Angie stood beside Joe, listening as closely as anyone.

Ed slipped over and beckoned her out of the pack. "Do you need saving?" he asked her.

She assured Ed that she was fine and went back to stand by her husband. She put an arm around his waist. Joe didn't appear to notice. Angie leaned in. Joe hesitantly put his own arm around Angie, draping it loosely around her waist.

Ed's defensive hackles rose, without reason. It was okay that Angie touched Joe, but Joe's touching Angie bugged him. It didn't seem right. But it was. Wasn't it?

Ed interrupted Joe. "Weren't they called Romans because they tended to wander around?"

"That's a popular misconception, Ed," Joe knowledgably acknowledged. "But the truth is they were called the Romans, because they were, in fact, from Rome."

"I think I see your logic," Ed nodded. "So did the Germans get their name because they're from Germ?"

"No. The Germans evolved from single-celled organisms," Joe informed Ed. "Along those lines, Bacteria is not the country of origin of the Bacterians."

"What?! Who else would live in Bacteria?!" Ed exclaimed. "Hey, wait! Are the Mormons really from Morm?"

"Well, *some* of them are," Joe admitted. "The rest claim to be, because they don't want anyone to know that they are from Jersey City." Joe looked up at Ed, and suddenly both of them burst into laughter. The others, who had been watching the conversation like it was a game of tennis frog, laughed uneasily.

Bill walked up. There was dancing downstairs, and he wanted to dance, but not with a woman who was not Cassie. He suggested that they find Roger and do the dance they did on the 'Let's Move' video. He told Joe he could sit this one out. Joe said, "Thanks, because this is something I would pay to see!" Joe held out his elbow for Angie, who took his arm and allowed him to find a way downstairs (though she knew a way already).

They easily found the dance floor. The light was muted, and the music undulated among the slow-dancing couples. Without pause, Angie took Joe's hand and fairly dragged him onto the floor. Joe put up little resistance, though he looked terrified. Angie pulled him toward the back of the floor and then encircled him with her arms. Joe reluctantly put his arms around Angie and danced like a tree. "Just move with me," Angie whispered. She swayed him back and forth, and slowly Joe responded, following, but lagging, her movements. Angie snuggled into his arms. She could feel his heartbeat and smell his perspiration. She could feel his warmth. She felt his damp back and his suppressed trembling. She immersed herself in Joe and in the music. Joe's arms held her with tentative tenderness. Angie would never before have imposed dancing on Joe, but here they were, together on the floor. Angie swelled with love for Joe.

The song drew to a close, and the DJ announced Ed, Roger and Bill, as the opening sequence for 'Let's Move' played. They took the floor and perfectly executed the dance, even modifying it on the fly to accommodate the extended dance version of the song. The song ended, and the trio yielded the floor to the other dancers.

The party continued. Bill accumulated a female admirer, who looked pretty good for 51. She followed Bill everywhere, and Bill had to admit she was good company, despite the fact that she was attractive, rich and drunk. Meanwhile, Ed managed to dodge en-twining encounters. He fell into a dour mood, mulling over his relationship with Vicky. Where was she tonight, for example? Every other young woman at the party became just another Vicky to him. What was the point?

Angie stayed with Joe every minute. She was taking their being in public as an opportunity to make physical contact with Joe. Usually at parties, Joe grew intense, but tonight he was so easy-going, it was actually relaxing to be with him.

The night evolved into early morning. Joe asked Angie if she were ready to leave, and she had the limo brought around. As they waited, Ed joined them. Bill had left already.

"With that woman?" Joe asked Ed.

Ed recoiled. "Are you kidding? Cassie would kill 'im!"

"Where's Roger?"

"I think he left early with someone."

The limo pulled up, and the trio got in.

Joe sagged into his seat. "That was a work-out," he sighed. "What about you, Ed, you holdin up?"

"I'm tired," he admitted, "but not as tired as I'm gonna be tomorrow. Uh, later today. I'm doing another demonstration at Giant Music, uh, today."

"Wasn't that yesterday? Didn't you do that already?"

Ed was surprised that Joe remembered his schedule. "Yes. They liked me so much, I get to come back." Ed shrugged and added, "It's okay, though; I never get a chance to practice." The limo joined the early rush-beater commuters on the highway. "What was that episode at the promoter meeting?"

"I dunno. Were you aware of a deal I made with the label?" Joe questioned.

"No, but I wouldn't necessarily. Michael wouldn't have been angry about it at the production meeting, though. If he knew about it, and you knew about it, why would he be yelling at you in the meeting?"

"Yeah, but they were being so obtuse, like there was something they didn't want to say, and they thought I knew what they were talking about. I didn't have a clue, so I just got stubborn and surly."

"Could you have a secret deal with Michael that no one knows about?" Ed offered.

Joe shrugged and looked to Angie.

"I wouldn't think so, the way you two always fight," she offered.

Joe said, "What if Stu was in on it, too? And they didn't want you guys to know? It had something to do with my talking to the press before coming in the promoter meeting. That's all I can figure. I doubt if it has to do with my Hot Rocks interview."

"Anyway," Ed said, "Bill told me you did a good job on the recording. You know what he said? He said he was surprised that you didn't once say, 'Is that what I really sound like?' Every person recording themselves for the first time says that."

"Actually, it's a weird thing, Ed. When I'm talking to you right now, to myself, I sound like I never have before. But when I heard myself recorded, or with the audio feedback, I sounded just like Joe Ecks. It's like I've never heard my voice from inside my own head."

"That is really weird," Ed agreed. The limo fell silent.

Joe nodded absently and gazed at the sunrise through the limo window. Ed looked at Joe, the new Joe. He seemed to have frozen. The light from the orange sun flashed on him without effect. Then Joe said, "I haven't turned back into Joe. It's been a week now."

Had it been a week? Geez, what a week, though; it started a hundred years ago, and yet it had flown by.

Still looking out the window, Joe added, "Yeah, it's been a week, and I'm still me."

Ed couldn't tell how that made Joe feel.

Chapter 13

Twinkle Twinkle

In the upstairs bedroom, Joe was practicing chord changes when Angie interrupted. In a hushed voice, she said, "It's Michael on the phone."

Joe picked up the extension and exclaimed, "Michael, good afternoon! How are you?"

"Joe, there's a problem," Michael announced. "We have to cut 'Sacramento' from the album. It's too close to a song Kubala put out last year called 'I Remember', and the legal team thinks it's actionable."

"Really? You mean for plagiarism?"

"You need to get me a replacement track by the end of Tuesday, otherwise it'll set back production by a month."

"Tuesday? You mean tomorrow? That's an aggressive schedule," Joe observed. He glanced at the clock, which read 4:05.

"If the album is out after the beginning of the tour," Michael continued, "sales for both will be severely compromised. Of course, this will influence the possibility of another contract. Since you've kept us from signing one already."

Joe rolled his eyes. "I understand. Do we have a studio?"

"The same one as before," Michael replied. "All you need is an engineer."

"Uh. Okay."

"Good luck," Michael sneered and hung up.

Angie asked, "What's going on?"

Joe reached for his shirt pocket that wasn't there. "A challenge," he told her. He explained the situation.

Angie fell into a chair. For a moment, she didn't speak. Then she said, "What are you going to do? What *can* you do?"

Joe's attention drifted away, as if he were watching a dust speck float through the air. Then he nodded and said to himself, "Okay." Returning his attention to Angie, he said, "Okay. I'm gettin the band together, and we'll produce a song in a day. It can be done, and we're gonna do it." Joe punched numbers on the phone. The force almost pushed it off the bedside table.

Angie opened her mouth. A day was an impossibility. The drum track alone for 'Calculator' took a week to record. It took six days to mix 'Mrs. Kisses'.

The phone was picked up. "Hello?" It was a woman.

"Oh. Is Ed there?"

"Sure, Joe." In the background: "Ed! It's Joe!"

A moment later, Ed was on the phone. "Yes?"

"Ed, it's Joe."

With mock suspicion, Ed said, "So it would appear. But why?"

Joe paused. "Ed, we're gonna have some fun."

"I'm up for fun," Ed said readily. "What do you have in mind? Does it involve nudity?"

Joe explained the challenge and concluded, "So we're gonna produce a song tomorrow. But I wanna go to the studio tonight and get everything set up."

"I gotta be at Morrow Motors tomorrow to sign autographs all day," Ed objected.

"You gotta postpone it," Joe urged. "This is critical. And call Roger, would ya? I'll call Bill. And Sam, I guess. We're gonna need an engineer. And I got a few cancellations to make of my own, I think." Joe looked at Angie, who nodded in confirmation.

Ed sighed. "Joe, you make my life interesting," he said morosely.

"Are you talkin about the Chinese curse, 'May you live in interesting times.'?"

"Uh huh."

"See you at the limo in half an hour."

Joe and Angie sat beside each other in the limo facing front. Angie watched Ed and his girlfriend Vicky approach the limo. Vicky had dark hair and big dark, excessively made-up eyes. She was Angie's height but with more curves, especially in the chest area. Angie, who had almost no curves, envied the women who did. Joe insisted that he was delighted with Angie's boyish figure, and she believed him, but she didn't think any woman would accept "boyish" as a positive description of her body.

Ed had had several steady girlfriends since high school, and Angie liked some more than others, but none ignited such a visceral distrust as Vicky. Vicky met Ed, and they became intimate almost immediately. She wedged herself deep in Ed's life, and she possessed him when necessary and ignored him when convenient. She was a partier. She flirted, she flaunted, and she thought a lot of herself.

The driver opened the door for Ed and Vicky, and they both got in. Even as Vicky climbed in the limo, she hung her over-stuffed bra inches from Joe's face, as if she didn't know exactly what she was doing. (Actually, she didn't, though, because only Angie saw that Joe politely averted his eyes downward.) Angie wondered if Ed were Vicky's only current boyfriend, but voicing her suspicions to Ed would just raise his defenses, not to mention his ire. So Angie could only watch as Vicky dismantled her brother.

Ed said, "I'm afraid I couldn't get Roger. He's not in his room. I left a message for him at the desk."

"Then this is it," Joe replied. He signaled to the chauffeur to drive.

Angie said, "Joe, this is Vicky." As she spoke, she put a possessive hand on Joe's arm and scooted closer to him.

Joe looked from Angie back to Vicky. "Uh. Vicky! Ed's girlfriend! Nice to meet you, finally." Joe held out his hand.

Vicky guardedly shook Joe's hand.

"It's nice to have finally met you after listenin to Ed talk about you all the time. He just can't say enough good things about you. He just goes on and on and on! Right, Ed?"

Ed wasn't sure he had *ever* mentioned Vicky to Joe since his transformation. "Yeah, Joe. But you know how sensitive I am about it. Sheesh."

"Oh, yeah, sorry."

The limo pulled out of the parking garage and onto the street.

Vicky looked at Ed. "He's not kidding, is he? About the amnesia?"

Angie hated Vicky. She had to have the attention of every male in sight.

Ed shook his head. "But we're not going public with it. It might just be temporary. The only people who know are the band members, you and Angie. I don't think Sam knows, but he knows something weird is going on."

The limo slid down the street.

"Do you think Michael is jerking us around?" Ed asked Joe.

"Well, he hates me, but why would he do *that*?" Joe asked. "He has a financial interest in our success. Hurting us hurts himself."

Vicky shrugged and suggested, "Maybe you do all this work, and then he keeps 'Sacramento' in the album. So he makes you do all the work for nothing. It shows he has the power and can make you dance." The others wordlessly agreed. Vicky snuggled up against Ed.

Joe was silent.

The limo turned onto the highway. Traffic was heavy.

Ed asked, "So what's the plan, Joe?"

Joe answered, "Plan A is to see if anyone has any nearly-finished song ideas we can polish and record. Like you. Got anything you been holdin back on?"

Ed smiled. "Me? No, I'm not the creative genius—" He shut up. He was going to say, "—that you are."

Joe frowned and brushed something off his thigh. "I disagree. 'Xylophone' was a hit. And 'Delta Kronecker'?" Joe smiled. "How many people have really understood the genius of that song?"

Ed frowned. "What do you mean?"

Joe quoted, "'When we agree, then we are one / But when we don't, then we are none'?"

Ed started to grin. "So?"

"The Kronecker delta math function? When x equals y, Kronecker delta equals 1? When x doesn't equal y, Kronecker delta equals 0? How many people get that?"

Angie and Vicky looked at Joe quizzically.

Ed grinned widely. "So far, only one that I know of. I never even told Bill. How did you make the connection?"

"'Delta Kronecker' seemed oddly specific. So I looked it up. I thought it might be a historical figure. And it is, sort of. Kronecker delta was named after Leopold Kronecker. The point is," Joe continued, "don't tell me you're not a creative genius. I know better." Joe settled back. "But, okay, maybe Bill or Roger has something."

Ed leaned back and tried to relax, though he sensed the tension. Perhaps Joe really understood the futility of what he was attempting. Ed suddenly wondered how Joe knew about the Kronecker delta math function now, when he didn't before his breakdown. Or maybe he did, and he never said anything. Frowning, Ed stared out the window at the usual landscape. Angie and Vicky tried hard to look at nothing. Eventually, the limo pulled into the studio parking lot.

Michael had said they were to use the same recording studio as before, which everyone but Joe knew was Studio 03B. They got a guard to unlock it. At 14' x 18', the studio was on the small side. Three of the walls had anechoic foam. The other wall was a big double-paned window to the engineer's booth. Unlike the studio in which they rerecorded the 'Shut Up and Suck' lyrics, there was no door between the studio and the booth. Both rooms opened to the hall; the studio door had an air-tight seal when closed. Communication was possible through an intercom.

So the foursome got busy schlepping instruments from the 4th floor to the 3rd. Early on, Joe asked, "Don't we have people that do this?" to which Ed responded sardonically, "*Real* bands do." Ed had long maintained that X Band was treated like a sub-star band, and he pointed out evidence that supported this assertion.

Most of the time was devoted to moving Ed's drums and their stands. At one point, Joe and Ed rode down the elevator together.

Joe declared, "Ed, you have a lot of drums!"

Ed looked at Joe. "This isn't the first time I wish I'd learned to play the harmonica."

Joe laughed.

Ed smiled. "Hey, I can use all my old jokes over again on you."

Joe shrugged. "Yeah, everything's new to me." He gestured to the bass drum Ed carried under one of his nine-foot long arms. The drum was black-and-grey flake, characteristic of the typical X Band colors. "I'll tell you what's cool, though: Gettin this close to X Band. Movin your equipment and hangin with you guys. Last week, I got vocal lessons from Bill Myers! How cool is *that*? Sometimes I'm just overwhelmed by how cool this really is."

The elevator door opened, and the two got off. Ed finally answered, "Yeah, I guess it *is* cool, when you think about it." And Ed continued to think about it.

Once several trips of drums and stands were in the studio, Joe suggested that Ed begin erecting the set.

"Do you need some help?" Joe asked.

"No," Ed answered. "I like to do it myself." He paused in reflection. "It connects me to my instrument. Sort of a Zen thing."

"I respect that," Joe told him and left for more equipment.

By 11:30, most of the equipment was in the studio. Ed had finished setting up his drums. Joe saw that, from the mixing room, Vicky was waving a phone at him. He sped out into the hall and back into the mixing room.

Handing Joe the receiver, Vicky said, "It's Sam."

"Dr. Sam! How are you?"

"Joe, I got your message. I thought it was a joke, but you're actually in the studio! Well, I'd like to help you out, but unfortunately I'm on another job now."

"You could call in sick," Joe offered.

"I can't do that. I'd get fired," Sam objected. "An engineer can't make talent wait. And that would be a whole day the studio isn't making money. I'd get fired twice. Sorry I can't help you."

"I'll pay you $2000," Joe pitched.

"Joe," Sam began.

"Okay, that's not worth getting fired for," Joe spoke exactly the point Sam was going to voice. "But this means a lot to the band. I mean a *lot*. How much do you make in a year? I'll pay you $100,000." Behind Joe, Angie gasped.

The phone was silent. Sam expected to get a nice bonus for sticking through Xylene, and if the album did well, he could command a quantum salary increase. But even if all went well, a salary of $100,000 was optimistic. In a low voice, Sam asked, "Are you serious? $100,000 for one day?"

"Sam, didja listen to my message? This one day could be the future of X Band. You bet I'm serious. But if I'm gonna pay you a year's salary, I want you workin for me for a year."

Sam hesitated. "How long do you have the studio?"

Joe glanced at his bare wrist and then at the clock. "Another 24 hours."

"Tell you what," Sam conceded. "I'll have Patty go over and set you up and record you if necessary. She should be able to do that. I'll go over when I'm done with my job. Should be no later than 5:00 or 6:00, but it could be as early as noon. Then I'll finish recording and mix. For this, all I ask is six grand, and out of that, I'll give Patty a nice bonus. No offense, but I don't want to work for you for a year. And, Joe, in 24 hours, I turn into a pumpkin. Deal?"

"Sam," Joe announced. "You're a good guy. When will Patty be over?"

"I'll call her and send her over now, if you think you'll be there."

Joe agreed. He posted Vicky in the lobby. Angie nodded off in the engineer's booth. Patty actually arrived at 1:50, still sleepy-eyed. She set to work running wires and referencing the board. It wasn't hard or complex work for a recording engineering intern who knew what she was doing. And thanks to Sam, she did. One thing Patty needed to know was if Joe planned to record "studio live". Then she had to explain that this meant to record all tracks simultaneously.

"Yeah, it would probably be more expedient to do it that way, don'tcha think?"

Patty stammered. "I-I don't know, Mr. Ecks. I don't know what you're going to do."

Joe laughed. "Neither do I! Do you, Ed?"

Ed looked up and smiled. "No, Joe. All you told me was that we were going to have some fun."

"That's right, I did. Are you having fun yet?"

Ed nodded. "Actually, I am." He was still pondering Joe's comment about how cool he thought this was.

Joe turned back to the intern. "Why do you need to know?"

Patty explained that the vocal and drum microphones would pick up each other in the small studio. Also, the amps wouldn't be necessary, since they could all listen to the outputs fed back from the board, but mixing is complicated by the cross-over. Ed watched as Joe listened carefully and asked several incisive questions. His questions showed he had a good understanding and was weighing the advantages and disadvantages. Then he ruled that they would record the instruments all at once and then add vocals afterwards.

Patty wondered why she had to explain all this to Joe, since he had now recorded three albums. Was he testing her? He didn't seem to be, and it puzzled her.

They set up mics and ran wires. One of the pre-amps they wired in proved to be dead, and they had to reroute eight channels, but first they had to spend almost an hour trying to figure out how to make it work. Later, a single channel stayed flat, until Joe saw a plug in the wrong jack.

Bill called in, and Joe apprised him of the situation and their status. Due to Joe's casual delivery, Bill thought he wasn't serious, but Joe convinced him that he and the situation were both serious.

Bill asked, "Is Stu there?"

"No," Joe answered, "I haven't seen any evidence of Mr. Stu Pidd, our esteemed agent. Hey isn't he *our* agent? Shouldn't he be protectin us from crap like this? Like runnin interference or something?! Where is 'e when the goin gets tough? What's he doin to earn his big, fat, bloated cut outa our earnings?"

Bill hesitated and promised to be in the studio in an hour.

Joe hung up and sagged. He suddenly looked overcome with weariness. He said, "I need more coffee."

Joe and Ed finished plugging in Bill's keyboards when he arrived at 6:30 and assessed the state of the studio. "Looks like you're ready for anything," he remarked. "What are we going to record?"

Joe smiled. "Well, I was hopin you would have something we could work out and record. Roger might have something, but I'd call that a long shot."

Bill looked at Joe and then at Ed, who shrugged.

"That's my Plan A," Joe said.

Bill hmphed. "There was one we worked on for 'Xenon', 'Bowling Angels', but you said it sucked, so we dropped it. I suppose we could try it out." He sounded doubtful. After Joe had critiqued his song, Bill had decided to save it for a solo album.

"Bill, I'm lookin at things with a whole new pair of eyes," Joe declared. "How does it go?"

Bill sat at his keyboard, set some switches and adjusted some knobs. Then his hands drifted across the keys, playing out a low rumble. He built on it and added some treble stabs like lightning. "Now the bass comes in throbbing on E flat, consonant with my foundation," Bill explained. Joe listened as Bill explained the piece in the same manner that he had described the songs on 'Xylene'. Ed vaguely remembered the song from before. Bill lost himself in the description. A few times, he would say something like, "Guitar sweeps through here," or "heavy guitar chord chops sustained," and Ed wondered how they would manage that. When Bill finished playing, Joe said he had a good idea of what the song would sound like. It could be done, and they could do it. But, Bill wondered, with the available time and resources?

"What didn't Joe like about it?" Joe asked. "Why would Joe say it sucked?"

Bill studied Joe and took a breath. "You said it wasn't right for X Band. You didn't like that the lyrics forced you to sing outside your normal range. And you said there wasn't time to fix it." Bill added,

"It's good for this particular crisis, because there's not much guitar."
Actually, Bill suspected that *that* was why Joe didn't like it.

"What do you think?"

Bill hedged, "Well, it's not the best song ever written, but I don't think it's the train wreck that you think it is. Or thought it was."

A wave of exhaustion swept through Joe. "Can you narrow that range a little? And be honest with me."

Bill straightened. "I think it's pretty good."

"Yeah, I do, too," Joe said. "Let's develop it."

Angie arrived with coffee and doughnuts.

Bill shrugged and turned to Ed. "Remember your part?" They walked through the interaction of drums and keyboard. They had the benefit of having worked on the song together already, so it came together relatively quickly.

Angie stood by with the last coffee mesmerized, as always, by this essential creative process. Bill and Ed were very different people with different skills, but they came together as they created music by collaboration. And their different skills fascinated Angie, surpassing her comprehension. Ed's sticks hit faster than she could follow, and each limb maintained different rhythms. Bill's hands worked the keys like they had their own brains, and while they were playing, Bill could be conversing with Ed. They ran through the song three times. Each time when they finished, they would both look at Joe.

"Sounds really good," Joe answered each time.

Bill struggled to recall and write down the lyrics. The simplest task seemed to take forever, like finding a piece of paper, and Joe was growing visibly anxious as the morning aged. Bill walked through the lyrics with Joe, drawing on his experience working with him on 'Stand Up and Shout'. Carefully, he suggested where to breathe and where to pay special attention to placing his voice. In two places, the vocals were just about a note beyond Joe's reach.

"Place your voice!" Bill snapped.

"Ah ayum!" Joe exclaimed.

"And don't sing with a southern accent," Bill admonished.

"Ah ain't!" Joe replied, then laughed when he heard himself. "Okay, I'll try."

They worked at it some more. Bill's frustration mounted. Finally, Ed stepped in and offered to work with Joe. Bill retreated to a corner of the studio. Ed was patient, but Joe was regressing.

Bill shook his head in exasperation. "Joe, what're you doing here?"

Joe looked at Bill with hurt and exhausted frustration. He collected himself and answered, "My best, Bill. I'm doing my best."

At 10:45, Roger glided in the studio. "You're here early," he greeted, and the others booed or moaned. Joe explained Plan A and their progress so far on it. Roger listened impassively. When Joe finished, Roger asked, "Are there any doughnuts left in that box?"

Joe pretended to gag. "Eat 'em all. I'm hungry, but I couldn't look at another doughnut." As Roger helped himself, Joe quietly asked, "Uh, Roger, can you play the guitar part for this song? Some of the parts Bill described sounded kind of hard, like beyond my abilities."

Roger looked up, piercing Joe with his light eyes. "No, Mike."

Joe pursed his lips. "We need this, Roger. It is not a good time to be dogmatic."

Roger was unmoving. "Why are you here?"

Joe looked at Roger abjectly. "I dunno, Roger. Tell me: Why am I here?"

"It's not for me to play guitar."

Joe looked away. "Roger, we have an objective that we *have* to meet. This is not an exercise or an option, this is the survival of the band, and we have to do this, now! Why would we not do anything we could do or use anything we could use to meet the goal?" Though frayed, Joe's zeal charged him.

Bill stepped forward, but Roger stopped him by producing a single capsule from his pocket. "If you take this, it will eliminate your fatigue, and that could be pivotal."

Joe stared at the pill, and then at Roger.

Roger said, "Why would you not take the pill? Why would you even hesitate?"

"You're right, Roger." Joe took the pill and swallowed it. "We should not put conditions on success. Maybe I'm not here for you to play guitar, but I'm not here for this band to fail, either. If this band goes down in flames, then I will want to know that I did my absolute fuckin best." Joe stopped and took a couple of breaths. "It would fuckin kill me if I let you guys down. Now let's get busy." Joe staggered and caught his balance.

Bill exchanged glances with Ed, and they shrugged. They agreed to record the keyboard, drums and bass first, then go back and add guitar and vocals. First, the three musicians ran through the song, then they cleared it with Patty that they needed a recording, but it was just a practice. They recorded. By this time, everyone was quite familiar with the song.

Joe sat in the booth with Patty and Angie and watched everything. He observed that professional recording took hours of painstaking preparation. He grew increasingly impatient with the methodical, plodding pace. But nobody else seemed frustrated at the pace. Nor did anyone seem aware that the hands on the clock were spinning around. Joe paced the booth, downing Diet Coke by the liter.

So finally Bill, Ed and Roger recorded their practice tracks.

"Okay, that was lousy," Bill groused when they were done. "But we can always do it over. Or not." He looked at Joe.

Joe sighed. "Let's listen to it," he said.

They replayed the track, confirming to Bill at least that the recording was substandard. Joe argued that it sounded good. Well, good enough. He admitted the possibility that he was compromising quality to keep to the schedule. Bill reluctantly conceded that they should move forward. He didn't like what was happening to his song, and he was feeling pushed into letting the song go bad.

Roger hefted Joe's guitar (the brown one), and Joe stood at the microphone. They ran through the song. Roger hit a couple of blips, and Joe started the second verse with the words of the first verse. But they got through.

Bill looked glum.

Before he could say anything, Joe announced, "You know, we should take a break. Let's go out and eat pizza." It was well after lunchtime.

Everyone in the room looked at Joe in disbelief. Ed said with amusement, "All of us? Like, go to a Pizza Hut?"

"Yeah, why not? We need some distance. We need a skull session," Joe declared. Then he explained, "A skull session is when the high school football team used to look at videos of their last game and go over what went wrong and why. It's like a strategic summit. An off-site, closed-door meeting."

"Do you know what would happen if we went to a Pizza Hut together?"

Joe rubbed his chin like he was pondering an immense philosophical conundrum. "Hoo! We'd get pizza?"

Ed explained, "We wouldn't get any pizza. Instead, we'd be constantly pestered by fans, if not overwhelmed." He turned to Roger. "Remember that time in the airport?"

Roger held out his arm. "See this scar?"

Bill barked, "Never mind!" Then he visibly controlled himself. He took a deep breath.

Roger asked, "Mike, what do you want to do?"

"I wanna look at our strategy. Maybe Plan A isn't the right thing for us. But I don't want us to realize that at 11:45 tonight. And I want everyone in on it, because nothin's gonna work if we're not all workin together. But my experience is that to change from tactical to strategic, you hafta remove yourself from the tactical. It's lunchtime anyway, so it seemed like a good idea. But I don't really care what the lunch is or where we eat it." Joe paused to get back on top of his weariness. "But I'm open for any ideas. Maybe we'll decide this is the way for us to go. Fine. It just looks like we're boggin down. Right? I mean, is everyone thinkin this is the best approach?"

The only movement among the others was a non-committal shrug from Ed.

Joe stared at them. "Then why are we goin through all this? Are you guys just amusin me until I give up or something?" Joe stared at them like he really wanted an answer.

Roger replied, "We have always followed you, because you have always been right."

Joe considered this, and then he inquired, "Have I?"

Roger acknowledged his error and answered carefully, "You have the same success rate as Joe."

Joe nodded slowly. "I take that as high praise. But now for the really hard part. We hafta decide what to put on our pizzas."

So they ordered pizzas. Until the pizzas arrived, the band searched for and found a room to meet and eat. It was the room in which their equipment had been stored. Already, Angie could sense the releasing tension of the band. Everyone was in the room: Angie, Patty, Vicky and the band. They sat on boxes, except for Bill and Angie. Angie stood just behind Joe's right shoulder.

"Okay," Joe said through a mouthful of pepperoni and bacon. "Let's talk about Plan A. The plan is to take a song from concept to completion. It's your song, Bill, how do you think it's goin so far?"

Bill sighed. "We can do it, I guess. It just won't come out the way I hear it. But it could do the job." Bill wanted to be cooperative. He wanted to be diplomatic and a team player. But he didn't think his song would come out good, and he wasn't very happy about that.

"You don't sound very happy about that, though," Joe observed.

"No," Bill agreed slowly. He decided to be forthright. "This song is close to me. I want to produce the song, but I want to do a good job on it. Not like this. Not just for something to fill space."

Roger abruptly asked, "Dude, what's Plan B?"

Everyone looked at Joe. He said, "Plan B is to take a song from the public domain and give it an X Band sound. One advantage to this is we don't have to worry about Michael pulling the song after the last minute for copyright problems. Another advantage is we can pick a song that I can actually play." Joe took some monster gulps from his 2-liter diet Coke.

Ed gaped at Joe. "You had a Plan B?"

Roger asked, "What song do you have in mind? The only complete song I've taught you is 'Twinkle Twinkle Little Star'."

Joe shrugged. "Okay, that's the song I had in mind."

Astounded, Ed exclaimed, "You want to put 'Twinkle Twinkle Little Star' on 'Xylene'?"

"Well, okay, it sounds stupid, but hear me out. For one thing, 'Xylene' has an edge to it, but I think it has too much edge, and this would balance it out. Plus, I can play it, and I already know the words. I can just play the melody, and you guys can be creative and improvise around it."

There was silence. Then Roger asked, "What's Plan C?"

"We jam," Joe answered, "actually *you* jam; I won't be able to contribute on that. So it might sound a little weird."

Bill narrowed his eyes. "Do you have a Plan D?"

Joe said, "Yeah, Plan D was for you to play some classical music on your piano. Maybe Mozart."

Ed blurted, "What?!" A pizza crust dropped out of his mouth and landed in his lap.

"Yeah," Bill said, thinking out loud. "Like Rick Wakeman playing Brahms' 4th symphony, 3rd movement on 'Fragile'. Okay, do you have a Plan E? How far into the alphabet do you go?"

Joe smiled. "No, D is as far as I got. But that doesn't mean those are our only options, just the ones that came to me. Of course, there's always Plan Z, which is to do nothing, but we're not gonna do that today."

Everyone chuckled. Even Patty seemed to loosen up. There was some idle talk about the pizza, and the quality of the pizza, and where one could find the best pizza. People had eaten heartily, but they were filling up. Joe had eaten a ton. When Bill commented on it, he answered that all-nighters had always burned a lot of calories.

Amused, Bill asked, "All-nighters?" To which Joe shrugged and said, "Well, that's what we called them." And Bill dropped it. He realized Joe was referring to his time at college, which he had never attended. It was impossible to talk to Joe when he got like that.

Joe had also drunk another whole jug of Coke. He had been looking alert after taking Roger's pill, which only Roger knew what it was. The Coke didn't seem to affect him beyond that. Nevertheless, he would struggle to find words in conversation, or simply lose his focus and drift. His accent seemed to thicken.

Ed finally asked Joe, "So what are we going to do?"

"Well, like I said before, I'd leave it up to the band. Personally, I think Bill's song has too much potential to use it as filler. On the other hand, what are we saving it for? If we don't succeed now, *today*, then there is no point in saving anything for later. Still, sometimes the success of a song lies in the details, and I'd hate for us to spend a lot of time to produce a song that just almost doesn't make it. But I don't wanna unilaterally ditch his song, apparently for the second time. Actually, I'd like to see how 'Twinkle Twinkle' sounds," Joe answered, and then he added, "but I could be swayed."

Bill said, "I like the words coming out of your mouth. I'm up for 'Twinkle Twinkle'. We can be as creative as we want, and it's fitting vengeance for Michael for putting us in this position. What about you guys?" he asked Ed and Roger.

They laughingly agreed, and the band went back to the studio. They decided to record the music first, and then the vocal track. This was in part because they didn't want Joe's mic picking up the drums and in part because Joe wasn't sure he could play and sing at the same time. Roger tuned Joe's guitar to exactitude.

Joe hefted the guitar and strapped it on. He stood facing the studio, conspicuously not looking at the guitar neck. Patty cued him, and he started. The guitar absorbed him, so focused was he in picking the correct notes. Even though he gazed over the others, he was blind. Joe had practiced the song endlessly, but his playing was so tentative, it didn't look like he could get through it five times without an error. Then Roger started with a countermelody. Bill punctuated it with chords. Looking in from the booth, Angie already felt attracted to the music. At the end of the first pass, Ed started up and added a beat. Into the second pass, Joe hadn't picked up the pace, but he was following Roger, so it was all right. He nodded his head to help reinforce the rhythm.

They entered the third pass. Ed turned up the pace a notch, and the song started rocking. The drumming grew a little more hard-hitting, and the keyboard more complex. Joe stood immobile, struggling to maintain concentration. The fourth pass, the others seemed to be competing for volume and complexity. As if they had been holding back, evaluating each other and now it was time to really dance. Joe played more by feel than from what he could hear through his headphones. Twice, he played wrong notes, but he got back on track without (literally) missing a beat.

The fifth pass, the energy slackened. Joe followed Ed's beat even as Ed faded away. Bill wound around and left, and Roger dropped off. Joe completed the song, and sight returned to his eyes.

Roger and Bill were doing high-fives. "We did it!" "That rocked!" they shouted. Angie and Vicky burst into the studio. Angie rushed over and gave Joe a big hug, then let go before Joe could react. Even Roger wore a trace of a smile. Then Joe saw Sam in the control room. "Hey, it's my dentist, comin in at the last minute! What did ya think, Dr. Sam?"

"I just heard the end of it. Let me play it back."

Sam rewound the tape and started it. He fed the sound back to the studio so the band could hear it, too. First, there was Joe's guitar. The amateurish picking was evident even to anyone's amateurish ear. Then the other instruments picked up and essentially drowned him out. As Sam listened, already he was adjusting the volumes, reining in Ed's drums and goosing bass. Sam's adjustments improved the song remarkably. When the song finished, Sam's whole face was a smile. He spoke over the intercom.

"Well, that's not bad for a rough draft."

The band cursed him roundly.

Sam answered, "I gotta make some adjustments, and then it's a do-over."

Joe said, "Uh, wait, I kinda liked the spontaneity of that first take."

Eyebrows went up all around.

"It's okay," Bill said, and he explained, "Now that we have a better idea of what each other is doing, we can do a much better job of working with each other. You'll see."

Joe nodded absently. He reached for his absent shirt pocket. He was very tired.

"Did you like the drums?" Ed asked.

"Uh, yeah," Joe said. "It meshed well with the, uh, pace of the song."

Ed looked like he was expecting more.

Joe added, "Well, not pace, because you really establish pace. It fit well with the, uh, tone? That's not the right word. Mood?"

Sam interrupted to announce he was ready for another take. The band settled into their positions. Joe started playing again. He messed up immediately. Do over. He started again. As before, the other instruments joined in, working with each other. Joe focused on playing each note. In the booth, Angie could tell that the band was more synchronized. More coordinated. Bill was right; the band did better the second time through. Especially in the way they exited the song, more uniform, with an equivalent style. Joe finished the last pass and looked up.

"Whaddaya think, Joe?" Ed asked. The others looked at him.

Joe looked back, gathering his thoughts. "Bill was right. The playin was much more, uh, orchestrated. Interactive. You guys play very well together."

The tension in the room seemed to relax in response to his pronouncement.

"Yeah," Bill said to Roger, "I liked the part where I did the A-G-C# chords, and you echoed."

Ed nodded and joined in the conversation, and the band compared opinions. Joe declined to offer any further opinion until he could hear the play-back.

Sam clicked the microphone. "Okay, that sounded okay from in here."

"Okay," Joe answered, "can you play it for us in here?"

Sam didn't answer. He just looked down, flipped two switches and turned a knob. The sound of Joe's guitar came through. As before, the playing seemed tentative, and the rhythm a little ragged. Then Roger came in, and the song jammed. In the control room, Vicky danced. The music wound down and stopped.

The others looked at Joe. "Okay, two things. Suggestions. I think five passes is cutting us short. I mean not giving us an opportunity to do our best. We oughta keep goin till we stop. Another thing is you guys oughta crank in the beginning, then pull back for the singin. Like one verse of singin. Then you guys jump back and continue the crankfest."

Bill thought to himself, "Here we go, as usual." As usual, Joe was turning something that could be simple into a major project. He couldn't just stop at one take, he had to tweak it and form it until it was excellent. And also, there was something else.

Ed said, "Joe, you're sounding like your old self. The way you correct yourself."

Joe looked from Ed to Bill. And he smiled. "That's good to know. Maybe it would help me imposter. I mean be an imposter. I mean, pose as Joe."

"Yeah, like that," Bill said flatly.

Joe laughed, "Yeah, but it's really irritatin. Even when I'm doin it, I'm irritatin mahself." Joe touched his eyebrow scar. "Okay, but what about the changes? Kin we do that? Kin we jus' give it a try an see how it sounds?"

Bill hesitated.

Ed said, "I wanna come in hammering after the interlude."

It was decided.

But Joe kept getting drawn off the beat, and they'd have to start over. Joe grew increasingly frustrated with himself. While playing, he didn't seem to lose himself in the music like he did before. He stood and declared, "God, I need a cigarette." Then he left the studio.

Bill looked at the others and asked, "A *tobacco* cigarette?"

Roger shrugged.

A few minutes later, Joe returned.

Bill asked, "Did you just smoke a cigarette?"

Joe answered, "No. I walked up and down the hallways. I needed a mental reset."

The reset was effective. He played the same tune over and over as the band jammed around him. Then they receded, and for a segment, there was only Ed thumping the bass drum that would keep Joe's singing on rhythm. Then Ed, as promised, hammered a drum repeatedly, and Bill and Roger joined him. The three of them worked the rhythm to its conclusion, and then they stopped.

Joe got into the next segment until, realizing he was on his own, he stopped. "That was great!" he exclaimed even before anyone could ask. "Let's record the vocals now. Then mix."

"Yeah, like that?" Bill asked, almost dumbfounded. He'd anticipated countless revisions.

Joe nodded. "Yeah, we gotta stay on schedule." Joe suddenly looked around at the others, like maybe he had put his stamp of approval on something that was obviously bad. "But what did you guys think? Do you think it's good enough?"

Bill answered, "Well, I guess so. I've just never seen you so decisive. Do you want to listen to it again?"

Joe agreed. "Dr. Sam" played it over for them, and everyone listened intently. Ed clearly liked it; Roger didn't seem to hate it. Bill was critical; he could find dozens of flaws, some that would take considerable effort to work out. Time that the afternoon stole away without remorse. In the booth, Angie thought the music echoed of their work on 'Xylophone', which didn't make sense, since now Shane was gone, and Joe was different. But it had that sense of spontaneity and fun.

When the song ended, they all looked at Joe. "I like it a lot," he declared. "I vote we move on."

"Like that?" Bill queried. "You like it just like that?"

Joe nodded. He replied, "Hey, the song is what it is. Could we polish it and make it better? Yeah, maybe. Or maybe we'd just make it more polished." Joe paused to recollect his thinning thoughts. "But it just wouldn't be... right. Y'know? If we made it a real production version, then it would just be another song, and not a very good one, since it's built around a fairly well-known melody. But if we leave it ragged, then it's a fun song."

"Yeah," Bill agreed reluctantly. He agreed with Joe, and that was still hard to accept.

Sam touched the intercom switch. "Okay, then, let's set up for vocals. And Joe, there's a phone call in here for you. It's Michael."

The room stiffened. Shouldering the weight of leadership, Joe left the room. When he entered the engineer's booth, Sam handed him the phone and left, as did Angie and Vicky.

"Good afternoon, Michael," Joe said with exaggerated politeness.

"What are you doing?" Michael demanded.

"We're recording the replacement for 'Sacramento'," Joe answered. He offered no further information.

"What are you recording?" Michael inquired like he really wanted to know.

"Uh, a remake," Joe answered.

"I'm glad you rethought your position, Joe. And how's the recording going?"

"Fine," Joe answered cautiously. He added, "Thanks for asking."

"Oh, so I'll have it by five o'clock?"

Joe flinched, and his eyes darted to the wall clock. 3:40. Joe reached for his shirt pocket. "Um," he said, gathering his thoughts. "We're on schedule to have it finished by midnight. You said we had all day today."

"Midnight?" Michael repeated with amusement. "No, I need it by the end of the business day. Business Day."

"Well then why not tomorrow morning? What's the difference between the end of the day today and the beginning of tomorrow?"

"I need to sign for it today and then give it to the courier."

"Well, can you stay late? Can you have the courier pick it up from us? Can you come here and sign for it before giving it to the courier here?"

"I'm afraid not."

"Michael, the band has been working on this all night; you can at least stay an hour or two late. Come on. Just a little more time, and you'll end up with a much better product."

"An hour or two or a day or a couple of weeks?" Michael retorted. "I don't have any faith in your promises, Joe. Five o'clock."

Joe said, "Okay, you'll have it by five o'clock."

"See you then." Michael hung up.

Joe cradled the receiver with exaggerated care. Then he noticed the illuminated intercom light. The others were in the studio, pretending to not be listening.

Joe left the booth and joined them.

"That was Michael," Joe said unnecessarily. "It's good that he called, actually. If he hadn't called, we woulda missed the deadline. Turns out, we need to have the song into him by five o'clock, not midnight." No one replied, or moved. "Sam, how long do you need to mix the song?"

Sam shook his head. "Joe, it depends on how good a job you want. We can record the vocal track and send it as is. But the more time we can squeeze, the better we can make it. You ought to know that."

"Besides," Ed added, "it'll take at least an hour to get from here to Theremin anyway. We'd have to leave now, and even then we might not make it. Especially with the rush hour traffic."

Joe stared at Ed.

"Hey, I'm just saying…"

Joe asked, "Does this building have a helipad? Or any buildings nearby? A helicopter could take it from here right to Van Nuys airport, which is practically right next door to Theremin."

Patty answered, "Sure it does, Joe. You flew in that way a couple of times." She had stopped wondering why Joe didn't know anything; she just accepted it.

"Yes," Joe agreed. "Patty, set that up, please."

"I can do that," Angie volunteered. "You need Patty to set up for vocals." Angie hurried out.

"Okay," Joe announced, "here's the new plan: We record the vocal track and send the tape on to Michael. Then we polish what we have until Sam's contract expires. Then we switch that tape with the one we sent to Michael. If it works, we buy ourselves seven more hours. If it doesn't work, we just have a crummy version of the song on our album, but the album meets the production schedule, and everyone's happy. Well, more or less. The thing is, how can we switch the tapes?"

"We ought to send him a blank tape," Sam said. "Or one that's broken or garbled. That way, it won't be used by accident."

"Yeah!" Joe agreed. "Good idea!"

Bill added, "Actually, then, we don't even have to switch tapes. Michael will probably listen to it when he gets it, and that's when he'll realize he needs another. That'll buy us a couple of hours, anyway."

"No, more than that," Sam said. "Because then he'll have to find someone, me, to have the replacement sent. And no one will find me until tomorrow morning."

Joe asked, "Does the studio here keep duplicates? Like back-ups?"

"Yeah," Sam confirmed with a grin. "And they're sometimes even filed where they're supposed to be."

Bill leaned forward. "I'm worried about the production deadline. We can't set back the album release."

"Good point," Joe commended.

Ed suggested, "Let's let the air out of Michael's tires. Or the tires of his car!"

Sam said, "I can call a guy at Paragon and buy us the extra time. Paragon Packaging is the company that actually makes the product. Well, for the west coast. For other regions, they lease the masters."

Joe said with a wry smile, "And you just happen to know a guy there who'll do us this favor?"

"Yeah," Sam explained. "Sometimes he has questions. We get routed to each other so many times now we just call each other up."

Joe smiled blankly back at Sam for a moment. "Okay, well, it sounds like we have a plan," he said. He outlined it again, checking for weaknesses. Then he looked around. "Why does it seem like none of you are as wiped out as me? Ed, you've been up as long as I have."

Ed said, "Uh, not exactly. I accidentally fell asleep while you were running wires."

Patty was ready to record the microphone. Joe adjusted it, commenting that he didn't need a music stand, because he knew the words by heart this time. He put on his headphones. The others left him alone in the studio with the abandoned equipment. From the booth, Angie informed him that the helicopter was on its way. Joe nodded and gave the thumbs-up as Sam started the music. Joe closed his eyes and regulated his breathing, which was his preparation for each of the takes. On the eleventh, Joe nailed it. Despite his exhaustion, his voice had a purity, a kind of weary innocence. Even Bill was satisfied. The team mobilized. Sam made a distorted copy, sealed it and turned it over to Vicky. Vicky was to take it personally to Michael from the airport and then return to the studio.

"Now I go to work," Sam declared. He looked around the room. "Who's staying?"

Bill said he'd stay. Ed wanted to put his drums away. Roger volunteered to stay and help Ed. Angie said she'd do what Joe did. Joe thought and concluded, "You don't need me here. I might as well go home and send the limo back for Ed."

Sam said, "I can't believe I'm saying this, but you could stay and help."

Bill added, "You've been with it this far, you might as well go the distance."

"Really?" Joe asked, surprised. "Uh, well, I'll stay until Ed's going back."

Everyone got busy. Bill and Joe and Sam went to work on the mixing. Patty put away the studio recording equipment. Ed and Roger put the drums in their cases and toted them back to the storage room upstairs. The pace was less hurried; the pressure was off. Progress was slow but steady. Patty finished the clean-up and helped Ed and Roger move the last of the instruments. Ed was exhausted, but happy. As Joe had promised, he'd had fun. And he was proud of the work he'd done. More than just *his* work, the work of the whole team.

In the storage room, Patty stopped Ed and asked him quietly, "What's up with Joe?"

Ed knew he was recognized as one of the top two authorities on Joe Ecks. He had to say something plausible. "Joe's been taking stock," Ed said. "He's been looking at his life and thinking about what's really important."

"Really?" Patty asked skeptically. "I thought he'd had a nervous breakdown. Is that what you mean?"

Ed laughed an easy laugh. A humble laugh. "That was the trigger. Do you remember today when Joe said he needed a mental reset? That's what he's done in his approach to his whole life."

The answer didn't completely satisfy Patty, but she figured that was all the information she was going to get. Of all the X Band entourage, she felt the closest to Ed, but she didn't think she could get him to tell her anything he didn't want to.

As the two left the storage room, Patty commented, "I like him a lot better this way."

Ed agreed.

They returned to the engineer's booth. The others were just ordering dinner. They played the mixed song for Ed, and he had to admit it sounded pretty good, despite the fact that the sound of his own drumming usually irritated him with its flawfulness. "Do we need to document the lyrics for Michael's guys?" he asked.

"What, for 'Twinkle Twinkle Little Star'?" Bill laughed.

"Yeah, so we could put the 'who' in writing," Ed explained to a room full of amused people. "You know? 'Twinkle twinkle little star, how I wonder *who* you are?' The second time he sings that line. Don't tell me you guys didn't notice that?"

Bill and Sam exchanged glances, then looked at Joe, who grinned mysteriously. "No, I didn't do it on purpose," he answered the expected question. "I hadn't even noticed that's what I said." To Ed, he said, "but I don't think we need to write down the lyrics for them. Let Michael's guys do some work. If he really needs them from us, then he can contact Mr. Pidd, and *he* can get them. Where the hell *is* he, anyway?" Joe sighed heavily. "Well, we got everyone here we needed, though, and we got the job done. Couldn't a done it without yer help, Dr. Sam. And Janet. Without you guys on the job, we would a been doomed."

"'Janet'?" Patty asked.

"Yeah, like the Evenings," Joe explained, and he sang, "Sam and Janet Evening!" to the tune of 'Some Enchanted Evening'.

People laughed. There was almost a giddiness in the relief after the recording pressure. The dinners came up, and everyone ate and told stories and laughed. They got back to work.

Vicky swept in, announcing a successful delivery to Michael at Theremin. He didn't bother listening to it, though. He simply asked Vicky if it was any good, to which she had replied it was okay. So he signed it off and gave it to the courier.

"He's going to be furious when he finds out what we did," Bill prognosticated.

Joe asked, "About switchin the versions?"

"No, you told him we were doing a remake. Well, you and Michael practically came to blows over it before. He wanted us to remake 'Fernando', and you refused. You said X Band doesn't do remakes," Bill explained, then added for Sam's and Patty's benefits, "Remember?"

Joe grinned devilishly. "So he probably thinks we remade 'Fernando'. He's gonna explode when he finds out what we actually remade." Joe laughed.

Vicky, Bill and Roger left for the hotel. The others went back to work. It was easy work, though. Eventually, Ed, Angie and Joe took the limo back to the hotel. Joe was dragging, and Ed was starting to feel sluggish. Angie was tired, but not as fatigued as the others. Like Ed, she'd also snatched some sleep. They were quiet in the limo.

Joe said, "So Ed. Didja have fun?"

Ed grinned a wide, tired grin. "Joe, I had more fun playing the drums today than I have had in a very long time. Thank you." He hesitated and asked quietly, "Joe, did you really say 'who' by accident? It fits just a little too well."

Joe answered sedately, "Honestly, Ed, I wish I *had* said it on purpose. It was just a lucky accident." Then Joe said, "I have a question for you: What do you really mean in the lyrics of 'Xylophone'? Is it a masturbation metaphor?"

Ed smiled. "No, it really is about doing anything you like for no other reason than just for your own fun. I guess that's what masturbation is, though, if you think about it. But I meant it more generally than that." Then Ed asked, "Why didn't you tell us you had a Plan B? Like an alternative to composing a whole new song?"

"I don't know," Joe answered slowly. "I guess I just assumed everyone knew there was a Plan B." He added dogmatically, "You *always* have to have a Plan B."

Ed asked, "Really? The big Plan A is for you to fake it as Joe Ecks until your Joe personality returns and saves the day. What's your Plan B for that?"

Joe gazed through sagging eyelids. "For that, there is no Plan B. Sometimes you have to make Plan A work."

Ed smiled. "You just contradicted yourself."

Joe was asleep.

Angie suspected that he did have a Plan B, and she wondered what it was.

Chapter 14

Vicky and the Press

By Friday, Angie and Joe were working out their morning routine. For Angie, the familiarity of routine meant she didn't have to think about everything she was going to do and how it might interfere with Joe and anything that he might want to do.

Angie still picked out Joe's clothes, but, to her surprise, she found that she didn't mind. She realized she liked picking out his clothes. After all, she had, in fact, bought most of his wardrobe, and she was going to add to it today. Joe seemed blind to the details of appearance, though he felt it important to have it mastered. And so, he appreciated what she did. At times, he would ask about her choices, but only in an effort to learn, never to be critical. So, without fear of having to get his wardrobe "right", Angie began to experiment in small ways. She could see his concept of "image" sharpening, albeit from that of a bowling ball to that of a nerf ball. And, Angie liked that the world saw Joe in the clothes that she bought and selected for him.

Angie also dried and styled his hair, unless she knew her work would simply be redone by professionals (as in the Fender photo shoot Tuesday). She liked the physical contact with Joe. She would stroke his hair or touch his head just to be in direct contact. At first, the touching made Joe uneasy, but he adapted and now he endured it as if it were a necessary part of drying his hair.

Wednesday, in an outburst of brazenness, Angie wore only her big fluffy bathrobe, and she left it barely tied. Mortified, Joe haltingly pointed it out, and Angie responded with a perfunctory effort to close the robe. Thereafter, Joe kept his eyes closed (except for frequent peeks) and sat rigidly. In fact, Angie noted with some satisfaction, every part of him was rigid. She liked the evidence that her appearance was provocative. Later, Angie felt a little shamed that she had teased Joe. But only a little shame, and even less remorse.

Over breakfast, she reviewed with Joe the day's agenda. "Roger's coming up for a lesson at 9:00. George Price is calling you at 1:30. The press conference is at 5:00, so you have to be in the limo at 3:00, latest. After that, there's the promotions mixer and after-dinner party."

As always, Joe listened thoughtfully. Angie was learning that Joe was always listening, even (or especially) when he didn't look like it. He would ask incisive questions. "What is your schedule today?"

Angie understood his underlying question of whether they would be together. "After lunch, I'll be out shopping. The press conference is only for Michael, Stu and the band members, but I'll join you after." Angie had hated band functions until recently. Now she used them as opportunities to drape herself all over Joe, and he had to pretend to be at ease with it. In private, he maintained a tangible personal shield, but not in public. She decided it was a concession he made for the sake of image. But the way he looked at her... How did he look at her? Not like how a dog looks at a big piece of fat. Not like how a shark looks at a fish. More like how a really hungry guy on a diet looks at a big, drippy cheeseburger.

Also this week, Joe had begun asking Angie questions about herself over breakfast. They were basic, harmless questions that one might ask a date. What's your favorite color? Do you have a favorite number? Favorite flowers, favorite animal, and so on. Thursday, he asked about where she had traveled, and was astounded by her range: All over North America, Europe, East Europe and Russia, Asia and Australia. He got her to talk about each place and listened raptly. Today, he asked about where she had lived and her earliest childhood. Angie felt uneasy talking just about herself. She feared she would bore Joe, but he wouldn't let her stop, and every time she asked, he assured her that he was very interested.

After breakfast, Joe practiced in the guitar room. He wore headphones now, but his playing was still audible downstairs. Wednesday, Roger had taught him 'Cincinnati Fan', and he had been practicing it doggedly. Even so, progress was glacial.

Roger arrived and joined Joe in the guitar room. During the lesson, the amps were on, and Angie could hear everything they played. Joe played through 'Cincinnati Fan', and Roger gave him some tips. They repeated some sections, and Angie couldn't always tell if they were doing anything different. During the lessons, Joe was intense; he never cracked wise, and he never strayed from the subject. Roger was infinitely patient. He was a guitar guru, and Joe his acolyte.

Angie sat in the den and answered fan mail. The fan mail was generally routed through Theremin to Stu. Usually, Stu had his secretary open and sort it. Much of the mail could be answered with one of several standard responses. However, Wendy had just left to pursue other career opportunities, and Stu hadn't replaced her yet. Until he did, all the mail came to Angie. Angie didn't have to answer the mail, but she felt strongly that it should be answered, and no one else would do it. Stu would have probably put the mail somewhere and then have it thrown away.

Angie took answering the mail seriously. First she sorted the mail by recipient. The amount of mail depended on whether the band was touring, recording, or promoting. Currently at a low level, Angie expected the volume to jump after 'Xylene' was released. Angie thought each letter should be answered with a reply that proved the letter had actually been read. Angie would write the response by hand and then type it, attach the appropriate glossy and mail it. It was an operation, but Angie didn't want it to become efficient. An impersonal response, she thought, could be worse than none.

The letters were from a wide spectrum of people wanting a vast variety of things. A lot of people posed suggestions. Some wrote for information, such as tour schedules, some wrote for advice, and some wrote just to express appreciation. Some wrote (often enclosing literature) to promote their own personal cause: Vegetarianism, creationism, alien abduction, socialism, animal rights, various conspiracies and so on.

The letters from admiring females bothered Angie more than they should have, she thought. Who were these women (or girls)? Did they know Joe was married? Did they think it didn't matter? How could they offer so much to someone they knew so little? Or was it just a pretense? What would happen if Joe showed up at someone's door-step and said, "I was so touched by your letter that I had to see you?" And what especially bugged Angie was that none of these girls had any idea what sacrifice was required to be Joe's chosen. What if they knew what Joe was like off the stage?

Angie looked at the boxes of letters and thought about Joe off the stage and sacrifice. She loved being Mrs. Joe Ecks, and she was aware that if Joe tired of her, she could easily be replaced.

Angie listened to Joe and Roger upstairs. She could hear their voices, but not what they were saying. Joe said something. Roger answered tersely and did something on his guitar. Joe followed with a clumsy imitation on his guitar. In the dining room, the hotel staff laid out a luncheon. When the hotel staff had left, Joe and Roger came downstairs.

"My brain is full, and my stomach is empty," Joe told Angie.

Roger joined them for lunch. Angie asked him how Joe was progressing. "Mike is an excellent student," Roger answered.

Joe smiled. "He means I compensate for my lack of talent with hard work," he explained. Roger bit into his sandwich, not disagree-ing. Joe added, "I may even be ready for the 'Cincinnati Fan' video shoot. What have you been doing?"

Angie explained about the fan mail. Joe asked a lot of ques-tions. Angie felt good when Joe showed interest in what she did. And Joe enthusiastically approved of her personal responses to the letters. Angie smiled proudly. Then he pondered their use as a marketing tool (How representative do you think they are?) and the benefit of Angie's personal answers (I wonder what impact that would have on brand loyalty?). Apologizing sheepishly, Joe returned to Earth, and said he was happy that fans who took the time to write were rewarded with thoughtful replies.

Roger left after lunch, and Angie got ready for her shopping trip. She didn't have to ask what Joe would do while she was away; she knew he would practice, unless he was going over the contracts with their accountant. She fussed with her appearance and gathered her things. Leaving was still awkward, but less so than it had been. Joe always saw her to the door, but he didn't kiss her goodbye or touch her. In fact, he expanded his personal space. And he watched her as the doors closed. Only when the car started its descent did he turn away.

Joe took the contracts up to the guitar room. He picked up his guitar and then noticed the phone. He stared at it and set down the guitar. He dialed a 617 area code number and listened tentatively. A recording informed him that the number had been disconnected. Joe slowly hung up. Then he dialed a 703 area code number. It rang seven times. A girl's voice asked, "Hello?" Joe replaced the receiver. His hand reached for his shirt pocket. Suddenly, Joe hurried downstairs until he got to the elevator, where he stopped short. "Damn," he muttered.

Just then, the elevator pinged, signaling an arrival. The doors opened, and Vicky strolled into the foyer. Her raven tresses bounced in coils about her shoulders and back, and her make-up accentuated her big, dark eyes and red lips. A thin white shirt with a deep V-neck conformed to her shapely torso. A red skirt went halfway to her knees, and even when her knees were together, its fabric stretched over her thighs. "Oh, hi, honey," she greeted, and she added coyly, "Were you waiting for me?"

Joe stepped back. "Uh, Vicky!"

She moved toward Joe, but he stepped back again, stumbling over the steps and crashing into the coat rack and umbrella stand and sprawling over them. Vicky altered course and headed for the kitchen. "Smooth move, Ace," she remarked.

Joe picked himself up and followed after her. He entered the kitchen to see Vicky tapping white powder from a vial onto the granite countertop. Her tight, white shirt wasn't tight any longer, because it was in a small pile on the floor. Vicky still wore her bra, a sheer white artifice that supported her without concealing anything. The bra could not, for example, be modeled by an actual woman in a TV commercial.

Astounded, Joe blurted, "What are you doing?!"

Vicky answered as if she didn't notice Joe's astonishment. "I thought we'd do some blow. And then *I'd* do some blow. You must be dying. Ange's been tight on you for about the last two weeks." Vicky smiled. "You're lucky I saw her leaving." She returned to arranging the powder in rows.

Joe swallowed, and he uttered, "Vicky, uh, we've been, uh, uh..."

Vicky laughed. "You really don't remember? I'm hurt, Joe." She shrugged. "Well, you'll know what to do."

"No, I don't think so," Joe said.

"No, you'll see once we get started. I just hope you haven't forgotten anything I've taught you."

In a stronger voice, Joe told her, "No. It's not gonna happen, Vicky. Not any more, if it ever did."

Vicky turned her attention to Joe. "Aw, honey," she pouted, slinking toward him.

Joe stepped back. "No, Vicky. No."

"You say 'No', but you really want me." Vicky didn't slow her advance.

Joe backed into the side of the kitchen doorway. "We can't. No, it can't happen. No, Vicky."

Vicky cocked her head and pouted, but she stopped her advance. "Joe, you're hurting my feelings. You don't want that, do you? Don't you like what you see?" She struck a practiced pose that accentuated her feminine attributes.

Joe swallowed and reached for his shirt pocket. "Swate Jasus! But no, I'm not gonna stray on Shelly. It's not gonna happen. I mean, Angie. I'm not gonna cheat on Angie. I'm sorry, uh, Vicky."

Vicky narrowed her eyes. "You're not seeing someone else, are you?"

For a second, Joe was more surprised than terrified. "Huh? No! As you say, how would I get a chance to, when Angie's been so close to me? But it doesn't matter, it's— Vicky, this isn't fair to anybody. Look at you: You've been the Other Woman. How is that fair to you? What do you get? This?"

Vicky smiled wickedly. "I get the part of you Ange can't get. I get the best part." When Joe didn't respond right away, Vicky frowned. "Omigod! You've been doing Angie! I don't believe it! You little shit!" Vicky sounded more irritated than betrayed.

"Uh, well, we sleep in the same bed. Sometimes," Joe pointed out. "It could happen."

"I thought," Vicky said testily, "that she didn't interest you anymore"

Joe blinked. "Uh."

"Yeah, never mind, Hot Shot," Vicky snapped, turning away. "So you don't need me anymore, huh? Is that it?"

"Truth is, Vicky, you deserve better than this. You shouldn't have to sneak around and grab whatever leftovers you can. You're better than this."

Vicky turned back.

Joe forged on. "Look at you. You're the sexiest, most desirable woman I have ever seen. And you really look good in, uh, practically nothing." Joe visibly reset his thoughts. "Everywhere you go, guys are staring at you. Swate Jasus, who wouldn't be beggin' to be your boyfriend? Guys would be on their knees if they thought they had a chance with you. And you're waitin' around for spare minutes with Joe? It's so wrong!" Joe argued the downside of being the mistress, much of it Vicky had already experienced.

She insisted, "But Joe, we *have* something. We click. I thought, maybe, it was possible that you were thinking we were a better match than you and Ange. That I wouldn't always be the other woman."

Joe considered this. "And then you an Joe'd get married? And everything would be okay from then on? Joe'd cheat on Angie with you, but he'd never cheat on you once you were married? But maybe Joe's been lying, dangling that carrot to keep you coming back. So you wouldn't feel so used. Apparently Joe's not completely trustworthy."

Vicky looked at Joe suspiciously. "Why are you doing this? What's in it for you? Maybe you don't remember what you've had, but you can see what you could have." Vicky arched her back and lifted the hem of her short skirt, the color of which her long nails matched. "Wanna see?"

Joe swallowed and ignored the invitation. "What's in it for me? I wanna be able to look Angie in the eye and know that she can trust me. I don't wanna hafta keep secrets from her."

Vicky smiled slyly. "It's a little late for that, isn't it?"

"Not for me," Joe stated. "I'm startin' over. Clean slate."

"You don't know what you're missing," Vicky spat, "and you don't even want to find out. Stupid. This is fucked up. And so are you." She turned and picked up her shirt. In a movement, she had it on, then carefully adjusted it to fit her curves. Ignoring Joe, she snorted up the powder on the counter. She dabbed the remainder with her finger and tucked it under her lip.

Joe stood by. "I'm sorry, Vicky," he told her.

Vicky snatched up her purse. "You don't even know how sorry you are," she said, pushing past him.

"Vicky," Joe said as she pushed the elevator button. "You were there for Joe, actually. He was in a bad state, and your comfort obviously meant a lot to him. You have a lot of spirit."

Vicky turned to Joe with a softening expression. "You're such a dork," she said and smiled sadly. She fished in her purse as the elevator doors opened.

Joe nodded. "Good luck, Vicky."

Vicky got on the elevator, and as the doors closed, she put a cigarette between her full lips.

The doors closed, and the elevator descended. Joe stood looking at the doors. "Damn!" he cried. "She had cigarettes!"

Joe was doggedly running fingering drills when George Price called at exactly 1:30, Pacific Daylight Time. He and Joe reviewed the historical earnings contribution of the different income streams. Price had itemized them, as the source determined the tax rate. Joe took a lot of notes in the contract's margins. Also, in the contract, Joe had written questions, which he posed to Price. At the first question, Price started to explain what Joe was really asking, but Joe interrupted and displayed a thorough knowledge of personal finance. Dismayed, Price simply answered the questions. Joe seemed to have learned a lot. As an aside, though, Joe asked about a line in the contract mentioning "production costs". "I don't see them itemized in the contract anywhere," Joe said. "Are production costs calculated from a standard formula?"

Price replied, "Not that I'm aware of. Shouldn't your agent know all about this?"

"I think my agent knows a lot more than he's telling me," Joe stated.

"I see."

Joe continued with his inquiries until he was done. Price answered him as best he could, and he wished he could have been more knowledgeable, because the questions were good ones. Finally, Joe's review of the contract was exhausted, as was Price. But before Joe could hang up, Price said, "There's one more thing: You never told me if you wanted to leave the Avon house in joint ownership."

Joe hesitated. "Joint ownership?"

Price explained, "Yes, when you had me put the other assets in your name only, you weren't sure about the house, and you said you would get back to me. That was, oh, two or three weeks ago. On the first, I believe." When Joe didn't reply, Price asked, "Joe, are you still there?"

"Yes," Joe answered quickly. "Yes. Okay. Leave it in joint ownership. Thank you for reminding me I'd left that open."

Price acknowledged, and asked if there would be anything else.

Joe hesitated. "Yeah, you know those assets you put in my name? I need you to put them in Angie's name only. And the house, too. Yeah. Can you do that tax-free?"

Price was confused. After Joe explained himself, Price was still confused, but he understood what Joe was asking him to do. And he was sure that *Joe* understood what Joe was asking him to do, even though, Price made clear, Joe would not be able to access the assets once they were in Angie's name only.

Finally, Joe hung up. And swore.

He sat for a long time staring at the same page of the contract. Then he practiced the guitar riffs for 'Cincinnati Fan'. The afternoon passed. Joe changed into his gray silk shirt, leaving the top three buttons unbuttoned (per Angie's instructions) and pin-striped suit. Joe had questioned the combination, but Angie had assured him he would drive the women insane. He hefted the contracts. He folded them in half, even standing on the folds to flatten them, but they were thick and sprang out. Frustrated, Joe tucked them in the back of his pants where they were hidden by his coat. Then he took the elevator down to the limousine.

The garage was packed with press and fans. The chauffeur had been by the door, and he immediately put himself between Joe and the fans. Then plowed through the people, and Joe stayed in his wake. Once Joe was in the limo, the crowd ignored the chauffeur, and he took his place at the elevator. Roger and Bill were already aboard. Roger wore a silk shirt that might as well have not had any buttons and a pair of tight pants. Bill wore a white dress shirt complete with bow tie, a top hat, and jeans. He interrupted himself to tell Joe good afternoon. Joe commented that the chauffeur did a good job as a bodyguard as well as a chauffeur.

"Yes," Bill answered, "these executive chauffeurs are well-compensated."

"Oh, so they already know they're gonna do more than just drive a long car?"

"Oh, yeah."

Joe frowned. "Is Ed late all the time? Like, is this common?"

Bill smiled. "Well, yes. But you're usually later than he is. We almost always wait for you. You don't like to wait for anyone."

Joe sighed. "That would be consistent."

"You know, since we have this time, I should tell you about press conferences," Bill suggested. "Our image to the press is critical to our success. This is all about the 'Xylene' release, so questions will be focused on that. Before each question, the person will state who they are and to whom the question is directed, but it will usually be you." Bill explained that, above all, the quality of the album is to be played up. "Don't say anything that could even indicate reluctance or regret or anything other than your belief that the album is X Band's crowning achievement. And everything is positive. You love X Band and Theremin and the studio people and Stu and everyone."

Joe grimaced. "Even Stu? Mr. Pidd?"

"Even Stu. He got us this job, after all. The press loves to exploit discord, and we need everyone to love us right now." Bill was interrupted by the limo door opening to admit Ed, who collapsed heavily in the available seat.

Joe remarked, "Ed, geez! Yer a wreck! The fans love you!"

Ed shook his head as the limo pulled slowly away. "Well, they do, of course, but not like Vicky. She was an animal! Wow!" Ed was visibly shaken.

The others smiled, but didn't ask for details. Nor did Ed offer any. Roger commented to Joe, "A gentleman doesn't discuss his romantic endeavors."

Ed replied, "That's probably true, Roger, but this is like pitching a perfect game in its amazingness. Or winning lotto or something. It was so incredible and so unexpected!"

Bill answered, "I was just telling Joe about how to answer questions at the press conference."

Ed was shocked. "Oh, right, and I'm sure Joe would rather hear you drone on and on than to hear about Vicky gone wild."

Irritated, Bill started to reply, but Joe said first, "Yes, Bill, tell me more about the press conference." Bill and Ed looked at Joe. "I want to know what I'm in for," he explained, smiling. "I've never done a press conference before."

Bewildered, Ed threw his hands in the air. "Great! I hope I never hit a hole-in-one! Who would I tell?"

Roger said, "Ed, you don't play golf."

"Yeah, exactly! See how amazing that would be? Swate Jasus!" Ed ranted. "No offense, Joe."

Joe shrugged. "I ain't Jasus."

In the following silence, Bill resumed his instruction on press conference behavior. The limo thumped along. Ed didn't participate in (i.e. interrupt) Bill's lecture, but he listened. Again, he found himself seeing the press conference through new eyes. Joe commented that the whole affair seemed like a lot of trouble for everyone when it was really just a sales tool, and Ed remembered thinking the same thing at his first press conference. After a while, he had simply stopped noticing the idiosyncrasies of this bizarre industry.

Joe asked, "What if there's a question requiring specific information that I don't know? Can I delegate it to one of you? Is that ever done?"

Bill thought. Protocol was loose on this, but if Joe thought he had to answer everything, then he would be under a lot of pressure, and it might revert him back to Old Joe. On the other hand, if performing in front of an audience didn't do it or getting shouted at by Michael or having to record a song in no time or singing a new vocal track or a magazine interview, he doubted a press conference would put him over the edge.

While Bill was thinking, Ed answered, "Go ahead and have someone else answer it. I know *I'd* like to say a few more words. Roger might be okay with the status quo, though."

Roger didn't argue.

Joe said, "I finished going over the contract, and there are a lot of things I need to clarify with Mr. Pidd. I'd like you guys to be there, too."

"I don't know if you'll be able to keep him still tonight, let alone get him out of the public," Bill said doubtfully.

Joe shrugged. "Yeah, I dunno. He seemed really eager to propose the contract to Theremin, but then he dragged his feet. Does he want to move on it or not? I have another question, too. What's this about shares? I think I know what it means, but what does it mean?"

Bill answered, "It's division of profits. If the band does something as a band, then each of us gets a share of the profits. Plus, Stu gets a share, because he's our agent, and you get an extra share, because you're you. For revenues related to a particular song, the song writer gets two extra shares, or if there are multiple writers, then the two shares are divided equally. So if X Band plays in a concert, that's a band thing. But revenues from the 'Cincinnati Fan' video, are divided like it's a song thing."

Roger added, "We vote the same way. Each of us gets one vote, and you get two, but Stu gets none."

Joe said, "So I always win. Unless all of you are against me? Yeah, it would take all three of you to overrule me. Do you think that's fair?"

Ed fielded this one. "No," he answered easily. "It's better than fair. You're the leader, and we follow you." Looking at Bill, Ed added,

"We all have the right to disagree, and heaven knows some of us exercise that right more than others, but when it comes down to it, we vote, and we live by the results. We move on. We stay a band."

Bill added, "Apparently the extra share started out as a tie-breaker. You had the tie-breaker vote. But it evolved into just another vote."

"Has Joe ever been overruled?"

Ed answered, "Once or twice. Well, once you wanted us to go on a long South American tour, but we outvoted you. Another time, you wanted to kick Shane out of the band, but we outvoted you."

"I thought Joe *did* kick him out of the band."

Ed emoted sheepishness. "Uh, well, we voted again later."

"So we can vote on the same thing more than once?"

Ed explained, "Yes, but the same person can't bring it to a vote. The second time, it was me who put it to a vote."

"I see." Joe leaned back, in thought.

The limousine thumped along with its cargo of rock musicians. Bill asked how the guitar lessons were going.

"Well, Roger says with practice, I'll reach Joe's skill level in 220 years," Joe answered.

Ed perked up. "You're doing better! Two days ago, he told me it would take 287 years."

Bill frowned. "Knock it off, Ed."

They discussed Joe's progress and Cassie's real estate discoveries, and a variety of other subjects. Before long, they were at the Hilton Hotel. The limo idled while a path was cleared and an aisle cordoned off between the limo and the side door. Joe was fascinated. "Look at how much trouble everyone is going to for us," he said, taking it in.

Bill explained, "It's typical of the entertainment industry. It's all about promotion."

Still looking out, Joe replied, "Yeah, but there are a lot of people involved in this, and we're the ones getting our pictures taken. I think we have the best jobs."

Bill found it hard to argue the point, so he kept quiet. When the preparations were complete, the band was ceremoniously paraded between banks of photographers to the building. Once inside, they all reflexively rubbed their eyes to banish the flash echoes in their retinas. Then they were led to a side-room for a light make-up and hair touch-up.

Stu breezed through, handing out encouraging banalities. He stopped by Bill. "Just an FYI, Bill, you may get some questions on 'Anesthesia', okay? Remember, there's no bad press. Joe, remember your PR training. Ed, try not to be disruptive. We'll get through this and look good on the other side." He hurried to the door.

"Stu, I gotta talk to you about the contract!" Joe shouted as he stood, startling his make-up girl.

"Yeah, Joe, we'll talk later," Stu called as he bustled through the door.

Joe sat back down disgruntled.

"Maybe he had to go to the bathroom real bad," Ed laughed.

Despite his frustration, Joe smiled. "Yeah, the one time I actually wanna see Mr. Pidd, and I can't nail 'im down."

Bill didn't try to explain Stu's behavior. He worried about what Stu had told him regarding 'Anesthesia'.

The band was touched up and ushered into a conference room large enough to house a convention. The band sat at a raised table and faced possibly two hundred press members. Joe was assigned the seat of honor, flanked by Michael and Stu. Though Joe was shown to his seat by an usher, the usher was cued by names taped to the side of the table.

As soon as the band entered the room, the room erupted in flash photography, which the band pretended to ignore. There was also applause and introductions announced through speakers, just to further confuse the senses. When Joe was shown his seat, though, he didn't sit. "I wanna sit with my band," he insisted.

"Don't cause a fuss," Stu admonished. "Sit down."

Joe stood firm. "I wanna sit with my band," he repeated. "We came together, and we're gonna sit together. We *are* together." Meanwhile the noise and flashes assaulted them.

Stu answered, "The seating is prearranged, see?" He gestured to the tape bearing the names of the seat assignee.

"I'm sittin' with my band," Joe replied, and he sat beside Bill (in the seat reserved for Stu).

Michael looked over from several seats away, his big bald head reddening.

Roger, from the opposite end of the seating, stood, glided through the confusion, and sat beside Joe.

Steamed, Stu sat in the seat vacated by Roger.

Michael clenched his jaw and stood to address the press. Bill handed Joe his microphone, a small omni-directional bud with a clip.

But first, Bill removed his own and said in a low voice, "Don't say *anything* that you don't want everyone in the room to hear." Joe nodded, and they put on their mics. The room rumbled to a relative quiet. Calmly and professionally, Michael opened with some introductory remarks, and then he talked a little about X Band and their first two albums. Bill was impressed with Michael's control and bearing. He had a public personality that quickly won respect. Then Michael talked about the release of the third album. When Michael announced the signing of the next three-record contract, Bill wasn't surprised. He had suspected an underlying reason for the press conference. He didn't know what else it could have been. Beside him, Joe didn't visibly react. Michael opened the floor to questions.

A middle-aged woman stood and introduced herself. "Bill Myers: How can you possibly justify preaching atheism to our children? Why do you think it's okay to use an entertainment medium for your own subversive religious agenda? How *dare* you say that God doesn't exist? Shame on you!" Several, and then many, others in the crowd loudly agreed, adding their own denunciations.

Bill stared back, stunned. Then he franticly dug around for the best (or any) response, resulting in a longer amount of time that Bill sat looking vacant. "Uh," Bill uttered, not really buying time. "I'm not really... I didn't intend to, uh..." He saw Joe looking back at him with a calculating expression.

Then Joe nodded imperceptibly and quietly muttered, "Okay." He turned to the indignant audience. "I'll field this one, Bill, if you don't mind," he said, cutting off something Stu was beginning to say. The loud voices in the audience abated. Joe's voice over the speakers was strong and confident. "First, I agree that it's a creepy song, and it gave me the willies when Bill first played it for me. But 'creepy' is really an under-exaggeration. The lyrics are literally diabolical. Diabolical as in Satan himself challenging Jesus Christ in the wilderness. Of course, Satan didn't sway Jesus' faith. He couldn't, after all. Jesus didn't have faith, because he had certainty, right? Doesn't faith pick up where certainty ends? Was *your* faith challenged by the lyrics to 'Anesthesia'?"

The room responded with silence.

Joe stood, leaned forward, and jutted his finger at the woman. "I'm askin' *you*. Was your faith challenged by the lyrics?"

"I don't have to answer your questions!" the woman declared.

"You came here to attack my friend with loaded questions presumin' yer own conclusions and condemnation, and you didn't expect to discuss it? Really?" Though Joe didn't raise his voice a decibel, his fury was clear. "Was your faith challenged by the lyrics?"

"No, it was not," the woman stated.

"Well, that's good, I think. Mine was, I admit. I pondered Bill's challenges for a long time before I came to answers that I could live with. Now my faith is as strong as ever, probably a lot stronger than it's ever been." Joe let this hang, then said, "Yeah, not really the point. I think what you're saying is you're upset with Bill for saying things that you see as blasphemous. Right? Yeah? Well, I can see why. See, the disconnect is you think Bill is attacking your faith, when really Bill is asking the questions whose answers support his own faith. They're not questions any more blasphemous than any Sunday school teacher might have to answer any given Sunday. In fact, if you want to answer those questions for Bill after the press conference, I bet he would really like to hear them. Can you meet with Bill later?"

The room was silent, except for the click of cameras. The woman asked scornfully, "Are you serious?"

"Aren't you?" Joe shot back. "Did you come here just to attack Bill or would you maybe like to do him some good? What would Jesus do?" Joe waited for the woman to answer, but she didn't. "Well, I hope for Bill's sake he sees you later. As creepy as it is," Joe continued, now addressing everyone, "I hope 'Anesthesia' does some good. If nothing else, it may get some people to think about their faith when they normally wouldn't. And that's a good thing." Joe leaned back. "Anyway, I'm sorry for takin' up so much time. The question was really for Bill about his song. If anybody has any other questions, go ahead."

When Joe bowed out, Bill thought the crowd might applaud. Maybe if someone had started, it would have caught on. The next questioner sullenly asked Bill about his religious background, which Bill could answer easily. Subsequent questions were easier. Once Bill was given questions that could be answered, he regained his composure and resumed his familiar teacher demeanor. He did reiterate the points that Joe had already made, and, since Joe had said them first, they sounded less like back-pedaling than they would have if Bill had lead with them.

Then the questioning shifted to Joe and followed more predictable patterns. Bill had a chance to breathe. His head had perspired excessively, and he really wanted to wipe it down, but he wasn't supposed to expose his bald head in public. Bill hated the restrictions imposed by having a public image, but then he thought about what Joe said in the limo: "We're the ones gettin our picture taken. I think we have the best jobs." Bill wasn't sure. He was the only one in the room who couldn't scratch his head.

He watched Joe convincingly field questions about an album he had never heard. Joe didn't have Michael's commanding presence, but he was skilled at public speaking. Also, Joe made it look like he'd been waiting for, and wanted to answer, each question. Just in the way he answered made the questioner feel good about the asking.

He told the story of the recording of 'Twinkle, Twinkle' that was factually accurate but seriously encroached on the fantastic. For example, "Mr. Rost wasn't sure we could produce a cut in time, but I told him I wanted to take that challenge if it would keep the album on schedule." Joe, Bill noticed, didn't take credit for anything, and one was left with the impression that the song was a massive collaborative effort, which it was.

Joe was asked about the new contract. "Theremin may be a little premature in the announcement," Joe offered. "There are still a few details to be worked out before it's a deal."

At which point, Michael stated that the contract conditions had been worked out with Stu, X Band's agent, and that Joe was unaware that the negotiations had concluded. Then Michael went on to speechify the future relationship between Theremin Records and X Band, and he effectively deflected Joe's reply by moving on to the next question.

The subject of the offensive lyrics in 'Shut Up and Suck' was raised, and Joe stayed with the story that he had told to the press before, about how he had intended it to be a private joke. He apologized again. Although the press responded to it, Bill didn't think you were supposed to apologize publicly, as if it admitted error or liability or something. He had heard from Ed about Stu's "working together as a team" lecture, and some possible implications concerned him. Joe concluded with an emphasis that X Band didn't intend to promote irresponsible sex or misogynist attitudes.

"What about you, Roger? Are you for or against irresponsible sex?"

"Wow," Roger said, thinking, and he admitted, "I'm against lying, I guess."

The crowd laughed.

"Do you have a steady girlfriend?"

"Every day."

More laughter.

The scheduled end of the press conference had passed long ago, but the conference rolled along. Officially, Michael would be the one to conclude it, but he didn't. The atmosphere had progressed from antagonistic through formal to casual. Roger got a few more questions. Michael discussed the schedule of video production and release. He only gave the barest of information on their content. Ed was asked if there were any hidden meaning in 'Xylene', the only song he had penned this album. Ed answered resolutely that there were no hidden meanings; the song was about xylene. He expounded, "Not many bands sing about hydrocarbons. I think that sets us apart."

Michael announced he would take one more question. Bill wondered if it would be a whammy.

"This is for Joe Ecks. Joe, what would you say sets X Band apart? How are you different?"

"Well, there's the hydrocarbon thing," he said, and the crowd laughed. "I would say it's our range. The intellectual dimension of our music. Well, most of it. Bill puts a lot of creativity into his lyrics, as does Ed. Bill's keys add a technical sound, and Ed's drumming style is decidedly nonstandard. I don't want to leave Roger out, though. He really is the stabilizing *bass* of our band."

Laughter rippled in the crowd. Bill found that he agreed completely. It did not escape his notice that, once again, Joe had side-stepped promoting himself. Michael made some concluding remarks, and, with a substantial applause, the band rose to leave. For the first time ever, Bill was relieved when a press conference ended. However, due to the contract announcement, he was sure there would be some fall-out with Joe. Although he seemed to take the news well, he still objected publicly to the signing of the contract.

As soon as Joe was through the doorway to the hall, he turned. "Where's Mr. Pidd?" he demanded. "Where's Stu?" An usher told him Stu had left the rostrum by the other door. Joe pushed his way back into the conference room. Bill followed in his wake. Joe threaded his way through the other door and down a hallway. He saw Stu and called out to him twice, but Stu obliviously got on a crowded elevator and escaped.

Bill caught up to Joe. Joe was fuming. Bill suggested, "Let's get some drinks."

Joe scowled. "I'm workin'. I'll drink later."

"Joe, you should be happy. We got the contract."

Joe turned on Bill. "Have you *read* the contract?" At Bill's hesitation, he demanded, "Then how do you know you should be happy about it? You don't. You just don't know. We've been railroaded."

Bill wisely kept quiet. They got on the elevator. It was fully loaded, but quiet; people wanted to listen in on the interesting conversation. Bill said quietly, "Thanks for answering that first question for me. I was really caught by surprise."

"It wouldn't have done the rest of us any good for you to look stupid."

Bill recognized the sentiment, and on the other side of it, it felt pretty ugly. He didn't think he had been that blunt with Joe after that first performance, but maybe he had. Maybe Joe thought so. Bill started to apologize when he noticed Joe smiling.

"Sorry, Bill," Joe said. "I didn't mean it that way. Although I believe the sentiment: We're a team, and what hurts one of us, hurts all of us. 'Never send to know for whom the bell tolls...'"

Bill was speechless. Not only had Joe recovered instantly from his anger, but he was correctly quoting classic literature! Still, Bill worried that Joe would make a scene over the contract. "Maybe you can talk to Stu about the contract after the festivities," he suggested.

Joe's face darkened. "No. Stu will leave early to avoid that. Stu's been bad, and he knows it. He won't talk to me unless he has to." Joe sighed. "So I have to make him have to."

The doors opened, and the crowded elevator emptied into a more crowded hallway. Joe and Bill were assaulted with flash photography. Joe waved and smiled and greeted as he was swept down the hallway to a larger room. Bill was separated from Joe, and he was detained by shaking hands and introductions. A man in a suit opined, "Well, they say there's no such thing as bad publicity, huh, Myers?" He had just been introduced, and already Bill had no idea who he was.

Another added, "Yeah, 'cept when everyone with a religion hates you."

"I didn't mean it that way," Bill explained.

"Oh, it doesn't matter what you said," the first man bellowed, "just what they thought you said."

Bill tried to defend his lyrics against ignorance, without success. Giving up, he turned to seek out Joe. He came upon Michael just behind Stu.

Stu asked, "You wanted to see me?"

Michael seized Stu's shoulder and growled, "That son of a bitch is going off about the contract again. Get him to shut up! Now!" Stu scanned the room for Joe. "That way!" Michael seethed, turning and pushing Stu in that direction. Stu spied Joe and threaded his way toward him.

Michael looked around and saw Bill. "Bill, get Joe to get with the program, will you?" Michael pointed to where Joe was holding court.

Bill replied, "I'll talk to him." He started moving through the crowd toward Joe. Then he encountered Angie. She looked good, as she always did for public appearances. She wore a dress snug enough to show off her lean figure, and her hair and make-up were perfect. She held a full glass of blush wine (probably because it matched her hair), and she listened patiently to a man explain something. She interrupted to snag Bill and ask him if he'd seen Joe. "Yes, he's this way about to have a very loud discussion with Stu."

Angie excused herself and departed with Bill. Progress was slow, due to the crowds and the number of times people tried to start a conversation with Bill. Bill and Angie caught up to Stu and Joe. They ducked into a service hallway and Stu led them into a laundry room that smelled sharply of bleach.

Before he even had the door fully closed, Stu was talking, "Joe, you remember not too long ago that we had that talk about teamwork, right? Now we're on the same team, right? You and Bill and the band and me and Michael and—"

Joe cut him off. "I don't feel like we're—"

"Hear me out, hear me out, hear me out," Stu repeated, holding up his hands.

Joe subsided, grumbling, "Well, get to the point. Please."

"Okay. You can't be making statements to the press that go against what other people are saying, people who are public relations professionals. It confuses the media, and you don't want to confuse the media. A confused media is not going to be helping us. There are people who have been trained to interact with the media to prevent confusion and help the media help us. People like Michael and me and others at Theremin and Tour Excellence and many others. All that time that you were learning the guitar, people like us were—"

"Why is Michael under the impression that we have a contract? Did they offer us one?"

Stu again held up his hands. "I'm getting to that, Joe, and then we'll get you out to the party so you can enjoy it." Stu took a breath and beamed. "Well, I have to admit, it's the culmination of a lot of hard work, and I'm proud to say that we have a second three-record contract with Theremin. And you and Bill and Ed and Roger have also worked very hard, and you should be proud of your contribution. It really was a little legal detail, and I don't normally bother you with the details of my job. I don't always have to trumpet my accomp—"

Joe was outraged. "Did you offer the contract to Michael after I told you I wanted to look it over first?" Stu started to answer, but Joe roared him down. "I thought I was clear on that! Was I not clear?"

Stu held up his hands. "I know you're surprised by this, Joe, but it really is a good surprise. You've been working for a second contract for a long time. And now, finally, you—"

"It's a *bad* surprise, Stu, a *very bad* surprise. How could you go against what I clearly stated I wanted?"

"You had told me you wanted to look at the contract for a day, and it's actually been several days since my girl gave you the contract. So that was done, and I moved forward. Michael is a tough negotiator, and we worked hard to—"

"But I haven't been able to talk to you since I got the contract," Joe objected. "No, correction, not since you *found out* I got the contract. What if I had a problem with something? Which I do, by the way, serious, deal-breaker problems. You have to invalidate the contract, now. That's the first thing." Stu had his hands out, deflecting Joe's words, clearly not listening. "All right, what?"

"Joe, I appreciate that you're taking such an interest in what I do, but I know the first time you read over a contract, the language can be confusing and frightening, but if you want me to explain the contract, we can get together sometime, maybe do it over lunch." Stu started to open the door.

Joe slammed it shut, the doorknob yanked out of Stu's grasp. "No. You're going to invalidate the contract, and then we're going to make some changes to it."

About four inches separated Joe's face from Stu's, and Stu backed away. "Joe, you don't want to do that. Now that it's been released that you've signed with Theremin, no one else will touch you. Severing the contract would just look bad. And then you have no contract, and Theremin is the only game in town. As you can imagine, that puts us in a poor negotiating position. But if you will tell me the major objections, I can work them out with Michael." For once, Stu stopped talking.

Joe stared at him.

Bill shifted, waiting.

Finally, Joe said, "Okay. There are three deal-breakers. Number one: Page 42, paragraph 3. I don't want to pay for production expenses. Especially undisclosed, unspecified expenses. Managing and recouping production expenses is Theremin's job. Number two: Page 24 and page 25. Transfer of rights. We are to retain the same rights that we did in the first contract. Number three: Page 61, paragraph 6 or 7. We are to retain the rights on the name of the band and on our own names and the names of our products. What's specified in the contract means Theremin will basically own us forever. I'm also not crazy about the 'product approval' clause on page 13 that allows Theremin to control whatever we do, but that was in the first contract, so I can't really claim that it's a deal-breaker."

Bill was simultaneously impressed by Joe's understanding and recall of the contract, and chilled by the ramifications of the clauses to which he had referred. He was sure Stu would correct Joe's interpretation of the clauses.

Stu looked at Joe in dismay.

Joe said, "Do you want me to write the deal-breakers down for you?"

Stu smiled, "The contract does *not* say that. Try reading it over again, and we can get together and discuss it."

Joe pulled the contract from where it had been tucked in the back of his pants. The contract was well-worn. Joe turned to page 42 and read paragraph 3. It did indeed say X Band was to pay production expenses.

"Let me see that," Stu said, reaching.

Joe pulled it back. "I would hope that you would be more familiar than I am with this contract, since you wrote it."

Stu frowned. "Well, Joe, these clauses are standard wording, and your interpretation is—"

"How can they be standard? They weren't in our first contract!" Joe exploded. "So far, we've had one contract, and none of these were in it. What are you calling standard?"

Stu stiffened. "I will take your concerns to Michael, and we will come to an acceptable resolution. Meanwhile, you can stop telling the press there's no contract. We don't want to confuse anybody any further. So you can relax and rest assured that everything will be smoothed over, and you can concentrate on what you do best." Stu was edging toward the door.

"You have three days to forestall Armageddon," Joe said. "Three days!" He allowed Stu to slither out. He turned to Bill and Angie and said, "I seem to keep losing my temper with Mr. Pidd. I'm sorry."

Bill smiled. "Yeah, you're usually the one defending him."

Joe considered this. "Well, that's too bad," he said. "Mr. Pidd seems to have gotten used to no one watching him."

Bill agreed and asked, "Shall we join the party?"

Joe nodded. "We shall." He held out his arm to Angie, which she dutifully took, and the trio re-engaged with the masses.

Chapter 15

Cincinnati Fan Video

The bedroom was dark, because outside, it was dark, still. The phone rang anyway. Angie slept on the far side of the super-king-sized bed, against Joe's back. The persistently ringing phone dragged her into consciousness. To reach the phone, Angie had to scooch across the bed in several scooches. She could have taken the bus, really. When she got to the phone, she fumbled the receiver behind the bedside table. Angie wasn't hung over. She never drank enough socially to be hung over. She was afraid that she would drink too much in public and end up on a tabloid cover. Then Joe would be embarrassed, or worse.

Joe sat up as she replaced the receiver. "Isn't it still yester-day?" he croaked. His long, black hair stuck out from his head. The imprint from a wrinkle in his pillow still creased his temple.

"No, Sweetie," Angie answered. "It's Saturday and time to wake up." Angie surprised herself by calling Joe 'Sweetie'. She hadn't ever called Joe any affectionate nicknames, but it wasn't because she had decided not to; they just never seemed to fit.

Joe looked up at Angie and smiled warmly. "Yeah," he said, still smiling, "it's another day."

Angie felt rumpled and unclean and a little embarrassed to be seen this way, though Joe had seen her every morning for years. She wanted to look good for him.

They worked around each other, preparing themselves for the day. Angie pulled Joe's hair back into a ponytail. They were due for a reception when they arrived in Cincinnati. If Angie styled Joe's hair now, it would look shabby later. Better to keep it casual. But she perfected her own appearance. Joe spied her at work and commented that every day she devoted a lot of time to her looks.

Angie shot him a glance in the mirror. "You don't think this beauty just comes naturally, do you?"

"Uh, yeah, I guess I did," Joe admitted. To Angie, he even looked disillusioned as he turned away.

They packed suitcases, anticipating a stay of several days. Angie found Joe packing soaps and shampoos. "I'm pretty sure they'll have those there," she pointed out. They left the suitcases in the foyer and headed down for the limousine. Joe wanted to know how the suitcases would get to Cincinnati, but Angie didn't know. Joe pondered this enigma as the elevator dropped to the garage. It was still dark as they got in the limo. There were no fans waiting for them. They were the first to arrive.

Angie slid in beside Joe. She was alert, but still sleepy. She felt like she could snuggle up against Joe and doze, but they were alone, and Joe radiated an aura of impenetrability. So they sat together, but apart, in awkward silence. Joe asked Angie what she liked better as pets, dogs or cats. Angie wanted to know why Joe was asking these questions. Was it to fill silence? Why would he want to know this trivia? She wanted to ask him; she knew he would answer, and the answer would be plausible. But would it be the truth?

She didn't have to reply, though, because Roger got in. Soon after, Bill got in and looked around. Roger was already asleep. Bill and Joe discussed Joe's readiness to play the song on camera. A long time later, Ed got in. The door closed behind him.

Bill asked, "Vicky's not coming?"

Ed shook his head. "No. She doesn't want to see Cincinnati."

The other three exchanged glances as the limo pulled away. Ed stared at the floor. No one spoke. They were all tired. The night had gone late, and the morning had come early. Today would be long, and they would be together for all of it.

Angie was troubled by Ed's despondency. She guessed that Vicky was the cause; that she had fought with Ed. Deep down, she hoped they would break up, but not if it made Ed this miserable. What she really hoped was that they would break up, and Ed would be happy about it. She hated that Ed was so in love with someone who was so bad for him.

Why did it seem so often that people did that? Why were people attracted to the very type of person that was wrong for them? And then they kept making the same mistake over and over? Angie remembered Lynn from high school. Lynn dated Daryl, who treated her like garbage, according to Lynn, who told Angie about it every day. And finally Lynn would break up with Daryl. But then the next day, or even the same day, they would be back together. It frustrated Angie beyond reason; once you decided to end a relationship, she contended, it was over and should stay over. Angie wondered what had become of Lynn and Daryl.

Bill was more puzzled over Ed's mood than he was worried. Bill was still glowing over the signed contract. Now they could move forward, and their future was all but secure. The worst thing that could happen was the band putting out a couple of dog albums, and Theremin losing interest. Even so, with a half-dozen albums cut, the band could tour forever, if you didn't mind venues like the Kansas State Fair. Bill shuddered and reminded himself that, okay, that was worst case. He was also happy that Cassie had found some property in Lakeland, Colorado that she had fallen in love with. To hear her gush about it made Bill's heart swell. He couldn't wait to see her again. Bill realized Ed was looking at him.

"Don't write any songs about Antarctica," Ed told him grumpily. "Or Hell. Cincinnati is bad enough."

"You don't like Cincinnati, Ed?" Joe inquired.

"Cincinnati's okay, I guess," he conceded. "But if you're going to write a song, why not write it about Hawaii or Fiji?"

Bill replied, against his better judgment. "Problem is, Cincinnati is the only place where you can find the Cincinnati Bengals."

Ed just scowled.

Joe commented, "There's a certain logic to that." Joe thought about it. "What if the Cincinnati Bengals were in Las Vegas? It wouldn't make any sense!"

Bill almost argued that if the Bengals were in Las Vegas, then they'd be the Las Vegas Bengals, but he restrained himself and sighed instead. Joe was getting as bad as Ed.

"'Sacramento' was a nice try, though, Bill," Joe commended.

The limo thumped along the highway.

"And there was 'Fort Wayne'," Joe added. "Bill wrote that one, too."

Bill didn't answer. Best not to encourage him.

Ed stretched his long legs across the car and leaned his head against the side. He wanted to sleep, but he knew he wouldn't. He watched Joe. Joe sat up, gazing out at nothing. He was motionless except for a slight twitching of his left fingers. Ed thought it odd. Then he recognized that Joe was pretending to hold down strings; he was practicing guitar. Since the 9th grade, Ed had been Joe's drummer. And throughout their careers until now, Joe had always been the major musical talent of whatever band surrounded him. It gave Ed security. Ed just had to be the drummer, and as long as he was with Joe, Joe's success would be his success. What would happen, though, if Joe crashed and burned? What would happen to Ed Brettington then? Would the band stay together? Ed thought Bill was considering a solo album; maybe he could play on that. And then tour.

There was the possibility that Joe's old personality would return and save the day. How would Joe see all the changes? Would he be able to perform with little or no preparation? Yeah, Ed decided, he would take everything in stride, and the rest of them would have to run to keep up.

The limo passed the airport exit, then got off at the next exit. After a few turns, it cruised behind some hangars and then pulled up to a small jet. Roger opened his eyes.

"Wow," Joe uttered, "we get our own plane. I was worried that we were gonna miss our flight."

Bill smiled. He had forgotten about the luxury it was to fly on a private jet. The band climbed aboard. Besides the flight crew, there was room for six.

Joe stroked the leather seats. "This is nice," he gushed. To Ed, he asked, "Do real bands get flown around in jets like these?"

Ed, folding himself into a seat, answered, "Real bands get much bigger jets and attractive stewardesses."

Disappointed, Joe asked Bill if that were true.

Bill was strapping himself into his seat. At Joe's query, he shrugged. "How would I know?"

"*I* don't know!" Joe exclaimed. "How would *Ed* know?" He turned to Ed: "How do you know about real bands, Ed?"

"Hey, I know things," Ed informed Joe.

Joe accepted this. Later, the jet took off and headed "back East". The direct flight was less than eight hours (7 hours, 51 minutes). Due to their eastward trajectory, the band saw the sun cross the sky at a faster-than-usual pace. Everyone slept at least some. Bill dozed erratically, but Roger was unconscious for the duration. When Ed wasn't sleeping, he was reading a thick book on the life of Robert Bruce. Over the roaring engines, Bill lectured to Joe the detailed procedure of filming a rock video. At last, the jet began descent toward Cincinnati National Airport, and something about the descent roused everyone, even Roger.

The jet landed and taxied to a position about a hundred yards (brightly lit by temporary floodlights) from the terminal. The copilot opened the door, and as soon as it was open, a youngish man appeared in it. "X-Band!" he exclaimed, "Welcome to Cincinnati!"

The man led them across the expanse of tarmac, an excellent photo opportunity for the press corps in the terminal. The band obligingly smiled and waved. Several ground crew came forward (apparently against orders) and shook hands. Joe told each of them they did a good job. Or he would comment on how nice it was to be in Cincinnati or how nice the airport looked. He wouldn't see the inside of the terminal, though, because the band was guided into a limousine in front of it.

"This guy got a really good space," Joe observed, getting in.

Their host got into the limo with them. He introduced himself as Tim Gelan, the deputy mayor of Cincinnati. His voice had more than a hint of the local accent: 'Deputy mayor', for example, became 'deppity mare'. He told the band how pleased he and the mayor and all the other citizens of the city were that they were honored by the song and video.

Bill was flattered, but Ed sneered, "Have you *heard* the song? It's about your loser football team."

Bill jumped in. "It's really about the bravery and character of the underdogs that meet their opposition with courage."

"There's nothing insulting in the song, is there?" the deputy mayor asked with concern.

Bill assured him there was not.

"I'd forgotten that the album won't be released for another, what, month and a half?" Joe mentioned.

Night had fallen. Dinner was late. The band was taken to a reception in the upper floors of the Cincinnati football stadium. Walking along the wide corridor, Deputy Mayor Tim Gelan pointed. "These doors lead to the premium skyboxes." Angie noted that the doors were far apart; the skyboxes must be big.

This reception was like others Joe had attended, and Angie could tell he was adapting. No longer was he agog at the expensive trappings or the exclusive guest list. The reception differed in that it had a particular focus: The 'Cincinnati Fan' video filming. And, holding court, was Director Bruce O'Reilly.

As director of the shoot, O'Reilly was the highest authority. Everyone, including X-Band, answered to him. It was his vision that the shoot was intended to articulate. O'Reilly had an "inner circle", and anyone making contact with his inner circle felt the privilege and power. Angie hadn't met O'Reilly, but she could tell who he was from the attitude and positioning of the others.

The social pull to connect O'Reilly and Joe was intangible and irresistible. On location, O'Reilly was a judge in his court, or a captain on his ship: The Highest Authority. At least on paper. But when O'Reilly connected with Joe, he had to acknowledge that, without Joe's cooperation, there would be very little to film. Plus, there was the fact that Joe was essentially the customer. Joe could get O'Reilly fired, but O'Reilly couldn't get Joe fired.

Angie saw that O'Reilly was a large guy, and his personality was larger. He held an oversized highball glass in his meaty hand, and even in semi-formal attire, he looked casually dressed. He and Joe greeted each other. Joe asked about the filming preparations, and O'Reilly answered in confident generalities: It was a welcome change of pace to get out of the office for a while; set-up had begun, but O'Reilly had to check on the progress before the night was over.

O'Reilly added he had had a team sorting through archival footage for appropriate visual spots. "It's coming out a lot better than I'd expected," he admitted. "I think you'll be pleased with the results. I can't wait to align it with the music."

Joe offered, "It's almost like you could do the video with just the football scenes."

Angie almost laughed. She recognized it as an opening move to escape the filming.

O'Reilly smiled widely. "Yeah, don't think I didn't think about it. Production is expensive, and you guys don't come cheap!"

"Okay, now that you have us, what are you going to do with us?"

O'Reilly shrugged. "The idea is that you're playing at halftime, so we're setting up a stage in midfield, and we'll film you playing on it. Then we'll shoot you coming out of the tunnel or in the press box. We're getting a bunch of extras, so we can make it look like you're coming to a game and sitting in the stadium. We can splice in pans of the stadium when it's full."

Joe shook his head and said with admiration, "You have such a cool job. You can put together all this stuff from different sources and in the end it's a beautiful orchestration. Man, that would be so cool to do."

For a moment, O'Reilly was at a loss. "Well, yeah, thanks, Joe, I like my job a lot. But you know, I'm just putting images to your music. You start with nothing and get music. You have fewer restrictions on your creativity."

Joe was about to argue when he was interrupted and pulled away. He (and Angie) was formally introduced to three team members and two coaches of the Cincinnati Bengals football team. Joe enthusiastically pumped each person's arm. "Man, I didn't think I'd get a chance to meet actual football players," he exclaimed. "And coaches."

The players were unusually reserved as if intimidated by Joe's fame. The right tackle said in a deep voice, "So?" At Joe's confusion, he explained clumsily, "You're Joe Ecks."

Joe came up short. "What? You can't possibly be thinking I'm more famous than you. Is that what you mean?"

The tackle smiled nervously. "I guess."

Angie took a mental note to discuss fame rankings with Joe. In the competition for fame, discussion of relative standings was not done. Although, at times, who was "bigger" had to be recognized, and even under the best of circumstances it could be awkward.

Joe stood up, indignantly straight. Even though Joe was relatively tall, the players all beat him by more than a few inches. He put his fists on his hips and glared up at them. "You gotta be kiddin' me. You guys are on national TV every week for a third of the year." Joe turned to Angie and asked, "Have I ever *once* been on national TV?"

"Uh," Angie stammered, unprepared for the question, "Well, yes. If you count your videos."

Joe answered, "Yeah, there's that. Okay, but shoot," he added, "you guys, if you play even one game, then you're immortal. Especially if you're a starter. Then you get in the statistics, and your name is in print for as long as football is a sport." Joe went off on a verbal bender, describing the permanence of sports data and recognized contribution. A few other people gathered to hear Joe's oration. "Plus, you guys play to a packed football stadium. How many people is that? Fifty thousand? X-Band has *never* played to fifty thousand people at once. And you guys do it every week!"

One of the players, the wide receiver, could not contain a laugh. The others were smiling.

"Am I right?" Joe urged.

Smiling, the tackle answered, "You're so full of shit."

Joe laughed an honest laugh. "Yeah, but am I right?"

Angie watched Joe interact with the football players. His tone and demeanor adapted and conformed until he was just like them. He asked the players about their positions and experience, noting the particular demands placed upon them. Then he drew the two coaches into the conversation. Angie didn't like football, but she found the conversation interesting. Bill came over and joined them. It was immediately evident that Bill spoke a fluent football. He engaged the Bengals, and Joe listened attentively. Angie felt like she was listening to people repeat telephone numbers to each other, and she lost interest.

Joe was urged to circulate further, and he spoke to a number of Bengal high-rollers, the men who paid top dollar for box seats that were more like furnished apartments in a very high-rent district. As a perk, they were invited to attend the odd Bengal event. Their satisfaction with the Bengals franchise was critical. As business magnates, they were used to deference, and so their position as Valued Customer fulfilled that expectation.

As before, Angie watched Joe circle and assimilate himself into conversations. He drove conversation without speaking much. Like with the football players, he deferred to the businessmen, which is what they expected anyway. They talked about business this and that, suits, private schools, investments and global generalities. Angie was swept along. The men looked at her like she was jewelry. Their wives regarded her banefully, judging her to be band-sluttage.

Twice, groups of men wanted their (and their wives') pictures taken with Joe. Angie worked the cameras. Better to be gracious about not being wanted in the picture.

Joe and Angie were introduced (as "Joe") to a foursome of 50-somethings, Mr. St. Germain and his wife Melissa and Dr. Geela and his wife Suzanne. (Angie noticed that the men typically had titles as first names.)

Dr. Geela glanced at Joe and commented to Mr. St. Germain, "I suppose I should have learned to play the guitar instead of going into medicine. Looks pretty easy to me."

St. Germain agreed and added, "And you'd be making a lot more money, too."

They laughed. Their wives laughed.

Angie felt Joe tense. "How long have you been a Bengals fan, Dr. Geela?" he asked.

The doctor assessed Joe. "He probably makes a lot more than both of us together. Yeah, it's a damn shame."

Joe admitted, "It does seem out of line with our comparative contribution to the hu—"

"No, what bothers me is that apparently any Joe Ecks Why or Zee can do well if they can play a guitar and say, 'Yeah, yeah, yeah!'" The doctor's companions laughed with exaggerated force.

Joe laughed, acknowledging the jab. "Yeah, I sup—"

St. Germain added, "They make so much money, they can't even count it."

Dr. Geela explained loudly, "But they can only count to four, can't they?" He asked Joe, "Don't you just count to four and start over? Here, I'll teach you something, Joe: Five. It comes after four." They laughed. Joe laughed politely with them.

"And what's with the hair? Are you trying to be a girl? 'Hi, I'm Joe Ecks, I have long hair and sing like a girl.'" More laughter.

Joe said, "Yeah, and don't forget about my clothes."

Dr. Geela took the bait. "Yes, where did you *get* that get-up? Do you have to shop at special stores, or did you mug someone weird?" Less laughter than before. "It hasn't been so easy since your mom stopped dressing you, huh?"

St. Germain commented to Dr. Geela, "That's probably enough, Walt."

Joe said, "I gotta move on." As he shook the wives' hands, he said, "It's been nice meetin all a you." He shook the men's hands. "Take care a yerselves." Joe turned and deftly inserted himself and Angie into another conversation in which a drunk businessman was urging Roger to plan for his financial future. Joe took a deep breath and sighed quietly. He asked the businessman how to account for uneven income streams.

Hours later, the crowd had thinned. X Band was collected, said farewell to, and escorted to their waiting limousine. Inside, and momentarily apart from the public, they relaxed.

When the limo started rolling, Angie said, "Joe, you really handled yourself there. Wow." She explained to the others about the hostile doctor and his friends. As she told the story, they looked at Joe with surprise. Bill kept repeating, "Really? Really?"

Joe shrugged off the attention. "It's just words," he said.

They were met at the hotel by staffers that escorted them to their rooms. Theremin had reserved the entire 14th and 15th floors for the band and executive production crew. Joe and Angie were assigned the corner room, the Presidential Suite. Joe sank into the loveseat and pulled off his boots. Angie slid beside him. Joe moved away.

"Why do you do that, Joe? Why do you move away from me?"

"Oh. So I can give you more room, I guess," he answered.

Angie should have known better than to have expected an answer that wasn't bullshit. She changed the subject. "What do you mean when you say 'It's just words.'? Like with that man insulting you."

Joe stared at his boots as he answered, "All that guy did was say words to me. He wasn't beating me up or stealing from me. I didn't need to have his approval for anything. It just didn't matter. You know?" He looked at Angie.

Even though what he said made sense, it seemed super-human to so effectively disregard someone's insults. She said, "Well, you really handled him well."

Joe picked up his boots and walked away. "I've been dealing with bullies all my life. This was easy."

Later, Angie studied herself in the mirror. It had been a long day, she reflected. The long flight and party. And tomorrow would start early and go long. And all the time, she would have to be attentive and alert.

Angie wavered. She was on the down-slope of a heavy buzz. She was tired and not realizing she was impaired. So she saw everything with a deceptively clear perception. Untethered, her mind floated from thought to thought. She saw herself drawn and wan. Her face had lost all color, and the light makeup no longer blended and had become a crude mask. For several days, Angie had made no effort to cover her freckles. Joe didn't seem to care, which was fine with Angie. Her bare face felt a lot more natural. But for actual public appearances, such as the 'Cincinnati Fan' reception, she covered them.

Not that it mattered. When Angie was seen with Joe, all anyone saw was Joe. But if she stumbled, it was caught. So did people notice her or not? Her presence augmented Joe's. Well, not always.

Angie sagged. She was tired.

She took a moment to envy Cassie, finding a home in Colorado. She was on her own, with no responsibilities, no deadlines and all the money she could spend. But no husband.

Angie scrubbed her face clean and changed into her tiny satin nightshirt. She found Joe scrunched up on his side of the bed, pretending to be asleep, as usual. She slipped in and scooted over, pressing herself against him. She suspected he was still awake. She snaked an arm around him, stroking his chest and other places, and found that he was indeed up.

Joe breathed, "Angie." Then he groaned, "Please don't do that."

She murmured, "I love you, Joe."

Quietly, Joe replied, "And Joe loves you."

Exasperated, Angie rolled over and fell asleep in thirty seconds.

A tear dropped from the bridge of Joe's nose to his pillow. Eighty minutes later, he joined Angie in sleep.

The morning started before morning. Costumes, hair and make-up. At dawn, the sky was partly cloudy, and O'Reilly was fully cloudy. Bill informed Joe that intermittent sunlight played hell with splicing scenes, and that complicated shooting.

Roger had a wiry girl wrapped around him who had been one of the servers from the party. Joe asked Roger if he was sure she was even eighteen. Distantly, Roger explained that he didn't ask if he didn't want to know. The girl told Roger he was funny. Ed had apparently gotten close to a Chinese girl who turned out to be one of the stage hands. They reluctantly separated so the girl could get to work, before O'Reilly sent someone over with a crowbar to pry them apart.

First, the band was filmed running down a hall. Then into the "tunnel". Then coming out of the tunnel. Each change in the shot required relocation of the camera, lights, screens, the extras and all the cables, fans, and other equipment. O'Reilly's crew knew what to do, however, and they set about it with energy. In each shot, O'Reilly had a definite vision, and he knew what he had to do to make it happen. He was often asked questions to which he fired off matter-of-fact answers.

Angie stood by, attentive. Joe watched everything. Uncharacteristically, he refrained from asking questions, but when he figured something out, he'd mention it to Angie. As in: "Hey. Diffusers broaden the source of light to reduce the *contrast* of shadows."

Between shots, there was a lot of standing around for the band. During this time, they were coached on the next shot by an assistant director. And their appearances were touched up by the experts. Several times, an extra would approach, but he or she would be shooed away by the crew.

By the time they got outside, it was late morning, and the puffy clouds had left. (O'Reilly took credit.) A rotating stage had been erected at mid-field with the band's instruments and a token amplifier or two. A camera track ran past the stage. Extras were positioned in the stands behind the shot.

The band climbed onto the stage, and, for a moment, looked for their positions.

"This is where I'm supposed to be," Ed declared, and he sat on the drum stool.

Joe put on his guitar and looked for the cord. Just as he remembered what Bill had told him on the plane, Bill muttered, "Don't bother looking for the cord. This is all for show."

"Attention!" announced O'Reilly's assistant. "We'll run through the song." O'Reilly's assistant actually announced everything and ordered people around. A stranger might have concluded that the assistant was really in charge, but really, O'Reilly was too important to be announcing things.

Bill's and Joe's eyes met. Joe nodded.

The stage lurched to a ponderous rotation. Then the camera started slowly along its track (pushed by two stage-hands). Someone started the song. The original version started with an announcer and crowd noises; this version started with the intro nearly over.

O'Reilly barked from off-camera, "Stand tall! Be proud!"

Joe complied. He was the only one who needed to. He focused his gaze on the rim of the stadium. Bill had warned him not to look into the camera.

"Ed! Match the beat!"

The camera crept past, zeroed in on Joe. Bill played to match the recording and pretended he was making the music. He saw Joe playing, aloof, oblivious to the camera. His fingering was off, but his demeanor didn't betray him. Bill wondered if he even knew.

Playing drums for video frustrated Ed. He had to synch with the music perfectly, because his instrument was more visual than any other (except singing, arguably). Once, when chided by Bill, Ed responded, "You could do *anything* and no one would notice! You could film a video wearing *mittens* and get away with it!" Then he added, "Though I don't know why a video would be wearing mittens..." So it was with increasing frequency that Ed drew O'Reilly's criticism.

After over an hour, O'Reilly changed tactics. He decided to film just Ed and synch him up in editing, a task that he did not want to do, and one that he resented having to do. Joe and the others stood aside as the camera crept by Ed, who tried to match his drumming in the recording. At first, O'Reilly harangued Ed, then he simply stood and stared at him darkly. At the end of the shot, O'Reilly asked, "Ed, do you even remember how you played this song?"

Ed rose from behind his drums like Godzilla coming out of the ocean to visit Tokyo.

O'Reilly added, "And if you don't, hasn't listening to it a hundred times reminded you?"

Ed turned and stepped off the back of the circular stage. He walked stiffly away from the film crew. Everyone stood unmoving, gaping at Ed and hoping secretly they weren't directly between Ed and O'Reilly. Ed nearly made it off the field when O'Reilly regained his voice.

"Ed! Goddammit, get back here! Where're you going?" O'Reilly progressed from irate to furious.

Bill said calmly, "Bruce, give him a minute."

If it had been suggested by anyone else, O'Reilly would have vented his fury on them. Instead, he subdued his anger.

Everyone watched Ed climb the stadium stairs up to the stratosphere rows. Then Ed stopped. He walked over six seats and sat down. He didn't look like he was planning to go anywhere anytime soon, although at this distance, it was hard to tell.

O'Reilly fumed. "This is fuckin great," he said.

Joe hopped off the stage. "Let me talk to him." He walked toward Ed.

To Joe's back, O'Reilly agreed.

Joe walked across the field and off. He threaded his way to the stands and ascended the stairs.

Ed slouched in his seat. His knees jutted upwards. He stared ahead glumly. He didn't seem to notice Joe climbing the stairs.

Joe dropped into the seat beside Ed, breathing heavily. He said, "You know, I'm not used to being in this good a shape. Still, that's a helluva climb."

Ed exhaled heavily but said nothing.

Joe settled into his seat. After a moment, he touched his eyebrow scar.

Ed didn't move.

Joe scratched his thigh.

Ed sighed. He finally asked, "Okay. What brilliant motivational speech are you going to ply me with now? What words of wisdom do you have that will get me out of this seat and back behind my drums without any wasted time? Go ahead. I can't wait to hear them."

"No, I got nothin'," Joe answered easily. "I just wanted to be here for you. And my bein' here keeps everyone else away."

Neither spoke for several minutes.

Indeed, back on the field, O'Reilly was squinting up at Ed and Joe. "What are they doing?" he asked Bill. "It doesn't even look like they're talking."

That's what Bill thought, too. "Joe knows what he's doing," stated Bill, even though *he* didn't know what Joe was doing.

"We're wasting time," O'Reilly decided.

Bill said, "Filming a video with a pissed-off Ed is wasting time, too."

O'Reilly silently agreed. Then he had his cameraman put on a telephoto lens and shoot them.

Back in the seats, Ed began to relax. He could feel it. He liked having Joe nearby, as long as Joe wasn't here to manipulate him. Ed relaxed further. He could smell the bleachers. He could hear the distant voices, with a backdrop of street noises. He thought about life. He was frustrated. Debi had been fun last night and this morning, but now she didn't seem to care about him; she probably never had. A failure; another false start.

He missed Vicky and what they had. Though she was a bit wild, Ed thought he could live with that. And she had a rather simplistic sense of humor. But they had been together for a while. Ed thought it might last.

Without realizing he was going to talk, Ed uttered, "Vicky's gone." He added, "She left." He clarified, "She left me." He didn't look at Joe. It was easier to keep looking ahead at the seats across the stadium.

"Ed. I'm sorry," Joe said. "Are you okay?"

Ed inhaled raggedly. "When I came back last night, I mean the night before, she was gone. She left a note. It was very well-written." Ed looked at Joe.

"I'm sorry she left you, Ed."

Ed sagged. "Well, I guess I should have seen it coming. Things weren't going so well. She was getting kind of distant, and I just didn't want to see it. I thought we were just getting past the honeymoon stage." Ed sat for a minute, miserable. "'Cept I had thought maybe she was involved with someone else."

"There in Los Angeles?" Joe asked.

Ed regarded Joe. "Joe, I'm going to ask you something straight out: Were you having sex with Vicky?"

Joe locked eyes with Ed. "I have no first-hand knowledge of it."

"Hmm," Ed frowned. "Okay. Joe, I suppose I need to tell you that a long time ago, we made a deal. If you cheat on Angie, I will hurt you bad. And you won't play guitar for a long time."

Joe said, "I'm glad Angie has you to look out for her."

"Yeah," Ed said, nodding. Apparently changing the subject, he said, "Good news. I found your elevator key card." Ed reached into his hip pocket and withdrew his wallet. "I guess Vicky found it when she was packing her stuff." Ed handed the card to Joe.

Joe accepted the card and said, "Thank you."

Ed leaned back and stared at the field. "You're welcome. And thank *you*."

The two of them sat quietly together for a long time.

On the field, O'Reilly gave up on Joe and Ed, and he shot close-ups of Bill and Roger. He had planned those shots anyway (if he had time), but this sequence was inefficient, requiring lengthy set-ups that would have to be undone later.

Bill stayed out of the way, except when being filmed. He stopped worrying about Joe and Ed. Ed lost his composure very rarely, and when he did, he and Joe were chilly toward each other for a long time, like weeks. The ice never really broke, either; it just thawed. But this new Joe didn't work that way. He wouldn't let Ed stay upset. He would face down Ed's upsettedness and obliterate it.

In the cheap seats, Ed was feeling restless, but he wasn't ready to return to filming. Then there would be the post-filming party and the red-eye back to LA. Ed sighed. "You know— well, I shouldn't be complaining to you, but sometimes it just seems like a lot of work."

Joe looked sidelong at Ed. "You know, Ed, we've only known each other, what, two weeks? But I'd like to think we're pretty good friends."

The comment surprised Ed. He'd forgotten for a moment that he was sitting beside Joe's other personality, and that surprised him. But also, he realized he *did* want to be friends with this new personality, as weird as that felt.

Joe continued: "So I'd hope you could talk to me about anything. Including complaints. You know, not too long ago, I saw my cousin Ray. He said he and his wife were working on having a baby. I was thinking, 'If you think *that's* work, what do you do for fun?'" Joe laughed.

Ed smiled, guessing where Joe was leading.

But instead, Joe reversed himself. "Hey, you've done this a million times, and you could do it in your sleep. For me, this is new and exciting, and I have to focus so I don't look like an amateur. It's easy for me to have fun with this. But if you're getting bored, that's a problem. Are you getting bored?"

Ed shrugged. "What do you mean?"

Joe nodded. "Yeah, things are getting routine. We gotta shake things up. We been tryin too hard to do things right."

Ed started to smile. "Like what?"

"I dunno, but we've been good boys long enough. Let's have some fun today. No, let's make it fun today for everyone else. Maybe we can even get O'Reilly to smile."

Ed's smile widened.

They were filming a shot across the stage, to capture Bill and Roger in the same shot. The camera would focus on Bill and then on Roger and then back. O'Reilly would splice it in later. No one saw Joe and Ed as they returned.

Joe approached O'Reilly directly, while Ed hung back. Joe said, "Bruce, we're sorry about the delay."

O'Reilly was unswayed. "We're really behind schedule. I'm going to have to sacrifice some shots because of this."

Joe replied, "Ed says he'll come back to work if you apologize and give him flowers."

O'Reilly stared at Joe. Finally, he said, "What?"

"And a pizza. He's *very* hurt."

O'Reilly straightened. "I'll hurt more than his feelings if you clowns don't get back on the stage right now!"

As they hurried onto the stage, Joe answered, "Okay, I'll tell Ed the pizza's a 'maybe'."

"Places!" O'Reilly barked. "For 14-1!"

The crew scrambled. The track was moved from its oblique path to an almost straight-on path. The lights were rearranged. The trolley was replaced on the track. O'Reilly studied the workings with the air of an Egyptian slave master.

Bill muttered to Joe, "Did you have a nice time up there?"

"You know, you guys looked like little ants from way up there."

"Joe, this is serious," Bill admonished.

"No, *you're* serious," Joe countered. "This is *fun*. Or at least it oughta be."

Bill glared at Joe.

Loudly and without shame, Roger farted.

Bill stifled a laugh and turned on Roger, but before he could speak, Joe guffawed. Ed joined in. Bill looked from one to the other and said, "Geez, you guys."

"Us?" Ed indignantly answered. "What about Roger? I didn't know he had it in him!"

Joe joined in. "He did! But now he doesn't!"

The banter continued between the three. Bill called Joe and Ed immature, and in turn, Bill was called stiff and tight. Both sides made their points. Several unoccupied crew members stood by and listened. And laughed.

"Places!" the assistant director barked, even though everyone was already in their places. O'Reilly studied the monitor, though he was distracted by the exchange.

"Cue sound," O'Reilly said.

The song came on, mid-intro.

"Camera," O'Reilly said.

"Speed," answered the cameraman.

"Action," said O'Reilly.

The band played the song, more or less. There were more takes. As the crew hurried to prepare for the next shot, O'Reilly regarded Joe and Ed, dourly, and this was an improvement from angrily. They were speculating on various uses for Bill's tightness. For example, Joe was saying, "If you were changing tires, then you could put on the lug nuts with Bill." Ed: "I used Bill to put a lid on my jar of pickles." Joe: "If you had a knot that you wanted to stay tied, you could use Bill." Long-suffering Bill pretended to ignore them, which only urged them on.

O'Reilly turned away, shaking his head.

"Joe, did he smile, just then, when he was turning away?"

"I don't think so," Joe replied. "We have to try harder."

"No, I swear I think he's laughing. Right now."

O'Reilly bellowed, "Places, for 8-1!"

And after that, there were different shots. O'Reilly still finished slightly ahead of schedule. He loudly attributed this to his hard-working crew and not to the professionalism of the "talent".

At the post-filming party, O'Reilly and Joe eventually met face-to-face. O'Reilly had a big stein of beer in one giant hand. He held out the other to Joe. Joe shook it enthusiastically. O'Reilly declared, "I had fun. I always have fun filming, but I had fun having fun. You understand?"

"I know what you mean," Joe nodded. "I hope we get to work together soon."

"June 3rd," O'Reilly stated. "That's our next shoot. For the band sequence in 'Contents Under Pressure'."

The airplane veered up into the night sky. Ed watched the lights of Cincinnati fall away, and he started to relax. He knew nothing would be expected of him for hours. Then he recognized his habitual thought path. Any time he had to do something, it was an opportunity to fail; something to fear. Today, the video had been fun to film, after a fashion. Ed looked across the aisle at Joe. Joe was leaning forward in his seat, studying the lights below. Then, like he knew Ed was watching him, he turned to Ed and smiled.

"I love flying," Joe announced. "It's such a miracle."

From the seat in front of Ed, Bill replied, "You like everything, don't you?" Bill was weary. And irritated with Joe. The shooting had been going fine until Joe interfered, and then it was going great. But in the process, Bill had been swept aside. No, not exactly swept *aside*; more like swept *past*. Bill didn't like it, but he had to concede that Joe *had* retrieved Ed, and he *had* enlivened the shoot. But did he have to be so flagrant about it? Did it matter? Was Bill wrong to be irritated? Shouldn't he feel grateful?

Joe replied, "I try to recognize the beauty that's around me." He shot a glance at Angie, who sat behind him. At the sight of his glance, Angie looked up from her book.

Bill didn't answer. Joe either didn't recognize Bill's barb, or he had chosen to ignore it. Which one? Duh. Bill had told O'Reilly, 'Joe knows what he's doing,' and he had meant it. Joe always knew what he was doing.

Joe asked Angie, "Angie, are we meeting with Mr. Pidd tomorrow?"

Angie shook her head. "No, I haven't been able to reach him. I left messages with his service, though."

"Service?" Joe repeated. "Doesn't he have a secretary? Wendy?"

"Yes," Angie replied. "Well, he used to. She left."

"That was sudden," Joe observed. "Well, the next message you leave, tell him if we don't talk tomorrow, he's fired. I mean that."

Bill twisted around. "What?" he exclaimed. "You can't just do that! You can't fire Stu on your own like that."

Joe faced Bill. "We need to talk to him. And he's avoiding us."

"He's not avoiding us, Joe. Stu isn't like that. You don't know him like the rest of us do."

"No, you're right," Joe agreed calmly. "What I know is that Stu knows where we are all the time, and he knows how to reach us at any time. So I don't know why we haven't heard from him in two days. I gave him three days to work out the deal-breakers, and since then I haven't heard a word about it. Have you?"

Bill was forced to admit that he hadn't heard any news from Stu. He had always trusted Stu to do his job without reporting details to the band. He said, "There are a lot of possible reasons why Stu hasn't gotten back to you. Be patient. Let him do his job."

Joe nodded. "Okay." He turned back to Angie. "Angie, the next time you leave a message for Stu, please tell him that tomorrow at 3:00, the band will be voting on whether to fire him. If he wishes to defend himself, he should see us before then."

Bill scowled. "If we vote to keep Stu, will you drop it then?"

Joe answered, "Bill, I hope we unanimously vote to keep Stu. I hope all my suspicions are proven wrong, and that we all decide that we have the best representation possible. Of all the outcomes I can think of, that's the best one."

Bill faced forward, ending the exchange. He should have known better than to argue with Joe. Joe knew what he was doing. Still, Bill had to defend Stu, because lately, Stu had been looking awfully guilty.

Chapter 16

Showdown with Mr. Pidd

In the limo, Ed watched the scenery and wiped his hands on his pants. He was anxious, and that bothered him. Absently, he overheard Bill explaining the rehearsal process to Joe, who listened closely. This was starting to feel familiar. And Ed predicted this is how it would go: Bill would explain everything to Joe. Joe would put forth an earnest try and fail miserably. Then he would do something unexpected and miraculous and save the day.

But today would be different. Because today would be interrupted by a showdown between Stu and Joe. Ed guessed that Stu would win, because Stu knew what he was doing, and Joe didn't. Either way, it would get ugly. Unless Stu called Joe's bluff and didn't even show up. But if Stu thought Joe was bluffing, then Stu was in for a surprise. This new Joe looked easy to manipulate, but if he had conviction, then he would stand firm.

Ed watched Joe absorbing everything Bill told him. Ed used to know Joe in the way a person would know his pet rattlesnake. You knew when it was okay to play with it, and you knew when to leave it alone. Now Ed didn't know Joe at all. But it didn't matter, because this Joe didn't have any hostility landmines. He was so stable and in control that he didn't seem real. And he was supportive. Ed recalled Joe defending Bill at the press conference. He recalled the way Joe had assembled the band and cut a new track from nothing. Or talking him down in the stadium bleachers. But this new Joe couldn't sing or play guitar. It would sure be easy if the old Joe came back. Ed sighed.

Joe asked, "Somethin on yer mind?"

Ed looked over guiltily. He said, "No." Then he realized he was obviously lying. "Just thinking about today."

Joe nodded, still spearing Ed with his eyes. Then he turned back to Bill and asked, "So what is the tour director like? David Burrill? No, he's called the 'performance director', isn't he?"

Bill had to search his memory. They had met the performance director at the tour company meeting. "We haven't worked with Burrill," Bill reminded Joe, "He seemed to know what he was talking about at his presentation. He has experience."

The limo pulled up behind a low, flat building. "We're here already?" Joe asked.

Their door was opened by a young man exclaimed, "X Band! Follow me this way!"

They complied. The young man walked in the back door and through a large utility room, and he led the band to a stage from the back. Their equipment had been set up already. Stage Manager Pete McCann and a dozen hands were standing by. To Ed, the assistants all looked young and eager. Burrill confronted the band immediately, re-introducing himself. He acted just as he had in the Tour Excellence meeting: Small, graying, and energetic.

McCann asked Angie if he could get her anything.

Angie asked, "Is there a place where I can spread out and make some phone calls?"

"I have a room for you." McCann ordered a stagehand to escort Angie there.

Joe looked around the auditorium, taking it in. Ed had been here before, on many long days, and he'd forgotten that Joe hadn't ever seen it. Relatively speaking, it was small, only seating about a thousand. The stage, likewise, was proportionately small. Ed knew that they would be playing on a variety of stages, so the moves they learned this week would have to be adapted.

"All right," Burrill said, rubbing his hands together. "We have a lot to d—"

One of the stagehands was whispering to another.

"Quiet!" McCann barked at him.

The hand snapped back into formation.

Burrill continued: "We have a lot to do, and not much time. First, is this configuration acceptable?" He gestured to the instruments on the stage.

"It looks about right," Bill answered.

Burrill looked up at Joe for an answer.

Joe said, "Yeah, it looks about right, looks right to me. I guess."

"This was your arrangement for the first two tours with Theremin," Burrill said in confirmation.

Joe said, "Uh, maybe you could move Roger and Bill up some so they're closer to the front of the stage."

"No, you'll need plenty of space here to walk back and forth," Burrill told Joe. Pointing to a stagehand, he snapped. "You! Get the white board!" The stage hand hustled away. Burrill asked Joe, "Do you have a playlist in mind?"

"What do you recommend?" Joe fired back.

"The way I work, it's all about pacing," Burrill said. He explained about pacing and how the songs carried the pace. Joe injected a comment, and there was rapid exchange between them. Ed scratched his goatee.

The group hashed out the sequence of songs. The first songs would be lively. Then the pace would slow until they played 'Anesthesia', and then they would play their most jamming songs to the concert's conclusion.

They planned out extras like introductions and solos. Joe started out with two guitar solos, but he didn't want to have any. Ed thought Joe might look humble to an outsider, but Ed knew the real reason was Joe didn't want to have to learn a guitar solo. Bill and Roger also had solos. Without mention, Ed was passed over. In the past, Joe had maintained that Ed wasn't capable. Ed's feelings would have been hurt, except he thought Joe was right.

But Joe stopped the discussion. "Wait, what about Ed? Isn't Ed doing a drum solo?" Joe asked.

Bill said, "It's up to you, Ed."

"Yes, I want one." Ed recognized the voice as his own. Shocked, he added, "I want to do a drum solo. If that's all right."

Joe answered, "I want you to do a drum solo, Ed. And you will do a good job."

"Thank you, Joe," Ed said. At the same time, he was assaulted by a paralyzing fear and a profound gratitude.

Burrill suggested that the best way for Ed to begin his solo was for the band to be playing a jamming song and then stop, and Ed could keep going. They picked two songs, in case Ed didn't feel right at the first one. And he could skip both if he really wanted. Then the discussion moved on, but Ed was already thinking about what he would do.

Angie interrupted to report that Stu would arrive at 3:45.

Joe said, "Please call Stu back and tell him the vote is at 3:00, so you'll call him at 3:01 and tell him if he has to bother coming in at all."

Angie hesitated. Her green eyes found Ed in an unspoken, "Ed, you gotta talk to Joe."

Ed said, "Joe—"

"Don't start!" Joe snarled. "It's a stupid little power maneuver. He wants *us* to wait for *him*. He controls the vote by setting the time. NO!"

Ed and everyone else took a step back mentally if not physically. Angie nodded once and left the room.

Burrill started to say something, and Joe interrupted. "I'm sorry everyone. I'm okay." To Burrill, he explained, "We're having a disagreement with our agent, and at 3:00 today, we're gonna need some time to work it out with him."

Ed heard someone whisper, "Denise was right." A reference to Denise Cody, who had directed them for the last two tours. Ed wondered if Burrill was their director now because Cody had declined. Or maybe refused.

Uneasily, Burrill continued. They plotted out the performance including the encore. Burrill promised to have the sequence typed, and copies would be hidden where the band members could see it.

Lunch. Caterers set up two tables with enough food to feed the entire building for two weeks.

Ed saw Joe at a table across from Burrill and surrounded by stagehands on his side. The only conversation was between Joe and Burrill; the stagehands were allowed to laugh. Ed saw that Joe's plate was piled with fried chicken. Joe, he observed, tended to eat a lot of only one thing. Ed had his own fans in tow, a boy and girl stagehand. He was only a few years older than them, but they seemed like kids, especially when they called him "Mr. Brettington".

Joe excused himself and left the room. Ed needed to talk to Joe about the upcoming meeting with Stu. He decided to wait a few minutes before following.

One of the stagehands asked, "Expecting trouble with your agent?"

Ed blinked. "I suppose it could get ugly," he allowed.

The hand grinned. "Don't worry, Mr. Brettington. We'll take him out if you need us to."

Ed wondered what exactly 'Take him out' meant.

Angie finished her hastily-made chicken sandwich (no mayo) provided by one of the caterers. She had set up her office in a room designed for presentations. She was transcribing dates from a list into her organizer when Joe came in. "Oh, hi," he said. Awkwardly, he sat across the table from her.

When Joe didn't say anything further, Angie asked, "Do you need something?"

Joe answered, "No, not really." He hesitated. "Well, I wanted to see you."

"What about?"

"Nothing." Another hesitation. "I just wanted to say hi. You're not busy, are you? If I'm interrupting, I could leave."

Angie smiled and said, "Hi."

Joe shifted. "I'm sorry I snapped at you earlier. It was rude."

"It's okay," Angie said. "It happens all the—"

Joe frowned. "Not anymore."

Angie thought. It was true. Joe had had a short fuse, and he would typically stay angry for a long time. But not now.

"Um," Joe said. He asked, "Where would you rather go for a vacation, to the beach or the mountains?"

Angie sighed. "Do you have a whole list of questions like that that you can ask people?"

"Well," Joe answered sheepishly, "actually, I do. But still, I actually wanna know."

Just then Ed entered. "Joe, I gotta talk to you."

Joe turned. "About Stu?"

"Yes." Ed sat down beside Angie, across from Joe. "Hear me out. You don't know Stu the way the rest of us do. We've been through a lot together, and Stu has proven that he really knows what he's doing." Ed waited for Joe to argue.

Joe said, "Go on. I'm hearing you out."

Ed noticed Roger seated at the end of the table. When had he come in? "Yeah, okay, look, Joe. Stu is a putz. He's annoying, there's no arguing that. But that doesn't mean that he's inept. He has always guided us to our goal." Ed described several instances in which Stu's advice had been beneficial. While Ed spoke, Bill came in and quickly understood the subject of the conversation. Ed concluded, "Stu knows what to do. We don't."

"Ed's right," Bill verified. Bill went into teacher mode, explaining in detail to Joe examples of Stu's business acumen. Joe sat patiently, listening. "So now you can see that we should let Stu do his job, just like he lets us do our jobs. You see that, right?"

"No," answered Joe levelly. "Stu's been—"

Bill interrupted. "Joe, we don't need to discuss this. I've—"

Meanwhile, Ed was grimacing. "C'mon, Joe—"

"Quiet!" Joe snapped.

Bill started to speak, but Joe yelled, "Be Quiet!"

Bill tried to talk twice more, but Joe kept yelling "Quiet!" until he was shouting. Finally, Bill was quiet. In a normal tone, Joe said, "I was quiet while you and Ed spoke. Now it's my turn. Then it's Roger's turn. Angie, do you have those contracts?"

Angie handed them over. They were worn, and had blue ink written all over them. Even the backs of some pages were covered with calculations.

Joe held up the contracts. "First, Stu wanted us to propose a contract to Theremin, which is hardly ever done."

Bill said, "That shows—"

"QUIET!" Joe screamed.

Bill decided to be quiet. Clearly, Joe wasn't going to budge until he had had his say.

"Thank you," Joe said, as if Bill had had a choice. "Okay, let's take a look at the contract that Stu submitted on our behalf. If our next three albums do as well as the average of the first two... I used the average of the two albums as a benchmark, just to show the comparison. So if they do as well, then we'll get about a quarter what we got on the first two albums, probably less. I'll concede that my numbers are fuzzy, because there are some things we don't know. For example, production costs. Do you know that with this contract, we are paying for all the productions costs, costs that are defined and managed by Theremin? Who's going to regulate what they consider a production cost? Do you know Michael's *salary* is a production expense? So Michael can set his own salary at anything, and we have to pay it. Under those conditions, he'd be generous if we got *any* money. And all this would be happening because we weren't allowed to see the contract. They'd be skimming, hell, *gouging*, and we'd never even know."

The door opened, and Stuart Cress walked in. He wore a suit with the collar open and carried a small notebook. "Here you are," he said. His eyes swept the room. "So you're talking about it anyway. Ed, didn't you talk to Joe?"

Ed squirmed.

Joe said, "Stu, I'm glad you came. You oughta take a seat."

Stu didn't budge. "Look, Joe, I know things—"

Joe approached Stu. "Sit down! Sit down!" he repeated.

Stu looked at Bill. Bill shrugged and said, "I'd sit down."

Stu started to say something, and Joe growled, "Sit down!" Joe was now practically on top of Stu. It looked to Ed like Joe was going to push him into the wall.

With an obvious disapproval, Stu sat down.

"Okay," Joe continued. "Maybe I'm wrong about the financials. There's still the rights. Theremin gets re-issue rights. If they rerelease an album, *which they can do even during the first production*, they own the profits. And not only that, Theremin has the rights to the name 'X Band'. They literally own us." Joe let that sink in. "And not only that, they own the rights to our individual names. So, Bill, if you ever wanted to cut a solo album, your name can't be on the jacket."

This shocked Bill. He'd been planning a solo career, and he didn't want Theremin to sabotage its success. "No," Bill objected. "They can't do that. Come on!"

Joe answered, "Taylor Wines, around 1970. One of the Taylor brothers left the company and started his own winery. The other brothers put an injunction on his use of his own name."

Bill looked over at Stu, who was flagrantly rolling his eyes and sighing in exasperation.

Joe said, "And by the way, Bill, you might wanna ask Stu why he hung you out to dry at the press conference. How did the Religious Right happen to get ahold of the lyrics to 'Anesthesia'? And how is it that so many got into a press conference that is usually limited to members of the press? And Stu preps you by saying 'there will be some questions' about it as he leaves the room?"

Bill hadn't thought about it. It almost looked like Stu had intended for him to be caught by surprise and crash and burn in full view of the press. And that would have happened, too, had not Joe stepped in.

"That's marketing," Stu declared. "You wouldn't know about it."

Joe continued: "And now that I think about it, it was the same plan with the 'Shut Up and Suck' lyrics, wasn't it? More publicity at our expense?"

"That was your idea!" Stu exclaimed.

"Yeah, that's what I figured," Joe grumbled.

Stu added, "And then you *apologize* for it? That wasn't in the script! It ruined the whole thing! Okay, may I speak now?"

"No, there's more." Joe brandished the second contract. "Here's our contract with Stu. You know what's interesting? It allows Stu the right to work with other groups. Not just other bands, but other entities in which a conflict of interest might be seen. Stu is poda be *our* agent! He's poda represent *us* and *our* best interest. Stu gets a decent percentage of our earnings, and I don't begrudge him that. In fact, I hope he earns a whole *ton* a money with his percentage. So why would he sell us out? Why? Because what he doesn't get from our percentage, he makes up for by also workin fer Theremin. He's on their payroll. He's getting paid by them to sell us off. And," Joe concluded, "the most obnoxious clause is the one in which we have to do a remake, selected by Theremin, every album." Joe turned to Stu and said, "I hate remakes, and you know it." Joe took a deep breath and let it out. "Okay, Stu, now it's your turn to talk. Then Roger's."

For a moment, Stu regarded Joe with apparent amusement. He chuckled, "You know, Joe, this would be amusing if the consequences weren't so serious. It's my fault it got to this point, I guess. We need to stay in touch, Joe. We should have lunch." When Joe didn't react, Stu continued. Bill thought he looked sharp. And confident. He walked through Joe's copy of the contract. One by one, he explained the language of the contract and why it was included. Many of the items that did not appear in the first contract were usually included, Stu said, only in the contracts of established bands. "To have the rights to your names allows Theremin to advertise. And issue press releases. Theremin likes you guys, and they're showing that they're in this for the long haul. Theremin is going out on a limb here. Rap is hot, and the labels are only signing rap groups." Bill had been swayed by Joe, assuming his claims could be proven. Joe was convincing in his confidence. But what Stu said made sense, too. Stu had pointed out that if someone examined any contract, such as that for a rental car, as cynically as Joe did, then you could find areas in which abuse could be leveraged. Bill looked over at Ed, and Ed was nodding. Joe was unmoving. Angie seemed on the alert for an outburst from Joe. Roger gazed at Stu blankly.

Stu began smiling with every point he made. Then he referenced the contract between him and the band and admitted that he was an employee of Theremin. But that allowed him free access to everyone in the building, so he could do his job. It showed Theremin's trust in him. Stu concluded his defense, hurt that they had doubted his very integrity. "And," Stu said, finishing, "bands do remakes. It's not the end of the world, Joe. Really." He gracefully yielded the floor to Roger.

Joe answered, "Well, Stu, I confess, I was just kidding about the remake clause. Okay, Roger, it's your turn to talk now."

Bill's head exploded.

Roger collected his thoughts. Finally, he said, "I vote we fire Stu."

"What?!" Stu erupted. "I've done a lot for you guys! We've got a good thing going! Look, first, back when we met—"

"It's not your turn to talk," Joe told Stu.

Stu turned to Ed, but before he could speak, Ed asked Roger, "*Why* would you vote to fire Stu, Roger?"

Roger said clearly, "I'm not qualified to have an opinion on the contract itself. But I do have an opinion on what Stu's recent actions say about Stu. Stu colluded with Michael to eliminate competition. He withheld the contract from Joe. Once the contract was obtained, with no help from Stu, Stu avoided all contact with Joe until, and even after, it was announced in public that the contract had been signed. He is only here now because he believes his job is threatened. My opinion is that these actions are not the actions of a man looking out for our best interests. These are not the actions of an honest man. That's why I vote to fire Stu."

Ed was following Roger's thoughts. Stu *had* been acting guilty. Joe had been telling them so all along, but Ed hadn't wanted to believe it. But did that mean he *was* guilty? Could the band survive without Stu? And the contract? Why should it have to? There were too many things to think about, and an answer was called for now.

"Ed talk some sense to Roger, would you?" Stu pleaded.

Ed realized he had to trust his future with one of them, and, to Roger's point, who had lately been acting the most worthy of trust? He turned to Stu. "Actually, Roger's been talking sense to me. I also vote to fire you."

Meanwhile, Bill had been sorting through the wreckage in his skull. Joe had baited Stu with his fictitious "remake clause", and Stu had fallen for it. Bill recalled the confrontation in the closet. Joe quoted from the contract, and Stu denied the existence of the clause Joe objected to. So Joe read the contract, proving Stu wrong. If Stu had written the contract, wouldn't he have remembered putting in those clauses? If he had written the contract, there was no way he would have thought there was a remake clause. But if he didn't write the contract, who did?

He heard Stu say, "We're the only adults in the room, Bill. Can you straighten out these kids? I've been honest with you all along. I've been working hard for all of you, and we need this contract."

Bill turned to Stu and asked, "Who wrote that contract?"

"Uh, well, what does it really matter? It's a good contract. I had a lawyer write it."

"What lawyer? Our lawyer?"

Stu sighed in exasperation. "What difference does it make? We need this contract, and Theremin has already signed it anyway. It would be very foolish for us to break this contract now. No one else would want to deal with us."

"Bullshit," Bill declared. "You sold us out. You're fired."

Stu turned to Joe. "All right, you made your point, Joe," Stu gritted. "They'll all follow you, no matter what. You win. You're in charge. Good for you. But we still need that contract.

Joe said, "I'm sorry, Stu. You're fired."

Stu sighed and forced on a smile. "We've been through tough times, and this is a tough time, too. It's also a critical point for the band. Remember how I got you into places you'd never been able to play? Remember how I got you much better money than you'd gotten before? I was the agent that got you places. Those were tough times, all right, but we got through them. I got you through them. We worked together—"

"Stu, the voting is done. I'm sorry," Joe said.

"Hear me out, Joe, I'm fighting for my life now. My life and the life of the band. Your lives—"

Joe said to Angie, "Have McCann send in three or four stagehands to escort Stu out of the building."

Angie rose and left the room.

"Joe, look, see, the band needs me, and, yes, I admit, I need the band. I'll work with Michael and change the contract. Do you want to sit in with us? You can work with us, and we'll formulate a contract that we can all live with. Joe, we can turn this around."

Six stagehands came in and headed for Stu. The one in front said, "This way, sir."

With pleas and begging, Stu was crowded out the door. Angie was afraid he was going to cry.

Joe grimaced and looked away. He looked back at the others. Sadly, he said, "Thank you for, well, for listening. And for your courage." He shook his head and muttered, "I didn't want to hafta do that. It's fer the best, though." Turning to Angie, he asked, "Do you have Michael's number? I need to tell him the contract is invalid."

The others stiffened. This was not a conversation they wanted to experience in any way.

While Angie dialed the number on the phone beside her, Joe said, "I really appreciate the trust you have placed in me. If—" Angie handed him the receiver. Joe listened.

Bill marveled at Joe's iron will. Any conversation with Michael would have ruined Joe's, the old Joe's, day or even week. This Joe looked like he was all business. And in the show-down with Stu, Joe was clearly in control. Finally, Joe spoke.

"I was calling for Michael Rost?" Pause. "It's Joe Ecks from X Band." Pause. "Oh, thank you. It's nice to hear that. Thank you for making it possible. When do you think Michael will be out of his meeting?" Pause. "Oh. Can I leave a message for him?" Pause. "Okay, please tell him that X Band fired Stuart Cress, and Michael can tear up the new contract he has with us, because it isn't valid." Pause. "Yes." Pause. "No, you know, it's actually not necessary for him to call me back." Pause. "Thank you." Joe hung up and sighed. "Let's see how soon Michael gets out of his all-day meeting."

Bill tried not to dwell on the fact that they had all just voted away their long-fought-for second contract. He decided to call his agent that night and have him begin the process of pushing a solo contract.

The phone rang. Joe picked it up and said, "Sam & Ella's Diner, this is Sam speaking."

Bill could hear Michael's shouting voice.

Joe answered, "Yeah, that's right."

Michael shouted some more. Bill could hear a string of bad language.

Joe said, "Our lawyer *is* aware of the situation."

Michael's shouting dropped a pitch.

Joe answered, "Then it's not appropriate for us to be talking, then. Please forward all communications through our lawyer." Joe hung up while Michael was still yelling.

Joe turned to Ed and asked, "Ed, do we have a lawyer?"

"Yes!" Ed exclaimed.

"Good, cuz Michael's suin us."

Bill blurted, "Suing us?!"

"Yeah, fer breach a contract."

Bill shook his head. "We're going to have such a bad reputation, no one will touch us."

Joe nodded, "Yeah, we're probably the only band to ever cause trouble."

Okay, Bill saw his point. Some bands not only had bad reputations, they seemed to thrive on the badness. Still, Bill didn't see how this could do anything but hurt them.

The phone rang. Joe answered it. Immediately, Bill could tell it was Michael. While Michael was yelling at Joe, Joe said, "We should not be talking." That didn't seem to deter Michael. Joe started to hang up the phone, but then he stopped and told Michael, "My advice to you is to try another way of interacting with us, because this way is not workin for you." Joe hung up. He said with amazement, "He's so *angry*!"

Bill was shaking his head. "Joe, did you have to *antagonize* him?"

Joe shook his head and admitted wryly, "No, I didn't *have* to..."

"Personally, I'm glad to see Michael get some attitude," Ed declared. "And it's even better that it comes from Joe."

The phone rang.

Joe sighed. "We probably should get back to work."

The phone rang again.

"Aren't you going to answer it?" Angie asked. "Do you want me to answer it?" She really didn't want to answer it.

"No, let it ring," Joe answered. "But if it ever stops ringin, could you call our lawyer and tell him or her what's goin on?" He started for the door. "Now for the hard part of today."

He was right.

The band returned to the auditorium. Burrill stood talking to an unusually tall woman. Addressing the band, Burrill was cautious. "So, how did everything go? All right?"

"No," said Bill.

Joe answered, "We got done what had to get done." He saw the stagehands coming in that had escorted out Stu. "Thanks, guys. Everything went okay?"

They shuffled. One said, "He fell down in the parking lot. I tried to catch him, but his face hit my hand."

"But he's okay, right?" Joe asked.

"He will be," the stagehand assured.

"Thanks again."

Burrill introduced the woman as Denise Enders. "She will be singing the part of Xylene."

"Hi, X Band," she said and offered a little wave. She was tall, dark and gorgeous.

Regarding Burrill, Ed commended, "This is *exactly* what I had in mind for Xylene."

Confused, Joe asked, "But Dawn Barlas sang for Xylene in the recording. Why isn't she touring with us?"

The people were momentarily quiet.

Bill began, "Dawn has an excellent voice..."

Ed finished, "Onstage, she wouldn't fit the image of Xylene."

"But she's the voice of Xylene," Joe insisted. "Denise won't sound like the Xylene in the song. How important *is* her image?"

Suddenly very serious, Ed explained, "Joe, it's an unfortunate fact that, in the entertainment industry, how a woman looks is very important. Much more important than it is for a man. It's not fair, but it's the truth. Look at Bill. No one would pay money to look at him, but we let him tour with us because he can play that thing, that keyboard thing. ("Knock it off, Ed," Bill was saying, but no one heard him.) But when Xylene is onstage, the audience will be looking at her closely. Critically. Denise can withstand that level of scrutiny."

"Oh," said Joe. "Oh. That's too bad. But good for Denise, right?"

The people agreed. And welcomed Denise to the show. Denise smiled and took a seat in the third row.

"Let's get to work!" Burrill exclaimed. They did, starting with the band's entrance. Burrill stood down front, in front of the first row of seats. He had the band come onstage and engage their instruments.

"This is important!" Burrill shouted. Burrill's shouting was not at all like Michael's shouting. Burrill shouted to vent his energy, and his shouts were more like encouragement, like a coach shouting at this team. "You're making a first impression here! The time between appearing on the stage and being ready should be minimal." So as soon as Bill reached his keys, he played something.

When they had done that to death, Burrill announced he wanted the band to run through the show once. Bill played the first chords of 'Tina'. Burrill shouted, "Joe, play those intro riffs!" Bill stopped playing.

"What?" Joe asked.

"Never mind," Burrill answered. "I'll take notes, and we can go over them at the end of the show."

Bill started over. Joe didn't play the intro riffs. He started into the beginning fingering, but he couldn't keep up with the song's pace. Roger and Ed joined in.

"Wait! Stop!" Burrill yelled. Everyone stopped.

Burrill approached the stage. "What's the problem, Joe?" he asked. His tone suggested that he thought Joe was having a problem with his guitar.

Joe knelt and got close to Burrill. In a low voice, he said, "David, can I talk to you?" He led Burrill to a corner of the stage. "Um, it's me. I had a migraine, so I took a pill. Several pills, actually. And since then I've had motor control problems in my extremities. My hands, especially."

Burrill narrowed his eyes. "Are you serious? When did this happen?"

Joe answered, "Two weeks ago last Tuesday."

Burrill stepped back. "Really?"

Joe said, "Yeah, you should have seen me before. Oh, wait, you did, when we played at Fooz. Remember?"

Burrill thought. "Wait! I thought you had a problem with your guitar! You didn't! It was you! Pete fired a stagehand for that mistake."

Joe stopped. "Really? Well, now Pete can hire him back."

"He filled the position," Burrill said impatiently.

Joe said quickly, "Okay, well, look, I need you to keep this quiet. I'm getting better. I'll be fine for the tour. It's just this."

"Did you see a doctor about this?"

"I saw a doctor. She said it's a rare but known side-effect, and I should wait it out. The drug company pulled the drug, and is now in a class-action law-suit over it."

Burrill vigorously rubbed his chin. "Well, we'll make the best of it," he said doubtfully. "But all of you are going to have to practice on your own. I don't want to be developing this show on the road."

Joe asked, "Will you be touring with us?"

"At first," Burrill replied. "All right, let's do the best we can!"

They did the best they could.

Bill saw that Joe's guitar-playing on 'Tina' was bad, but it was a hard song to start with. For 'Let's Move', he knew nothing. But he made an honest, but futile, try. Burrill had a tape deck plugged into an amp, and they played with that. Joe's singing wasn't bad, though. Bill could see that he was employing the tips that Bill had taught him. Bill had to admit he felt sorry for Joe. And, despite constant failure, Joe kept trying. He kept his composure and even displayed his sense of humor on occasion.

The day was long and grinding. They ate a heartless dinner, and then threw themselves back into it. Bill had expected they could run through the show twice and call it an early day. Instead, it was a late night, and they had plowed not even halfway through the show.

At eleven o'clock, they climbed into the limo, exhausted. It was the first time they had been alone since firing Stu. "Guys," Joe said, "I am *so* sorry."

Bill was frustrated and angry, and he wanted to yell at Joe. But Joe had been the focus of everyone's ire, and he had tried his hardest.

Ed said, "You should try harder."

Joe looked up with an expression of disbelief.

Ed smiled.

Joe grinned. "Yeah, an' maybe I'll try practicing." He laughed. "You know, I used to have dreams, nightmares, really, that I had to go on stage, and I had no idea what to do. I thought that was weird, because I never had to go on stage for anything. Well, except for my salutatorian address at graduation."

"Hey, what did you tell Burrill that got him so cooperative?" Ed asked.

"I told him it was from a drug reaction, a side-effect." Joe added, "Did you know McCann fired a guy because he thought he'd screwed up my guitar at Fooz?"

"Hmm," said Ed. "Did you know that Stu fired Wendy?"

Joe's mouth dropped open. "You mean she didn't leave on her own?"

"No, Stu fired her."

"Why? Because she gave us those contracts?"

"Well, Stu said her work was sloppy. She made a lot of mistakes."

Joe moved to push up his glasses, then touched his eyebrow scar. He stated, "That is wrong. Angie can we find Wendy and hire her?"

"I suppose," Angie hedged. "What would you have her do?"

"She could be the band secretary. Uh, Administration Manager. Angie, yer doin a full-time job already, an yer just handlin me. She could do the mail." Addressing Bill and Ed, Joe asked, "What are you guys doin with your mail? How do you process it?"

They both looked at Joe blankly. (Roger didn't look like he was listening.)

Joe turned back to Angie. "Are you doing their mail, too?"

Angie said, "I do now, yes."

Joe said, "They can get more done, or done right, and you get a huge amount of your work done. Well, think about it. I'll pay her salary, of course."

Angie made a note in her organizer.

The band discussed the rehearsal. Joe was determined to rehearse as much as possible. He said he wanted to know the show so he could practice it before the tour.

Bill asked, "So what are you going to do about getting an agent?"

Joe sighed. "We have to find someone we can trust, but I'm wondering what the odds of that would be. I should ask around. Or, to be truthful, I should make Angie ask around." Joe looked at Angie. "Hail, Stu's been makin' Angie do half his job all along! If we got a new agent *and* we got Wendy, maybe Angie would have some free time."

"There's no 'if'," Bill admonished. "You *have* to get a new agent."

Joe regarded Bill. "*I* have to get a new agent? Don't you want to be a part of that process?"

Bill was wondering himself why he had said 'you'. Was he disassociating himself from the band that quickly? "Well, yeah, sure," Bill mumbled. Fortunately, the limo reached the hotel, interrupting the conversation.

It was late; they went in the front door. Miguel handed Angie a thick wad of phone messages. Angie flipped through them as they walked to the elevator. Once the elevator got started, Angie said, "Seventeen messages from Michael. It looks like he called every half hour and finally gave up. Stu left only one message. He wants to set up a meeting."

Joe nodded without answering.

Bill, Ed, and even Roger counted their messages from Michael/Stu. Angie noted that Stu's message for Joe was really for her.

The elevator stopped at each floor to let the others off. When they were alone in the elevator, Angie said to Joe, "You used to have a recurring nightmare that you were looking at your exam schedule, and you realized you had forgotten a class you were supposed to take. You had only a short time to learn the material and take the exam. It used to really freak you out, even though you'd never been to college." Angie hesitated. She said, "And now you're pretending to be a college graduate."

Joe said, "Maybe we've been having each other's nightmares. Now I'm *living* mine."

The elevator stopped, and the doors opened to their suite. Joe entered, with Angie behind.

"What are you going to do?" Angie asked. "Do you want to stop?"

Joe turned, smiling. "Heck no, I'm havin too much fun! And, I want to succeed so I can live Joe's life." Sobering, he answered, "Really, there's too much at stake for me to stop. People—a *lot* a people—are dependin on me. For their sake, I can't stop."

Angie mentally stepped back. She had been working around this new personality for weeks now, but, in the back of her mind, she'd assumed he would eventually revert back. Suddenly, she realized he might *never* revert back. She didn't know what to do about that.

She heard Joe say, "Ange?", and she blinked. She answered, "Yes?"

"Um, I'm a little wired still, so I'm gonna practice some. Okay?"

"You know, you can practice too much," Angie pointed out.

Joe smiled. "That's what undisciplined people say to rationalize not practicing." He headed up the stairs.

Angie sighed. That sounded like something Joe would have said. Both personalities had a ruthless determination.

When he was upstairs, he called down, "Good night!" and disappeared into the guitar room.

Later, Angie lay in bed. She could hear Joe's bad guitar-playing through the wall. He always wore headphones, but she could still hear the strings. She wondered: Was *she* a part of Joe's life that this Joe wanted to live?

Chapter 17

Turnabout

The band and Angie were in the limo heading for the second day of rehearsal. The mood was glum. Ed wasn't looking forward to rehearsal. But he remembered that yesterday's predictions had been 100% wrong. He looked over at Joe and saw that Joe was smiling.

Ed asked, "Is something funny, Joe?"

Joe's smile widened. "No, I'm just thinking about how much fun I'm having."

This got everyone's attention. Ed sputtered, "For real? You're having *fun*?"

Joe answered, "If I start feeling down, I take a deep breath and look around. I'm ridin in a limo with X Band. I suck at guitar, but you guys are all being really supportive. And—"

Ed interrupted, "Joe, you're too hard on yourself. I think you're actually past 'suck', and you're well into 'stink'."

Joe mused, "Maybe not *really* supportive."

"Hey, that's progress!" Ed assured.

"Okay, then, what's the level above 'stink'?" Joe inquired.

Ed said, "Oh, uh, 'bad'."

"I haven't even gotten up to 'bad'? That's disheartening."

"Keep practicing," Ed advised.

Angie assured, "Oh, he's practicing!"

"And," Joe said, picking up from Ed's interruption, "I'm married to the most beautiful, supportive, generous, *tolerant* woman in the entire *pantheon* of wives."

Ed saw Angie blush bright red. He laughed. "I won't argue with you there, Joe. Except you forgot 'modest'."

"Point taken." Joe turned to Bill. "How's Cassie doin?"

Bill had talked to her last night, mostly about his solo album. "She's fine," Bill answered.

"Are you going to see her soon?"

"Yes. I'm going up to Colorado in a few days."

Joe turned to Angie. "We can take time off?"

Ed answered, "No, we're almost done here. Then we can do what we want until the tour starts. Except for promotional gigs and video shoots and stuff."

"That's a relief," Joe said. "I was worried that the pace never let up."

Angie said, "Well, you're booked out for another week or two, but..."

Ed finished, "But without an agent, you may find your schedule opening up."

"Hmm, yeah," Joe agreed.

Having reached its destination, the limo stopped. The driver opened the door, and the band climbed out. Walking in, Joe asked Angie, "What do we do when we're finally done?"

Angie answered simply, "Go home."

"Oh. To Connecticut?"

"Yes, to our house in Avon."

Joe seemed to ponder this.

Then came Hurricane Burrill, and rehearsal was underway. Joe was trying hard. Burrill would make suggestions, and Joe would write them in his show outline. Today, Angie sat in the seats and processed mail. Bill was losing patience, as evidenced by the increasing frequency of negative, sarcastic comments. Ed was getting embarrassed at Bill's tone. It no longer sounded as if he were joking. Throughout the rehearsal, Joe actually did seem to get better, though Ed was not ready to concede that he had achieved badness.

Lunch came. The caterers set up tables, and the food was precisely arranged. Ed saw the lunch spread as way overdone, the way he imagined Joe would see it through his new eyes. It was just lunch, after all. He recalled eating pizza with Sam and Patty at the studio. It was just carry-out pizza (and not very good pizza at that), but it was a good meal, memorable in its casual friendliness.

Today, the food was outstanding, but the mood was oppressive. Ed saw Joe and Roger seated together. Several stagehands sat around the two of them. Ed moved to sit by Joe, and the stagehands jumped to make room for him. Joe's plate, Ed saw, was piled with rolls.

"What do you think of the lunch today?" Ed asked Joe.

"Well, I'm only qualified to evaluate the rolls," Joe pointed out. Several stagehands laughed. "But the spread is fabulous, especially considering, y'know, this is just a rehearsal. What do you think?"

Ed smiled and admitted he was thinking pretty much the same thing. They talked about trivial things, like what happened to the extra food.

Soon, lunch was over. They took their positions on the stage and resumed. It wasn't long before Joe messed something up. He said, "I messed that up."

Bill snarked, "Again."

Joe sighed and very carefully set his guitar in its stand. "Mr. Burrill, can you and your people give us a few moments, please?"

The request was spoken in a level, conversational tone. Yet the staff climbed over each other in their hurry to comply.

Joe stood and fixed his eyes on Bill across his keyboards. Bill glared defiantly in return. When the stampede had left the room, Joe spoke quietly, yet his voice could be heard throughout the silent auditorium. "Bill, this isn't like you. Something is really under your skin. Wanna talk about it?"

Bill angrily clenched his jaw.

Joe said, "Is it something to do with Cassie? Bill, we're family here, we can open up about anything." Joe looked at Ed and Roger. "Right?" Ed found himself nodding. Roger was, too.

"Oh, for Christ's sake!" Bill shouted. He disgorged bad language, directed at Joe. He paced around his little space behind the keyboards, hollering and waving his arms. He hurled his headphones at an amp, and they broke into about four pieces. He pointed right in Joe's face and continued his verbal torrent, ending with, "And it's your fucking fault! It's entirely your fucking fault!" Joe didn't move. Bill stopped to catch his breath. If *this* didn't start a fight, nothing would. It didn't. "How can you be destroying the band and at the same time make being in it so goddamned enjoyable? *Fuck* you! *And* it's because of you," he seethed, "that I'm going to pass on a solo career and stay with this band that, by the way, is a fucking train wreck *because* of you."

Joe said, "You were going to quit the band today?"

"Yes," Bill grumped.

Joe said, "But you're not?"

Bill answered, "No. It's a stupid, dumbass decision that goes against all common sense. I don't see how this can possibly work, but I'm all in. As if going down on the Titanic would have had any chance of stopping its, uh, sinking."

"We'll make it work, Bill. You heard Ed. He said I was almost up to 'bad'."

"I didn't say 'almost'," Ed interjected.

Bill sighed. "If I left the band now, I'd regret it for the rest of my life, you little shit. Because there is a chance we can get through this, and if we do, all this grief would be totally worth it." Bill looked around. "Now I've got to call my agent. He's expecting my call before the end of the day."

"Wait," Joe said. "You have an agent? An agent that's not Stu?"

"Yes. For my solo career." Bill suddenly felt shamed. He wanted to say it wasn't what it looked like, but it was. "I wanted to keep my solo identity distinct from the band's." Not to mention hidden from Joe.

"Is your agent any good?"

"He was going to get Bill a solo career; he must be a magician," Ed pointed out.

"Knock it off, Ed," Bill grumbled.

Joe inquired, "Where did you get an agent that's not Stu?"

"Actually, I got him from Shane Skinner," Bill explained. "He's also Shane's agent."

Ed asked, "You'd trust your solo career with the agent that masterminded Shane's meteoric trajectory from stardom to obscurity?"

Bill turned to Ed. "Do you know when it's time for you to be quiet? When you're talking."

Ed grinned. "You love us, Bill! You decided to stay!"

Bill retorted. "I'm starting to change my mind."

"Do you think your agent would want to represent us?" Joe asked.

Bill rubbed his bald head. From his agent's off-hand comments about Joe, it seemed as though he wouldn't care to. But now... "I don't know," Bill finally answered. "I can ask."

Just after Bill left the room, Burrill poked his head through the door and asked, "Should we resume?"

Joe smiled. "Yeah, it's safe. Come on in."

The tension released, though not completely. Burrill and his staff clearly wanted to know what the drama was about, but no one would ask. Burrill did feel bold enough to ask, "So, it's good between you and Bill?"

Joe replied, "Yeah, it always was." He smiled. "When we're bein honest with each other, it gets loud."

Bill eventually returned. "Well, he wants to meet with us. I at least talked him into that."

"I would have thought he'd jump at the chance, actually," Joe said. "Seems like guaranteed big money."

Bill sort of shrugged. "Sometimes the big money still isn't worth it. But I convinced Richard, that's my agent, Richard Sheriden." Ed started to say something, but Bill interrupted, "He goes by *Richard*, Ed! Anyway, I talked him into meeting with us tomorrow night."

In the theatre seats, Angie consulted her book. "All right," Joe said. Ed thought if anyone could win over the agent, it would be Joe. They got back to work. Bill felt strangely at peace. He had committed to a course of action. His internal conflict, of which he hadn't been aware, was resolved.

Like the day before, progress was stop-and-start. The rehearsal session went late, but they had gotten to the end of the show. Ed, in particular, was relieved that he wasn't asked to frame a drum solo. When they returned to their hotel, it was late enough that the band could enter through the lobby. Angie picked up the messages from Miguel.

In the elevator, Ed asked, "Joe, if you're not too tired, could I talk to you tonight?"

Angie wondered what was up. Ed seemed particularly anxious.

"Sure, Ed, c'mon up," Joe replied

Roger and Bill got off on their floors. The elevator rose to the top, and the door opened to the penthouse suite.

"Do you want me to leave?" Angie asked.

"It's not really a big deal," Ed said. "You can even join us if you like."

The trio sat in the lounge. Ed looked at Joe and asked bluntly, "Why did you push for me to have a drum solo?"

Joe answered, "I was under the impression that you wanted one. Bill told me that."

Ed sighed. He asked, "But what if I screw it up?"

Joe chuckled and said, "Ed, I think I'm gonna win on the number of screw-ups."

"Um, okay, I'll concede that. You see, Joe, the old Joe, wouldn't let me have one, because he knew I wasn't ready. You don't know that."

"No, I know that you *are* ready."

Ed scoffed, "You *couldn't* know that."

"Ed, I've been listening to recordings of you for years." Joe leaned forward. "Lemme tell you something." Angie noticed that Ed was so nervous, he was almost shaking, and Joe looked serene. Joe said, "You know Nick Mason, right? Pink Floyd's drummer?"

"I don't know him personally," Ed admitted. "But I know who he is."

Joe said, "His drumming has an erratic style that I like. Reminds me of Bill Bruford, only Bill is tight and crisp, and Nick is not. I was under the impression that Nick Mason is really not that good, but his style was perfect for Pink Floyd. But between 'Animals' and 'The Wall', someone taught Nick how to play the drums, and now he sounds like 99% of everybody else."

"Pink Floyd broke up a couple of years ago," Ed pointed out. He stopped. "Wait. What are you saying?"

Joe shifted position on the loveseat. He said, "Suppose Phil Collins had been Pink Floyd's drummer. Pink Floyd would not have had the experimental sound that they had. Pink Floyd wouldn't a been as good. Nick Mason was perfect for Pink Floyd. When I listen to X Band, I listen for you. You're an integral part of X Band's music. You're not simply keeping the beat for the band."

"I've been told that," Ed told Joe.

"Right," Joe said. "You are playing your instrument with the band. You are contributing to the music." Joe sighed. "Ed, look. Three weeks ago, I was just a fan, like millions of other people. But if I had the incredible opportunity to give Ed Brettington my opinion, and I thought there was any chance he would listen to it? I would tell him not to change a thing. You want to be better? I say fine, but be better in the way that you are. Be a better you, don't be more like everyone else. That's not better."

Ed studied Joe. He finally said, "Joe, I will think about what you told me. I really will."

Joe reached for his shirt pocket. Realizing that he didn't have one, he moved to push up his glasses, then conspicuously put his hands in his lap.

Ed asked, "How do you know so much about drummers?"

Joe replied, "I listen to a lot of rock and roll, and I pay attention to it."

Ed nodded. Joe suddenly seemed to know a lot. Ed asked, "I meant to ask you: When we were talking about the new contract with Theremin, how did you know about the Taylor Wines license thing? Was that BS? Did you make that up?"

"No, that's a real case," Joe said. "Look it up."

"Look it up where? The encyclopedia? Where do you look up stuff like *that*?"

"I dunno," Joe admitted. "I learned about it in a business law course. At Harvard."

"You know, I'm reasonably sure Joe never went to Harvard," Ed mentioned.

Joe nodded. "I seem to know things that Joe didn't know. That would be fair, since Joe obviously knows things that I don't know. Like how to play guitar."

"How is that possible?" Ed asked.

"Angie's theory," Joe said, gesturing to Angie, "is that Joe was exposed to the information and forgot it. For example, Joe took swimming lessons, but never learned to swim. Yet I can swim. Apparently, I processed the training into a usable skill."

"No excrement?"

Joe shrugged. "It's a theory."

"What else do you know that you didn't used to know?" Ed inquired.

"I'm not sure," Joe said. "I can fix cars. Did Joe ever work on his car?"

"Never," Angie said.

"Okay, well maybe I don't really know how to fix cars," Joe said. "Maybe I just think I can fix cars. And there's all the bogus personal stuff that has no practical value."

"Personal stuff?" Ed asked. "Like from an imaginary background? How thorough could that be?"

"You'd be surprised," Joe told him. "My address, the layout of Dad's garage, where the tools are, my sisters' birthdays, my teachers from the first grade on, the campuses of UVA and Harvard, my classes, and more. The more I remember back, it seems like there's more underneath that to remember. There's memories all the way down." Joe sighed. He said, "I try not to think about it too much, though. I'm lovin it here, doin this, and all y'all, but sometimes I really do miss my family. My pretend family," Joe added sadly.

Ed saw the genuine sadness. Ed asked, "What are they like?"

Joe made a noise. "Hail, you don't wanna hear all that. Besides, what difference does it make?"

Angie asked quietly, "Do you have a girl?"

"Not really," Joe answered frankly. "There's a girl I date, Shelly, but it's not, I dunno, permanent. I had just graduated, so I was movin out. Shelly still has two years left, so she's not gonna follow me or anything."

Angie asked, "What did you have planned for after graduation? At Dr. Vrakas' office, you said you were all set for the rest of your life."

Joe visibly shuddered at the phrase. He answered, "No, I didn't say that; my roommate did. I got in the GE Management Training Program. I don't start until August, so I was gonna go spend the time at home."

Ed inquired, "And where is home?"

"2112 on route 80, Davenport, Virginia," Joe replied as if he had said it a thousand times. "Sort of across from the post office."

Ed commented, "Your memories sure are thorough."

"Yeah," Joe answered absently. To Angie, he said, "What's on the agenda for tomorrow?"

"Tomorrow, you're doing call letters for Castleview Communication Network." She explained: "Castleview is a network of 145 radio stations. So you will be doing the station identifications for them."

"Oh, yeah, I've heard that done," Joe said. "I always wondered how they did that."

Angie smiled. "Tomorrow, you'll find out."

"I'm sleeping late tomorrow," Ed said. "I'd better get started on that." He stood, towering over them. "Thanks for what you said about drummers, Joe. You gave me something to think about. For a snotty college guy, you're all right."

Joe replied, "Thanks, I think."

At the elevator, Ed hesitated. He wanted to tell Joe that he liked him this way, but he didn't want to be disloyal to Joe, and there was also this pesky guitar thing, upon which his career depended. Finally, he said, "Good night, Joe. Angie."

Angie went to bed. As was becoming usual, Joe stayed up to practice until he fell asleep in the practice room. In the morning, they dressed and ate breakfast in an increasingly refined routine. They elevatored down to the parking garage. Since it was just the two of them, they took the car. Angie drove. Joe sat quietly and looked out the window. They rode in silence. Angie felt herself growing less self-conscious about her driving, since Joe hadn't even seemed to notice it at all. He watched the desolate landscape speed by. Compared to Connecticut, southern California was a wasteland. And everyone was poor. As seen from the road, anyway.

Joe remarked, "There sure are a lot of old cars on the road here."

Angie hadn't noticed before, but since Joe mentioned it, she did see a lot of older cars.

Joe said, "I guess the weather doesn't age them as fast here as it does in New England."

"I suppose so," Angie agreed. "Plus, we put down sand and salt when it snows."

A few minutes later, Joe said, "I really appreciate your driving today. You could be doing a lot of other things besides this, and those maybe are even more fun than this."

"Um, you're welcome," Angie said. What exactly did he mean by that?

"I mean, besides the driving, thanks for just coming along and bein with me."

Angie hadn't realized she'd had a choice. Old Joe would have expected her to be with him. If she'd thought about it, she would have realized Joe, New Joe, didn't demand that she attend him; but he preferred her company. That's what he seemed to be saying. Joe was looking at her, expecting a reply. How would Joe answer? Angie smiled. "I want to keep you out of trouble. You're still learning how to be a celebrity rock star."

Joe nodded and looked back out the window. He looked back with a grin. "But I'm getting better, right?"

Joe was never going to get his hair to look the way it had, but he didn't burn it anymore, and he could keep it from standing out. And even though he was wearing his own clothes, they didn't look like they fit quite right. Even when accounting for the few extra pounds he'd gained. "Better?" Angie asked. "Yes. You no longer suck. You're well into the Stink range, almost up to Bad." She smiled.

Joe laughed out loud. He said with satisfaction, "That's progress."

Angie pulled into a freshly-paved parking lot. A new sign proclaimed, "Castleview Communication Network World Headquarters". The building was surprisingly small, but the parking lot was nearly full. Angie pulled into a Visitor space near the front door. The lobby was expansive and included a rather large fountain. Before they got far, a dark woman in her twenties intercepted them. "Welcome to Castleview," she announced, shaking Joe's hand. She wore a business suit and skirt that, Angie noted, fit snugly around the hips. She shook Angie's hand, "Welcome," she said.

Joe said, "Oh, this is Angela Ecks, my beautiful and charming wife. And you are?"

"Betsy Abetes. It's nice to meet you, Mr. Ecks."

To Angie, she seemed a little deflated that Joe had brought along his wife.

"Thank you," Joe replied. "It's nice to meet you, too."

"Uh, right," Betsy Abetes said. "I'm your recording specialist today."

Joe said, "Did you make somebody mad? Are you being punished?"

Betsy looked confused at first, but then she laughed a fake laugh and replied, "No, it's my job." She turned and walked. Joe and Angie followed.

Angie told Joe, "You're getting more like Ed all the time."

Joe smiled. "Really? That'd be okay; I really like him. Do you think I'll start getting taller?"

Angie smiled up at him. "Actually, you have been already. You used to be only 5'11"."

Joe exploded laughter, then stifled it, though he still drew the attention of everyone else in the lobby. They passed through a door into a hallway. Joe continued to snicker. Eventually, Betsy led them to a room divided by a Plexiglas wall. Betsy took Joe in the opposite side, which could snugly accommodate two people. Angie noted that Betsy tended to crowd Joe, and Joe tried to make room for her so that after thirty seconds, Joe was flattened against a wall. Betsy showed Joe where to sit. His only control was a button that would pause the recording if he had to sneeze or something. Betsy returned to her side, where she sat before a bigger panel with more buttons.

There was no extra chair that Angie could use. "Is there an extra chair?" she asked.

"Yes, you can take one from one of the other rooms," Betsy said as she adjusted her panel.

Angie went and got a chair from a conference room. When she returned, she saw that Betsy had removed her suit. Her tailored blouse fit as snugly as the skirt. Strumpet.

Joe held up a piece of paper. "Can I start?"

Betsy pushed a button. "Don't rattle the paper. The mic will pick up the noise."

Joe put it down and deliberately flattened it. And stared at Betsy. "Can I start?"

Angie put her chair against the wall where she could see both Betsy and Joe.

"Okay, yes, you may start now," Betsy told Joe.

Joe took a breath and said, "I'm Joe Ecks, and you're listening to KDKM, Kay-Dee 93.1 FM." He looked at Betsy.

Betsy smiled and gave him the thumbs-up.

Joe read off the next four lines. When he read the next one ("I'm Joe Ecks, and you're listening to KBRO, Kay-Bro 101."), he added, "No other station can make that claim."

Angie looked up. Betsy pushed the button. "Mr. Ecks, please just read the line."

"Okay," Joe said agreeably. He read it correctly. Next one: "I'm Joe Ecks, and you're listening to KLNT." Next: "I'm Joe Ecks, and you're listening to KNTC, the only station that uses these particular letters in this exact order." Joe held up his hand and read it correctly.

Betsy looked over at Angie and sighed.

Angie smiled.

Betsy frowned and glared back at Joe. She pushed the button. "All right, Mr. Ecks, just say each one correctly. We have to be done by one o'clock, because that's when someone else gets the booth."

Joe checked his watch, saw that he didn't have one, and located the wall clock. He said, "I'm KTTG, and you're listening to Station Joe Ecks." He paused and said, "I'm Joe Ecks, and you're listening to Station KTTG-FM, FM 103." He read off several more perfectly, and then he said, "You're listening to KCUT, Kay-cut 99, the home of rock and roll, and I'm Joe Ecks." Then he read it correctly.

Betsy turned to Angie and asked, "Why is he doing this?"

Joe no longer surprised Angie with any crazy thing he did anymore. So Angie answered, honestly, "I don't know. Why don't you ask him?" Angie hoped she would, because she wanted to hear his answer. Not that she would necessarily believe it.

But Betsy didn't ask. She looked at the clock. It was 11:14.

Joe continued with a pattern of reading several correctly and then one creatively. Angie had to admit that his impromptu changes amused her. They did not, she observed, amuse Betsy. She sat and tagged each correct line. Joe also muffed lines for unintentional reasons, and several times Betsy had him repeat lines that Angie thought had been done well.

"I'm Joe Ecks, and you're listening to Station WPLR, instead of doing your homework, which you really should be doing."

Angie snickered. Betsy didn't move. Joe read it correctly. Betsy tagged it.

Joe read the last one at 12:51.

Betsy pushed the button. "All right, Mr. Ecks, we're done." She released the button and added, "That took a lot longer than it needed to."

Joe came out of the booth. He exclaimed, "Whew! Well, thank you so much for your patience, Betsy."

Betsy replied, "Yes. You're welcome."

She showed Joe (and Angie, by default) to the door with somewhat less admiration than she had in the morning.

It was hot and dry out. Angie got behind the wheel and backed out of the space. Joe looked out the window. He didn't look especially pleased with himself. Finally, Angie asked Joe why he did it.

Joe answered, "Otherwise, it would have been way too boring. Swate Jasus! Betsy wasn't amused, though. She was annoyed."

Angie thought it unusual for Joe to do something consciously that he knew would bother someone. Except his confrontation with Stu, of course. Angie hoped he would be better with Richard Sheridan.

Joe asked, "So is that it for the day?"

"Until our meeting with Bill's agent after dinner."

Joe nodded. He said, "It sure was nice today to not have some critical challenge to meet. Or survive. This was something I could do. I didn't have too much southern accent, did I? I wasn't paying attention all the time."

Angie looked over briefly. "It wasn't really obvious. But I'm getting used to it, so I might not have noticed. I wasn't listening for it."

Joe nodded. They rode the rest of the way back to the hotel in silence. Angie fell into a thoughtful mood, but her thoughts seemed to cycle without purpose.

For the afternoon, Angie would have gone through the mail, but it was still going to Stu's office. Stu and Michael were calling with less frequency now, but their messages showed an increase in desperation and hopelessness. Angie decided to find Wendy and, if possible, hire her. But she didn't know Wendy's home number. She wasn't even sure about Wendy's last name or where she lived. She wondered if Sam knew. Angie recalled that Wendy called Sam at the studio often to arrange times.

Angie didn't have Sam's number, either, but she knew his last name and the town in which he lived. It was the middle of the day, but she called, hoping that Sam had an answering machine. To her surprise, Sam himself picked up the phone. "Hello?"

"Um, Sam? Is this Sam?" Angie asked.

The line was silent for two long seconds. Then Sam asked, "Angie?"

"Yes, excuse me, Sam, I didn't expect you to pick up," Angie explained, regaining her composure. "I guess your hours aren't nine-to-five."

"Not anymore," Sam grumbled. "The studio fired me last Thursday."

"Fired? You were fired?" Angie fairly stammered. "May I ask why?"

"'Unauthorized use of company equipment,'" quoted Sam. "Remember your emergency recording session? It was that. Patty was fired, too."

"Sam, that's terrible!" Angie exclaimed. "You were fired for helping X Band? Really?"

Sam sighed. "No, they said it was because I was paid under the table. Totally against company rules." To Angie, Sam didn't seem to believe what they had said. Sam asked, "So what can I do for you, Angie? I hope you don't need help mixing another song."

"No," Angie answered. "Do you remember Wendy from Stu's office? I'm trying to reach her."

"She's not at Stu's office?"

"No, she's, uh, she's not there anymore," Angie said, hesitant to explain that Wendy, too, had been fired for helping X Band.

"Why don't you call Stu?" Sam asked.

Angie explained, "X Band fired Stu."

"Oh."

"I don't think he would want to help us right now."

"I doubt it," Sam agreed. "Why do you want to contact her?"

Angie plunged forward. "Joe thinks Wendy was fired because she helped the band, him, really, expose some shady business things that Stu was doing. Joe feels bad about her being fired, so he wants to hire her himself."

"Oh," Sam said levelly. He allowed, "That's awfully stand-up of Joe."

"It is," Angie agreed. She hesitated, then said, "Sam, do you think you would want to work for X Band?"

Sam chuckled drily. "As what?"

"I don't know," Angie admitted. "But we're going on tour soon, and we don't have anyone to run the board."

The phone was silent for so long, Angie thought Sam had hung up on her. Sam said finally, "I'd do that. If you'd asked me that two weeks ago, I'd've laughed in your face. Or worse! But now? Yeah, I'd do that. What about Patty?"

"Her, too," Angie said. "But don't say anything to her; I want to make sure it's okay with Joe, first. But I think it will be."

Sam told Angie everything he knew about Wendy, and they hung up. Joe was upstairs practicing. Angie went to see him. When she got to the room, she saw Joe standing. He wore his guitar and was running through a succession of chords without playing them. He looked up.

"These are the chords for 'Tina'," he explained. He ran through them quickly and only fouled up one. He shrugged. "I'll get there. What's up?"

"I was looking for Wendy, and I talked to Sam," Angie began.

"How's he doin?" Joe asked.

"Well, not so good. After he and Patty helped us record 'Twinkle Twinkle', the studio fired them."

Joe blinked. He said, "See if they wanna work fer us. I think Burrill needs someone to run the board when we're on tour."

Angie was proud to have anticipated this new Joe's direction. Hiding her smile, somewhat, she replied, "Sam will work for us. I don't know about Patty yet."

Joe's eyebrows went up. "You already asked Sam?"

"Yes," Angie answered, starting to glow. "I thought that's what you would want."

"Good girl!" Joe beamed.

Angie left, thoroughly satisfied with herself. She spent the afternoon on the phone, connecting Sam and Patty with Burrill. Joe spoke to Burrill and emphatically endorsed Sam and Patty.

Angie was late calling for dinner, and dinner was late besides. They were meeting Richard in one of the hotel conference rooms downstairs. On the way down, Joe commented that he was nervous; he wanted to make a good first impression on the agent.

Angie walked in first, and immediately she could sense something wrong. Everyone was standing and gaping at her with a confused horror. Then Joe came in behind her. Joe's eyes swept the room. He regarded one man, who stood nearby.

Joe uttered, "Skinner? Shane Skinner! Wow, it's great to mee—" Hand extended, Joe stepped toward Shane. Shane put both hands up in a defensive posture and backed away. "What—" Joe's eyes found the only other individual in the room with whom he wasn't familiar. "And you must be Richard Sheridan."

Richard was slender and about Joe's height, and he looked surprisingly old to be representing rock 'n' roll bands. Bald on top, the remainder of his greying hair was pulled back into a ponytail. His green eyes darted to Bill.

"My mistake," Bill admitted.

A long silence followed.

Joe's eyes narrowed, and he asked Bill, "Shane's playing guitar with us now?"

"Uh," Bill stammered. "Well, yes, us. Um, not you."

"What?"

Finally, Richard said, "Joe."

Joe said, "Oh, not me, though. I'm not one of 'us' anymore."

"Yeah, that's how it goes," Shane sneered. "You kicked me out, and now suddenly I'm in, and you're out. How fast the tide turns!"

"Indeed," Joe agreed, coming up to speed. He stepped over to Roger and shook his hand. "Thanks, Roger, for all your help. I wish I had been a better student."

Blankly, Roger said, "So long, Mike."

Joe turned and shook Bill's hand. "Goodbye, Bill. No hard feelings."

Bill's brain had completely lost the ability to form words.

Joe shook Ed's hand and said, "I think I'll miss you most of all, Scarecrow."

Ed said, "I doubt it, actually, since you're married to my sister."

"Yer right," Joe agreed, and he shrugged and added, "For now. Ya never know, she might *also* decide to replace me."

Joe swept out of the room.

Angie stayed behind. Glaring at them all, she seethed, "I cannot imagine anything more loathsome you could have done. You are all despicable shitheads." She fled to catch up with Joe. Behind her, she heard:

Shane: "Such language!"

Roger: "Shut the fuck up."

Angie had to practically run, because Joe was taking full advantage of his long stride. She got in the elevator before the door closed. Joe stared straight ahead. Tears ran down his face. He grimaced in a failed attempt to mask his quivering chin.

Chapter 18

Falling Home

The door opened to their suite before either of them had said anything.

Angie asked, "What are you going to do, Joe?"

Tears streaked Joe's red, puffy face. He said, waveringly, "Watch TV. And drink a lot of beer. Can you call down and have them send up a case of, uh, well, we have money, I can celebrate big-time. Have 'em send up a case of Moosehead."

"Moosehead?" Angie repeated. "*Beer*?" She'd never heard of Moosehead, but it didn't sound especially expensive. She picked up the phone.

"Meanwhile, I hafta goto the bathroom," Joe said over his shoulder.

Room Service was just answering the phone, but Angie slammed it down and ran up the stairs, pushing past Joe. She hurried into the bathroom. Joe came to the door just as Angie was leaving, carrying a lot of things wrapped in a towel.

"What've ya got there?" Joe asked, confused.

"Your pills and straight razor," Angie told him bluntly. "And if I hear the tub running, I'll kick this fucking door down myself." Angie glared up at him defiantly.

Horrified, Joe blurted, "Swate Jasus, I wasn't gonna do anything like that!"

Angie was unmoved.

Joe explained, "I just wanted some privacy to, you know, collect myself."

Angie wanted to tell him he didn't need privacy. That she would help him through his despair. That she wanted Joe to need her at his darkest moment. She dropped her towel of things and grasped Joe in a hug. Joe stiffened, then wrapped tightly around her. She felt his body shudder with quiet weeping. They stood that way together, not moving. At last, they released each other. Joe blotted his face with his sleeve.

"Use the bathroom, if you want to," Angie said. "I'll order the beer."

Joe went in. Almost instantly, she heard sobbing. She listened as it carried on, neither abating nor escalating. And she heard nothing else to indicate danger. Quietly, she turned to order the beer.

And then she sat at the dining room table from where she could hear Joe and get to the door. The beer arrived. Angie had the deliverer set the case on the kitchen counter. It was warm. She put three bottles in the freezer and the rest in the refrigerator. She returned to her seat in the dining room.

Usually, when she had a spare moment, she had to call someone. But there was no one to call, no appointments to plan, nothing. She felt unreal, as if none of this were really happening. She wondered what she and Joe would do now; Joe had invested every effort toward developing himself for the band, and developing the band, too, for that matter. "There is no Plan B!" Joe would declare. "Sometimes you just have to make Plan A work."

The phone rang, startling Angie. She picked it up. "Hello?"

"Angie, it's Ed."

"What do you want?" she snapped.

"Do you need help with Joe?"

It wasn't a stupid question. In the past, Joe had sometimes been unmanageable by Angie alone. "No. Anything else?"

"Angie—" Ed began.

"What were you thinking, Ed? You'd go behind Joe's back and do something like this to him? He's your *friend*! He trusted *all* of you!"

"I know," Ed said in a low voice. "Richard called back Bill—"

"At least when Stu got fired, he got a chance to defend himself, and you wouldn't even give Joe that consideration!"

Weakly, Ed said, "I want to explain—"

"This is *not* a good time!" Angie declared. "Try again tomorrow! Or next week!" She slammed down the phone. And considered hurling it against the wall. She saw Joe in the doorway.

He looked a lot better, more composed. He asked, "Was that your mother?"

"No, I wouldn't talk like..." Angie stopped. "You're making a *joke*?"

"Yeah," Joe admitted, "A bad one, I guess. Was that Ed?"

"Yes. He wanted to explain about what happened." Angie sighed and asked, "Joe what *did* happen? I've seen you work a room until you could get everyone to do anything you wanted. But today you gave up. You didn't even try. Why not?"

Joe answered, "Do you know why they met and planned this behind my back? Because they were afraid that's exactly what I would do: work the room. But keeping me in the band wouldn't have been in their best interest, and they knew that. Bringing back Shane Skinner keeps the band together, and it keeps their public identity intact."

Angie stared at Joe, sifting the meaning of what he'd said.

Joe added, "It's a good idea, actually. For the band, though, not for me personally. Is the beer here?"

"Yes. It's in the refrigerator. I put a few in the freezer, so drink those first."

Joe grinned and disappeared. Angie met him in the lounge. Joe came in holding a full beer bottle.

Angie quipped, "Aren't you going to drink your beer?"

"Yeah," Joe answered proudly. "This is my second." He sat in the loveseat.

"I left you a glass on the counter."

"I saw that. Thank you." Joe drank from his bottle, just like Ed would have. Men.

Angie sat on the sofa. She asked, "Are you okay?"

Joe nodded. "I felt really sorry for myself, and I had a good cry. Now it's time to move on."

"Move on to what?" Angie inquired.

"I don't know," Joe said, as if he had been asked tomorrow's weather. "Tonight is not the night to think about the future that can be, but rather to mourn the future that is not to be." Joe drank from his beer and held it up to Angie. "Do you want one?"

"Maybe just one," Angie surprised herself by saying. "I'll get it."

"No, I'll get it," Joe said, springing out of his seat. "I need another one anyway." Shortly, he returned and handed Angie hers (in a glass).

Angie set it down and picked up the remote. "Is there something in particular you want to watch?"

Joe grinned. "When I would come home from college between semesters, I'd watch TV. All semester, I'd be workin like crazy, and TV was such a luxury; such a flagrant squandering of time. So I don't care."

Angie flipped through the channels, seeing each one for about four seconds.

"Wait, stop!" Joe cried. "Back up!"

Angie backed up to a black-and-white movie on the Old Movie Channel. "This?"

"I like this movie. 'Here Comes Mr. Jordon.'" Joe finished his beer.

Angie watched it for a minute while Joe got another beer. Joe could determine the movie from watching it for four seconds? He sat in the loveseat. He seemed so composed. "How are you doing?" Angie inquired.

Joe sagged. "I'm doing okay." He stared into space for a moment. "D'ya know what I'll especially miss? Those guys. I'll see Ed, I guess, on holidays and weddings and stuff. But I'll never see Roger. After all those lessons, I still don't know hardly nothin about him. He's a mystery. Bill could be a putz, but he was okay. He's like a teacher when his kids are clownin around. He wants to laugh, but he feels like he can't. But I'm gonna miss playin with them. Yeah, I know I never did, not really, but I could see how it could be. How cool is it to be a member of such a team, with everyone so in synch that they can play music?

"Roger used to talk about language. You can learn the words and the grammar, but you're not really speaking it; you're translating. And then you get it. I could sense it getting close, feelin how it might be in short bursts. And then to combine that with others, workin in harmony. Well, yeah, literally. *That's* what I'm gonna miss, even though I never had it. Only now I know I never will." Joe sat glumly. He sighed.

Angie felt terrible for Joe. She wanted to give him something, a consolation. "You could still learn guitar," she offered. "You won't have trouble getting a band together, when you're ready."

"Another band, like a *different* band? With different people?" Joe thought on this as he finished his beer. "That's an idea. We'd never get to where X Band is, but we could probably find places to play. Even if we didn't, we'd still be a band, playing together." He stood. "I'll give it some thought. Thank you." Joe headed back into the kitchen.

Angie was pleased. She made Joe feel better, and she gave him something to work toward.

Joe returned with a beer and sat in the loveseat. She squeezed her little self between Joe and the arm of the seat. Joe stiffened, and he scooched away a fraction, but he didn't flee. She snuggled up against him. The action felt entirely unfamiliar, but good. Joe's rigidity didn't decrease. Tentatively, he put his arm around her. Angie snuggled into a better fit. This is what she sought: Closeness, contact. Slowly, Joe relaxed. Angie relaxed. Joe had said he wanted to go home. She was home at this moment.

Content, she watched the movie, wondering what was happening. She didn't just enjoy snuggling with Joe, she reveled in it. She caught him sucking the fumes out of his empty beer bottle. "I'll get you another," she offered, rising.

Joe said, "Don't get up. If yer not gonna have yerze, I'll have it before it gets warm." He leaned forward and picked up the glass.

Angie resettled in his arms. She didn't normally drink beer. From Joe's attitude, she thought that Moosehead might be a good beer, but it really wasn't. Angie's typical drink was white wine, or a vodka Collins. She inhaled Joe's scent, which had changed since his memory loss, but it was still his.

Joe set down the empty glass and belched silently. To Angie, he felt very relaxed. Very snuggly.

Joe shifted.

"I hafta go to the bathroom," he confessed.

"Oh, okay," Angie said, disengaging herself from him.

Joe stood, wobbly, and, with deliberation, walked into the kitchen. Angie's attention returned to the movie. She expected him back soon, but when soon had passed, she sat up, suddenly alert. She scanned the room. She hurried into the kitchen. And the dining room. The downstairs bathroom door was open. Angie bolted upstairs to check the master bathroom. But in their room, she saw Joe sprawled across their bed, sound asleep. (She checked his breathing to make sure he was just sleeping.)

Angie drifted back downstairs. An open beer was in the kitchen. She carried it into the lounge and sat in front of the TV, still on. She decided that she needed a little "beer and TV time", too. Her mind passed over the events of the day. Then, without meaning to, she thought ahead to tomorrow. But then Angie came up short. There would be no meeting to plan the upcoming video shoot for 'Contents', at least not for Joe. Later in the week, he wouldn't be on the Hank & Pete morning show. Angie wondered if the press would pester them. Probably. Joe would need an agent.

Angie thought about Joe not working the room. 'It wouldn't have been in their best interest,' he had said. He had forfeited a pitch to stay in the band for the benefit of the band. The band that had just betrayed him. Had Joe *ever* urged anyone to do anything that would hurt them? Angie couldn't think of one. In fact, when Joe found out Wendy had been fired, he took responsibility. The same with Sam and Patty. Even his drive to succeed with the band was, in part, fueled by his duty to the people who depended on him.

Angie thought about Ed. She and Ed were very close, even for siblings. Ed going behind Joe's back was a betrayal to both she and Joe. She was going to have to confront him, eventually. For Bill and Roger, she would have to be content with hating them forever.

Angie was looking forward to going home. She'd been out here for months, and it had been a non-stop sprint. Especially lately. And maybe without the band's success on his shoulders, Joe could relax. Angie glanced back up in the direction of their bedroom. Well, maybe not get *this* relaxed.

The next morning, Angie woke surprisingly rested. Joe was no longer sprawled on the bed. He had still been in the same position when Angie went to bed, and she'd expected to see him in the same position when she woke. She wondered where he was; it was silent in the guitar room. Angie scooched on her shorts and went looking. She found him on the balcony, leaning on the railing, looking out over the city. Angie joined him at the rail.

"Oh, hi," Joe greeted.

Angie said, "Hi. How are you feeling?"

"I have a headache," Joe admitted.

"I thought you might." Angie held out a pill bottle. "These will help."

Joe dry-swallowed two of the pills. "Thank you," he said.

They looked out over the desert landscape.

"It's desolate," Joe commented.

Angie agreed and thought 'desolate' was a word not often used in conversation. She asked, "Have you thought about what you're going to do?"

"More or less. I gotta make money, so maybe I can do endorsements or get on Hollywood Squares or something. But I can't play guitar, so actually being a musician is out. I need an agent, and Los Angeles is the best place to get one." He sighed. "I'm not up to it, though. I need a break. Let's go to Connecticut and relax for a while. Maybe the agents will come to me, if they're interested."

Angie had no doubt that agents would come to Joe. Side-by-side, they looked out over the desolate landscape.

Joe said, "If I can't capitalize on my fame, maybe I can open a guitar store, 'Joe's Guitars'."

Angie said, "Seriously? There's already a Joe's Guitars in Wallingford!"

"Where you grew up?" Joe asked. "How far away from there do you live now?"

"Well, Avon's far enough from Wallingford, I guess," Angie admitted. "If you wanted to have your store nearby. That's what I assumed."

"Yeah, me, too. Or I can open a garage. I know how to fix cars. And I think what I learned in business school will really help."

"You don't know how to fix cars, and you never went to business school," Angie reminded Joe.

Joe remained silent. He looked at Angie. He said, "It's not what you signed up for. I'm not a rock star anymore. I'd be a store owner." Joe tried to hide a wince. "Do you think you could live with that life?"

Angie had considered this as well. Joe had been broke when they married, and at that time, she didn't really think he would make a living as a musician. So, yes. "Your career would be different, but you'd still be the Joe I married." Instantly, she regretted saying that.

Joe's face fell. He looked out at the terrain and sniffed. He didn't move for a long time. Finally, he said, "Well, we ought to pack or eat breakfast or something." Turning to go indoors, he avoided her eyes.

They spent the day lazily packing. A few times, Angie picked up messages at the desk, but she didn't comment on their content to Joe. Ed had called once, as had Bill. Stu left the usual number of messages. Angie called Douglas and informed him of their return.

When she hung up, Joe asked, "What is Douglas like? Is he a caretaker?"

"Yes," Angie answered, "and butler and chauffeur, and he pays the bills. He's an estate manager."

Joe asked, "And maid and valet?"

"We have a maid service," Angie said. She withheld the comment that *she* had been Joe's valet. She added, "We also have a landscaping service."

"What do you do all day?" Joe inquired, not being in the least sarcastic.

"Me?" Angie asked.

"You plural, I mean. You and Joe."

Angie smiled. "Not chores." Realizing that that didn't answer the question, Angie said, "I don't know. We have people over for business or friends over to be social. You write music. Or we go to things. Events, you know, fund-raisers and so on."

Joe was still looking at her, baffled.

Embarrassed, Angie laughed. "We always have something to do. We're busy."

Joe nodded slowly. He asked, "Is Joe a philanthropist? What does he donate to?"

"No, not a philanthropist," Angie replied. "Um, you donate to the American Heart Association, I know."

"That makes sense," Joe commented, "since the AHA is focused on education and prevention. Right? Because if his father had known he was having a heart attack, his death might have been prevented."

Angie agreed that it made sense. She felt strangely uncomfortable that Joe was figuring stuff out about himself that even she hadn't noticed. But then... "Joe, do you think your memory is returning?"

"No," Joe answered, holding up a shiny grey shirt. "Joe really wears this?"

Angie grinned wryly. "Not so much anymore." She heard Joe mumble, "Good," as he tossed it in his suitcase.

After a few minutes of ruminating, Joe asked, "What about cooking? Who cooks?"

"Cheryl does," Angie answered. "You met Cheryl through the band. She was your vocal coach for a long time, and that's how you met Douglas, because they're married. Cheryl just started cooking for everyone on her own."

Joe looked up. "Do they live in the house?"

Angie smiled. "No, they live in the back, in the guest house. Ed calls it the 'little house', and our house is the 'big house'."

Joe smiled and repeated, "'The big house.' Geez, Angie, this hotel suite is bigger than anyplace I've lived. The big house is bigger than the guest house? What's it like?"

Angie gave a cute, little-girl shrug. "You'll see." She was looking forward to seeing Joe's first impression of the house. She wondered why Joe was eager to go home, when he didn't remember it at all. Maybe, surrounded by everything familiar, Joe's memory would return, and this thought gave her hope. She'd been thinking Joe's new personality would be around for a while. Stress hadn't scared it out of him; even the loss of the band hadn't revived the old Joe. Maybe the old Joe would return to familiarity.

They finished packing and put the suitcases together in a pack near the foyer. Joe came down the stairs with two guitar cases.

"Did you put away Good Guitar?" Angie asked. She knew Joe wouldn't touch it, it being the personal domain of the old Joe personality. It presented a quandary.

Joe answered, "Yes. I used pillow cases so my hands weren't actually touching the guitar. I hope Joe will see that I respected his dominion as well as I could." Joe chuckled. "At least there won't be any fingerprints." Joe rolled his eyes. "Of course, if I *did* leave fingerprints, they'd be Joe's anyway." He surveyed the sea of luggage. "Will this all fit in the car?"

"We're not carrying the luggage, Joe. We pay people to do that," Angie explained. To herself, the words sounded of a class-conceit that she genuinely didn't feel. She hoped Joe understood.

Joe shrugged. "That's convenient, if you can afford it. *Really* convenient. This would a taken several trips."

It sounded to Angie as if he understood.

Joe went directly for their car. Angie took a detour to drop off the key-cards and check out. The people at the front desk seemed genuinely sorry that Angie and Joe were checking out. "And will the rest of X Band be checking out, too?" the woman, a young woman, at the front desk asked, possibly just for conversation.

"No, just us," Angie answered. She didn't want to have to explain. She realized she felt shame at being, what? Voted out of the band? Kicked out? Exiled? Maybe exile was a most accurate term. And she felt that, not just Joe had been exiled; she had been, too.

The woman handed Angie the receipt folder, and Angie headed for the car. She wondered if Joe felt the same shame at being exiled. Probably not. He wouldn't submit to a petty emotional response like that. She approached the car. No mob of fans pressed. It was quiet. Joe was in the driver's seat; Angie got in the passenger side. As soon as she thumped the door closed, Joe pulled out.

"I assume we're flying out of LAX," he said.

"That's right," Angie confirmed.

"What time's our flight?"

"When we get there," she said.

Joe drove on. Presently, he asked, "Aren't private jets really expensive?"

"It's just a charter," Angie explained. "We don't own the jet."

"I didn't think we owned it," Joe said. "I was just thinking about the flight."

Angie said, "Compared to first class, it's not so bad, actually." Only about double or triple.

Joe turned onto the entrance ramp.

Angie asked, "Joe, do you feel shame at having been exiled from the band?"

"Yes!" Joe cried. "That's *exactly* how I feel! I used to be a member. I *belonged*. And now I don't." Joe glanced over. "I like your use of the word 'exile'. Pretty accurate."

Angie hadn't expected that. They rode in silence. Presently, they got bogged down in traffic until they were about sitting still. Angie watched Joe. His demeanor was the same on the open road as it was in the jam. Joe flipped on the radio. It was set on a station selected by Joe before his change. 'Stairway to Heaven' came on. Joe said, "Led Zeppelin songs have a lot of energy, don't you think?" Joe had hated Led Zeppelin. He said their songs were simplistic.

"I suppose so," Angie answered. They were too hard rock for her taste. She said, "They're too hard rock for my taste."

"I suppose they would be," Joe agreed.

They inched forward in traffic. 'Stairway to Heaven' was replaced by 'Life in the Fast Lane'.

Angie said, "I like the Eagles."

"Well," Joe said, "'Life in the Fast Lane' was the second-best thing the Eagles ever did."

"What was the best thing they ever did?"

"Break up."

"You don't like the Eagles?"

"No," Joe said, "but once they broke up, the members went on to record some pretty good music."

They discussed the Eagles, and as songs came on, the conversation floated over bands, albums, musicians, songs. Angie liked this conversation. Joe obviously knew what he was talking about, and Angie's opinions were different from his, but they didn't argue. They traded opinions and observations. And, Joe was pliable. He listened. Angie actually won him over to the Bee Gees. Okay, not completely, but he stopped hating them a lot, and that was progress. Joe's taste in music had only slightly altered at his change. Angie recognized that his perspective of music was that of a listener; no longer a musician. And, of course, now Joe didn't see every other band as competition.

Before long, they reached an exit, and Joe took a detour. He drove down a street with about 37 stoplights per mile, then took an entrance to another highway. This one was crowded but moving. When they got to the airport, Joe took the almost invisible route to the private plane section. "Um," Joe said, "which one is our plane?"

"That one," Angie said, pointing. A uniformed man stood in front of a small jet. He held a professional sign that read simply, "Ecks".

With a slight smile, Joe said, "Oh, yeah, I saw that, but I didn't want to make assumptions."

"Uh, huh," Angie said, not buying it.

Joe pulled up to the jet. He and Angie climbed up the short stairs and sat down. The jet had only four tiny seats behind the pilot's. The pilot boarded behind them. After installing himself in his seat, he contacted the tower and exchanged incomprehensible phrases. Joe looked out the window.

Angie said, "Someone will return our car."

Joe tore his eyes from the window and looked at Angie. "Traveling with you is very easy."

Was that a compliment? Probably not. "It's all services we pay for," Angie explained. "If you have enough money, you don't have to do anything you don't want to."

Joe considered this. "I suppose not," he observed. "Free enterprise abhors a vacuum."

Angie smiled. She said, "You used to say, 'Imagine what you could accomplish if you didn't have to do the shit.'" She thought, for Joe, that might have actually been true. He worked harder on music than he did on laundry. He wasn't just avoiding the labor.

Joe looked out the window. Self-consciously, Angie drew a paperback from her purse. She knew Joe would ask about it.

Joe looked over.

"Okay, it's a guilty pleasure," Angie confessed.

"Reading?" Joe inquired.

"No. Reading trash." She held up her book for Joe to see its cover.

Joe smiled easily. He said, "Everyone should be allowed their guilty pleasures."

Relieved, Angie said, "I suppose so."

Joe asked, "What does Joe read?"

"You are not really a reader."

Disappointed, Joe said, "Oh. What would Joe do in an airplane for long flights?"

"Fidget. Complain. Sulk. You can stand it, but just barely." Then Angie recalled the trip back from Cincinnati when Joe had exclaimed, "I love flying! It's such a miracle!" She shook her head.

Joe nodded vaguely and looked back out the window. Presently, the pilot drove the jet around on the runways and eventually took off. Joe stared out the window the whole time. Angie wondered what he was looking at. The jet was loud enough that conversation was possible, but too difficult to maintain. After about an hour, he gave up looking out the window. He slouched down and tried to sleep. Finally, he shouted to Angie, "Do you have anything to read?!"

In the pouch before her, she saw the corner of a magazine. She pulled it out and held it up. Woman's Day.

Joe shrugged and took it.

Joe read the magazine, flipping through the pages. He seemed superficially engrossed. Last night, he seemed to have accepted the decision of the band, but Angie could tell he was not okay. Well, there was the crying episode. That was expected. His calm afterwards was surreal in its under-exaggeration. And there were signs: He was distracted. Anxious. Now today, he didn't even mention it. It wasn't natural. No one got over a loss of this magnitude so quickly.

Joe put the magazine in a pouch. He looked over and saw Angie was looking at him. He smiled. She smiled back. He looked out the window, but there wasn't much to see except a solid floor of clouds. She would have to keep an eye on him. She'd get Douglas and Cheryl to help.

She guessed that Joe was safe from suicide, but he could do something else self-destructive, or have a mental breakdown.

After a few hours, Angie put down her novel. This was the part she hated. She couldn't read any more, and there was nothing else to do. Conversation wasn't possible. In fact, occasionally, the pilot would turn and speak to Angie (and, less often, to Joe). But no one could understand him, and eventually he gave up.

Angie was getting increasingly excited about returning home. They'd been in Los Angeles for a long time. And yet, it had never felt familiar. Or comfortable. Maybe it was the stress. But even without stress, Joe could nurture his own stress. But probably he wouldn't now. Angie looked over and saw Joe sleeping soundly. Yeah, until now, he had never been able to sleep on airplanes. As if by doing so, he would allow himself to be vulnerable. What would he be like now, at home, with no band? And no deadlines.

Maybe they all had it wrong. Maybe the switch back to Joe's regular personality wouldn't be triggered by stress; what if it was the lack of stress? Didn't Dr. Vrakas suggest that? That Joe might return when it was safe? The more Angie thought about it, the more she could make herself believe it.

Eventually, the jet landed at Brainard Airport. Bradley International Airport, to the north, was bigger, but there was a lot of construction going on with the new added concourse. Brainard was closer and cozier and far more convenient. Joe woke suddenly when the wheels touched down. One side of his hair was flat, and the impression of a seam remained on his face. He had been sleeping soundly.

When they stepped down out of the jet, Angie inhaled deeply the smell of Connecticut. She was happy to see the familiar landscape, complete with hills. The vegetation, and even the dirt, looked familiar. "There's Douglas," she told Joe over the jet engine whine. Douglas stood beside their car, a white Cadillac. As Angie and Joe approached, he opened a back door for them.

Douglas was short and dumpy with thick, greying hair and a perpetually calculating expression. "Good evening, Mr. Ecks. Good evening, Mrs. Ecks," he said, nodding slightly. Angie always expected Douglas to have a proper English accent, but it was pure American. And he struggled to suppress the New Bri'ain oddi'y, the glo'al stop (as Ed would say). It was a very localized tendency to drop internal 't's.

"Good evening, Douglas," Angie said. "Thank you," she added as she got in the car and slid to the other side.

Joe held out his hand. "Good evening, Doug," Joe greeted. "It's nice to finally meet you."

Angie had warned Douglas of Joe's temporary condition. Nevertheless, Douglas hesitated. He formally shook Joe's hand and replied, "Yes, sir."

Joe got in the car and commented, "He seems like a nice guy." Joe looked around the interior of the caddy. "Wow, this has more legroom than the limo!" Joe powered the electric window down and up. "Cool!"

The car pulled away. Douglas deftly maneuvered the big vehicle around some obstacles and out of the airport.

"What're ya gonna do when we get home, Ange?" Joe asked.

Angie sighed. Joe used to call her 'Ange', though she hated it. The luggage wouldn't be coming until later. There would be mail, though Douglas had forwarded the important letters. But even though she had been sitting all day, Angie really just wanted to rest. She answered, "Relax."

Joe nodded. "Yeah, that sounds good."

Angie said to Douglas, "Douglas, please have drinks ready for us in the den when we get home."

"Yes, ma'am," Douglas answered. He picked up a phone and spoke into it.

Angie said to Joe, "After that, I'll show you around."

The car rolled through a commercial area and into suburbs.

Angie asked, "Does any of this look familiar?"

Joe shook his head. "I've flown in and out of Bradley before. In some ways, it's more convenient than Logan. And I've driven through Connecticut once or twice."

That wasn't what Angie really wanted to know. She was hoping the familiar surroundings would encourage his memory to return. The car came down a steep hill and made a right turn. "We're almost home," Angie told Joe. The car turned into a driveway and stopped at a wrought-iron gate in a brick wall. Beside them, a box with a speaker and keypad stood on a pedestal. Douglas pushed a button on the visor, and the gate slid open. The car passed through, and the gate closed behind them.

The driveway curved through close trees, and then they opened. Across an expanse of perfect lawn loomed the Ecks mansion.

Constructed of brick, it towered two stories with a gabled attic. A front porch spanned the front with two-story columns. The driveway looped by the front door, and the walkway to the porch was guarded by two marble lions. But Douglas took the Caddy around to the back of the house. The back yard was expansive. The caretakers' quarters (the "little house") were over a four-car garage, across a driveway that was more like a parking lot. A volleyball net was set up in a flawless yard. Between two trees in the back, in the distance, a sand trap could be glimpsed.

Joe said, "You have a *golf course*?!"

Angie laughed. "No, what you see is part of the course belonging to Avon Country Club."

"Whew," Joe exhaled. "I was afraid I'd have to learn how to play golf!"

The car stopped. Angie and Joe got out. The back of the house was only slightly less ostentatious than the front. It sported decks on the first and second floors. A woman stood by the back door. She was slightly shorter than her husband and slightly thinner. She had long hair tied back, and the part in her blonde hair was brown.

Joe held out his hand. "And you must be Cheryl," he said. "Nice to meet you. Angie says you're my vocal coach."

Like Douglas, Cheryl tentatively took his hand. She said, "Yes, sir." To Angie, she said, "Drinks are in the den, ma'am."

"Thank you, Cheryl," Angie said as she breezed through the door. Joe followed. A wide hallway took them to a lowered room dominated by an imposing stone fireplace. Drinks sat beside two chairs. Angie fell into an overstuffed armchair. She kicked off her shoes. Smiling up at Joe, she sighed, "It's good to be home."

"I guess I sit here," Joe commented as he sat beside the other drink. He looked around. He inspected everything without moving from his seat. He finally commented, "This is a nice room. It would be cozy if it weren't quite so overpowering."

Now Angie looked around the room, seeing it from Joe's new perspective. Yes, actually it was a bit too much. "What did you think of the outside of the house?" she inquired. She didn't want to hear the criticism, really, but she figured he would be critical, and it was better to get it out in the open.

Joe said, "Joe is very proud of his success, isn't he?"

Angie knew what he meant. She replied, "You worked very hard to get what you have. Yes, you're proud. And you should be."

Joe took a swallow of his drink and sighed. He gazed at the huge fireplace. "I really have failed, haven't I. Because of me, everything that Joe worked so hard on is ruined." He said it as a statement of fact. No recrimination, no self-flagellation. Not even remorse.

Angie didn't know what to answer. He was right. Before the change, they had been making progress in mixing the album. They were going to get another contract and tour. They had made it. Yes, this changed Joe had failed, but to agree seemed especially heart-less. Yet he was right.

Joe said, "But Joe still has you, doesn't he?"

Angie smiled. "Yes, you do."

Joe frowned and nodded.

Chapter 19

Half Rest

After a drink or three (silently replenished by Douglas), Angie introduced Joe to his house. She thought, for a change, that she wouldn't have to restrain her pride; after all, she was showing Joe what he had earned. At the doorway to the dining room, Angie announced, "Here is the dining room." Angie entered the room.

Joe looked back and forth. "How often do you and Joe eat here?" he asked.

"We only eat here when we entertain," Angie explained.

Joe nodded. "Well, you can entertain a lot of people all at once."

From the dining room, Angie guided Joe through the sitting room, the library, the living room, the indoor swimming pool, the pantry, the kitchen. In each room, Joe showed an appropriate awe.

In the kitchen, he asked, "Where do you usually eat? You and Joe?"

"When we eat together, we take our meals in the solarium."

Joe turned his head. "You don't always eat together?"

"No," Angie answered. She started to explain, "We're not always, our, uh, things to do... Never mind, it's not really important. No, we don't always eat meals together." At times, Angie grew annoyed with having to justify to Joe the habits that she and Joe had developed.

Joe nodded and asked, "Now that I'm unemployed, can we afford this place?"

"It's paid for," Angie replied. "But there are taxes. And the maintenance. Maybe you should talk to George."

Douglas appeared. He said, "Sir: Thomas Sparks from Wheel-Well Guitars is calling."

Joe said, "Really? On the phone?"

"Yes, sir."

"I guess that makes sense."

"Will you take the call, sir?"

"Sure. Yes."

Douglas handed a cordless telephone to Joe. Joe looked at it.

Douglas explained, "To speak with Mr. Sparks, press the 'Answer' bu'on."

Joe searched the keypad and pressed a button. "Hey, Thomas?"

Joe held the phone away from his ear. Angie could hear the caller. "Hey, Joe? Is this a good time?"

"I guess so, otherwise I wouldn't be answering the phone."

Thomas laughed. "When you're right, you're right! Hey, Joe, Mr. Ecks, what's going on with X Band? I've been hearing the strangest rumors."

Joe replied, "I couldn't tell you about X Band, Thomas. I haven't been in that band since yesterday."

"Is that so? Are you going solo, then? Wheel-Well wants to be sure everyone they sponsor is active in the biz."

Joe made a noise. "Don't sweat it, Tom. It's all publicity and negotiations. Hey, I gotta go now, call me next week? Thanks." Joe searched the keypad and pressed a button. Then he pressed another button. Angie heard a dial tone.

Joe handed the phone back to Douglas, who disappeared. Joe said to Angie, "I need an agent."

"I'll find you one," Angie told him, not knowing how she would go about finding one or where to start.

"Well," Joe said, "we'll work together on it, hey?"

"Okay," Angie agreed. "How?"

"Well, we'll probably hear from a lot of agents, and we'll hafta evaluate them for honesty and skill level. Like in an interview or something. We'll have lunch with them."

"Why?"

"Lunch is good. It offers a distraction, and it paces the conversation. You have a feel for how long the conversation will be," Joe explained.

"And this is something you learned in business school?" Angie asked skeptically.

"No, this is something I observed when I was interviewing. They'd never teach anything so practical in business school," Joe answered wryly.

Shaking her head, Angie led Joe to the solarium. It was night out, and the floor-to-ceiling windows became mirrors. "During the day, the view from here is amazing," Angie told Joe.

Joe shrugged and muttered, "It's not too bad now, either."

Angie realized he was referring to her. She blushed.

Joe asked, "What's next?"

Angie finished walking him around the first floor, and then they went upstairs, where Angie showed him the bedrooms and the TV room. Joe was taking it all in. Angie finished with the master bedroom suite. Standing in the expansive master bathroom, Joe commented, "Yeah, I think this upper floor is much bigger than my whole house." He amended, "My imaginary house. Doesn't Joe have a music room?"

"Right!" Angie answered. "It's in the basement. You have to go through the theater. Do you want me to show you?"

"Yeah," Joe answered. "Right now, I don't think I could even find the basement on my own."

Douglas liked his job. It wasn't really a job; it was more like a role. Behavior and bearing were as important as execution. Several years ago, when he recognized he was sliding into the position, Douglas ducked out while the Eckses were away and took the ten-week Epicorps Estate Management Course down in Greenwich. It paid off almost immediately, because when Joe offered him the job, Douglas was fully aware of the scope and responsibilities that the job could be, and in ten minutes of discussion, he nearly tripled his salary. And rank, because instead of being a caretaker or butler, he was all of these under the official title of Estate Manager.

Douglas didn't care for Mr. Ecks's music, the product that bought the estate for which Douglas cared. But Douglas respected Mr. Ecks's determination and skill. He felt a satisfaction in doing his small part to make Mr. Ecks successful. And Douglas knew that Joe recognized, and respected, his modest contribution.

The first morning after the Eckses had returned, Douglas was surveying the house, assuring himself that everything was in place. He heard a periodic thumping noise in the kitchen. Investigating, he found Mr. Ecks opening and closing the cabinet doors.

"May I help you, sir?" Douglas inquired.

Douglas' voice startled Joe. He recovered and said, "Oh, good morning, Doug. How are you?"

"Fine, sir, thank you for asking," Douglas replied. He repeated, "May I help you with something, sir?"

"Well, yeah," Joe confessed. "I'm looking for the cereal. Where does, where is it? Do you know where it is?"

Douglas answered, "In the pantry, I imagine, sir." Douglas opened the pantry door.

"Thank you, Doug," Joe said, squeezing past into the pantry. He found the cereal and, back in the kitchen, he filled a bowl with it and added milk. He sat down. He ate a bite. He looked over his shoulder at Douglas. He asked, "Do you want something?"

"No, sir."

"Have you had breakfast?"

"Yes, sir."

Joe ate a few mouthfuls of cereal. He said, "Doug, do you wanna sit down?"

"No, sir."

Joe ate two more spoonfuls of cereal, deliberately not paying attention to Douglas, who stood nearby. Finally, Joe turned and asked, "What are you doing?"

"I'm standing by, sir," Douglas responded. And that was exactly what he was doing; if Joe needed something, he would be available to satisfy that need. "In case you need something," Douglas clarified.

"Well, please sit down."

Douglas balked. It was against the rules to share a table with your employer. And yet, it was exactly what his employer had requested. Douglas warily pulled out a chair. "Very well," he conceded. "If you insist." He sat stiffly and hoped Joe detected his reluctance.

Joe took a breath. "Doug, Angie told you about my mental state, didn't she?"

"Yes, sir," Douglas allowed. He noted that Joe seemed neither embarrassed nor proud of unusual condition.

Joe frowned. "So you see, I don't know you at all. Tell me about yourself, Doug."

"What shall I say, sir?" Douglas had no idea at what Joe was getting.

"Well, I dunno!" Joe blurted. "What's yer last name? I don't know even that!"

Relieved, Douglas answered, "Douglas, sir."

"Doug D—? Oh." Joe chuckled sheepishly. "What's yer first name, Mr. Douglas?"

"Charles, sir," Douglas stated.

"Oh," Joe said. "I see. So you prefer Mr. Douglas then?"

"Simply Douglas will do, sir," Douglas answered.

"And yet you call me Mr. Ecks?" Joe inquired. "That doesn't seem equitable."

This new Joe was perceptive as well as open, Douglas thought. No, what they called each other wasn't equitable. But neither was their relationship. He said, "It's what I prefer, sir."

Joe studied Douglas and said, "Very well, Douglas. It is no longer necessary for you to share my table."

"Yes, sir," Douglas said with relief and stood. "If you will excuse me, sir, I'll just be in the next room if you need something." Douglas resumed his stand-by out of sight.

Joe finished his cereal.

Later that same morning, at 10:26 Eastern Daylight Savings Time, Angie opened her eyes. She remembered where she was. She listened and could not hear Joe's breathing. It was typical. He had become an early riser.

An hour later, Angie held a giant coffee mug in her tiny hands. She walked up beside Douglas, who stared into the back yard. The summer sun was strengthening. The insects were quiet. Traffic could be heard on nearby route 44. Joe moved back and forth along the back wall. Angie and Douglas watched.

Finally, Angie had to ask: "What is he doing?"

Douglas didn't move. "He's gathering golf balls, ma'am."

"Why?!" Angie exploded.

"I don't know, ma'am. He's been at it for over an hour." Joe's behavior had been vexing him for the last 24 hours, and it seemed to equally vex Angie. And she had been with him like this for a long time. Douglas asked tactfully, "Has he lost more than his memories?"

Angie sighed. "No, he's not insane," she said. Then why did everyone think so? "But he's not like he was." Angie carefully sipped her bowl of coffee. She had sincerely missed Douglas's coffee.

Douglas offered, "I suppose if I were to meet him for the first time, he might not seem… irrational. Not if I were not expecting him to behave like Mr. Ecks."

Angie nodded. Joe had stopped patrolling the wall. He stood and seemed to be having a conversation with God. "What is he doing *now*?" she asked.

"I don't know, ma'am," Douglas answered.

Angie handed him her coffee, and she strode out to Joe. As she neared, she could hear two voices. Joe was conversing with a man sitting on a high branch at a tree. The man was in his twenties with unruly hair and a 5-day beard stubble. A camera with a huge telephoto lens hung from his neck. He saw Angie and suddenly seemed afraid.

Joe saw Angie and smiled. "Hi, Angie. This is Steve."

"What are you doing in our tree?" Angie demanded. She was furious. When she was in public, she expected to be scrutinized, but when she was at home, she expected privacy.

"It's really not our tree," Joe pointed out. Indeed, the tree trunk was on the other side of the wall. Joe turned to Steve and said, "Although, to Angie's point, you *are* in our air-space."

"Get out!" Angie shouted. "This is our house!" She looked for a rock to throw.

"I gotta go," Steve said. He scrambled back toward the other side of the wall. He dropped out of sight, with a grunt.

Angie was relieved at Steve's retreat. She really didn't want to throw a rock at him.

"All right, see you, Steve!" Joe called out.

"Bye!" a voice called out. Footsteps pounded into the distance.

Angie faced to Joe. "Don't encourage stuff like this, Joe! We get little enough privacy as it is."

"Yeah, okay," Joe said, "Sorry."

"And why were you picking up golf balls from the yard?" she demanded. "Douglas thinks you're crazy."

Joe raised his eyebrows and started to smile.

"It's not funny," Angie groused. "When are you going to start acting normal?"

Joe said, "If my behavior was normal, then I *would* be acting."

"Stop that," Angie snapped. She was in no mood for witty word-play.

Joe stopped. A profound sadness passed over him. He said, "I'll go practice." He walked past her toward the house.

Angie saw his rejection. "Um, while we're out here, I can show you the garage." The garage was actually on the way back to the house, sort of.

Joe turned and looked. "I thought the Douglases lived there. This is 'the little house'?"

Angie explained, "The garage is the first floor. The Douglases live on the second and third floors."

Joe looked at the four garage doors. "Oh. We have four cars? Or do the Douglases have one or two?"

Angie smiled. She said, "Wrong," and she let him in the side door. When she turned on the lights, she heard Joe literally gasp. The garage was two-deep, with room for eight cars. Two of the bays featured car lifts. At present, the garage had two empty spaces.

Angie explained, "They're all ours, but the Douglases are allowed to drive them. Some of them."

Joe drifted between the cars, and he came to a stop before Joe's crown jewel. It was on a lift, elevated enough to lift its tires from the floor. It wore a fitted cover that sported the tasteful logo of Ferrari. Joe gestured at the vehicle. "May I?" He peeled over the cover. "Oo, it *is* a Ferrari!"

Angie answered, reciting from memory, rather than knowledge, "A Ferrari Testarosa TX2N3 turbo fuel-injected flat 12, 5.8 liter with overhead cam... 5-speed. Red."

Joe gently touched the fender. "Can I get in it?"

Angie smiled at his unnecessary politeness. "Of course. It's your car."

Joe smiled back. "Well, not really," he said. "Not to me. Maybe on paper, it is." And then he added mysteriously, "Well, no, not even then." He smiled again. Then he reached up, opened the door and climbed in. The door closed with a solid thump. Angie slid over a step-stool and got in the passenger side. She watched Joe caress the three-spoke steering wheel, the shift knob, the controls. He moved to adjust the seat, but found he didn't need to. "This is so cool," he marveled. "I once worked on a Ferrari when I was workin in Charlottesville. Just a brake job. Didn't really need it. Only 195 miles on it?"

Angie said, "You had to have it, but you haven't learned how to drive a manual transmission yet."

"He bought the car, but couldn't drive... These go for about $87,000, you know," Joe told Angie.

Angie looked away. "You paid a bit more than that, Joe."

Joe studied Angie long enough for her to grow uncomfortable. She studied her perfect nail polish, which happened to match the Ferrari's perfect red exterior.

Finally, he concluded, "Joe collects his treasures. But he doesn't know how to fully appreciate them."

Angie wasn't sure what he meant. What other treasures besides the car? The house, maybe? She said, "The salesman said they don't come in automatics."

"No, they don't," Joe confirmed. "I approve. Something this fine shouldn't be automatic. When you have an automatic, you're just ridin. But when you have a stick, it's a whole different experience. You're *driving*. You and the car come together as one."

"Where did you hear that? You can't drive a manual, Joe."

Joe grinned. "Oh, I can drive a stick, and I *can* appreciate *this* treasure. But I haven't experienced anything this beautiful and elegant." Joe turned the key. The Ferrari coughed and hummed. Joe listened analytically. "It *has* been awhile," he figured, and glanced at Angie. Angie wondered if Joe could really tell how long the car had sat just from listening to it idle. But then she realized that of course he couldn't tell. He was Joe, and Joe was no automotive expert. Joe said, "I'd give it some dry gas. Gasoline decomposes into water and some gases, and dry gas'll get rid of the water." He cocked his head. "I'd goose the octane with a booster, too. When was the last time the tank was filled?"

Angie shrugged.

"I can't wait to take... Can I take you for a ride sometime?" Joe asked. "Y'know, in the car, I mean?"

"Sure, that would be fun," Angie said. Recalling the trouble Joe'd had with it before, Angie guessed he wouldn't be able to get it to the street.

Joe switched off the engine. He looked at Angie. He said, "A machine this fine... I never thought I'd ever get to drive anything like it. I figgered I would just hafta admar it from afar." Joe sighed.

They climbed out of the car, exited the garage and headed back to the house.

Douglas waited for them. As they approached, Joe commented, "Do you think the house needs a coat of paint?"

Suddenly, the house's exterior looked shabby. Angie hated it when Joe did that: Change her perspective on something with which she was familiar. "You're not thinking about painting the house are you?" she asked.

"No, not me," Joe assured her. "Fer somethin like this, I'd call in the professionals." They reached Douglas. Joe said, "Douglas, if anyone calls about being my agent, please forward them to Angie. Angie, I would like for the two of us to interview candidates one per day at 1:30 pm, over lunch. Would that be okay with you?"

Angie realized that Joe had delegated the administration to her. She asked, "You're telling me to keep track of all the scheduling and everything?" She should have been annoyed, but instead she felt pride that Joe trusted her to handle the details.

"No, not telling you, Angie," Joe said. "Well, you've been keeping track of all the schedules and everything up until now, and you've done a great job at it, so I figured you would want to stay in charge." Joe shrugged. "I'll keep track of everything, though, if you don't want to. I'll need a piece of paper."

"Well, I've never been 'in charge', but I'll do it." At times, Angie recognized Joe's new motivational tactics.

Joe rewarded her with a smile. He said, "Thank you. I guess I'd better go learn how to play guitar now. See ya." He left Angie and Douglas and headed for the house.

Angie and Douglas watched him go, then exchanged glances. Douglas handed the giant coffee mug back to Angie. The coffee was still warm.

Anechoic foam covered the practice room walls but didn't make them soundproof. Angie could hear Joe practice from just about anywhere in the house, but it got worse with proximity. In the study, she could usually tell which particular song he was butchering. In more remote rooms, such as the solarium or the master suite, she could only sense that he was playing, as if it were a mere vibration in the ether or a disturbance in the Force.

He still practiced the X Band songs, because they were the only songs Roger had taught him.

Occasionally, Joe took a break from guitar and practiced singing instead. He wrote down a song's lyrics, memorized them, then sang them a hundred times. No, that was an exaggeration; Angie thought it was probably only forty or fifty times. She guessed this new Joe had a specific number and counted.

Joe didn't ask Cheryl Douglas for vocal instruction, even though she was his coach. When Angie heard him singing, she summoned Cheryl and directed her to work with Joe. One day, as Cheryl was leaving the basement, she commented to Angie, "He really is starting completely over. It's as if I haven't taught him a thing."

Joe took his meals with Angie in the solarium. He was deeply interested in her day. He admitted that he didn't have much to talk about, since he was doing the same thing every day. Sometimes he would ask about the lyrics, either what they really were or what they really meant. He noted discrepancies between the lyrics on the album covers and what he thought was actually sung.

Angie took phone calls from agents. She scheduled interviews, and, as Joe had prescribed, they ate lunch with them in the dining room. Joe didn't want to conduct business in the solarium, to preserve the sanctity of their personal space. And the dining room was also imposing. The first interview was mostly Joe and the agent chatting. Joe seemed to like the agent, and Angie thought he would hire him, and so did the agent, right up until Joe shook his hand on the way out and said, "I don't think you have the right experience to represent me, but I hope you do well." To Angie's surprise, the agent agreed and left happy.

When the next day's agent left, he was not as agreeable, nor as happy. Joe shrugged off the unpleasantness. To Angie, he said, "The objective is to find a good match. A bad match makes everyone unhappy."

Joe elected to keep the house's existing color. He told Angie, "When Joe comes back, I don't want him to be upset with all my changes." Later Angie reflected that when Old Joe returned, of the changes that upset him, the house color was not likely to appear in the top six.

Douglas selected a painting contractor. First, the painters set up elaborate scaffolding around the house. On days of clear weather, the contractor's crew arrived and advanced the prep-work. They chipped off the loose paint, and they power-washed the house's exterior, further littering the hedges with paint chips. For Angie, the air compressor and blasting drowned out the sound of Joe floundering with his guitar. Douglas supervised the painting process, but the contractor did all the yelling.

Joe avoided the press. It wasn't that hard, since he rarely left the basement.

But avoiding the press wasn't keeping him out of it. Angie read, in Rolling Stone, about X Band bringing in Shane Skinner to replace Joe Ecks. Bill Myers was quoted as having said he was happy with the change and looking forward to working with Shane. Bastard. Angie threw away the issue. She didn't mention it to Joe.

Selecting an agent was taking a long time. They had interviewed a lot of candidates. Two of them seemed like they would be pretty good agents, but Joe didn't like them, and his reasons seemed trivial. Almost as if he knew he was going to reject them and only needed a reason. Increasingly, Angie became a part of the process. At first, she was a mere spectator. But she realized she didn't want to have to manage Joe's schedule like she had. First, she asked if they managed Joe's schedule, and everyone said yes. Later, she started asking *how* they managed his schedule, and not everyone had a ready answer.

Most agents had some degree of arrogance. Angie wondered if it were a personality characteristic necessary for one to be an agent. But Stu wasn't arrogant. He was extremely self-assured, though, and that was different. Today's agent, though, was exceptionally arrogant. His name was Arthur Lee, and before he even sat down, Angie knew Joe would reject him.

Douglas brought out the lunches, tuna sandwiches and tater tots. It was the same lunch every day. Angie didn't know why Joe specified this particular meal, but she knew there had to be a reason.

"Why do you need an agent, Joe?" Arthur Lee questioned.

"Because I don't have one," Joe replied.

Arthur Lee picked up his sandwich. "No, not after X Band kicked you out," he said and took a bite.

"You're right," Joe agreed. "It would have been awkward for me to have kept the same agent."

Arthur Lee swallowed and said, "Rumor is you're difficult to work with."

Joe smiled. He said, "Joe Ecks has a public persona."

"Well, you fired your agent, then the band kicked you out, even though you are, or, you *were* the central figure of X Band. Hell, X

Band is practically *named* for you." Arthur Lee shrugged. "And now they're not even asking you back."

Mouth full, Joe asked, "Why would they?"

Arthur Lee raised his eyebrows. "You don't know?"

Joe stopped. "I guess not."

Neither did Angie.

"You don't know."

"No. Tell me."

"Oh, Skinner left X Band. He got a contract with Distinction Records. Now X Band's got no one, and they're *still* not interested in you. That tells me a lot. You know what that tells me? It tells me you need an excellent agent. You *need* me."

Joe seemed to calculate the square root of 625 while Arthur Lee smirked. Angie snapped, "Joe is *not* difficult to work with. Not any more than any other creative genius."

"And I can trust your unbiased opinion," Arthur Lee sniped.

Joe put his napkin on his plate. "I'm afraid I'm going to have to cut this interview short. Thank you for visiting us, Mr. Lee."

Arthur Lee smiled and rose. Douglas appeared and escorted him out.

"I'm sorry he talked to you that way," Joe said.

Angie leaked fury. She fumed, "He wasn't like that when I talked to him on the phone!"

"I would guess not," Joe said. "Are you okay?"

"Yes, Joe, I'm okay." Angie dabbed her napkin under her eyes, not okay.

Joe studied her and called out, "Douglas, could you bring me the phone? And Angie would like a glass of white."

Seconds later, Douglas appeared with the telephone and a glass of white wine. Angie sipped the wine. Joe asked, "What's Ed's phone number?" Angie told him.

Joe punched the numbers and waited. "Ed, it's Joe."

Ed said something.

"Ed, I was wonderin. I kin still sing like Joe. What if I just did vocals and we got some other schmuck to play guitar? We'd still sound like X Band."

Ed said something.

Joe answered, "Yeah, okay." He pushed the Disconnect button.

Angie's curiosity replaced her anger. "What did he say?" she asked.

Joe grinned. "He said he'll be over in twenty minutes."

"It's a thirty-minute drive," Angie mentioned.

Douglas brought Ed to the den, where Joe and Angie waited. "Edward Brettington," Douglas announced, then he disappeared.

Joe rose. "Ed, it's good to see you!" He shook Ed's hand. To Ed, it was a little formal. They never shook hands before. "Have a seat," Joe offered, gesturing to an available chair.

Everyone sat. Ed said, "So you don't absolutely hate us?"

"Oh, Angie does," Joe said.

"I do not!" Angie snapped. "I'm very angry, though, and Joe should be, too."

Ed said, "Can I explain? Please?"

Joe said, "Sure, go ahead." Angie glowered.

Ed said, "The timing was bad. We'd just slugged through two days of rehearsal to go over a two-hour show. Sheridan offered Shane to play guitar, and you could sing. We were okay with that. Well, you know how important the voice is to a band's identity."

"That sounds like something *I* would say, actually," Joe commented.

"Well, actually, you *did* say that," Ed confirmed. "But when Shane showed up, he would have none of it. He insisted on doing guitar *and* vocals. And kicking you out of the band." Ed studied his fingernails. "I think that's all he wanted. He didn't have a problem leaving us behind when he got another deal." He looked up to see Joe searching him with his eyes. And Angie seemed not at all appeased.

Ed looked down. "We all feel really bad about what happened, by the way, and especially the *way* it happened. No one really wanted it, but we couldn't have Shane *and* you, and it seemed like the right thing to do. No, maybe like the only thing we could do to save our asses, which is not always the right thing to do. Everyone regretted it later. Except for Roger, I suppose, who regretted it right away." Ed summoned the courage to say the next words: "Will you forgive us?"

"Oh, hell yes," Joe stated. "Seriously. What you did made sense. I really didn't like it, but under the conditions, I understood it."

Ed looked up.

Joe continued. "So do you think it's possible I could be X Band's vocalist?"

Ed raised his voice. "Hey, Douglas, could you get me a German beer?"

"Yes, sir," Douglas said from the other room.

Ed smiled. "We could use your voice, Joe. And you."

Angie said, "Cheryl has been working with him. She says he's learning."

"'Learning'?" Joe repeated. "Where's that on the scale? Is that better than bad?"

"'Learning' isn't a skill level, Joe," Ed informed him. "It just means you're getting better."

Angie said, "Cheryl told me he's pretty good."

Joe brightened. "Hey! See? In vocals, I'm 'Good'!"

Ed admonished, "No, she said 'Pretty Good'. That's not as good as 'Good'."

Joe pouted.

Ed stroked his goatee thoughtfully.

Joe said, "So. Just to be clear, am I back in the band? Because in case this isn't clear to you, Ed, I really want to be in the band. A *lot*. And I'll tell you this: With me in the band, we might fail. But we are *not* gonna fail because I didn't care enough. Or because I didn't work hard enough."

Ed smiled. "I don't think that was ever in doubt."

Joe looked at Ed. "So?"

"Yeah, Joe, you're in," Ed said.

"Don't you need to talk to Bill and Roger about it?"

Ed said, "Yeah, no. Bill and Roger and I talked about it already. We didn't know how you would react, so they wanted me to talk to you."

"Oh. I see. Well, thank you for taking me back," Joe said. He asked, "What will Sheridan think about my rejoining the band?"

"Bill told him I was gonna talk to you," Ed said. "Sheridan thought I was crazy. He thought anyone who reached out to you would pull back a bloody stump. He doesn't know you like we do."

"What about Sheridan? How is he workin out?" Joe asked.

Ed said, "Oh, for one thing, well, we showed him the contract Stu wanted to offer Theremin. Sheridan said it was obvious from the contract that Stu and Michael were working together. Sheridan called the whole situation 'insidious'. He was impressed with you."

Douglas appeared with a sweating green bottle and a glass for Ed. "Can I get you anything else, Mr. Brettington?"

"No, thank you, Douglas," Ed said. He drank from the bottle.

"So Sheridan's workin on gettin a guitarist for the tour?"

"He's working on it," Ed confirmed doubtfully. "He's not connected like Stu was, and he's not getting much help from Theremin or

Tour Excellence. Already, I can tell it will take a lot of time. I was hoping we could get Steve Hackett or maybe Steve Howe to tour with us."

"Seriously?"

"Hell, Bill Bruford toured with Genesis on the Duke tour. It could happen." Ed knew that it wouldn't happen. X Band is no Genesis.

"Okay, yeah, it could happen," Joe admitted.

Ed finished his beer. "Yeah, I know. It's a long shot. Worst case is that Sheridan can't get anyone." He asked Angie, "If the worst happens, has he been practicing guitar?"

Angie rolled her eyes. "Constantly."

"And?"

"I don't know how *you* would rank him, but I think now he's better than 'Bad'."

Joe smiled proudly.

Ed said, "Mediocre?"

"Yeah, not quite competent."

"I'm only a level away from 'Competent'?"

"Can you play the show by October? As a fall-back position?"

Without hesitation, Joe replied, "I can. Look at the progress I've made since, uh, a month ago. I've spiraled up from 'Sucks' to 'Competent'."

"Angie said 'Mediocre'," Ed reminded Joe. "And there are a whole lot of levels between 'Mediocre' and 'Joe'."

"Joe has a level named after him?"

Ed said, "Joe, lemme tell you about Joe. Old Joe. We had a harpist come in to record some bits for 'Anesthesia'. Rhonda Cushman. Now I don't know if she was any good or what, but when the session was over, you asked if you could play her harp. Well, she agreed, and you played it pretty well. Then she started crying. She said it was the most beautiful harpistry she'd ever heard."

"Wow," Joe said.

"Yeah, this was an instrument you'd just picked up. You've been playing guitar for years. How good do you think you are on that? There are skill levels between 'godhood' and 'Joe'."

Ed continued: "I'll tell you a joke. Shane Skinner gets hit by a bus, and—"

Angie snarked, "I like it."

Ed smiled. "There's more to the joke, actually. So Shane goes up to heaven—"

"'Heaven'? *Shane*?" Angie questioned.

Ed pretended to summon a great patience and said, "Shane's at the gates of heaven, and he's talking to St. Peter. Not too far away, he sees Joe Ecks jamming on the guitar. He says, 'I didn't know Joe Ecks was dead!' St. Peter sighs and says, 'That's not Joe Ecks. That's God. He just *thinks* he's Joe Ecks.'"

Joe chuckled. He said, "Fortunately, I don't have to be as good as Joe. I just have to be Good Enough."

Ed looked at his empty beer longingly. He said, "I suppose you're right. Hey, 'Contents Under Pressure' is due to be released in a couple of weeks. Keep your fingers crossed. Sheridan says Rolling Stone is going to review the album."

Douglas replaced Ed's empty bottle with a full one.

Joe said, "Wait. I thought 'Cincinnati Fan' was gonna be pre-released. That's why we filmed the video already."

Ed explained that that had indeed been the original plan. But Michael had been overruled. 'Contents' would be pre-released, and 'Cincinnati Fan' would be released the first day of football season. The change had thoroughly ruined O'Reilly's schedule, as had X Band's new habit of changing guitarists.

"Why, did you already film the 'Contents Under Pressure' video?"

"Yeah, just a few band shots. Most of the video is the story." Ed grinned. "Shane's in it as the guitarist of the band, lip-synching to your voice. It's such a glaring inconsistency, but I don't know what's to be done about it. Sheridan thinks they may just scrap it, but, assuming you actually agree to come back, he wants to reshoot it."

Joe nodded. He asked, "So how are *you* doing, Ed?"

Ed sighed and put down his empty bottle. "Y'know, life in a rock and roll band is like shooting the rapids. You get knocked around, and you're barely in control of your destiny. It's exciting and scary, and you get swept along with the current, and you don't know what's coming up next. But lately it's been crazy, Joe. Uh, no offense. The band changes, our agent changes, our label is in limbo. I'm wondering if we will ever see another three-record contract." Ed paused and looked around the cavernous den. "I'm not sleeping well."

Douglas provided Ed with another sweating bottle and removed the empty.

"Ed," Joe said, "everything will work out. It really will."

Ed smiled and sighed. "I suppose."

Joe asked, "Hey, how's yer drum solo comin? Have you been workin on it?"

Ed looked surprised. He answered, "No. When Shane took over, he nixed my solo." Ed smiled. "You still want me to do it?"

"Of course!" Joe cried. "I really wanna hear what you come up with! Tell you what: Put something together, and I'll stop by yer house and listen to it in a couple of weeks."

Ed looked at Joe. "You're really not mad we kicked you out of your own band? Really?"

Joe said, "No, I'm not mad. Really."

Ed looked at Angie.

"He's not. He never was," she fumed.

Ed shook his head and said, "You're a better man than I am, then."

"Not as tall, though," Joe pointed out, and he changed the subject. "So, now that Vicky's history, are you dating again?"

Ed smiled as the last of his tension dissipated.

They talked for hours.

Chapter 20

Getting Set

One day, Angie set out to call each agent with whom she had scheduled an interview and cancel it. She learned that, if there was one characteristic that all agents shared, it was that they excelled at not taking rejection personally. However, they each had to take a parting sales shot, "in case things don't work out as planned. (You never know.)" The task dragged unexpectedly long and exhausted her.

—X—

One day, Angie's alarm rang at an absurdly early time. She nudged Joe and told him it was time to get up. He had a 6:00 flight from Brainard to John Wayne near Anaheim. Joe sat up and said, "I should have my own alarm clock. Why should you have to get up to wake me up?"

Angie mumbled, "It doesn't matter. If your alarm went off, I'd wake up anyway."

"Hmm, good point," Joe said. He went into his closet to change. When he came out, dressed, Angie was curled up on her side, with only her face visible. Joe padded around and kissed the exposed forehead. Then he ducked out. When she heard the door close, Angie smiled.

Joe drove himself to the airport in the '84 Jaguar XJS V12 (an automatic transmission). Outside the plane, the pilot and co-pilot took his bag and guitar case. "You can take a seat if you like, Mr. Ecks." the pilot offered. "We're ready to go when you are."

Joe climbed in. He was asleep before the plane left Connecticut airspace, and he slept heavily until the plane landed in Detroit to refuel. After that, he was awake for the flight to John Wayne. Joe climbed out of the plane and got into a waiting limousine, where he slid in beside Ed.

"Ed! This is a surprise!"

"Yeah, I just got in from Dallas." Ed felt like he had run the whole way.

As his bag and guitar were placed in the trunk, Joe asked, "Did they fit your whole drum set in the trunk?"

"I won't be playing my own drums. They'll already have everything set up for us when we get there. We do our thing and leave, and they put our toys away."

There wasn't much more conversation until the limo arrived at the studio. Ed and Joe were escorted to a set, upon which authentic-looking concert equipment had been set up, validating Ed's first prediction.

Bruce O'Reilly was talking to Bill, who wore a ridiculous, black jumpsuit.

Ed and Joe approached.

O'Reilly held out a hand like an oven mitt. As he and Joe traded greetings, Bill excused himself and moved away.

Ed called after him, "Hey, how've ya been, Bill? Nice jumpsuit!"

Joe and Ed were hurried back to "wardrobe", as Joe called it. The room was crowded with people helping. Instructions were shouted back and forth. The Wardrobe Manager, a woman in her 50s, greeted Joe and Ed, "All right, boys, strip down."

"I can't tell you how many times I've heard *that*," Joe remarked. He saw that Ed was complying. Joe followed suit. Soon they were both wearing ridiculous, black jumpsuits to match Bill's. Then they had to hold still for make-up.

When Ed and Joe took the stage, Ed said to Bill, "Sorry I made that crack about your jumpsuit. Actually it's starting to look pretty good. It grows on you."

Joe said, "But nobody can wear it as well as Roger does."

They looked at Roger. Holding his bass, he stood at his mic. He wore the same black jumpsuit, but Roger's unblemished dignity made the jumpsuit look even more ridiculous. Roger looked over.

Joe cleared his throat. "And make-up?"

Bill said, "Under the bright lights, you'll look normal."

"Joe, you ought to take those lights home," Ed said from behind his drums.

Joe had to laugh.

"Knock it off, Ed," Bill said sullenly. He put on a Mickey Mouse cap.

Ed's second prediction had been correct. As soon as they were in place, O'Reilly was shooting the first angle. As before, they played through the song while the camera filmed them. Then the crew mobilized to prepare for the next angle. The band stood around. A table had doughnuts and fruit. And coffee, which Ed was drinking plenty of. To Ed's surprise, Joe went for the fruit; bananas, especially. Joe said, "This standing-around part feels familiar."

"It does," Roger agreed.

Joe shook Roger's hand. "Roger, it's good to see you again. Really good."

Blanketed in serenity, Roger said, "Mike, you're a good man."

O'Reilly approached. "Joe, we're set to film 'Xylene' on August 9th. I checked it with Sheridan. Uh, he's still your agent, right?"

Joe blinked. "Well, yeah, sure."

O'Reilly went away.

Joe turned to Ed. "Why wouldn't Richard be our agent?"

Ed answered, "He's pretty sure you'll fire him. Actually, he expects you to call a vote on it today."

"Really?"

Ed nodded. "Bill's a little nervous, too."

"Bill is? Bill's n— Bill thinks I'm gonna *fire* him?" Joe looked around. "Where is he?"

"I dunno," Ed said.

Roger shrugged.

"Places for 2-1!" O'Reilly's assistant shouted. Joe got onstage and directly approached Bill, who was already behind his keyboards. "Are you worried that I'm gonna fire you?" Joe demanded.

Bill looked up at Joe, fearing the worst. He uttered, "I think it's a possibility, yes."

"Stop it," Joe told him. "Nobody's gettin fired. And if you talk to Richard, you can tell im that, too." Addressing Roger and Ed, he said,

"Fear is bad, counterproductive. So is insecurity. We need to communicate, okay? And to do that, we have to feel secure. What about you, Roger? Are you worried that I'm gonna fire you?"

"Not really."

Joe glanced at Ed. "An I know yer not." Joe called out into the bright lights, "What about you, Bruce? Are you worried that I'm gonna fire you?"

O'Reilly muttered something to his assistant. The assistant yelled back, "Mr. O'Reilly is worried that he's not going to stay on schedule!"

Joe smiled. "Yup. We have a job to do." He picked up his guitar.

Bill took a breath. He felt safer, but not safe.

They filmed another angle. The shoot went according to plan. The synch problems were few. The song didn't have any guitar bits that Joe couldn't fake his way through, and Ed tracked okay on drums, and O'Reilly took it easy on him anyway.

During breaks (for the talent), Bill lounged with the others. He was glad Joe wasn't being openly hostile. But, Bill figured, maybe that was because he was in public. This new Joe had plenty of discipline, but he still had feelings.

By 10:45, the work of the talent was complete. The crew busily and methodically disassembled and packed the equipment. They had a long night ahead.

The band changed out of their jumpsuits in the wardrobe room. Bill was a little worried that this was when Joe would chastise them all, or worse. It was his last chance before they went their separate ways.

Joe asked him, "Bill, are you going back to Colorado now?"

"I've got some appearances in the Bay area," Bill said.

"When you're in the Northeast, can you stop by my place? We need to go over some things."

Mentally, Bill gulped.

"Like the 'Perihelion' duet. There's gonna be no substitute for us doin it together in the same room."

Joe's plans included Bill. Yay! Bill smiled. "You're right, Joe. I think I can get there in a couple of weeks. Would that be okay?"

"Perfect," Joe assured. "What about you, Ed? Where're ya goin next?"

Ed started out the day looking worn out. Now he looked like he was sixty years old and worn out. "Back to Houston," he answered.

"You came here from Dallas," Joe pointed out. "At least that's what you told me this morning."

Ed looked over at Joe. He said, "Back to Texas. Jerk."

"'Jerk'?" Joe repeated. "I think I like you better when you're afraid of me."

Ed didn't want to be afraid of Joe ever again. He said, "Back to Texas. Sir."

"What about you, Mike?" Roger asked.

"I'm goin back home. I gotta lotta stuff I hafta learn." Joe looked at Roger. "An by the way, Roger, yer welcome at my house *enny* day. My last lesson was over a month ago, an I'd like some new material."

Roger smiled placidly. "Is there an empty seat on your flight back?"

—X—

One day, Joe asked Angie about seeing fireworks on July 4th. Angie said no. The Avon fireworks committee chairman had asked her if Joe could play before the fireworks, and Angie said he would be out of town. It would look bad if Joe were seen anywhere local.

—X—

One day, Joe and Angie waited in the dining room. Douglas appeared in the doorway with Richard and announced, "Mr. Sheridan."

"Good afternoon, Richard," Joe greeted. "Thanks for coming out here." They shook hands.

Richard wore the same dismantled look he had sported on the day Joe had been ousted. "You're welcome," Richard said. "Thank you for not firing me, by the way."

They sat at the table, in the same seats as Joe and Angie had sat when interviewing prospective agents. Angie wondered if this was, in a way, also an interview. "How've you been?" Joe inquired, as if they were old buddies.

"Fine," Richard answered. "Fine." He regarded Joe critically. "Joe, we need to talk."

"Because your ESP isn't working right?"

"I've received a telephone call from Lawrence McDermott himself. Lawrence McDermott, as you probably know, is the president of Theremin Records. He has requested a meeting with the two of us. He offered to fly us to California to meet with him."

"Is he flying us back here, too?"

"Of course."

Angie recognized that Joe's attempt to keep the conversation light wasn't working. He adjusted his demeanor to match Sheridan's gravity.

"What would be the purpose of this meeting?" Joe asked.

"He hinted that he may want to offer us a three-record contract."

"Why does he want me there?" Joe asked. "Negotiating contracts is your job."

"Negotiating contracts was also Stuart Cress's job, but you undermined him," Richard recounted. "If you're going to involve yourself in the negotiations, then, to save time, you should be present at the negotiations. But, personally, I would rather not have you looking over my shoulder."

Joe's eyes cut Richard like scythes. He said carefully, "I undermined Stu Cress because I didn't trust him, and that proved to be justified. I will trust you to do your job when you have earned my trust. And right now, you're pretty deep in the negatives. Do you understand?"

"I understand," Richard replied, cowed. "If you give me a chance, I will earn your trust."

"I hope you will," Joe said. "When do we leave?"

"Friday morning."

—X—

One day, the painters transitioned from surface prep to actual painting.

—X—

One day, Joe boarded a private jet at Brainard and flew to Van Nuys Airport, the same airport to which he had sent Vicky with the garbled master of 'Twinkle Twinkle'. He left the jet and got in a waiting limo to sit beside Richard, who had taken an earlier flight from San Diego.

Aside from greetings, Richard didn't say much. The limo left the tarmac and cruised along residential roads.

Finally, Richard asked, "I've heard that you've lost your memory. Is this true?"

Joe answered, "Yes. But I've learned a lot, and I'm not stupid."

"I was told that as well."

"How's your search for a guitarist goin?"

"Uh, slower than I expected," Richard admitted. "Roger says you're picking it up quickly, though."

Joe smiled. "Roger said that? What did Ed say?"

"Uh, he said he hasn't heard you lately."

"I guess that's true. The last time he heard me play, I was in the Stink range."

Richard nodded.

"How's 'Contents' doin? Did Theremin release it last week?"

"Yes," Richard confirmed, now on comfortable ground. "It's at 87 this week." Noting Joe's expression, he added, "You can't tell anything from its rank the first week, you know. It's good that it's in the top 100."

Joe said, "You've got kids?"

"One of each. My son is at college, and I never see him. My daughter lives with her mother."

"That's too bad," Joe said. "How did you end up representing rock and roll bands?"

Richard thought back. He said, "That's a long story, really."

Joe said, "We've only got a few minutes, and I'd hate to short-change you. Maybe you can tell me after the meeting."

Soon, the limousine pulled into the Theremin parking lot. Richard and Joe waited in an upstairs lobby.

They were eventually shown into Lawrence McDermott's expansive office. It was obviously decorated by someone paid to decorate the offices of powerful executives. The office was big and powerful and devoid of personality. Lawrence McDermott's big, wide, glass desk was completely bare. Lawrence himself was in his 40s and lean. Also, big and powerful and devoid of personality.

They shook hands and exchanged small talk about their flights and the weather.

Then it was time. As casually as he had discussed the weather, Lawrence asked, "What's after the tour for you guys? Have you a contract from anybody else?"

Richard answered, "You know we don't."

Lawrence smiled. "You're right. I know you don't. Maybe lightning will strike if the tour's good. And you're depending on us, indirectly, to manage the tour. It's almost a conflict of interest for us, don't you think?"

Joe replied, "The tour will have a more direct effect on the sales of 'Xylene', and that will directly benefit you."

Still smiling, Lawrence said, "Correct. But suppose I offered you a contract today, but you had to either sign it or reject it before leaving the office. Would that interest you?"

Richard leaned forward.

Joe asked, "Have you fired Michael Rost?"

Lawrence answered, "Michael Rost has been severely reprimanded. He will not, repeat, *not* think about anything like that again. Naturally, we've assigned a new producer to your band, and that hits Michael right in the wallet, where it will hurt."

Joe said, "I don't think you realize how much damage Mr. Rost did with his shenanigans. I don't think you're taking what he did very seriously."

Lawrence seemed to be losing his good nature. "Believe me, Joe, we take it very seriously."

"Eight point two million dollars," Joe said. "That's how much our lawyers estimate it cost us. We're planning to sue."

Richard looked at Joe in alarm.

Joe said to him, "I'm sorry, Richard, was I not supposed to tell him?"

Lawrence chuckled. "Everything was legal. You can't win that case."

"I know," Joe agreed. "But the details will be made public."

Lawrence reddened. "Get the fuck out of my office, you little pissant! Fuck you and your puny lawsuit! Get out!"

"Okay," Joe replied, rising. "Come along, Richard." He bounced out the office, Richard trailing.

Richard used the lobby phone to summon the limo, and they waited. The lobby had big, comfy chairs, but they stood, expecting the limo to pull up momentarily. Joe gazed sedately through the giant windows. Richard was about to blow a brain vein.

He hissed, "Joe, are you insane? We could have had a contract! You want that, right? Because I just want to make sure we're on the same page."

Joe replied, "If he's not gonna offer us a competitive contract, he's not taking us seriously, and I'm not interested."

Richard took a few measured breaths. He whispered, "Christ, Joe, we're not in a position to be picky. Let me go back and take a look at the contract."

"No."

They stood. Five minutes went by. No limo.

Joe observed, "It looks like we have time for that story of how you became a rock-n-roll agent."

Richard looked at Joe like he'd started speaking Norwegian for no reason.

A man entered the lobby from the building. He wore a white shirt with the sleeves crisply rolled up, and his thick hair was parted perfectly. He said, "Gentlemen."

They turned.

He said, "I'm Henry Cort. I'm your new producer." He held out a hand.

They shook. Joe said, "Good afternoon, Mr. Cort."

Henry gestured toward the interior of the building. "Can we talk?"

"Sure," Joe answered, not budging.

"Inside?"

"Our ride will be here any minute."

Henry said, "Um, would you want to review the contract before you go?"

"Yes!" exclaimed Richard.

But Joe frowned. "I'd like to take the contract home and review it. We'll give you an answer in one week. Or so."

"You know I can't let you do that," Henry said, uncomfortable.

Joe shrugged.

"Um, how did you arrive at a figure of eight point two million dollars?"

"I dunno," Joe admitted. "I'm really just repeatin what our lawyer told me. I'm sure it'll be detailed in the complaint. You can look it over then, if you want; it'll be available to anyone."

Henry looked around the lobby. "How determined are you to file that suit?"

An hour later in the limo, Richard clutched his head. "Goddamn, Joe, what the hell just happened?" He massaged his temples like he was grinding out twin cigarettes.

Joe answered, "Negotiation, I'd say."

Richard said, "Joe, if you're going to do something like that, you have to tell me ahead of time. Okay?"

Joe shifted. "Yeah, sorry. Mr. McDermott took that condescending attitude with us, and it made me mad." Joe looked out the window. "These guys are slick. Did you see how they held up our limo? And Mr. Cort already knew about our eight point two million dollar figure. He'd been briefed that quickly."

Richard asked, "What adds up to eight point two million anyway? You got that from the lawyer? Which lawyer? Jonathan?"

"No, I made it up," Joe smiled. "It gave us a negotiation starting point."

"Christ." Richard groaned, returning to brutally massaging his temples. "Not that I'm complaining, but we still don't have a contract."

"The contract they offered woulda been garbage anyway. Anything we hafta sign on the spot is *not* going to be competitive. So it's no loss. The problem is, these guys think we're desperate for a contract, so—"

"We *are* desperate for a contract," Richard reminded Joe.

"Sure we are!" Joe agreed. "But the problem is they *think* we are. That's most likely why I was invited. Because Mr. McDermott thinks I'm more desperate than anyone. It's unfortunate that they all think we're a bunch of stupid kids. We will never get a good deal from Theremin until we get a competitor's offer."

Richard sat staring at Joe, re-evaluating him. "Shit," he said. "You're not stupid, I can see that."

Joe smiled. "Thank you, Mr. Sheridan. Geez, I can't wait to tell Angie how it went. Whaddaya gonna do with your haffa mil?"

—X—

One day, Angie decided to eat lunch with her husband, even though he was eating lunch with Roger Novak. For a long time, Angie didn't especially care for Roger. He seemed to be in a drugged state all the time. His vacant stare and absent conversational skills made her uneasy. When Roger was in the room, she tried to not be distracted by his presence. However, this would not be easy at a table with just Joe and Roger.

But since the 'Contents Under Pressure' video shoot, Roger had been coming to the house on and off. Angie was happy that Roger was helping Joe with guitar. He could use it. And Roger had told Shane to shut up when Shane was being snide. Space cadet or not, that had endeared Roger to her. Maybe she had misjudged him.

Joe and Roger took lunch in the dining room. She arrived with her plate in time to hear Joe ask, "Why the bass, Roger? You can play guitar as well as anyone."

Roger swallowed his food deliberately. He posed, "If a person plays the bass and the guitar, why should he play the guitar?" He took another bite.

Angie sat down and wondered what particular branch of chemistry Roger was studying today.

Joe considered Roger's words. He said, with some surprise, "I have a bias! I think guitar is *better* than bass. But, okay, still, why do you play the bass if you could play either? What draws you to the bass more than what draws you to the guitar?"

Roger's sky-blue eyes gazed ahead. "I like to be the fabric."

Angie wondered if maybe it would have been better for her to have eaten alone. Hell, she was practically eating alone right now.

Joe asked, "Angie, how did Roger and Joe meet?"

And with that, he deftly pulled her into the conversation. On familiar ground, she talked about those early days. Even Roger said a few things. Angie realized that, for the first time, she felt at ease with Roger. Just in time for her lunch to be eaten. She excused herself and left the room.

Roger watched her go and looked back at Joe. He said, "The first time you and I met was in your penthouse suite for the band meeting. You walked up to me and said, 'You must be Roger Novak.'"

Joe smiled and said, "Yes. I remember *that*."

—X—

One day, Joe accepted the telephone from Douglas. "Good afternoon, Richard," Joe said into it. "How are you?"

"I'm fine, Joe," Richard answered.

"Hey, where are we in the standings?"

"The charts? 'Contents' is at 53 this week. The Xylene album is at 122," Richard reported.

"Hmmm. How's your search for a guitarist?"

"Good. I've been talking to Nan Barbins. Remember her album two years ago 'Anyway, Thanks'?"

"Yeah," Joe said. "I'm surprised, though. I didn't really think we were her style."

"Well, we'll find out when she auditions," Richard answered. "But the reason I'm calling is because the Cincinnati Bengals want you to sing the national anthem on August 18th. I know it's just a pre-season game, but it coincides well with the release of the 'Cincinnati Fan' single."

"Absolutely not," Joe answered.

"Wh— Huh?"

Joe described his encounter with Mr. St. Germain and Dr. Geela. He concluded with, "So if there's any possibility of encountering them again, I'm not gonna take that chance. They made the Bengals looks bad, and they made all of Cincinnati look bad. So you may politely turn them down."

"Um. Shit. What were their names?"

Joe repeated them.

"Uh, what if they apologized?"

Joe chuckled. "It would have meant a lot more to me if they were sorry *before* there were consequences, but it's too late for that now. Why don't you ask Bill? I know he can sing, and, after all, he *did* write 'Cincinnati Fan'."

"Yeah, I could ask him," Richard said.

"Anything else?"

Richard sighed. "I guess not."

—X—

One day, Joe and Angie were eating lunch in the solarium. An animated Angie was describing a Six Flags roller coaster when Douglas appeared. "Mr. Myers is here to see you, Mr. Ecks. He has an appointment."

Joe checked his bare wrist.

From behind Douglas, Bill said, "I'm sorry I'm so late, Joe."

Joe said, "Oh, hey, c'mon in, Bill. Hava seat."

Bill hesitated, holding his derby in both hands. He had to know up front: "Are you still mad?"

Joe rose. "I was never mad. Very disappointed, yes. Also tristful."

Bill said, "Okay. What's that mean?"

"Sad. Very sad," Joe explained. "*Angie* was pissed, though."

"I wasn't *pissed*," Angie snapped. "I was *furious!*"

Joe said, "Siddown, Bill. All is forgiven. Right, Angie?"

"No."

"Okay, mostly forgiven. Have you had lunch?"

Eyeing Angie warily, Bill sat at the small table, still holding his derby. "I got something on the way from the airport," he confessed.

"How's Denver?" Joe asked, sitting.

"We're looking around Lakeland now," Bill said.

"And how's Cassie?"

Bill sighed and told Joe, "I love her more every day."

Joe said, "That's great. I'm happy for both of you. Have you heard about Richard getting a guitarist?"

"Nan Barbins? She auditions next week. We'll see." Bill sighed. "It's problematic. The big names want to charge us so much, we'd lose money on the tour. Anyone else any good is booked out, and anyone else *not* any good can't learn the material in time. And Richard can't explain why when Joe Ecks is on the stage we still need a lead guitar."

"He's not telling anyone about the amnesia, is he?"

Bill answered, "No, but the rumors are flying."

Joe said, "I'm surprised we've kept it a secret this long, actually."

Bill leaned forward. "If Theremin found out, we'd be done. And Richard says you ruined our chances of getting a contract from them."

"It was a lousy contract."

"It was a contract, though. And you didn't even see it."

Joe replied, "How good could it have been if they only gave us a few minutes to look it over? With no chance of a counteroffer from other labels? Don't forget the herd mentality, Bill."

"I haven't forgotten that," Bill grumbled indignantly. "I'm the one who told *you* about it."

"At least I squeezed 'em for some spending money," Joe said.

Bill nodded. "Yes. Thank you for that, by the way. At least they didn't cancel our tour."

"Not yet, anyway," Joe commented.

Bill glared. "Don't joke about that, Joe. We really need that tour."

"So do they. Look, Bill, we've put out three good albums now, and we're headlining our own tour. We deserve a decent contract."

"Don't believe your own fan mail, Joe. 'Three good albums' an exaggeration," Bill told him. "'Xylene' is only at 91."

Joe got serious. "Don't you be believing your crooked produc and your scheming, traitorous agent, neither. Both of them had a reason to make you believe your work was inferior. Neither of them had your best interest at heart. Bill, I heard 'Xylophone' and 'Xenon' as an objective consumer when they came out, and I can tell you 'Xylophone' is a great album. I'd put it in my top five. 'Xenon' is pretty good. It's worth buyin. 'Xylene' is between them. It's a solid third album. And, by the way, 'Contents' is at 38 and still climbing. Don't let anyone convince you that you're not worthy of a good contract."

Bill leaned back, studying Joe. Could he be right? Had Bill's whole perception of their floundering success come from Michael and Stu? No, he'd heard good things from other people. But Stu and Michael would say, 'Don't start believing your fan mail,' effectively discrediting any opinion but their own. And those exact words had just come from Bill's own mouth. Michael and Stu had been manipulating him. Ergo, Bill had been underestimating X Band all this time. Bill admitted, "Maybe you're right. Maybe we are all that." Bill thought for a moment. "Some humility is necessary, though, otherwise, we end up like Shane. And also I don't want us to get complacent."

Joe smiled and said, "We're not ever gonna get complacent, because we're gonna keep havin fun explorin our music. You know what the secret hit of 'Xylene' is?"

Bill smiled. "Yes. 'Twinkle Twinkle'. It's getting requests."

Joe nodded. "And that was you guys just havin fun. How much work was that?"

"It seemed like work at the time," Bill said, though he knew as soon as he said it that it was bullshit. They had had to set up, and there was plenty of deadline stress, but once they started playing, it *had* been fun. And it had happened due to the leadership of this Joe. "But it was fun. Yes."

Joe said, "Let's go practice the 'Perihelion' duet. That'll be fun."

"Okay. Help me bring in my gear." Bill rose. "And thank you for recommending me to sing for the Bengals," Bill said, thanking Joe for much more than that. "Thank you."

—X—

One day at lunch, Joe seemed uncomfortable. He asked, "ie, uh, do you wanna go out?"

"Out?" Angie asked. "Outside?"

"No, uh, out, like together. Do you wanna see a movie? Or something?"

Angie saw that Joe was actually perspiring. She smiled. "Are you asking me out on a date?"

Joe nodded.

"Well," she said, thinking. "You know whenever we're in public, we attract attention."

"Yeah, yeah, you're right," Joe stammered, wiping his forehead. "Going out is probably not a good idea."

Angie said, "We could dine out. Avon Old Farms is just down the road. I could reserve a room for us."

Stricken, Joe uttered, "A room? No, not like—"

"A private dining room for us, I mean. So we won't be bothered."

Joe brightened. "Oh. Yeah, that would be good. And we could have dinner."

"Yes. What day would you like me to make reservations?"

"Today? Tomorrow?"

"I'll make reservations for tomorrow," Angie told him.

Angie was unexpectedly happy about the date with her husband. In the morning, she had her nails done, and later, she had her hair done with fresh highlights added. She showered and dressed, even taking care in choosing sexy lingerie. She picked out a long, green dress, to match her eyes. The neckline was a deep V to draw one's eye to Angie's sternum.

Darkening her normally invisible eyebrows, she recognized Douglas's knock at her door. "Yes?"

Douglas entered with the telephone. He announced, "Telephone call from Middlesex Memorial Hospi'al."

Angie's heart dropped. She took the phone. "Hello?" she asked with dread.

"This is the Middlesex Memorial Hospital Emergency Room," a woman's professional voice said. "Have I reached Angela Brettington Ecks?"

Frozen, Angie said, "Yes."

"We have been asked to inform you that Edward Brettington has been admitted into our care." The professional voice had become quite antiseptic.

"Why?"

"I'm sorry ma'am, we are not allowed to give that information."

"Is he okay?"

"I'm sorry ma'am, we are not allowed to give that information."

"Damn!" Angie exploded. "Well, what *can* you tell me?"

"Edward Brettington has been admitted into our care."

"Fine," Angie snapped. "We'll be right there." She disconnect-ed and told Douglas, "Ed's in the ER."

"I'll drive you, ma'am," Douglas asserted and disappeared.

Angie scanned the room. She snatched her book and shoved it in her purse. She glanced around for anything else she might need. For what? She didn't know anything. She slipped on flats and hurried from the room. She found Joe, predictably, in the music room. He wore his suit, complete with striped power-tie (poorly knotted). "Ed's in the hospital," Angie told him. "Let's go." Joe followed.

They hurried out and slid into the idling Cadillac.

Douglas drove. He knew the way. Angie told Joe everything, which was nothing. Douglas pulled up to the ER entrance, and they rushed in. They were directed to Ed, in a bay with an unconscious black man. Ed lay under a thin sheet. He wore a particularly drearisome hospital gown.

"Ed!" Angie cried. "Are you okay?"

"You came down here?" Ed asked. "Really?" To Angie, he seemed weak.

"The hospital called us," Angie said. "What happened? Are you okay?"

"Physically, yes, but I am a bit chagrinned. Um," Ed said. "Yeah, I'm okay. I just drank too much."

"What?"

"Yeah, sorry. I was drinking grain. It sneaks up on you, y'know. I was partying with Tom and Todd and Debbie and Kitty, you know, from high school?"

"No, I don't remember them," Joe said.

Angie asked, "You're not dating Kitty again, are you?"

"I was hoping to," Ed said wistfully. "Anyway, I decided to relax on the floor, and I guess I fell asleep. The next thing I knew, I was s'rounded by ambulance people. Okay, well, what happened was Kitty saw me sleeping, and she freaked out and called 911. The ambulance people were worried that I would vomit and aspirate, so they took me here for observation."

Joe said, "You don't seem very drunk, Ed."

Ed yawned. "It was grain. I just drank too fast, really, but not too much." Concentrating, he looked from Joe to Angie. "You two really dress up nice for the emergency room. Classy."

"That's not saying much, considering what you're wearing," Joe pointed out.

Ed chuckled. He said, "True. But I wasn't wearing this when I came in, y'know. I changed into this when I got here."

"Good," Joe said. "Because that's not really impressive party-wear. Kinda drab."

"Yeah, I guess. I was wearing better party clothes before. And they covered nearly my whole ass." To Angie, Ed said. "I'm really sorry, Angie. I didn't mean fer you to come out all this way."

"Is there anything we can do for you?" Angie asked.

Ed answered, "They're gonna let me out early for good behavior. Like in an hour. Then could you take me home? My car's not here. Can you believe they wouldn't let me drive here? They pretty much insisted on driving me here themselfs. So when they release me, could you take me home?"

Angie would have stayed up all night with Ed, but she didn't want to speak for Joe.

Joe answered, "Sure, Ed, yeah, we'll take you home." He turned to Angie. "Is that okay with you?"

Surprised, Angie replied, "Yes, uh, it's what I would have chosen to do."

"Good," Joe responded. "I'll go tell Douglas what's going on."

Angie stopped him. She asked, "You don't mind about our date?"

Joe commented, "It's not really what I had in mind for our first date, but we're sitting together and talking; it's not too different from having dinner." He appraised Angie and added, "You look really good." He looked away sadly. "It's not right for me to be dating a married woman anyway."

—X—

One day, Douglas announced that the painters were done. Joe wanted to inspect their work, and this worried Douglas. He'd already checked it, but he was certain Joe would find something he missed, even if he hadn't missed anything. Joe, Douglas and the painter surveyed the house's exterior, taking a slow walk around. When they had completed the circuit, Joe said the job looked good. "Pay the man," he told Douglas.

—X—

One day, Angie was reading her book in the library. When Angie read, she liked to read in the library. The library was a cozy room. Three walls were floor-to-ceiling bookshelves filled with books. She reclined in one of the two big chairs that faced the doorway. On this day, her head hurt with an ache that wouldn't go away, and cramps wouldn't leave her alone. She felt listless and tired and irritated. Reading was about all she could manage without resorting to TV.

Joe charged past the doorway. He stopped and backed up and looked in. "Oh, hi," he said.

Angie could tell he was anxious. "Hi," she replied. "Is something wrong?"

"Huh? Oh. May I sit down?" He gestured to the other chair.

"In the chair?" Angie asked. She was testing to see how anxious he was.

"Yeah," Joe answered.

He didn't play along with the comedy. He was very anxious. "Yes, certainly," Angie replied.

Joe sat in the chair, tight as an E string.

"Are you taking a break?" Angie inquired.

"Yes," Joe told her. "Before I started breaking things."

"Is it not going well?"

"It is going decidedly NOT well."

"Can I get you anything?" Angie asked.

"No, but thank you. I just wanna sit here," Joe said, "with you."

"Okay."

They sat for a few minutes. Joe's breathing was measured. Angie considered returning to her book, but she thought that would seem rude. Dismissive. Joe wanted something. He had sought her for a reason. Her headache tightened, and she winced.

He stood. "I should practice. I should get back to practicing. I should work on the 'Perihelion' duet." He didn't move. "But I don't want to. I want to do something else." He stared for a moment vacantly. Then he looked at Angie. "Do you want to do something? Like, together? With me?"

Angie closed her book. She asked, "Like what?"

"I dunno. We oughta do somethin *fun*. What do you like to do that's fun?"

Actually, Angie had been managing to enjoy reading her book, and Joe had interrupted that. She answered, "I don't know."

"Well, what were you planning to do later?"

Nothing, really. "Maybe update the X Band scrap book. I need to touch base with Richard."

"Or are you too busy being Joe's slave to consider doing anything fun?" Joe's voice had an edge, like he was blaming Angie.

Angie normally would have mentally retreated, giving room to Joe's ire. But Angie's head hurt, and she was confused by what Joe said. Was Joe annoyed, why? Because she did everything she could do for him? "No. I don't know what you mean." She put down her book and stood.

Joe hesitated. It looked like he might turn and leave. But he held his ground, despite an obvious increase in his level of discomfort. He started to talk and stopped himself several times.

"Just say it," Angie told him. She wanted to sound supportive, but she sounded as irritated as she was.

Joe knotted his fists at his sides. "Fine. You're so busy, dedicated to serving Joe. You do everything for *him*. You don't have any idea. You're so busy serving Joe, you don't know what you want or who you are."

Angie felt struck. "I've been helping you," she whined, hating the way she sounded.

"Everything you do is for Joe. You don't have any of your own friends or hobbies or interests. Yer like not even a whole person!"

The words were like nails driven into her heart, and Joe was the nailgun. Because she knew it was true, and Joe didn't care. She'd invested her whole self into Joe since she was a girl. Until... And now... Enough! Her plunging despair inverted into a towering rage. "You! You're one to talk!" she screamed. "You're so busy being everybody's best friend, you don't even know who you are! You want to do something that's fun? No! You want *me* to do something that's fun! You couldn't do something fun unless it was doing something for someone else!" Angie was radioactive, enraged, beyond control.

Joe stood dazed. "Ange..."

"Don't call me that!" Angie snapped. "Joe used to call me that even though he knew I hated it. So don't you start."

Joe stood, fixed in place. His face was an unreadable mix.

Angie plunged on. "You hypocrite! Damn you! Everything you do, and don't do, is for Joe. All the hard work, all the time and tough situations, everything is for Joe Ecks. And not one damned thing for Mike Smith." As she finished, she held one finger up in Joe's face. He didn't flinch or even take his eyes off Angie's. "So don't accuse *me* of being Joe's slave."

"Oh, Angie," Joe uttered, and his arms wrapped around Angie and enfolded her into a tight hug. When they hugged, she really did feel surrounded. And safe. They didn't hug this way often, and not at all since the change, except for when Joe had been ousted. Despite the suddenness, she settled in and allowed herself to relax against Joe.

After a few moments, they parted. Joe quickly turned away, a strange glint in his eye.

"Joe?" Angie asked. "Are you crying?"

"Oh," he said in a shaky voice. "Yeah." He wiped his eyes.

Angie didn't ask.

Joe sniffed and faced her. "You called me Mike."

Then Angie thought. Yes, she had. And she realized it was easier to think of him as Mike, a distinct, separate person, than to think of him as an aberrant, defective Joe. It made sense, and everything made sense. She looked up at Joe and asked, "Is that okay? Isn't that who you are?"

"It's who I believe myself to be," he answered slowly. "But you should call me Joe to avoid confusion, or leaking the truth. I think."

Angie nodded, feeling vaguely disappointed. She could see him as Mike, but even he didn't seem to accept it.

"You're so right, though. I work so hard at the interpersonal development. It's so important to get everyone's buy-in and cooperation. I don't want to miss any opportunity to improve my chances for success."

Angie pointed out, "See, you're doing it right now. This is exactly what I mean. You're pushing down your own needs to do what Joe wants."

"No, Angie, it's for me." Joe reached for his shirt pocket, then went to push up his glasses and lowered his hand. "This is what *I* want to do. More than anything. We just have to get past this, this trial. I have to get good enough." Joe sighed and looked at Angie. "You know what I'm afraid of? I'm afraid there will always be an upcoming trial to overcome. And it will never end. Was that Joe's downfall? He was always working on the next thing, and he couldn't ever relax? Because there was always a next thing?"

"It's not the same thing. Joe was *always* freaking out about something. He always needed to have something to obsess about. But it's not the same for you." Angie thought about all the trials Joe — Mike — had confronted: learning to sing, recording 'Twinkle Twinkle', the contract, etc. It did seem that Mike had faced a succession of trials, but he had met them. The trials did not possess him. Mike's focus was broader. Not every little thing was a looming catastrophe.

"Well, I'm glad you see it that way," Joe said. "I think once the tour gets underway, the worst will be over. I hope."

Angie touched Joe's arm. "I know it will, Mike." Angie saw Joe's uncertainty fade as he smiled faintly. She liked that she could comfort him.

"I want to go bowling," Joe stated. He looked at Angie. "You wanted to know what I want to do. I want to go bowling."

Angie uttered, "Bowling?"

Joe smiled warmly. "Yeah. I like bowling, but I haven't been in months. A high-class woman such as yourself, though, you've probably never even been in a bowling alley."

Angie recalled her friend Marcy's birthday party at Colony Lanes. She bowled four frames before giving up and keeping score for everyone else. "I have *too* been in a bowling alley," Angie asserted indignantly.

"Yeah, but bowling ain't your sport," Joe mused. "I'd guess your sport would be... archery."

Angie smiled. "I never tried archery, but I've always wanted to. At least try it. I don't know why. It's kind of a strange hobby."

"Shootin arrows in targets don't seem no stranger than knockin down pins."

"I suppose that's true," Angie agreed, happy with that rationalization.

"I spose Joe Ecks can't go bowlin in public," Joe figured. "We oughta rent the bowling alley, maybe at night, after they would normally close."

"The whole alley?" Angie asked.

Joe looked off. "The two of us, three games, would take a lane for an hour. It would cost us maybe $9. Up here in New England, maybe $12. So if an alley has fifty lanes, the most they can make on it is $600 per hour. Yeah, for a thousand dollars, they might do that. Do you think Ed wants to join us?"

Angie repeated, "A thousand dollars?"

Joe said, "This month alone, I extorted a million dollars from Theremin, before taxes. 'Contents' is at 40, and 'Xylene' is at 85 this week. That's gotta be worth somethin."

Angie smiled. She said, "I'll make some phone calls. Mike."

Joe smiled. "No, let me. It's my thing."

—X—

One day, Angie sat in the solarium alone. It was uncommonly early. Angie's hair stuck out, and she cocooned in a big, white bathrobe. The sun beamed optimistically on the garden outside the windows. Angie had before her a giant mug of Douglas's Good Morning® coffee, extra strong.

Angie had a virus or something that kept waking her with random symptoms. Her stomach had hurt, next her nose had clogged solid. She medicated and still spun in bed. Dreams plagued her and seemed to drag past when she was awake, variants of the same dream over and over: She had to get Joe ready for the tour bus, but she kept remembering things she'd forgotten. Joe kept asking her when she would be ready, but it was already hours too late. They were back in the California penthouse suite, then they were back in Connecticut. At which point, Joe called to ask when she would be ready. "I don't know. I'm hurrying." To which Joe replied, "Ange? Are you dreaming?" "I'm not sleeping!" Angie insisted. She saw another empty suitcase. What was supposed to go in that? And they were back in California. An alarm went off, the fire alarm? Angie floated up through sludgy sleep. It was the phone beeping, because the receiver was between the bed and end table. Angie replaced it, and then sat up, grateful to be awake.

Her restlessness hadn't disturbed Mike, since he hadn't come to bed. That was fine with Angie. She didn't want to bother him with her illness.

Even now, Angie felt like being awake was less exhausting than being asleep.

"Is there anything else I can do for you?"

"No, thank you, Douglas," Angie answered, although actually she wanted him to kick her in the head until she was unconscious. She felt woozy, and the dream residue felt like it would never leave her head. "Is there more coffee?"

"I'll make another pot, ma'am." Douglas left the solarium.

Angie sighed. If she had a virus, there was nothing to be done except try to be comfortable and wait it out. Maybe the doctor could help her be comfortable. Maybe he could give her something to help her sleep. Angie sipped her coffee. Anything to avoid another night like last night.

The phone. Had Angie dreamt Joe was calling and then picked up the phone in her sleep? Or had someone else called? Angie figured she could ask Mike if he had heard the phone ring.

—X—

One day, Ed opened his front door, because, minutes earlier, Joe had rung his doorbell.

Joe: "How're ya doin, Ed? Yer lookin better than the last time I saw you. Yer certainly much taller, and yer dressin better, too."

"Ha ha," Ed smiled. "Yeah, today I got to pick out my own clothes."

"And you picked out those?"

Ed laughed. "You win. How's Angie? Is she over that cold?"

"Mostly. Poor thing. She was a hurtin unit there for a while. Do you want to sterilize me before I come in?"

"I guess not," Ed decided. "Come on in."

Joe walked in and surveyed the expansive foyer. Doorways led to a living room and a dining room. Wide stairs with polished wood banisters led up. "Nice house, Ed. Very stately."

"Thanks," Ed shrugged, aware of how modest his house was compared to Joe's. "The houses here along Ridge Road were built just a couple of years ago. You should see the view out the back."

Ed led Joe to the back den, with its nearly floor-to-ceiling windows, and looked across the valley contoured with rows of grapevines. "Wow," said Joe. "This is nice!"

"Yeah, it is." Ed sighed. "All right, let's get to work."

A third of Ed's basement was his practice room. The walls and ceiling were covered with soundproof foam. Ed's drum set dominated the room. Empty drum cases, unused cymbal stands and other artifacts jumbled against the far wall. "Nice set-up," Joe appraised.

"When you play the drums," Ed commented, "you don't have a lot of options as to where to practice." He gestured to the whole room. "Now I do."

"These aren't the drums you played in LA."

"No, that's my studio set. I have another set I play on tour."

Nodding, Joe pulled out a drum stool and sat. "Okay, I wanna hear what you got."

Ed got behind his drums and sat. Here goes. With a drumstick, he depressed the PLAY button of a cheap boombox on the floor. 'Cincinnati Fan' played, starting near the end. Ed matched his drumming to the song, and then the song ended. Ed forged forward with a simple beat. Then he added other rhythms with other limbs. Then he hit the cymbals, and as their sound died, he fell into a drum roll. He kept this up and added other toms and cymbals. He concluded with rolls on descending toms. He looked up at Joe.

Joe frowned. He said, "Technically, it's perfect, and it fulfills the requirement of being a drum solo. There's nothing wrong with it."

Ed leaned back. "Why am I not feeling a glow of pride with your assessment?"

"It's not a solo I would expect Ed Brettington to play. Maybe Phil Collins..."

Confused, Ed stated, "Phil Collins is a great drummer! I wanna be more like Phil Collins!"

Joe shook his head. "Yer no Phil Collins, Ed, and you never will be. But I would also assert that Phil Collins is no Ed Brettington, and *he* never will be. You two are different, but that doesn't mean that Phil is better, just different."

"Well, what do *you* think I should do?"

Joe seemed to grind his teeth. "All right, Ed, look. You're essentially writing a new song with your solo. How do you develop the drum line in any other song?"

"I dunno," Ed answered, having no idea where Joe was going. But *that* wasn't a new feeling anymore.

"On 'Entertainment Tonight', you said you play what feels right for the music. True?"

Ed couldn't remember being on 'Entertainment Tonight', but it sounded right. "True, I guess."

"But you can't do that for a solo, because there IS no other music. No wonder you're gummed up." Joe stood. "I wanna try somethin. Lemme git my guitar." He hurried out of the room.

Ed watched him go, without a clue as to what Joe had in mind. He drank from a lukewarm water bottle containing vodka.

Joe returned with his flying V2 guitar and a tiny amp. "Okay," Joe said, plugging everything together. "I'm going to make the music to which you can play what sounds right. Okay?" Joe crudely tuned his bass E string only. "And when you're playing your actual solo, you can imagine this music in your head."

Ed started his tape and played to it. The song ended, and Joe kept playing, but only a simple one-note beat. Ed stared and then smiled. He played the drums. It was easy.

—X—

One night, Angie stood beside their back driveway. She wore a tube top with an open button-down shirt tied at the waist over a pair of snug shorts, because Joe had assured her it was proper bowling attire. A garage door opened, and Joe backed out the Ferrari, top up. He swung the car around so the passenger door faced Angie. "Excuse me, miss. Might you be in need of a ride?"

"Why, yes, thank you, sir," Angie replied, getting in. She buckled her seatbelt and saw Joe looking at her with a stupid grin.

He said, "Yer wearin blue-collar clothes, and you still look elegant. How do you do that?"

Angie blushed. "Just drive," she said. "And keep your eyes on the road."

Joe cruised up to the gate, waited for it to open, then exploded onto Nod Road. Angie noticed that Joe had had no problems getting the car out of the driveway. She anticipated that he would give her a wild ride. In seconds, they came up to the stop light at route 44.

"I put in some dry gas," Joe told her. "And some octane booster. It's running better, but it needs a new tank of gas, really. Did Joe fill it with regular gas?" Angie didn't know.

The light turned green, and they leaped forward onto route 10. The narrow, two-lane road wound through woods and past golf courses. Angie had ridden it a thousand times. But not like this. Joe drove the Ferrari fast and kept it in the lane precisely. Angie was frightened at first, until she realized Joe had control of the car. She had nothing to fear. In fact, it was exhilarating. They left route 10, took a connector and got on I-84. Angie marveled at Joe's casual command of the vehicle. The clutch was not a problem to him now. It was a tool. Once on 84, Angie expected Joe to open up, but he kept the same speed (maybe a little more) as traffic.

Joe turned on the radio and left it on the Springfield station. As they cruised, the musical wallpaper was Phil Collins and Men at Work and commercials. Then a familiar voice said, "I'm Joe Ecks, and you're listening to Station WPLR instead of doing your homework, which you really should be doing." The disc jockey added, "Except school's out now, so if you still have homework to do, I'm sorry for that. Here's Tom Petty."

"Hey!" Joe cried. "They used it! They used my funny one! Did you hear that?"

Angie nodded. She recalled Betsy's disapproving frowns and savored a secret satisfaction.

Joe pulled into the Bowl-O-Rama on the Berlin Turnpike. Angie recognized Ed's turbo Z in a front parking space. Joe pulled in between the Z and a Corolla. When he switched off the Ferrari, he gazed at Angie and said, "What a work of art."

They went in and saw Ed with a young woman over six feet tall with Nordic blue eyes and a sharp nose. Ed introduced her as Cynthia, a senior at UConn on a volleyball scholarship. "You're Joe Ecks!" Cynthia exclaimed, shaking his hand. "Wow!"

"That's what they claim," Joe said. "And this is my beautiful wife Angela."

"What's it like being married to such an amazing man?" Cynthia gushed.

Angie looked up at Cynthia.

Ed intervened. "Angie wouldn't know, for reasons that are obvious."

"Oh, ho!" Joe exclaimed. "Ask her what it's like to have a brother with social skills!"

"Hey! I have social skills! I even got a date! And my date's *taller* than your date!"

Joe eyed the two women, comparing Cynthia's 6'+" height with Angie's 5'2" height. He conceded, "Well, maybe in heels. Okay, point taken."

Ed looked around. "We need to find bowling balls that fit our hands."

Joe said, "No, you don't. One of the perks of renting a whole bowling alley is you get free, custom-fitted bowling balls."

Cynthia had brought her own bowling ball and shoes. Angie, Ed and Joe had their hands measured. While their balls were drilled, they sat at a wobbly Formica table and drank cheap beer from a plastic pitcher. Ed bragged that he and Cynthia could beat Joe and Angie at bowling. Cynthia proposed that the competition should be men versus women, but she wanted a handicap. Angie, recalling Marcy's birthday party, didn't want to be involved in any competition. Joe suggested that the four of them should strive to beat a 600 combined. He explained that, this way, they would all be working together toward a common goal.

Ed accused Joe of trying to avoid getting whooped by him and Cynthia. Joe insisted that he didn't want to compete against friends. He added, "What I really love about being in a band, Ed, is that we each contribute to the whole, and none of us succeed unless all of us succeed. If bowling were like a band, we'd each have our specialty, and we'd play like a real team. More like volleyball." He gestured to Cynthia. "Right?"

"Yeah, I guess so," Cynthia laughed.

"Play to our strengths?" Ed queried. "How so? Aren't we all just rolling balls?"

"Hell, no!" thundered Joe. "Spose Cynthia was our first-ball. Then maybe you were good at picking up spares. And maybe I'm the split guy. Angie can be good at high pin-counts after spares. I dunno. We would have to do better as a team that way than as a set of individuals playing."

Angie was watching Joe. In this milieu, it was easy to see Joe as a different person.

"Do you want to try it?" Ed asked.

Joe said, "Yeah, let's each bowl our own game. Then we'll bowl four more games as a team and see if we beat the first total. We need a captain, though, to keep us organized. I nominate Cynthia."

"Me?" Cynthia laughed. "Why?"

"You obviously know more about bowling than any of us," Joe told her. "You're the only person who brought their own ball."

Ed added, "He's got a point."

"Really? Okay!" Cynthia smiled.

When they started on the second pitcher, they discussed "the charts". 'Contents' had slipped from 40 to 47. 'Xylene', the album, had jumped to 48. 'Xylene' the song was due to be released in five days, and Ed suggested that its release would further help the sales of the album.

Ed then asked, "Joe, have you been keeping track of the tour bookings?"

"Not really," Joe said, "but I've got Richard updating me on the date of the first one. Now it's September 30th at Virginia Tech." He made a face.

Ed nodded. "I thought so. That's the important one, isn't it? And what's with the face?"

"Ah, Virginia Tech and UVA are rivals."

"Oh, right," Ed said, recalling that Joe now believed he had attended UVA. "Are you getting nervous?"

"Oh, I passed nervous a month ago, and I'm well into the 'stricken mad with terror' category."

"Maybe it would help if we played someplace, sort of as a practice."

"You and I?" Joe asked.

"No, Roger and Bill could fly in. We'd do a surprise performance someplace. Like at the Half Moon. We used to play there all the time back when we were getting started. You need to get in front of people and realize it's no big deal."

Joe regarded Ed. "That's a surprisingly good idea, coming from you."

Ed smiled. "I wish I could disprove your assumptions, but it was actually Bill's idea. He told me to talk to you. Y'know, Bill, being a former music teacher, has seen a lot of newbies perform for the first time."

Cynthia laughed. "Mr. Ecks, you've played hundreds of concerts!"

Joe glanced at Cynthia and explained, "It's a running joke between us." To Ed, he said. "Yeah, let's set that up."

Angie made a mental note to contact Richard.

Ed said, "Great. I'll tell Richard, and he'll handle the details."

Angie recalibrated. Richard wasn't Stu. Richard handled details.

As they drained the second pitcher, the balls were delivered. Angie liked her ball. It was light, and had taupe swirls. As it should have, it fit her delicate hand perfectly. And on her first roll, she dropped her new ball in the gutter. Joe coached her patiently and with encouragement. By the second ball of the third frame, she got the ball to go all the way down the lane to the pins. She knocked down seven of them. Her four-frame score was already higher than it had been at Marcy's party. Joe cheered deliriously.

After the first game, Cynthia had the best score, with a 167. Joe had a 151, Ed a 135, and Angie had a 44. For a total of 497. Ed accused Joe of holding back to prove his point. Joe declared that the four team games would add up to over 600, so far over 497 that Joe's theory would be proven.

"Okay, Cynthia," Joe said, "Just to keep the experiment fair, each of us has to roll a ball every two frames. Frames one and two, each of us must bowl. But if there's a strike, then someone doesn't hafta bowl."

Cynthia had herself go first in the odd frames and Ed would attempt the spare. Then Joe would roll the first ball on the even frames, and Angie would try to get the spare. If either Joe or Cynthia got a strike, then Angie wouldn't have to bowl.

Ed started to say something, but Joe cut him off. "Did our captain ask you for your advice?" he demanded.

Ed lowered his head and muttered, "No, sir." (Cynthia laughed.)

They bowled. The bowling alley staff of three sat at a table to the side and watched. Joe and Cynthia rolled good first balls, but Ed wasn't very good at getting spares, and Angie was worse. The first game was a 130.

"Four times one thirty is five twenty," Ed informed Joe. "Five twenty is less than six hundred."

Cynthia reversed the strategy. Angie and Ed would roll the first balls, and she and Joe would go for the spares. Angie was getting better at missing the gutters, but she never hit the head-pin. Following her, Cynthia still blasted a lot of spares. Ed would get eight or nine pins (and one strike), and Joe picked up three out of four spares. The second game score was 165.

Joe told Ed, "Now our total is two ninety-five. Two times two ninety-five is five ninety. We're almost on the pace."

"Five ninety is less than six hundred," Ed observed.

Cynthia made another adjustment. Ed went first, and if he got a strike, then the next frame was Cynthia and Joe. Cynthia seemed better on the big-count spares, so if Ed left a lot standing, Cynthia, instead of Joe, would go after Ed.

Angie saw herself doing better, too. Joe stopped telling her what to do, but never restrained his encouragement.

The third game score was 160. Cynthia kept the same strategy. They only needed a 145 to break 600, a goal they had all adopted. In fact, on the fourth game, they bowled a 181. Joe had made his point, but, more importantly, they had all had fun.

"I had so much fun!" Cynthia announced. "You both are so famous, and here you are bowling just like regular people!"

Joe replied, "We actually are regular people."

Ed said, "Yeah, but we have pretty cool jobs, though."

They carried their balls to the front desk to trade in their shoes. The woman at the desk said, "You can't just carry your balls like that! Hold on." She disappeared in the pro shop and returned with three bowling bags and handed them out. "Use these," she said. "And let me know when you want to do this again. I'll throw in some shoes for you."

Joe thanked all of them, and they exited into the cool night air. And, at 2:45, it was quiet. No cars drove the Berlin Turnpike or even any roads within a few miles. They put their bags in the trunk and drove away. Joe didn't drive especially fast, even though the roads were empty. He'd drunk a lot of beer, but Angie didn't think he was too drunk to drive.

Joe said, "Angie, thanks for playing along. You bowled great, and I was really proud of you. I had a lot of fun tonight."

"Thank you," Angie blushed. "But I bowled worse than everyone."

Joe took the ramp to I-84. To Angie, they seemed to be sitting inches from the road.

"The thing about bowling is what really matters is how you do relative to yourself. Look how much better you were doing towards the end. Geez, at first, you couldn't keep it between the gutters, and that last game, you picked up a spare! You were able to aim at a specific pin and hit it. You'd gotten a *lot* better. More confident, too."

Angie thought about it. She said, "Thanks. Mike."

Joe smiled at the windshield. "And you looked really good, too. Those shorts of yours were quite a distraction."

They left the highway and turned onto what Angie thought of as the final stretch, the last, winding few miles of route 10. Joe continued his moderate driving pace. They came over a hill, and the road abruptly turned left. Joe hadn't anticipated the turn. The right tires went on the gravel, and Joe whirled the steering wheel. The Ferrari turned, but the right tires dropped into a ditch. The car lurched up, bottomed out and slid. The right front fender hit a tree, jolting the car to a stop.

"Angie! Angie, are you okay?" Angie became aware that Joe was searching her face.

"I'm okay," Angie responded. Joe had a small cut on his nose that emitted a single drop of blood.

"You're really okay? Thank God!" Joe opened the door and got out. He staggered through the brush to the front of the car. Angie also got out, rubbing her neck. Joe gaped at the ruined fender and mis-aligned front tire. He looked at Angie rubbing her neck. "Damn!" Joe cried. "Damn!"

Angie said, "Joe, it's okay, really." She stepped closer.

Joe backed away. Gesturing vaguely to the car and Angie, he said, "This is why I can't have anything nice." He gritted his teeth. "I ruin everything I touch."

Angie mentally stepped back. She started to say, "You haven't ruined me," but she realized that he hadn't touched her. Not really.

"Ma'am, is everyone okay?" a voice called from the road. A car idled there.

"Everyone is okay," Angie confirmed. "But we'll need a tow truck."

The car drove away.

Angie's neck ached. Joe rubbed her neck and shoulders, and that felt good, but it wasn't really necessary. He apologized about a dozen times.

A police car pulled up, lights flashing. Seconds later, another police car pulled up. Angie gave her account of the accident, and the policeman asked Joe the same questions. Meanwhile, the tow truck arrived, and the driver set to work preparing his gear. The policeman was about their age, stocky, with a buzz-cut. He regarded Joe. "Do I smell alcohol?" he asked.

Joe answered, "I drank some beer tonight, sir."

The officer said, "I'll drive you home, then."

They sat in the back of the patrol car for a few minutes, then the officer got in and took them home. No one spoke on the short trip. The radio blurted incomprehensible phrases. The officer pulled up to the keypad and punched in the numbers Joe gave him. The gate opened. He drove to the loop at the front door. Angie and Joe got out. Joe said, "I really appreciate the ride and everything. We're gonna be playing in Hartford in January, I think. Do you want tickets?"

The officer told him, "We're not allowed to accept gifts. If you're okay, I'll be on my way." He circled and drove out to the road.

Joe watched him leave. He said, "I should have gotten in trouble."

Angie replied, "I suppose you could have."

Joe shrugged. "It's good to be king, I guess." In the east, the sky was lightening. "Let's go to bed."

—X—

One day, Ed arrived at the jet at stupid thirty o'clock in the morning. The sun was just coming up. He knew which jet was his, due to the fact that standing beside it were two uniformed men and Joe Ecks. He pulled his Z in beside Joe's Jag and joined him at the jet. They all piled in. The jet taxied and took off, bound for Hollywood Burbank Airport.

The jet was quieter than most; conversation was possible.

Joe asked, "What happened to your Z's fender? It's dented."

"I hit a mailbox or something."

"'Or something'?"

"Well, it wasn't a dog or a person, because there's paint on the dent." Ed hoped Joe wouldn't ask any more questions, because that was about all he knew.

Joe said, "This 'Xylene' filming has been making me anxious for a long time. I really appreciate your coming along for moral support."

Ed made a noise. He said, "I'd pay *big* money to see this video filmed."

Joe said, "I thought I'd misjudged you, Ed. Guess not."

Ed grinned. He watched Joe trade some banter with the pilot and co-pilot. Then some turbulence woke him up. He looked out the window and saw endless farmland. He looked over at Joe. Joe was reading a book. The jet touching down woke Ed a second time. He felt a lot better now. He'd needed more sleep than he realized.

They left the plane, walked about twenty feet to the waiting Cadillac limousine with the open door and got in. The driver, a young woman in her twenties, put their carry-ons in the trunk, then got behind the wheel. Pulling away, she said, "Good morning, sirs, and welcome to California. My name is Melissa, and I'm from the service. If there's anything you need while you're here, I'll get it for you."

Ed said, "I need a sense of purpose."

"Your purpose is to entertain people by playing the drums," Melissa told Ed.

The reply was so perfect, that Ed was speechless.

Smiling, Joe said, "See, Ed?"

Ed cried, "I can't believe I didn't see it all this time! Thank you, Melissa-from-the-service." She really made a good first impression.

The limo made slow progress through traffic.

Ed asked, "Joe, did you get any sleep on the plane?"

"Yeah, I did," Joe answered. "I'm fully rested."

"Good," Ed approved. "Big day today."

Joe sighed heavily. He was quiet. Finally, he asked, "Do you know what Bruce has in store for me today?"

"Not exactly," Ed answered. "Why?"

"Because I fear the unknown more than anything else."

Ed studied Joe. Joe was nervous. Very nervous. Ed felt responsible, because he had suggested the concept of a woman crawling all over Joe. He'd wanted to see Joe uncomfortable and maybe squirm a little. But this was too much. Ed wondered what Joe would say if the roles were reversed. Ed said, "This will be the first time you actually act."

"What do you mean?"

"Yeah, you've been filmed a bunch of times playing guitar, which is acting in a way. But here, you're actually playing a role. You're acting." Ed didn't know where he was going with this. He hoped Joe would pick up the fumble.

"Acting," Joe repeated. "It's a role."

"Yeah. Have you ever acted in anything?"

"No. You?"

"No, not since that disaster when I was Pig Pen in the school play." Ed scowled.

Joe looked at him curiously.

"Don't ask. And don't ask Angie, either. She doesn't remember it right." Quickly returning to the subject at hand, he said, "But anyway, I'll bet you'd be good at it. And you know what? The woman is acting, too. She's a professional. For her, it's just another job."

"Hmm, yes, it's just acting," Joe mused. "But, you know, I bet it would be funnier if it were you instead of me."

"Nope," Ed stated.

"Yeah, there's that Pig Pen stigma that follows you. Forget it."

"I'd like to," Ed assured.

The Cadillac turned into a parking lot. Joe wiped his hands on his pants.

In the studio, Ed and Joe were confronted with three different sets of a house interior. And O'Reilly. O'Reilly shook Joe's sweaty hand. He said, "Morning, Joe. Ed. I've been going back to your comment, Ed, at the production meeting, where you suggested that Xylene is a metaphor for a woman. So of course, I need to know what kind of woman Xylene would be. I've listened to the song about a hundred times now." O'Reilly turned to a guy standing by and said, "Get Tsuzi and bring her here." The guy took off. O'Reilly continued, "So what I understand is this: Essentially, Joe is strongly attracted to Xylene, though for him, the relationship is destructive and ultimately fatal. Xylene, though, is indifferent to Joe. You follow me? That sound about right, Ed? It's not what you brainstormed in the meeting, though."

Ed stroked his goatee in thought. No, it wasn't. And it didn't sound as much fun.

"Um," said Joe. "Whaddaya thinkin?"

O'Reilly grinned. "Imagine a boss in a large company falls for a secretary, who could care less. Now imagine they're at a company function or party or whatever, and the boss makes a total fool of himself and ruins his career."

Joe tilted his head. "And Ed's the boss?"

O'Reilly glanced at Ed and back to Joe. "No, you."

The guy returned with a woman. She was medium height and Asian. Ed thought she looked like she was about thirteen years old, but his estimate was contradicted by her obvious frontal assets, which, Ed speculated, were retrofits. Her long hair swayed in a ponytail, and she wore ultra-conservative office-wear. This contrasted with the fact that she fairly glowed with sexual heat, though she didn't seem particularly interested in anyone around her.

"This is Tsuzi," O'Reilly introduced. "This is Joe, of course, and Ed Brettington is here."

Joe held his hand out to shake. Tsuzi ignored it. Joe withdrew his hand. "In character already," he said. "Good."

O'Reilly said, "Throughout these scenes, the music will be playing, but we're not synching to the music. If anything, we will be recording the audio, and we may let it bleed through the music." O'Reilly ambled toward one of the sets. "We're shooting the party scenes first, because they're gonna be the hardest." He gestured to a host of office workers on the set. "Everyone, meet Joe Ecks, and this is Ed Brettington. Joe, these will be your coworkers." He gestured to an older man. "Eric is your boss. He's the one who will be particularly displeased with your foolish behavior."

The older man smiled and waved. "Hi, Joe."

O'Reilly sent Joe to wardrobe.

Ed followed. The room was even more chaotic than usual. Ed retreated to the studio. He perused the breakfast table. The bagels looked good, but Ed picked up a fruit bar. A guy wearing a headset stood next to him studying the breakfast table critically. He picked up a doughnut and saw Ed. "Ed Brettington?" he asked.

"In person," Ed confirmed. They shook hands.

"You wrote 'Xylene', right?"

"Co-wrote it," Ed said. "I wrote the lyrics."

"Is this what you had in mind?"

"Not really," Ed admitted. "But I think it's a fair interpretation."

"Hey, what about 'Xylophone'? Was that about, uh, what was that about, really?"

Ed smiled. "It was about doing something that has no purpose other than to give you pleasure. And, yes, that would include masturbation."

"So it's not really about that."

"Not specifically."

The guy looked up at Ed and said, "I understand. Hey, I gotta go. Thanks!"

Ed thought maybe he actually did understand. Ed ate his fruit bar, which had the flavor and consistency of sticky sawdust. Joe, surrounded by people, appeared onstage. He ineffectively tugged at his suit. Ed found a chair and watched.

O'Reilly arranged people in their places. "Now, Joe, you come in through that doorway with, uh, Peter. You see Tsuzi. Her name is Xylene, of course. You light up and ignore Peter and horn in on the conversation. Eric, be sure to give me some disapproving looks. In fact, you guys should be also noticing Joe."

O'Reilly stepped back and nodded to his assistant. "Places for six one!" the assistant shouted.

The actors were all pretty much in position already, but they morphed into character.

"Sound!"

"Hot," a remote voice reported.

"Camera!"

"Speed."

"Action!"

The actors began a convincing buzz of party talk. Joe and Peter came into the room. Joe saw Xylene and approached her.

"Cut!" O'Reilly shouted. He spoke to his assistant.

The assistant went to the set. He gave some direction to Joe and finished with, "Places for six one!"

Ed checked his watch and wondered how many days they would be shooting this video. He wished he had brought a book. Melissa appeared beside Ed. She dragged over a chair and sat. They exchanged hellos.

Ed asked, "What's your function in this vast project?"

Melissa answered, "I handle the talent."

Ed nodded. He pondered the immense scope of the term 'handle'.

They watched another iteration of scene six one. Joe laughed and patted an actor on the back and returned to his place.

Ed said, "Bruce is really working hard on this video. This is much more elaborate than usual."

"He wants a Moonman," Melissa said. "Last year, MTV started giving out awards for music videos like the Grammys. Mr. O'Reilly really wants the award. It's called a Moonman."

"Why?"

"You know, the astronaut with the MTV flag on the moon? That's the trophy." Melissa watched Joe on the set and said, "You know, Joe Ecks has a reputation for being a major asshole, but he doesn't seem to be. Is he?"

Ed answered, "Joe and I have been friends for a very long time. I've never thought of him as an asshole. But I guess he has been that to a lot of people. Lately, though, he's been a changed man. Even I don't recognize him."

"What happened?"

"Well, I guess he didn't like who he had become. So he changed."

Melissa said, "People can't change that much and stay that way."

Ed pondered this. He said, "It wouldn't kill me if you were wrong."

They watched the filming of six one through six six. Day turned into night. Then the crew started set-up for seven one. Joe stopped by. After hellos, he said, "How's it going so far, Ed? Enjoying yourself?"

"Not really. I was expecting to see a sultry biker chick invading your personal space. This is boring."

Joe said, "Bruce says it's going well. He asked me if I had any acting experience." Joe laughed. "I'm hittin on a beautiful woman and gettin rejected an lookin stupid! This isn't actin at all!" Joe laughed heartily. "I don't think we're gonna finish these scenes today, though."

Ed said, "At this rate, I don't think you'll finish this week."

Joe pointed to the set, on which a guy stood. "Look!" he exclaimed, "I gotta *stand-in*! Is that cool or what?"

Ed said, "You can cross that off your bucket list."

Joe made a noise. "I don't have a bucket list *that* cool."

Ed opened his mouth, and then he smiled. He said, "Maybe you should."

Joe thought about it, and he said, "Maybe I should. What about you, Ed, what's on your bucket list?"

"Places for seven one!" O'Reilly's assistant shouted.

"Now I gotta go do something. See ya." Joe turned and headed for the set.

Melissa said, "I don't think that guy could even *act* like an asshole."

Ed agreed.

Melissa sat with Ed for the duration, and she got him whatever he wanted. As Joe predicted, the filming went late, and they still had a scene to shoot. O'Reilly released the talent, and Joe left to change from his business suit to the T-shirt and jeans in which he now looked natural. He was one of the last to leave the dressing room. He and Ed went out to where the limo idled.

Three young men stood beside it. "Hey, here he is!" one exclaimed. They crowded Joe. They asked rather innocent questions ("Hey, how are you?" "What were you working on inside?" "Hey, I play guitar, do you need a back-up?"). They ignored the woman commanding them to back off. Joe and Ed politely worked their way to the car. Melissa grabbed the hair on the back of one guy's head and yanked him off his feet. She twisted the wrist of another, and he threw himself on the ground. The third wisely stepped back.

Ed and Joe got in the car. A second later, Melissa got behind the wheel. She said, "I'm sorry, sir. They weren't there before." She pulled away.

Joe looked behind them and saw the men getting up. He said, "Wow. Thank you."

In the rear view mirror, Melissa winked.

In the elevator, she told Ed, "Your room is on the 5th floor."

Ed said, "Thank you. I'm going up to Joe's suite first, though."

Melissa led them to the Presidential suite, and told Joe, "I'll pick you up from your room at nine o'clock." She stood by while Ed and Joe went in the door and closed it.

Joe put his bag on one of the beds.

Ed said, "Nice place."

Joe smiled. "Do you ever stop thinking about the over-kill? I just wanna *sleep*, not move in. What are you doing here anyway?"

Ed was on the phone. "Send two six-packs of Moosehead beer to the Presidential suite, please. Thanks." He put down the phone.

"Are you ordering room service and charging it to my room?"

Ed answered, "What I'm doing is keeping you out of trouble."

"By buyin me beer? Where were you when I was in college!"

Ed explained, "When two six-packs are delivered, maybe Melissa will realize I'm going to be here awhile, and she'll go home."

Joe blinked. He said, "Oh." He moved to push up his glasses and stopped. He looked up. "Ed, you are a good friend. And a good brother. And very tall, of course."

Ed literally blushed. He changed the subject. "Did Sheridan tell you he got Dan Dumbrowski for the tour?"

"Dan Dumbrowski?"

"He's known for the single 'Not So Fast'? He fronted Journey last year," Ed explained.

Joe nodded. "Yeah, he oughta be capable. Can he learn the material in time?"

Ed said, "Sure. He'll learn the songs, and then we'll get together in LA in a couple of weeks with Burrill and McCann. Richard's setting it up."

Joe looked doubtful.

Ed continued, "He has a head start, because he already knows how to play guitar. But keep practicing, and maybe you can play something yourself."

The beer arrived, which enhanced the conversation in the same way that gasoline enhances a lit match.

The next day, Joe woke up in the hotel bed. He uttered a bad word and checked his wrist, then looked at the clock. "7:17?" he mumbled. "Oh, west coast. Right." He lay back down. A few minutes later, someone knocked lightly on his door. Joe tip-toed over and peeped through the peep-hole. It was Melissa. Joe quietly backed away and took a shower.

He was refreshed and ready by 9:00. Someone knocked on his door. Joe checked. It was Melissa and Ed. Joe opened the door. "Right on time," he commended.

Walking down the hall, Melissa asked, "How did you sleep, Mr. Ecks?"

"Soundly!" Joe answered. "I almost overslept."

Ed replied, "That's good. It may go late again today."

Joe wiped his hands on his pants.

After shooting the last party scene, O'Reilly switched to the office sets and the scenes in which Joe discovers Xylene and she is indifferent to him. Then he shot a series of short fantasy scenes in which Joe and Xylene kiss passionately. This was what Ed came to see. Joe was, as Ed had hoped, delightfully uncomfortable, but, he was so awkward at kissing passionately that it was embarrassing to watch. O'Reilly and his assistant cleared the set (including Ed and Melissa) and gave Joe instruction, presumably using Tsuzi as a prop.

After that, Joe almost looked natural. But O'Reilly kept shaking his head and filming the scenes over again.

It was another late night, but the video was in the can. Joe returned to Ed and Melissa. He was wrung out. He said, "What happens now, Melissa? Are we flying back tonight?"

Melissa answered, "You're not flying back tonight. I'm to take you back to the hotel. I'll drive you to the airport tomorrow."

O'Reilly appeared. "Joe, as always, it was a pleasure working with you." They shook hands.

"Sorry I made it take so long," Joe said.

O'Reilly answered, "Stop saying that. You're a natural, but I wanted every detail perfect."

Melissa asked, "Do you think it's Moonman-worthy?"

O'Reilly answered, "I wouldn't rule it out. I'll know more after editing."

It occurred to Ed that 'Xylene', the title track, had been released that day. O'Reilly was under a lot of pressure to get it done.

Melissa drove them back to the hotel and escorted them both to Joe's room. Joe had requested that Ed join him.

In the room, Ed saw that Joe was miserable. Joe said, "Ed, I spoze yer the last person I should be confessin to." Ed noticed his accent was especially prominent. "I did some things. Things Angie wouldn't like. Like me to do. Bruce told me to, and I didn't object."

"Joe, did you do anything that wasn't necessary for the video?"

Joe looked around. Finally, he said, "No. But I don't think we needed to do all that. An all that kissin! Swate Jasus." He kept reaching for his shirt pocket. "Angie's gonna see that video," Joe moaned. "A *lotta* people are."

Ed offered, "Angie doesn't have to know how many takes there were of you and Tsuzi kissing."

Joe paced. "Kissin and *stuff!*" he cried cryptically. "Ah caint keep that from Angie. I don't wanna be keepin secrets from her. Or anything! I gotta teller."

Ed regarded the agitated Joe. He knew that Joe was capable of harboring secrets. Or of at least not telling the whole truth. He said, "Joe, I think you ought to tell Angie everything. I am positive that she will understand and forgive you. If she doesn't, I'll talk to her and set her straight."

Joe stopped pacing and grinned wryly up at Ed. "As if Angie would listen to you."

Ed chuckled. "Well, there is that." Suddenly serious, he asked, "What is Angie to you, Joe?"

"Oh, I'm crazy in love with her. I've been with her almost constantly for months now, and I still feel like I'm gettin to know her. An with every little discovery, I lover even more. You know, a couple a weeks ago, she started calling me 'Mike'."

"So?"

"She doesn't just see me as a crazy Joe. She sees me as a different person."

Ed stroked his goatee and wondered if *he* saw New Joe as a different person. He knew he was different, but it was hard to see it, because he was Joe. He was in Joe's body. "And this is important why?"

"I need her to see the distinction, because I want to win her over. I want her to love *me*."

Ed was about to exclaim, "Of course she loves you! She married you!" But he saw that she had not. Not Mike. He asked Joe, "So you want to steal her away from Joe?"

"Yes."

"You realize she's married, right? Married to Joe?" Ed couldn't believe he was having this discussion with Joe. It was getting unreal.

"Yes," declared Joe. "But really, she belongs with me. She'd be happier, I think."

"Happier with you than with Joe?" Ed asked. "Do you think she would actually consider divorcing Joe to be with you?"

"No, I dunno," Joe admitted. "She's been with Joe for a long time." Ed started to speak, but Joe said, "Wait. She wouldn't have to. Hey!"

"Yeah," said Ed drily. "Maybe you've got a shot."

"Yes, I'm sure of it," Joe stated. Now resolute, he said, "Thanks, Ed. I will confess to Angie. I'll beg for her forgiveness. Thanks."

Leaving the Presidential Suite, Ed wondered if monogamy was a worthwhile goal. The next morning, Joe met Melissa and Ed at his door, and Melissa took them to the airport.

—X—

One day, Joe stood in his music room and picked his way through 'Mrs. Kisses'. It had two main guitar tracks, rhythm and lead. When there had been a danger that Joe would have to play guitar, he and Bill had decided that Joe would play lead, and Bill would fill in rhythm when possible. So Joe figured out what he was going to play, and he had pretty much figured out how he was going to play it. Next, he was going to play it at about one-tenth speed, until his mastery allowed him to play faster. Angie had observed this process repeatedly.

Joe smiled when he saw Angie in the music room doorway. "Angie, hi." Behind him, amps were stacked imperfectly. A rack held several pre-amps with wires coming out from all over. The room contained about a dozen guitar stands, but only three of them held guitars, none of them Good Guitar. Six pedals were lined up in front of Joe. The equipment heated the room, and even though Joe had the air conditioner on, he still set it at about 90°. He wanted to simulate ""the temperature on stage. Joe wore a Fender baseball cap primarily to act as a sweatband.

"Hi, Mike," Angie answered. She held up her camera. "I want to take some pictures. Do you mind?"

"No, I don't mind," Joe said. "But I'd a thought this was a period you'd prefer to forget."

Angie regarded Joe softly. "No. I want to capture you in your natural habitat."

Joe looked back and forth critically. "Uh, okay. I should tidy up."

"Don't. I want the picture to be natural."

"Okay, how should I stand?"

"I want the picture to be natural," Angie repeated. "Just do what you would do if I weren't here."

"You want me to ignore you?"

"I guess. Yes."

"Okay," Joe half shrugged. He mentally reset and returned to fingering 'Mrs. Kisses' with exaggerated slowness. He stood straight and stared at the walls, though it really looked like his eyes had stopped seeing.

Angie had a purpose for taking pictures of Joe in his music room. Since the 'Xylene' shoot, he'd been particularly anxious. She wanted to see him comfortable in an environment that was under his complete control. The stacks of amps, the disorganized wire, it was all a consequence of Joe's new, different, touch. Angie wanted to get it in the background, but still keep Joe the focus of the picture. She carefully orbited Joe, evaluating.

Joe obeyed Angie precisely by ignoring her completely. She orbited again, snapping pictures from the vantages she thought best.

She was satisfied with her shots. But she would know for sure once they were developed. "I'm done now," she told Joe.

"I can stop ignoring you?"

Angie smiled. "Please."

Joe said, "You seem to know what you're doing."

"Thank you, but I don't. There's a lot to photography, and I'm just scratching the surface. I like trying to find the best shots. But I just have this camera, and I don't even know what all of it does." Angie actually had two other cameras, both more simplistic than the one she held.

Joe regarded Angie. "You should learn," he encouraged. "You could go to classes, or even get one-on-one instruction. Why not?"

"I don't want to start anything I couldn't finish," Angie explained. She was afraid of liking it and having to give it up for some reason. Some reason like it interfered with something. Something with the band. Something of Joe's. She was afraid of liking it and feeling guilty about its burden on Joe, if he allowed her to continue at all. She looked up at Joe, who seemed to understand her mental journey. "If it interfered with anything."

"Like what?" Joe asserted. "Set a schedule. We'll work around it, if we can. If you get private instruction, then you have a lot of flexibility. If you need more cameras, we'll get them. If you need a darkroom, we'll build one for you. As long as you enjoy it. But if you lose interest in it, that's okay, too."

Joe made it seem so simple, but he couldn't know how crazy the schedule got sometimes. Usually. She hedged, saying, "Maybe I'll look into it." She left the room.

—X—

One day, Joe saw Angie in the library. He entered. Angie looked up. She wore a heavy cotton shirt and snug jeans. It was late summer, but the house was cool.

Joe said, "I need to tell you something."

Joe's serious tone made Angie a little nervous. "Yes?"

"Shooting 'Xylene', I did... things. Wrong things."

Angie hadn't seen the video, because it hadn't yet been released. The song had debuted in the top 100 at 39 without even an associated video. "What things?"

Joe said, "There's a scene where Joe is fantasizing about his love interest, Xylene. Well, several scenes, really. Uh, Joe and Xylene kiss passionately."

"For the video, right?"

"Yes, yes. But I wasn't very good. Not on film. Bruce made us kiss a lot until we got it right."

Angie didn't really want to hear this. "Okay. Is that it?"

"No," Joe admitted miserably. "Bruce had Tsuzi touch my pants."

"She touched your pants?"

"Yes. In the crotch area. Bruce wanted us to be close in this scene, like we were, uh, lusting for each other. He said I was, like, I had a personal barrier. And he made me touch her."

"Where?" Angie asked with trepidation.

"Right there in the studio," Joe said. "No one else was there, though."

"No, I mean what part of her did you touch?"

"Oh. I touched her bra."

Angie was relieved, actually. A confession that started like this was likely to be distressing. "You touched her bra?"

"Yes. I'm sorry, Angie. He made me do it, and I didn't fight it. I'm really sorry."

Angie said, "Well, Joe. I don't think it's right that you've been more intimate with a stranger than you have been with me."

"What?"

"Yes," declared Angie. "You have to passionately kiss me. It's a rule."

"I... What?" Joe stammered. "Why?"

"I'm sorry, I don't make the rules," Angie said, making the rules. "Now show me what you learned."

They kissed. Joe's lips were soft, and Angie melted. Joe wrapped her in himself. Kissing Joe, as Mike, was so different. So... mutual. Then Joe left her standing. Angie caught her breath and focused. Joe was looking at her uncertainly. Angie said, "Tell Bruce I said 'Thank you'."

"Really?"

"You're not done atoning," Angie told Joe. "Now you have to touch my bra."

Joe looked at Angie uncertainly.

She said, "Stand behind me and reach into my shirt."

"Uh," Joe stuttered. "Okay." He moved behind Angie. "Okay," he wavered, "I'm reaching now. Okay?" His hand advanced down into Angie's shirt. Suddenly, he was alarmed. "Angie, you're n—"

"No, I'm not," Angie confirmed.

"Oh, God!" Joe blurted stepping back. "Oh, God! I'm so sorry, I'm so sorry! Oh, God! Angie, I'm so sorry!"

"Joe, it's…" Angie said as Joe fled the room. "Joe?" she called. "Mike?"

He was gone. And she hadn't even gotten to touch his pants in the crotch area.

—X—

One day, Angie apologized for tricking Joe, and Joe apologized for over-reacting. The incident was forgotten, but not really.

—X—

One day, Cheryl climbed the stairs from the basement after having coached Joe on voice. Seeing Angie, she commented, "He's coming along, but he's no Joe Ecks." Walking away, she muttered, "Thank God." Angie couldn't stop pondering those last two words. It wasn't the last time she would hear them.

—X—

One day, Angie realized she was lonely. Keeping busy helped. She read books and bought presents for upcoming birthdays. She studied the charts until she had them memorized.

'Contents' dropped off the top 100. The 'Xylene' album had got up to 48, then slid to 52. But when the 'Xylene' song was released, it rose to 24. The song itself was at 15, and the video was getting a lot of interest. Angie saw it on the sly, then wished she hadn't. Almost in tears, she called Ed, and the first thing Ed said was, "Yeah, that guy can act! You would never have guessed how uptight he was!" It was exactly the right thing to say. Never one to know when to shut up, Ed continued: "And, you know? I think he actually learned how to kiss." Yeah, Angie thought. There is that.

Angie missed Mike. He practiced for hours. During the day, she only saw him for lunch, either in the solarium or in the dining room with Roger. Then he'd practice for more hours. Learning and mastering guitar possessed him. Okay, Old Joe had always been fixated on something, but he, well, he always involved Angie, even if her involvement was just managing the schedule. Or calling who he told her to call.

Angie followed the music news to see what the press was saying about X Band. She cut out articles for her scrapbook. Following the music news was how Angie discovered that Dan Dumbrowski had checked himself into a 90-day drug rehab program. She wondered if anyone else knew. They did not. And they wanted to know if Joe had been practicing. Except Roger.

—X—

One day, at breakfast, Angie asked, "Do you know whose birthday it is today?"

Joe looked up in alarm. "It's not *yours*, is it?"

"No, it's your sister Susan's. Joe's sister." Angie sometimes lapsed in the Joe/Mike distinction.

"Yer kiddin! I shoulda gotter something. Dang!"

"You did," Angie assured Joe. "You sent her a sweater and enough money to buy a thousand sweaters. Well, officially, *we* did."

"Oh. That was nice of me. Us. You." Joe looked uncomfortable. "Thank you for doing that. I hope she gets a chance to use it, y'know, living in Florida. Do they get much sweater weather?"

"I thought so," Angie said with some doubt. "You can ask her when you call."

"What?"

"Joe always calls her on her birthday."

"That's today!"

"Right, but you shouldn't call her until evening, when she's home from work."

"Swate Jasus! What would I say to her?"

"Well, ask her how she likes her present?" Angie didn't think Joe would have a problem maintaining a conversation with anyone. "Ask about sweater weather in Florida."

"I suppose it's relevant," Joe agreed, "but I hate to fall back on the weather so early in a conversation."

Angie said, "Joe's talks with Susan are usually pretty short."

Joe looked over. "I should have guessed. Joe and his sister aren't close?"

"Well, you, I mean Joe and Susan were never really close. But once the band started making money, they've been fairly distant."

Joe rolled his eyes. "I should of figured."

"It's not what you think," Angie said. "For as long as I've known you and Susan, I mean *Joe* and Susan, she's always maintained a birth-order superiority over Joe. But when X Band started getting successful, she was downright insulting for a while in an unsuccessful attempt to keep Joe in his place."

"I suppose Joe took exception to that."

Angie said, "Joe overlooked a lot, and he forgave a lot, a lot more than I did. Bitch. Now that she has to admit that Joe is a big success, she's just sullen. When she can't avoid you. Joe."

"And yet, Joe sends her money?"

Angie grinned slyly. "Every time she cashes that big check, it reminds her how successful Joe is."

Joe said, "Oo, Joe has a spiteful side."

Angie's grin widened. "No, that was *my* idea."

—X—

One day at lunch, Joe said, "Oh." He pulled a small notepad from his pants pocket. "I called Bengston Photography and talked to Christine Bengston. She'll be over at 2:30 to talk to you about photography stuff. If yer busy, I can call her back and reschedule."

Angie looked up. "You called a photographer?"

"It was presumptuous, so I'm sorry if I overstepped." Joe shifted. "I didn't think you were going to call anyone."

Angie wasn't sure what to think. It was presumptuous, sure, and it was exactly what Angie didn't know she wanted: Actual evidence that Joe supported her hobby. Angie smiled and said, "Good man!"

Joe smiled back.

—X—

One day, Richard Sheridan visited the Ecks Estate. He sat with Joe at the dining room table, as he had before. He discussed the arrangements he had just made with the owner of the Half Moon. As he talked, Angie entered and sat in her chair. Richard said he had arranged for them to play one set.

"One set?" Joe asked. "Which songs should we play?"

Richard answered, "'Contents Under Pressure', 'Cincinnati Fan', 'Stand Up and Shout', and 'Twinkle Twinkle'. Bill thought you would be comfortable with these songs."

Joe considered this. He asked, "Not 'Xylene'?"

"No, I don't want to fly Denise here just for this."

"Why, who's payin? I thought the label would pay for it. Doesn't this count as promotion? Hasn't Theremin been buggin you to circulate me?"

"Well, yes, they're paying, uh, some."

Joe let it drop. He repeated the songs.

Richard nodded. "Yes, you should definitely finish with 'Twinkle Twinkle'. It's your tour encore, after all. You know, it's still getting a lot of requests, and Theremin is going to issue it as a single."

Joe asked, "Will it also have a video?"

Richard answered, "All live footage from the tour." He added, "The 'Xylene' single is #3 this week, and the album might even crack the top ten. Tour Excellence is adding a lot of dates."

Joe suggested that the band meet before the Half Moon to rehearse the set.

Richard replied, "I'm afraid that would be impossible. Everyone is booked. Bill said not to worry; it'll be okay. Have you been practicing?"

"On and off," Joe replied. "I take breaks to go to the bathroom."

Richard chuckled.

To Angie, that sounded about right.

—X—

One day, Angie's subliminal hearing registered that Joe was playing the same chord over and over. Then he started shouting, and she heard banging. She grabbed the emergency six-pack of Moosehead and hurried down to the music room. By the time she got there, Joe's tirade had ended. She saw him seated on the floor, back to the wall. She handed him a beer and bottle opener. Joe popped the top and guzzled the beer. He said, "I'm never gonna get this." His eyes sweated tears of frustration.

"What are you working on?" Angie asked.

"The 'Xenon' solo," Joe answered. "It's difficult." He opened another beer.

"Yes it is," Angie agreed.

"It's got so many tricks in it, so many technical challenges. But if I can play this, I can play anything. Well, I will have the skills I need to play anything. Swate Jasus."

"Did you ask Roger for help?"

"Yeah, I ask Roger for help on everything." Joe set down his empty. He reached for another, but held back. "Roger says I'm thinkin too much. I don't know how else to learn somethin hard."

Angie said, "Joe worked hard on the 'Xenon' solo when he was writing it. And when he finished, he was proud of it."

"He should a been. It's a masterpiece. Joe's a genius."

"You're a genius," Angie defended.

Joe wiped sweat off his forehead. "Not a musical genius. Not like Joe."

Angie looked over at Joe. "No," she said. "Not like Joe." They sat quietly for a few minutes, then Angie stood. "I should let you get back to it."

Joe handed her the diminished six-pack. "Ya might as well put this back in the fridge."

Angie took it and left.

Joe practiced until breakfast, at which he reported that he had made pretty decent progress.

—X—

One day, a limousine grumbled across a gravel parking lot. "Here it is," Richard told the driver. "Stop here." The limo slowed and stopped.

X Band got out the back doors. Following Ed, they hurried up an alley. Bill and Roger had never played at the Half Moon, and Joe had only recently learned where Wallingford was. A familiar guy (to Ed) opened a side door. "I can't believe you're really doing this," he said. The band hustled past him. Keeping a tight formation, they muscled through the pressing crowd to the stage.

Joe put on a guitar and fiddled with the strap. "Good evening, Wallingford!" he exclaimed into the microphone. The crowd cheered. Ed saw that the small restaurant was packed. No one was supposed to know about the surprise performance. Oh, well. "We are X Band, and this is the first stop on our North American tour!" Cheers. Bill tested his keyboards. All were hooked in. Roger played a bass riff. Ed kept quiet. He knew, in this venue, amplification of the drums was not necessary. They'd played in a lot of tiny restaurants, and Ed had thought they never would again.

"Thank you for coming here tonight," Joe said. "We'd like to play a few of our latest songs. Starting with 'Contents Under Pressure'."

Ed counted off, and they started. It wasn't long before Joe was off on the timing. He stopped and rejoined them, managing to stay more or less on the beat. Ed was impressed, though; he hadn't seen Joe play anything on guitar since their tour rehearsal. Joe sang the lyrics, but got them confused, borrowing a line from the second verse. He managed to stay with the band, but Ed could tell he was concentrating. He stopped completely to sing the second verse, then he rejoined the band with the wrong chords, but it was admittedly hard to tell, because they were so rough. Joe figured it out and started again.

The guitar solo for 'Contents' was simple, and Joe nailed it. On the third verse, Joe turned away from the mic for a line, and no one heard it. Mercifully, the song finally ended. The restaurant patrons cheered. Ed was grateful they were all drunk.

Their next song, 'Cincinnati Fan', having been written by Bill, was heavy on the keyboard. Joe turned down his guitar and tried to follow. He sang the correct lyrics in the correct order, just not with the rousing emotion captured in the recording.

Their third song was 'Stand Up and Shout', but Bill waved Joe over. "Let's go right to 'Twinkle Twinkle' and get out of here." Joe nodded and passed the word to Ed and Roger.

"Okay," Joe told the crowd, "This is the first remake X Band ever did." Joe dutifully played the simple melody while the other three jammed. Ed thought they sounded good. They stretched it out. When the song finally ended, Joe thanked the audience, and the band pushed through the crowd and out the side door. A few people had waited for them outside, but the band raced past them down the alley and into the limo.

The limo started up and left the parking lot.

"What the fuck, Joe!" Bill yelled. "What the fuck!"

Richard looked like he was about to cry tears of blood.

Joe had his head between his hands. He moaned, "I know. I know."

"We can't play professionally like that! Fuck! We need the show to be solid so the labels will see that we're viable! That's not solid! I thought you'd been practicing!"

Joe said, "I couldn't hear you guys. All I could hear was my own guitar. I couldn't track."

"And the lyrics!" Bill screamed. "Memorize the lyrics! Oh, Christ!"

"Bill," Roger said evenly, "shut the fuck up."

Bill shut up.

Roger said, "It's legit that Mike couldn't hear us. No one did a sound check, and Mike didn't know enough to stop the performance to fix the problem."

"Oh, shit. Shit!"

Roger said, "I'll stay here in Connecticut to work with Mike on timing. He has worked a lot, but it's been almost all on his own, and he needs experience playing along with others."

Bill regarded Roger. "Will it be enough?"

"It will," Roger answered factually.

Ed said, "Hey, party at my house! Anybody coming?"

—X—

One day, when Angie and Joe were to take dinner in the solarium, Joe appeared with his guitar strapped on.

"What's this?" Angie inquired.

Joe sighed. "Roger says I'm not familiar enough with my guitar. He says I hafta have it on for 36 hours." He sat at the table. The guitar was in the way. Joe had to stand back up.

Angie had to smile. "Oh, my. Is it working?"

Joe glowered. "Yes, dammit."

—X—

One day, X Band started the 'Xylene' tour.

Chapter 21

The Joe Show

Tour Excellence, Inc. had added a show at the Roanoke Coliseum a day ahead of Virginia Tech. That afternoon, Joe and Angie, aboard a commercial airline, arrived at Roanoke airport. They flew commercial for one reason: Their walk through the Roanoke airport would generate some footage for the six o'clock news and provide free advertising. Angie and Joe, having flown first class, were the first passengers to emerge through the gate. In the jetway, two men stopped Angie and Joe. One of the men told Joe, "You go out first. I'll be behind you. Angie and Tom will follow." Joe nodded.

A large crowd had assembled at their gate. They were cordoned off to give Joe room to walk by. Bright camera lights were in his eyes, and the crowd cheered. Joe smiled and waved and walked past. Around the corner, Joe's escort came to his side and guided him out of the airport into a limousine. A few moments later, Angie joined him.

"Swate Jasus," Joe breathed.

The limo pulled away and took them to the Roanoke Coliseum, a short trip. (In Roanoke, VA, nothing is very far away from anything else.) The limo ducked into a small garage underground and stopped. Joe got out and came face-to-face with Sam Foley and Patty Clark.

Sam grabbed Joe's hand and shook it. "Thank you for getting me and Patty this job, Joe. After everything, I really appreciate it."

"Yes, thank you," Patty echoed.

Joe looked surprised at first, but he quickly recovered. "That was terrible about your job loss. I'm just glad both of you were able to take the job. Nobody knows our sound like you two, and it's a godsend having you come on the road with us. Thank *you*."

Angie asked if she could watch the show from the control room. Sam agreed. Joe wanted to see the stage. Sam took them there.

Joe walked on from the wing. He looked around at the thousands of empty seats. He saw the equipment. "What?" he uttered.

Sam said, "It's Metro Gnome's. Your equipment is back there on casters. When Metro Gnome is done, it just gets rolled out."

It was quiet, nearly silent. Joe said, "It's hard to believe it's going to be so noisy and hot and, uh, critical."

"Doors open in half an hour," Sam mentioned.

Joe sighed. "I gotta get ready anyway. I just wanted to see the stage this way." He turned.

Angie said, "I'm going to go up to the control room now, so I won't see you until after the show." They hugged and parted. "You'll do well. Break a leg."

Joe went downstairs. It was quiet, with a few people hustling around. It was early to even get the Metro Gnome band ready. He looked around the sprawling basement complex. He saw two guys talking. One of them looked familiar.

"Carp?" Joe said. "Jack Carpenter?"

The man stood up straight. "Joe Ecks! It's nice to meet you."

"The pleasure is mine," Joe said, shaking his hand. And he shook Carp's friend's hand. "What're you doing here? Here in Roanoke?"

"I'm Metro Gnome's bassist. After my band broke up, I got some guys together, and we started a band."

"How's it going?"

Carp grimaced. "So much drama! Frankly, I'll be surprised if we survive the tour."

"Well, break a leg, Carp," Joe said. "I gotta get goin."

As Joe departed, he heard Carp's friend say, "Damn! That was Joe *Ecks*! He shook my hand!"

Richard found Joe in the labyrinth, and dragged him back to an office. David Burrill and Pete McCann were both there, as well as Ed and Bill. Richard left to find Roger.

"How's that nerve problem with your hands?" Burrill asked tensely.

"It's much better, thank you."

"It didn't go so well at the restaurant, though."

"That wasn't because of my hands."

Burrill studied Joe. "If you're not ready to go on, tell me now, and I can get some damage control in action. Otherwise, everything will fall on you."

"Yep," Joe replied.

Burrill consulted his notes and reviewed the show for the band. Everyone memorized the order and the transitions. Ed confirmed that he had developed a drum solo. (More or less...)

Burrill stood. "I hope you do well tonight. I'll be in the control room, and we'll go over notes tomorrow morning."

"Not too early, I hope," Ed said.

"Oh, it will be," Burrill assured, and left.

McCann, left behind, said, "I'm in charge now. If you need anything, see me." And he went out the door.

Ed called after him, "I need a sense of purpose!"

McCann pretended not to hear.

"Ed, your purpose is to entertain people by playing the drums," Joe reminded. "Remember?"

Ed looked over. He said, "Oh, that's right."

They settled under a blanket of silence. Joe asked Bill about the Lakeland house. Bill said the offer had been accepted.

"Excellent," Joe said. "Hey, how difficult is it to get a mortgage if your income is as erratic as, uh, ours?"

Ed asked, "Does it have rooms for bambinos?"

Bill said to Joe, "You can't. Bankers are robots. If you can't show them W-2's, they can't compute it." He turned to Ed. "And, yes, Cassie and I are planning for children."

"What about you and Angie?" Ed asked Joe.

"Huh? Well, to tell you the truth, Ed, not that it's any of your business, that's too far outside my planning horizon. And for another thing, Angie's married, fer Christ's sake. Swate Jasus."

"To you," Ed pointed out.

"To Joe," Joe emended, perturbed.

"So, wait," Ed said, "So you and Angie have never—"

"Okay, that really *is* none of your business."

"She's my sister!" Ed declared.

"Then ask her yourself."

Ed pictured Angie's reaction to such a question and flinched. "Uh, maybe not."

Quickly changing the subject, Joe asked Bill when he was closing on the house. Bill answered the closing was in two weeks. Cassie was going to have to handle it on her own, though, unless the tour was cancelled before then. Joe asked Ed if he had seen Cynthia in a dating situation. Ed said that they had dated twice since the bowling night, but now that the tour had started, they would be apart for a long time, unless the tour was cancelled.

"Swate Jasus," Joe stated. "Kin we stop talkin like that's a probability?"

Sounds filtered through the building. Joe consulted his bare wrist. "Have they opened the doors yet?"

"A while ago," Bill confirmed.

Richard came through the door with Roger. "Here he is. Where's Burrill?"

"In the control room, I imagine," Ed said.

Richard said, "Let's go over everything one more time."

Around the corner was make-up and wardrobe. The Metro Gnome musicians were getting worked over by the crew. X Band waited until they were done, then it was their turn to get worked over. The crowd noises rose and fell. Metro Gnome left for their show.

"Relax," Bill told Joe. "They've got a half hour, then another twenty minutes for the stage crew."

McCann escorted in Denise Enders, the embodiment of Xylene. "Hi again, X Band," she said, as tall, dark and gorgeous as the day of the rehearsal, a million years ago.

The band echoed her greeting.

Denise undressed for her wardrobe.

Ed asked, "Hey, Denise, do you know all the words in their correct order?"

Pulling up her elastic pants, Denise asked Joe, "Are your hands better now?"

"Yes, thank you."

McCann asked, "Joe, is everything okay?"

Ed said, "I think he's nervous."

"Oh, I'm past nervous," Joe admitted. "I'm petrified. I can barely remember my own name."

"Or Joe's name," Ed commented.

"Huh?" Joe asked. "Oh. Well aren't any a you guys nervous?"

"A little," Bill allowed.

"Yeah, I am," Ed said. "Big drum solo."

"What if ya screw up?" Joe asked. "Aren't you afraid people'll think yer a fraud?"

Bill and Ed exchanged glances. The make-up personnel bustled around them like bees around flowers. Bill said, "If I make a mistake, I just keep going. Most of the time, people won't notice. Or it won't decrease their enjoyment of the music."

McCann seemed worried. "You *have* done this before, right, Joe?"

"Of course I have," Joe assured the stage manager. To the others, he asked, "Is there anything I need to know?"

Ed shrugged. "It gets really hot on stage."

Bill said, "You can't really see the audience, because of the lights."

McCann laughed uneasily.

Make-up was done. The band cleared the room for Metro Gnome's return. They ended up in the actual green room. A few others were in the room: Richard, and two make-up people pretending to do finishing touches. There were assistants of assistants standing by. Through the bones of the building, they could hear Metro Gnome's concluding notes and the cheering crowd.

Joe stood and addressed everyone in the room. "Excuse me," he said, and everyone was quiet, watching him. "Y'all have done a great job, and we appreciate it. Now it's time for the band to meet privately. Please excuse us."

Wordlessly, the staff filed out. "You, too, Richard. Just the performers."

Denise stopped her exit and sat. Dismayed, Richard left.

The room was silent except for the ubiquitous crowd noises seeping through everywhere like a pervasive chill. Joe regarded his band. "Okay, this is it. Any last words? Denise?"

"I'm really excited to be performing with X Band. Thank you for this opportunity."

"Roger?"

Without hesitation, Roger said, "What will be will be."

"Very profound," appraised Ed. He saw that Joe was looking at him. He added, "My last words would be, 'Let's get out there and do our jobs.'" He looked at Joe with a half-grin.

Joe nodded. "Bill?"

Bill stood. "This is it. This is what we practiced for these months. This is the culmination of every music lesson we ever took, every press conference we sat through, every note we recorded. If we blow this tonight, everything we've done will be wasted, and X Band will end. But if we're good..." Bill let the sentence hang.

Ed spoke up, "Then we get to play at Virginia Tech tomorrow."

Joe laughed as Bill said, "Knock it off, Ed."

Roger spoke. "What about you, Mike?"

Joe just smiled. "People do their best work when they're having fun. So let's have fun."

Roger, Bill, and Ed agreed. Denise wondered at the fatalism.

"Can you do me a favor, though?" Joe asked. "Can you give me a few minutes? I just need to focus."

"Um, okay, see you in the wing." They left and headed up the two floors to the wing. From there, they could see the stagehands finishing the transition. The crowd noise swelled.

Ed said to Bill, "Sam will make sure Joe can hear everything. I warned him about it."

Bill nodded. He asked Roger, "Do you think he can do it?"

Roger answered, "He has accomplished an amazing feat. He's memorized the sequence of about three hundred thousand notes."

Bill nodded, though he wasn't sure that was a good answer.

They waited. The stage crew finished and left the stage. Lights raked across it randomly.

"Where's Joe?" Bill asked. "He ought to be here by now."

McCann ran up. "Are you ready?" he demanded.

"We're waiting for Joe," Ed told him.

"Where is he?"

"Never mind, here he is," Bill announced gratefully as Joe glided up.

Roger said, "Welcome back, Joe."

Angie liked the control room. It was privilege, and it was comfort. It had a clear, though distant, view of the stage. You had a seat, but you could get up and move around. You could have a runner get a soda for you. And you were an insider, so you could watch the manipulation of sound and lights.

Everyone else in the control room was an insider, too: Sam and Patty, Burrill, a quiet guy running lights, and a runner. Cassie was also in the control room, and she was quite chatty.

During the Metro Gnome performance, Sam and Patty ran the board, continually making adjustments. Angie knew that Sam had studied their songs ahead of time and had spent some time with McCann. And Sam received some direction through his headset.

"They're finally coming on," Sam told Patty.

Patty nodded.

Cassie was telling Angie details of their house in Lakeland.

X Band came onstage. The crowd cheered. Ed snuggled behind his drums and struck each one. Bill hit a few chords on his keyboards. Roger played a little riff. Joe donned his guitar and stood at the mic. "Are you ready to rock and roll?" he thundered.

Angie sat up and stared through the window. She shushed Cassie.

The crowd cheered.

"I said, 'Are you ready to rock and roll?'" Joe hammered a chord and drifted away with a little riff.

The crowd cheered.

Burrill shouted to no one in particular, "What is he doing?"

"That's not Mike," Angie said.

"What?" Sam asked.

Angie turned and looked at Sam and said, "He's back."

'Tina' was to be their first song, but the band launched an intro for something else. Sam looked into space as he received a message from his headset. "What? 'You'!? It's not even on the— Yeah, I can manage, I mixed it. Okay, bye." He turned to Patty. "They're changing the order. 'You' is first." He fired out orders, and Patty obeyed as Sam raked his own board.

The band launched into 'You'.

Sam said into his mic, "So what's next?" He listened. "You don't— If *you* don't know, who does? What, are they making it up as they go along?! Shit!"

Sensing something wrong, Cassie looked out the window. Angie couldn't look away.

Joe concluded 'You' with a swipe on his guitar. "How was Metro Gnome, huh?" Joe shouted. The crowd's response was lukewarm. "Okay, well, here's some X Band!" And Joe launched into 'Let's Move'.

"It's 'Let's Move'," Sam said. He told Patty what to change and what to watch. Shaking his head, he adjusted his own board.

Angie watched. Joe was perfect. X Band followed him perfectly. Joe indulged in three guitar solos, each one more amazing than the last. Angie noted that Ed did not perform his drum solo. Bill was to solo on 'Anesthesia', but the band played it as it had been recorded. Even then, Joe punctuated it with spiky riffs. The set finished with 'Cincinnati Fan' and 'Xylene'. The first encore was 'Contents Under Pressure', and the second encore was 'Tina'. 'Twinkle Twinkle' was noticeably absent.

Exhausted, Sam set down his headset and collapsed into a chair, which he hadn't used until now. Patty parked the channels and powered them down.

"Good show, huh?" Cassie asked.

"I guess so," Angie allowed. She knew she had to see Joe.

But not for a while. Joe was surrounded by adoring fans and sycophants and gushing members of the press. Angie watched from afar as Joe absorbed the adulation.

Roger, of course, disappeared immediately. After a half hour, Ed and Bill retired, allowing Joe sole possession of the spotlight. Angie searched the coliseum for Ed, but couldn't find him. This first night, the band was staying at the Roanoke Holiday Inn; thereafter, it would stay at the bus. Angie couldn't find anyone. Eventually, she returned to the green room where Joe had held court. Only a few toadies remained. Joe dismissed them. Members of the crew remained.

Joe had been triumphant, and now he was fiercely defensive. Had 'Anesthesia' been the right song to follow 'Perihelion'? Why wasn't this transition as smooth as it should have been? He got in a shouting match with Burrill until the director raged out of the room. Richard was more cooperative, but ultimately, he walked away shaking his head. Then Joe turned on Sam. Angie watched helplessly while Joe tore down every working relationship that Mike had built.

Joe was displeased that Angie couldn't find the other band members. He had to settle for outlining changes for the next day's show. As directed, Angie took notes. But she didn't want to be Joe's secretary, not anymore. And later, she was other things she didn't want to be anymore.

Chapter 22

Extraction

Late that night, Angie lay curled on her side of the king-sized bed. She was afraid to sob; afraid that it would wake Joe. Tears flowed freely down her face into the sheets. She was miserable. Beside her, Joe slept soundly. Angie wept. She had been unsuccessfully date-raped by her husband.

"I've waited so long for this," he had declared. "Mike probably did you every night, right? But I want you to know that while you were sleeping with Mike, I was faithful the whole time. I was faithful."

Angie couldn't stop crying. The sentence assaulted her like a mantra: "I was faithful to you the whole time." Finally, Angie asked herself, "Faithful, when?" *Where* was Joe when he was being faithful? Where was he when he was looking forward to 'having fun' with her? Where?

No one had asked Joe where he'd been for the last few months. Everyone assumed he was just gone. But Angie wondered.

And she recalled that night, a hundred years ago, that she had slept feverishly. She dreamt that Joe had called her, but was it a dream? The receiver had been off the phone. She had picked it up. Why?

She began to perceive that the room was lightening. Dawn was approaching. Angie had to put together a plan. She was exhausted, and her brain was spinning.

She put on yesterday's clothes in the bathroom. She padded into the bedroom to get her suitcase.

The light came on. Joe said, "Where're you going, Ange? I'm ready to snuggle. I'm rested, so I think I can do it now."

Angie lifted up her suitcase, unopened from last night. She said to Joe, distinctly, "Fuck. You," and she walked out the door, not reacting to Joe's surprised expression. She strode down the hall, hoisting her heavy suitcase. She wanted to look strong. Joe's door opened. "You walk away now, and you're walking away from everything," Joe called down the hallway. "I mean, *everything*." She hobbled down the hallway to the elevator. She really didn't care about *everything*. Joe said, "Okay, fine, you've made your point. Fine. Okay. Well, when you realize the mistake you've made, let me know."

Angie pushed the elevator button. Joe looked at her from the open doorway. Angie pulled off her rings and threw them down the hall. "Here are your rings." The door opened, and she got on.

It was too fucking early, and Ed was hungover, but not as hungover as he was going to be. The rising sun blared into his open, second-floor window. Ed pushed himself to close the drapes. In the parking lot, he saw a black stretch limousine. What? Then he saw Angie lugging a suitcase toward it. Ed came out onto the balcony. "Angie!" he called.

Angie stopped and looked up. Then continued toward the limo. The trunk opened.

"Shit!" In sweatpants only, Ed raced to the stairs and ran onto the parking lot.

Ed caught up to the limo as Angie was closing the door. "Angie!" Ed yelled, banging the window.

The window powered down.

Ed said, "What are you doing, sis? Where are you going?" He noticed that Angie was a fucking mess. No make-up, eyes swollen, tears, hair in disarray, etc. No slap marks on her face, though. "What's going on?"

Angie sat in the limo, not making a move to get out. She said, "I've left Joe. I'm going to go find Mike. He lives in Davenport, and that's not too far away."

Ed's brain raced through the sludge to do the calculations. He repeated, "Find Mike? Mike Smith? There really *is* a Mike Smith?"

"There is," Angie told him icily, "and I'm going to find him."

Ed's eyes widened. "Wait!" he blurted. "Wait wait wait wait wait!! Can you wait for fifteen minutes?"

Annoyed, Angie looked at her watch. She asked Ed, "Wait for what?"

"Fifteen minutes!" Ed cried. "Trust me, okay, sis?"

Angie looked forward. "Very well." She motored up the window.

Ed raced away from the limo and up the stairs. He hammered on a door. Then he hammered on another door. Then he returned to the first door. Eventually, Roger and Cassie opened their doors. Moments later, Ed, Bill and Roger argued on the walkway. Then they walked down and got on the elevator. Angie sighed and looked at the time. The sun had risen enough to be too bright to look at. Angie checked the time again.

Suddenly, Ed knocked on the window. Bill and Roger stood behind him. Angie lowered the window. Out of breath, Ed said, "Let us in."

They climbed in the limo. Ed sat beside Angie, and Roger and Bill sat across. "What do you want?" Angie asked crossly. "Because I'm not going back to Joe."

Ed said, "That's not what we're doing."

Bill said, "We want to join you on your quest to find Mike Smith."

"What? Why?"

Bill answered, "We just fired Joe, and we need a guitarist by tomorrow. I mean today."

Angie gawped. "You fired Joe? Really? You fired him from the band? X Band?"

Bill looked away. "We did, God help us."

Angie looked at the three of them. "What happened? What did he say?"

At first, no one spoke. Finally, Roger said, "He thanked us."

The band members ran back to their rooms to put on clothes. They were back in ten minutes, out of breath and perspiring. Angie pushed the intercom button. "All right, we're ready to go now." The limo rolled up to the road and left the parking lot.

Bill asked, "Do you know where to go?"

Angie held up a roadmap. "I got this at the front desk. We take 81 south to 460."

Ed asked, "How is it that you're being driven in a stretch limousine?"

Angie smiled. "This is still being rented from yesterday. Richard was using it, and I asked him if I could use it."

"Does he know we're going to get Mike?" Bill asked.

Angie answered, "No. When I talked to him, Joe was still in the band."

Ed and Bill looked at each other. Ed said, "We gotta tell Richard. Otherwise, who knows what he'll do."

While the limo got on the I-81 entrance ramp, Bill called the hotel and got Richard. He explained that Joe had left the band, and they were going to get a replacement. It was a long, painful conversation in which the phrase "trust me on this" was overused.

Bill hung up. He looked at the others. "I can't believe I'm betting everything on this craziness. Do you realize what we're depending on? That Joe and Mike literally switched bodies. Even if there is an actual Mike Smith, it must be someone that Joe met, and Joe assumed his personality after the seizure. We will probably find Mike Smith, and he won't know us or how to play guitar. *Then* what are we going to do?"

Angie said, "If you're right, and Joe concocted an accurate representation of Mike Smith, then I still want to know him."

Bill and Ed looked at each other. (Roger was asleep.) Ed said, "Okay, then *we're* screwed. Figuratively."

Bill asked, "Do you know his address?"

Angie said no. She was hoping to get to Davenport and ask around.

Ed said, "2112! That's his address. He mentioned it once, and I remembered it, because it's a Rush album."

Bill asked, "What album?"

"2112," Ed elaborated.

Bill nodded. "Okay, thanks. What street?"

Ed said, "He said it was on the main road, near the border of the county. Uh, the road had a number."

Angie consulted her map. "Only one road with a number goes through Davenport. Route 80?"

Ed shrugged. "I dunno. Could be. He told us, but I didn't remember it."

The limousine cruised down the highway.

Angie picked up the phone.

"Information."

"Virginia?"

"What city, please."

"Davenport?"

"Yes."

"Smith."

"First name?"

"I don't know. The address is 2112."

"I'm sorry, that's not enough information."

"Uh, route 80?"

"I'm sorry, that's not enough information."

"Okay, thank you." Angie hung up grudgingly. She told the others, "I'm sure he never told me his father's first name."

"Did he tell you anything else that could be helpful?" Bill pressed.

"No," Angie said. "Maybe. To be honest, I wasn't really listening. I thought it was all made-up."

Ed said, "I know what you mean. I don't remember anything he said about his personal life, either, except for the address. I didn't think there really was a Mike Smith." He frowned. "None of us did." His eyes fell on Roger. "Except Roger. He knew all along."

Bill sat up. "Yeah, and he spent a lot of time with Mike."

They impolitely awakened Roger.

"What's Mike Smith's father's name?" Bill demanded.

Roger blinked his clear, blue eyes. He said, "Michael. Mike is a junior, but he didn't tell us, because he didn't want us to call him 'Junior'."

Angie picked up the phone again. This time, the operator rewarded her by saying, "I can connect you."

"Yes!" Angie said to the others, "It's ringing!"

The phone rang seven times before it was picked up. A girl's voice: "Hello?"

Angie steadied herself. "Could I speak to Mike Smith?"

"Junior or Senior?"

"Junior!"

"He's in the grodge. Kin Ah take a message?"

Angie said, "Don't let him leave, *please*. We'll be there in two hours. It's important."

"Who's callin?"

"*Please* don't let him leave!" Angie hung up. Her heart was hammering as she repeated the conversation to the others.

Bill said, "That's interesting. There is indeed a Mike Smith junior and senior."

Ed asked, "Why didn't you tell her who you are?"

Angie glowered. "He ran away from us once. I'm not going to let him do it again."

The limousine turned onto route 460. They passed Virginia Tech. Angie was asleep by then. So was Roger. Ed watched his little sister. She had been put through the wringer. He looked at Bill. They all had. Ed's head hurt like shit, and he wanted to throw up. After a time, Bill nodded off. Ed took the map from Angie's sleeping hands and directed the driver to stay on route 19 and to turn onto route 80. After a half hour on route 80, Ed asked the driver to look for address 2112.

The black stretch limousine rolled to a stop before 2112 route 80. The occupants, shielded by tinted windows, assessed the lair of their quarry. The house was a smallish split level, set high up the hill. Angie opened the door and got out. The others followed. Ed said, "Showtime!" Bill responded with, "Knock it off, Ed." The steps that led up to the front door were uneven and tilted, homemade-looking slate slabs. Hardy grass squeezed through fractures in the slabs.

Angie led the band up the uneven steps. They assembled on the stoop. The house itself was brick painted white, except where the paint peeled away in thick curls. The front storm door was tarnished aluminum, and the door a faded red. The limo, far below at the street, still looked large. Angie pushed the yellowed doorbell. There was no sound from inside the house.

"Maybe it's one of those silent doorbells," Ed suggested.

Angie shot a glance at her brother. She decided to knock on the door, when it opened. Fear shot through Angie.

But it wasn't Mike. It was a younger girl, perhaps twenty years old. She was Angie's height, though about ninety pounds heavier with long lifeless blonde hair. Acne scars punctuated her face. "May Ah help yew?" she asked through the storm door screen. "Did you call earlier?"

Angie answered, "Yes. We're looking for Mike." When the girl didn't answer right away, Angie added, "Mike Smith? Junior?"

Roger asked, "Are you Beth?"

The girl was confused, not just because there were four unknown unexpected guests at the door, but also because they had come from a stretch limousine. "No, I'm Sarah," she answered. No one had ever confused her with Beth before. "Mike's down in the grodge." She indicated a second building, down the slope and just off the road. The building was chipped-white cinderblock with a flat, mossy roof (visible from the front stoop). A dirt path led from the side of the house down to the garage. "I'll take you," Sarah offered. She came out the door and bounced down across the yard toward the path.

The others followed. They stepped carefully over the uneven ground as they worked their way down to the side of the garage. As they neared the front of it, they could hear their recording of 'Stand Up and Shout'. The sound reproduction was all mid-range, from an inexpensive player. The song came to the end of the verse, and a voice shouted with it. Although Angie had never before heard it, the voice was unmistakably that of Mike Smith.

They rounded the corner to the front of the garage. It had three bays with generous room around and between, though the room was more often claimed by stacks of tires or motor oil or air filters. The air was thick with the smell of new tires and lubricants. The walls, those not supporting overflowing shelves, were festooned with graying fan belts. Except space had been spared for two posters. One was the "Pinko Flyd" Dark Side of the Moon poster. The other was the X Band Xenon Tour poster.

Bill liked that poster. They were on a tight stage in Boston, so they easily fit in the same shot. Joe was leaning over his guitar, cranking. Bill was to the side with Roger and Ed behind. What Bill liked most was he and Roger were looking at each other, and also, everyone looked like themselves. Except they looked like they were having fun.

A green Pacer with wood trim sat in the nearest of the garage bays. The center bay had a red pick-up on the lift, halfway up. Sarah led the band around to the third bay, which was vacant.

"Junior?" Sarah called out. "Some people here to see yew."

The band rounded the back of the pick-up and saw, for the first time, Michael Koop Smith. The pick-up's front wheel was off, and Mike was on the brakes, with his back to the door.

Angie wanted to freeze this moment, because in the next second, it would be decided. Had Joe and Mike mentally switched? Or had Joe developed a personality that was a copy of Mike's? Would Mike even recognize them?

Mike turned to face them. He was short, 5'6", and chubby. His blue shirt had permanent oil stains, including the shirt tail, stained as much as of the rest of the shirt. He wore baggy blue jeans with the cuffs rolled up about four inches. He had a round, baby face, except for his sparse, blond whiskers. His hair was cut short, but even that short length had irascible waves.

He dropped his pliers. He stared. He wore glasses that were just big. The lenses were wide and thick so they magnified his green eyes to a freakish proportion. And the lenses were supported by a tortoise-shell structure, much like Bill's. Mike's front teeth jutted and over-lapped, with one of them almost sideways. Shiny braces gripped his teeth, but had obviously not yet corrected them. The teeth pushed out Mike's upper lip, and it had obviously suffered as a result. A thin but jagged scar ran up from his mouth halfway to his nose. A scar on his chin marked where a mole had recently been removed.

His eyes went from one of the band members to the next. "Swate Jasus," he uttered, and he pushed up his glasses.

For a long time, no one spoke.

Finally, Ed broke the silence. "Tell us something only Joe would know."

Mike thought. "Okay. One of Joe's testicles is slightly larger than the other."

Roger, Ed and Bill exchanged glances, then looked at Angie. Angie blushed bright red. "I didn't know that!" she cried.

"Damn," Ed said. "It really *is* something only Joe would know!"

Bill barked, "Cut it! Bottom line: Have you been Joe? Do you remember us?"

For a moment, the world stopped.

Mike answered, "Yes. I remember everything."

"Amazing," Bill uttered, voicing everyone's thoughts.

"Mike," Ed said, "we need you in the band. We fired Joe."

Mike raised his eyebrows in surprise. He pushed up his glasses and reached for his shirt pocket. The pocket was empty, but its vicinity was heavily grease-stained. Mike sighed. "I can't. My job starts in two days. I'm flyin to LA tomorrow." Mike looked up at them. "Do you think you can get Joe back?"

Bill sputtered, "Mike! What?"

Ed stepped in. "Mike is it the money? How many years of working at GE would this one tour pay for? Look at what Joe has, his house and cars and portfolio. Are you going to earn that working for General Electric?"

"No, probably not. But my career at GE is what I've been trained to do. Look at me. I'm not a rock star. I'm just me." He pushed up his glasses. "See if you can get back Joe."

As they spoke, Sarah circled around to stand beside her brother. Her eyes wandered to the Pinko Flyd poster, then to the X Band poster, then to the people facing her and Mike. Then back to the X Band poster. Then back to the visitors. Her eyes widened.

Ed spoke. "I can't believe you'd give up the band for a career in GE."

"The GE Management Training Program is big," Mike informed Ed. "They take the best of the best, train us and assign us top management positions. I could be president of a division in ten years."

Ed: "And you would leave us, just like that? I remember you saying you would fucking die if you let us down."

"I didn't let you down. I gave you back Joe."

Angie had been silently assessing Mike. He had all the New Joe's mannerisms. And his stance, his carriage. And his speech was identical. Except Angie could see he was extremely agitated. She doubted the others recognized it. She could see he was being torn, and the tear was going deep.

Mike added, "Look: I have no talent with the guitar. I can't sing or dance, and I'm not good to look at. I'm no Joe Ecks."

"No you're not," Ed echoed.

"Thank God," Bill uttered.

Mike clenched his teeth and reached for his cigarettes. Then he pushed up his glasses and reached for his cigarettes. "Damn it!" he exploded. "Damn it! Why did you fire Joe? And why did you find me and come and get me? Why?! I did everything I coulda done to get you through, and more. I pushed myself as hard as I could... and at the end, I got outa the way so Joe could take you the rest of the way. I woulda— I fuckin ripped my goddamned heart out and walked away so you could succeed! And, what, you fired Joe, and you're comin back fer me? Didja fergit all about Plan A? Remember that? That we would fake it and stumble through until we could get Joe back? Swate Jasus! What happened to Plan A?!" He tore off his glasses and savagely wiped his eyes.

"We have a new Plan A," Ed said quietly. "Plan A is to get you back in the band and finish the tour."

Mike slowly replaced his glasses and glared up at Ed. "What's yer Plan B?"

Ed planted himself and glared down at Mike. He said, "There is no Plan B. Sometimes you just have to make Plan A work."

They stared at each other for a long time. The difference in their heights would have been comical if they weren't both so intense. Ed knew in a battle of pure willpower, he would lose. Mike had a steel backbone. But in this case, Ed couldn't afford to lose. He could not leave here without Mike. And if he backed down now, there would be no second try. But as long as Mike was arguing, they had a chance.

Mike said, "Then you will fail."

Bill huffed in frustration.

Ed persisted. "But, Mike, you had fun, didn't you? It seemed like you were really having fun."

Mike clenched his fists. "Swate Jasus, yes, I had fun! And I loved every damned minute of everything. And I had my time in the sun! But it wasn't really me. It was me inside Joe. It was me wanting to be Joe so bad that I *was* Joe. And I did what I was supposed to do, and when my time was up, I took a bullet for the team, and you got Joe back. But now you're back here, and I don't understand. Didn't I do enough?" Tears ran freely down his cheeks, and his breath caught. "Swate Jasus!" No one had anything to say as Mike composed himself. He saw Angie.

Angie felt his anguish. They were getting close to the point. She could feel it.

"Why are *you* here?" Mike asked her sullenly. "Shouldn't you be standing by your man? You *can't* be here to get me in the band."

Then Angie understood, and she couldn't contain it. "No, I'll tell you why I'm here. I'll tell you exactly why I'm here." She was suddenly radioactive with emotion. And what emotion was it, really? It wasn't fury or terror or elation, though it was as intense as all three. It was the indignancy of being right, and the determination to jam that rightness down Mike's throat. "I'm here, because I love you, and I want to be with you.

"But you don't believe that. You don't believe it's even possible that someone like me could fall in love with someone like you. Guys like you don't get girls like me, whatever that really means. So you think I'm wrong. Maybe I'm infatuated. Maybe I'm lying to you, for a reason I can't imagine. But you can't imagine that I could love you, and you can't get past that.

"Mike, before you, I was living every day on a balance beam. I did everything I could do, and I tried so hard to get everything right, because I thought maybe if I just stopped fucking up, then Joe would love me." Angie choked back a sob. Her eyes brimmed, and tears ran down her cheeks. "But not you. You treated me with respect always. You were polite. You listened to me. You cared about me. And I started trusting you. I started letting myself be me. And I'm learning about me. I took photography lessons! I *never* would have done that before. And I learned to love you.

"I've seen you brimming with happiness and excitement, and I've seen you plunged into despair. I've seen you behave with sincerity, and I've seen you laugh until you were out of breath. I've seen your acts of compassion and generosity, and I've seen you behave with dignity and strength under amazing pressure. And you don't think I know you well enough to love you? Bullshit. I know you better than anyone, Michael Koop Smith, *Junior*. I know you better than you do.

"And I know why you abandoned us."

"Plan A," Mike started to say.

"Don't give me 'Plan A'!" Angie shouted. "That's an excuse, and you know it, just like my being... Well, never mind. You didn't learn to play the guitar and then practice it for a billion hours so you could duck out at the last moment."

Mike said, "Okay, but that would have pretty audacious of me to ask the band to fire Joe and hire me. And for me to ask you..." Mike frowned and shook his head slowly.

"Right, Mike, because you're just not capable of being audacious. Give me a break. No, you didn't give us the option, because you were too scared the band would reject you. And this time, they'd be rejecting *you*. Because that's too personal for you to handle, and rejection would cut you too deep. Hell, rejection would cut you to pieces, because you wanted it so much. And your conviction that you ruin everything you touch. So it was easier for you to walk away and convince yourself it was never really an option."

Mike regarded Angie sadly.

"And what about me, Mike? That's also why you fled from me. Because you were sure I would see the real you and reject you. You couldn't see any other outcome. But I left Joe on the hope that you actually existed, and I came here to find you. And I did find you, and I'm looking at the real you and telling you that I love you. You've been wrong about that, you see. Guys like you really *can* get girls like me. And now I'm hoping that girls like me can really get guys like you."

Ed and Bill had marveled while Angie railed.

Sarah was lost. Mike was in X Band? He lived with the redhead for months?

Mike looked weighed down, like his body weighed five hundred pounds. "What about you, Bill? Is it your turn to deal on me now?"

Bill just said in a calm voice, "I gave up my solo career. I bet it on the success of the band. Because I wanted the band to succeed, and I thought it might. Today, Roger, Ed and I fired Joe just on the hope that there was really a Mike Smith that had been Joe Ecks. That's our show of faith. That's our commitment. What's going to be yours?"

Mike looked down, nodding slowly. Then he looked up at Roger.

Roger met his gaze, saying nothing out loud.

Mike looked away. He looked at Sarah, then he looked back at the band. "I really appreciate your coming for me. It means more to me than anything else. You're right, Bill, it's an incredible statement of faith. Thank you. I had so much fun with you guys, and even when I was working hard, I was *still* havin lots of fun. And you guys as people. First, I was overwhelmed by your fame, and then I got to know you. And I liked you even more." Mike's eyes rested on Angie. "Except you, Angie. I fell in love with you as soon as I looked up from the floor and saw your face. And since then, everything I've learned about you's made me love you more. But, but." Mike took a calming breath. "But you were in love with Joe. Guys like me don't get girls like you. Guys like me 'specially don't win girls like you away from good-lookin millionaire rock stars like Joe. But now. You're here. You came with the band to find me. And you're lookin at the real me and tellin me you love me."

Ed interrupted. "Dude, you're wrong about one thing. *She* didn't come with *us*. *She* was determined to find you. *We* tagged along with *her*."

Mike nodded to himself and turned to Sarah. He said, "Tell Mom and Dad that I've left home to join a rock and roll band."

Chapter 23

What Happened

The band rode in the limousine as it negotiated the twisting Route 80. Mike sat in the seat facing forward, between Angie and Roger. Mike said, "I really appreciate your comin to get me. Thanks."

"Stop saying that," Ed admonished. "Swate Jasus."

"Are you guys gettin hungry?" Mike asked. "There's a pretty good pizza place comin up."

Ed asked, "There's a pretty good pizza place in Davenport, Virginia?"

"We're not in Davenport anymore," Mike said indignantly.

Bill said, "We're on a schedule. Let's hit a drive-thru."

Mike said, "There aren't any drive-thrus until we hit 460. There's a Subway, though. We could probably go in without being mobbed."

"You don't have to worry about that," Ed said. "Yet."

Route 80 was narrow and steep, with treacherous switch-backs awkward for a stretch limousine to negotiate. The band explained to Mike about the Joe Show.

Mike said, "So all this time, you've been praying for Joe to come back, and when he did, you fired him twelve hours later. That's what I don't get."

Bill answered, "What do you want us to say, Mike? Joe has the technical skills, but he was insufferable to work with. Speaking for myself, I was dreading going on tour with him."

Mike said, "Hey, at least you got all the scouts to see the band performing well. Right? Weren't they all gonna go to the first show? Has anyone offered you a contract?"

Bill said, "No. Roanoke was added late, and all the scouts already had plans to see us at Virginia Tech. So nobody saw us. They will tonight, though."

"Oh," Mike said. "Tonight is the important show."

Bill said, "They may as well see you as part of the band."

Mike smiled.

Bill rubbed his bald head. "You know, it's really weird hearing your voice coming from a body that isn't Joe's."

The limousine rolled into the Subway parking lot. Mike and Angie went in to get sandwiches for everyone. As Mike paid, the cashier asked, "What's with the limousine?"

Mike answered, "I got a special ride to the X Band concert at Virginia Tech."

The cashier didn't ask any more questions. Mike and Angie carried the subs to the limo and got in. The limousine got back on the road. Everyone ate their subs. Angie fell asleep with her head on Mike's shoulder. Quietly, Mike said, "She's really tired."

Ed commented, "I don't know what happened last night. It was bad."

Bill asked, "How is it that you and Joe changed back at just the right time? Do you know?"

"Yeah, I know," Mike grated.

—X—

"Can you do me a favor, though?" Joe asked the band. "Can you give me a few minutes? I just need to focus."

"Um, okay, see you in the wing." They left.

Joe sat in his chair, alone, amidst the cheering of a thousand fans. His eyes fell on a pack of Newports on the counter with a lighter beside it. Joe withdrew a cigarette from the pack and passed it under his nose, then put it in his mouth. He lit it. He took a puff and inhaled deeply and exploded in coughing. Such a full-body cough that it doubled him over. He didn't hear the knock, and when he could finally straighten, he found himself looking into a round face topped with short curly blond hair.

Joe stopped. He finally said, "Joe."

"Mike," said Michael Smith.

"We meet," Joe grinned.

"No kidding," Mike said. "It's time for us to switch back. Vacation's over. Time for us to get back to work. I pushed back your GE start date to the 4th. You leave on the 2nd."

Joe frowned. "I don't want to."

"What? What are you thinking?" Mike demanded. "You're going to go onstage and replace me? Really? You don't even play guitar!"

"I took some lessons," Joe explained. "And I practiced a lot."

Shaking his head, Mike chuckled. He gestured to the cigarette. "Am I going to have to quit smoking again?"

"No. But I don't wanna hear any complaints, since I had to face down your cocaine addiction."

"I wasn't addicted. I could have quit at any time," Mike maintained. "You didn't tell anyone about Vicky did you?"

"No, but I'm pretty sure Vicky told Ed."

"Did Ed threaten to beat you up? To a pulp?"

"No, he gave me a pass because I ended it. But I don't know how he would feel about you."

Mike frowned. "Still, I'm glad you ended it. She was making my life too complicated. Vicky landed on her feet, though. Or maybe her knees. Now she's dating that musician who toured with Kansas." Mike hesitated, then asked, "You didn't tell anyone about my sexual preference, did you?"

"No," Joe said, flicking ashes to the floor.

Mike exhaled in relief.

.   "I think Dr. Vrakas knows, though."

"You saw the good doctor? Yes, she knows. I think she wanted to convert me." Mike smiled. "So that's good. Anyway, you'll be happy to know that I ditched your gold-digging, barnacle girlfriend Shelly. And, look, I lost over forty pounds for you. You're welcome." When Joe didn't answer, Mike continued. "We've got to switch back now. At this time. Otherwise, the band crashes, and everything is lost. Only I have the ability to save this show. Act. And how do you think Ange will like losing everything due to the pretentions of a man who is not her husband?"

"I think I can do this. I can do this. I can live your life, Joe. Why didn't you study up on business?"

Mike laughed. "We were never meant to live each other's lives. We were only supposed to see, experience, how the other side lives. I got to fuck around all summer, and you got to be a big rock star and fuck my wife. And now we are meant to return to what we do best."

Joe scowled. "You have no appreciation for Angie."

"Now that I've got her trained just right?" Mike sneered. "You bet I do. But we're out of time. Tell me, Mike: Who do you think the band wants as their guitarist? You or me?"

Joe admitted, "You." He closed his eyes and sighed. "Okay, so how do we make it happen?"

"It's done. It's been done," Joe said. He noticed the cigarette in his hand. "Here ya go." He handed it to Mike. "Now if you'll excuse me, I have a band to rescue." Joe opened the door.

Mike said, "You know what our curse is? We're both really good at something that doesn't interest us."

Joe, in the doorway, answered, "That would be true if you were good at anything." And then he was gone.

Mike stood for a few long moments. Then he dropped the cigarette and crushed it. With a vacant, unreadable expression, he left the dressing room. He walked down several corridors, unnoticed, and out an emergency exit. Outside, he could hear the announcer announcing and the crowd cheering. Then he heard the opening chords of 'You'.

Mike sat heavily in the grass and sobbed.

—X—

Mike told them, "Joe started out with the correct assumption that we had switched bodies. And, he had assumed that, on command, we could switch back. Problem is, he didn't prepare at all for his—my—upcoming management job. He should have. Joe's a smart guy; in five months, he could have learned enough to get by, and then he would have *excelled* at that job. Instead, Joe took the time as a well-deserved vacation. And then he came to see me at the last minute.

"Meanwhile, he dropped my girlfriend, spent all my money and ruined just about every relationship I had." Mike growled under his breath, then admitted, "To be fair, I owe Joe a lot. He had this wart removed." Mike pointed to the scar on his chin. "And he got me to quit smoking. I never smoked when I was Joe, and since Joe lived through the nicotine withdrawal, I decided not to go back. He gave me some grief about it, though, but I told him I had to live through his cocaine withdrawal, so I didn't want to hear it."

"Cocaine?" Bill exclaimed. "You— Joe was on coke? Where did he get it? Roger?"

Roger said, "Hey, I don't do coke, man. That shit's addictive." To Joe: "What do you know about cocaine withdrawal?"

"I went to UVA," Mike explained. "I didn't do coke, but everyone else did, and a few of them tried to quit."

"Well, if not Roger, where, then?"

"He had a contact," Mike answered vaguely. "But he doesn't anymore." He pushed up his glasses. "But, look, Joe got my hair... better. And he got me braces so maybe someday my teeth'll be normal. Most of all, though, is Joe lost forty-five pounds while he was me."

"Off you?" Ed asked. "Really?"

"Yeah, I was a fat guy. Forty-five pounds is a lot of weight when you're short. Joe must've been starving all the time. I still have about fifteen to go, and then I'll be where I was before college. I couldn't have got there if Joe hadn't given me such a head start."

"What about your glasses?" Ed asked.

Mike chuckled. "I'd love to get rid of these things, but I can't wear contacts. I have an astigmatism."

They rode in silence for several minutes. The limo got on route 460.

Bill commented, "I almost feel sorry for him, actually. Joe lost everything."

Mike said, "Everything he didn't want."

Ed said, "Angie? He wanted Angie."

"No, he didn't," Mike stated harshly. "He did not."

Ed and Bill exchanged glances. Ed said, "Is there something you're not telling us, Mike?"

"Yes."

Ed said, "Okay, well, do you have any other inside information about Joe?"

Mike grimaced. "I've said way too much already. At least I didn't let it slip that Joe was the real Son of Sam. Oops."

Ed said, "And Joe caused the Mianus River Bridge to collapse?"

Mike nodded sadly. "I don't know what that is, but, yes, that, too."

Bill said, "We'll get to Virginia Tech by about 2:00. I'd better call Richard and let him know."

The limousine rolled across the Virginia Tech campus, past buildings of quarried stone. Classes were changing, as evidenced by thousands of students blithely crossing the street. Mike looked out the window. "So this is Virginia Tech," he mused.

Ed asked, "Is this how you expected it to look?"

"Not at all," Mike said. "The roads are paved, and the students are all wearin shoes."

Ed commented, "Big words coming from a resident of Davenport, Virginia."

Eventually, the limo pulled up beside an especially imposing stone building. Burruss Hall. The band was just getting out of the limo when Burrill and McCann were on them. "What the hell is going on here?" Burrill screeched. "Who the hell is thish?"

"Mike Smith," Mike greeted, holding out his hand.

Burrill ignored the hand. "My whole band was gone! Where have you been? And where's Joe?"

Bill explained, "Joe quit the band last night. Fortunately, Mike Smith here was available. We're ready to go."

Burrill yelled, "Joe quit! What the? A guy can't just shtep in and take over for Joe! Are you crazy? Where's Joe?!"

Bill explained, "Mike knows as much about the show as anyone. He will get the job done."

Burrill gestured at Mike. "He's a fucking garage mechanic! Are you sure he can play guitar even?"

Bill said, "Burrill. It's our careers on the line here, too. This will work. He knows the show. Better than Joe did last night."

Burrill threw his hands up and marched back into the building.

McCann asked Bill, "He really knows the show?"

"As well as anyone," Ed said. "Maybe better."

Bill nodded. "I'd bet my career on it."

"You are," McCann said, and he also went into the building. "This way to the green room."

The band followed. Richard was in the green room. "Oh, hi, Richard," Bill said.

Richard looked about 150 years old. "Bill, are you trying to kill me?"

"Richard Sheridan, meet Mike Smith." They shook. "Joe quit the band, and fortunately, Mike was available."

Richard regarded Bill. He said, "Joe told me you fired him."

Bill answered, "Uh."

Mike answered, "The official version is that Joe left to pursue other opportunities."

Frantically indicating Mike, Richard demanded, "Who the fuck *is* this?"

"He's Mike Smith," Ed reminded. "Didn't we go over this already?"

Richard shook his head. "All I need to know is: Can he play guitar? And: Does he really know the show? You realize that all the industry scouts are here to see if the band is viable. Rumors are flying. And for good reason!" Richard looked down at Mike. "Is he joining the band, then? Can I tell the press and everyone else that he's replacing Joe? Christ, can *anyone* replace Joe in this band?"

Bill assured factually, "He has replaced Joe. Yes."

Richard shook Mike's hand again. He said, "Welcome to X Band. I'll draw up the necessary contracts, then. But first, I've got to go talk to some guys. I don't know how I can assure people that the band is stable when you guys just fired Joe. Joe Ecks! Of X Band!"

Ed said, "This is how you earn the big bucks, Richard."

Richard groaned, "You really are trying to kill me." He walked out.

The band was left alone in the green room. Mike said, "I really appreciate that you guys found me and got me."

Ed said, "Stop saying that."

Angie came in the room. "Hi," she said. "I held back because I thought my presence would raise a lot of questions." She approached Mike, and they hugged. Then they kissed. The lips were different, and the height was different, but it was the same kiss. Angie gave in to it.

Bill cleared his throat.

Ed said, "Uh."

They separated. Angie blinked herself back into reality. She said to Mike, "I'd better go. I'll be watching the show from the control room. Break a leg." They kissed again, enough to embarrass Bill and Ed. Then Angie left.

Ed said to Mike, "That stuff you learned at the 'Xylene' shoot came in handy, didn't it?"

Mike grinned. "Perfect timing, too."

The band hung around. There were still five hours until they had to go on. Mike wanted to see the stage. Bill took him up, and they walked on from the wing. It wasn't a bad size, Bill thought. But it was crowded, because the road crew was setting up their equipment on the stage. The band looked out over the seats. There weren't many, Bill thought. Burruss Hall only seated three thousand. There'd been over ten thousand at Roanoke. Well, better to start Mike with a smaller audience. Except that what the audience lacked in size, it would compensate for in clout.

Ed sensed something wrong. The crew was setting up their equipment. Only their equipment. Ed walked over to the guy setting up microphones around his drum set. "Hey," Ed said, "where's Metro Gnome's equipment?"

The guy answered, "I don't know. They told us to just set this up."

"Hey, Sam!" Ed shouted up to the control room. "Get McCann! We need to see him!"

Another guy ran off the set and appeared minutes later with McCann. "You're not in the green room," McCann told Ed.

"What happened to Metro Gnome?" Ed asked.

"Burrill told me they broke up, and yes, you have no opening band."

Burrill appeared on the stage. "We're losing thirty minutes of show and twenty minutes of intermission," he told the band. "Okay, so, how long's the show we've got planned?"

Bill answered, "We don't know. We've never played it through."

Burrill glared at Bill. He said, "Tell me this is a practical joke."

Sam was between sound checks. Patty had left to forage some food. It was just Sam and Angie in the control room. Angie pointed to Mike. "Sam, do you see that man? In the blue shirt?"

"Yeah, who's he?" Sam asked.

"He's Mike Smith. He's replacing Joe as lead guitar."

"Oh, lord! What happened to Joe? Is he okay?"

"Yes. But he left the band, and Mike's replacing him."

Sam looked at Angie strangely. "Where's Joe now?"

Angie shook her head. "I don't know."

Confused, Sam inquired, "Well, Angie, why are you here, then?"

Angie said, "It's really a long story. Do you have a couple of minutes?"

Sam looked down on the stage, where everyone seemed to be yelling at everyone. "Fifteen, I imagine."

Angie sighed. Here goes. "Sam, remember when Joe had that seizure?"

And then Patty returned with the food. "There's not one place to buy food on this whole stupid campus!" she exclaimed. "I had to walk about two miles away." She handed out bags of Burger King food-like products.

And then Sam had to do another sound check.

The band and some others were back in the green room. Bill admitted, "We probably should have played the set together as practice."

Mike was examining his hand. "You know, I don't have calluses. On my fingertips."

"That's probably not good?" Ed guessed.

Mike said to the runner, "I need something called 'cut patch'. It's sold in bowling alleys. If you can't find that, I'll need super glue."

The runner fled.

Another runner appeared. He asked Mike, "Are you right- or left-handed?"

"Left. But I play as a righty."

The runner departed.

Ed said, "We ought to start doing costumes and make-up soon. Mike, are you nervous?"

"No," Mike said. "I'm not."

"Really? You were terrified last night."

Mike answered, "Yeah, I was. But tonight, I'm not worried about being exposed as a fraud. Remember when I gave you that speech about how you're no Phil Collins, and you never will be? I should have listened to myself. I'm no Joe Ecks, and I never will be. But I *am* Mike Smith."

McCann came in. "It's time for wardrobe and make-up, guys." He said to Mike, "Um, Mike? Would you be comfortable wearing those clothes for the performance?"

Mike looked at his clothes. He still wore what he was wearing when he was doing the brake job on the pick-up. He answered, "Actually, I *would* be comfortable wearing this. Why?"

McCann said, "That's who you are, and I want the audience to see that. No pretension. You're a garage mechanic replacing Joe Ecks." Plus, they didn't have anything Mike's size.

Mike said, "I like it. But do me a favor. Before we go on, just announce only me. I'll go out, and then the other guys will come out, and we'll play. It'll be a hoot."

McCann looked at Bill.

Bill said, "Do it."

Chapter 24

The Mike Show

Bill thought the crowd was loud, but not nearly as loud as the one in Roanoke. Bill distractedly wondered if they knew Joe had been replaced. The band huddled off-stage in the left wing, surrounded by McCann and two impressive security guards.

Roger spoke into Mike's ear. He said, "Don't play the notes. Play the music."

Ed grabbed Mike's stubby elbow. "We are *not* going to give you a minute to yourself."

Mike looked startled. "Uh, I gotta go to the bathroom."

Ed didn't budge. "That won't work, either."

Bill rolled his eyes. He was wearing a Fighting Gobbler hat.

McCann spoke into his headset, and then told the band, "It's time."

A voice boomed over everything, "Ladies and gentlemen, Mike Smith!"

Mike bounced onto the stage as the cheering dissipated in confusion. When Mike reached the mic six weeks later, the auditorium was nearly quiet. Mike donned a guitar. The microphone was positioned about a foot too high. Mike unhurriedly adjusted the height and said into it, "Hi. I'm your opening act today." Mike played the first chord of 'Tina'. A voice in the seats said quietly, "Hey, that's

Brettington there." "And Bill Myers." "The whole band!" Oblivious to X Band plugging in behind him, Mike said, "I'm Mike Smith." He smiled. "But you already know that." Ed tapped his sticks together. Bill began the intro, and Roger came in. Mike still stood at the mic, unaware of the song beginning. Ed set the beat, thunderous on the floor toms. Mike hesitated. The song rocked on, lacking only the guitar. They came around for another pass. Mike started chopping and met them at the strong intro chord.

The band had debated leading with 'Tina'. It was their best-known "signature" song. It had been their One Hit when X Band was a One-Hit Wonder. It had always been in their encore as the anchor. Also, it had a challenging mix of chords and lead-work. "It's better to play it after you've warmed up," Roger had advised.

Mike, as Joe, had said, "So, then, we put this song at about 1993?"

Whatever connection Mike had had with the audience, it was lost as he bent to concentrate on his fingering. Bill smiled (on the outside) and played on. He wished they had taken Roger's advice. Mike was hacking it up. But he played on courageously, and the tune was recognizable. The guitar line dropped into a slow fade. Mike sang quietly, "My soul awoke when we first met..."

Bill had heard Joe sing 'Tina' a thousand times. He had heard, over the years, others sing it, too. But he had never heard it sung with such feeling of love and sacrifice and grief. Even Ed looked up. At the end of the verse, Mike turned away from the audience. He looked weak, stricken. And determined. He locked eyes with Ed, and Ed understood.

Once, Mike (as Joe) had told the band, "Oh, I've been singin these songs since they first came out. Only, as Joe, I sing them like Joe." Now Ed knew what Mike had meant, and he knew to whom Mike now sang. Ed nodded his encouragement to Mike. Mike nodded back. He paced in a slow circle as he played, returning to the mic. This was supposed to be a sustained Tina. Mike got started, but choked off. His play, though, was uninterrupted. His eyes were bright. On the verse, his voice was quiet, but steady. The band played a few measures, and Mike returned to the mic. On the chorus, his voice was an odd mix. It wavered badly, but Mike forced it out strong. He forced out the last two lines like he was scrubbing a wound.

> I loved you so much, but even so
> I loved you enough to let you go.

At this point, the music ended, but Mike unexpectedly stood planted, and he sang in the silence lyrics that had never before existed.

I loved you enough to set you free.
Thank God, you didn't let go of me.

Mike turned away. Tears flowed down his cheeks.

At the board, Sam was stunned. He thought, "He's *good!* Is he really that good?" He turned to Angie to get her opinion, and he saw that she was sobbing without shame. He turned back to the board and thought, "He really *is* that good!" Beside him, Patty sniffed wetly.

Ed started thumping on the bass drum. Mike looked up and locked eyes with Ed, and he seemed to remember where he was. Ed added snare, and Roger came in. The beat was strong, persuasive. Bill played the intro to the next song. Mike grinned and swang back to the mic. He shouted, "Let's Move!"

'Let's Move' was a good intro song. Strong beat, simple melody. It engaged the audience and won them over. And, it warmed up the band. Ed could feel himself warming and loosening. Mike played with enthusiasm. Bill watched him critically. He realized that it was now possible to see him play and to judge him for who he was. Before, it had been impossible to see him as anyone other than Joe. And, as a result, always lacking. Now, Bill could objectively rate Mike as a competent guitarist. Well, almost competent.

And he sang well. Aside from the different voice, Bill could recognize his training. After the train wreck that 'Tina' had been, Mike surprised Bill by singing 'Let's Move' fluidly. Bill smiled (on the inside).

'Let's Move' ended. The audience cheered. When the cheer ebbed, Mike picked the intro to 'Contents Under Pressure'. The studio version was too complex to replicate in concert, so the band had constructed a simple approximation, and this is what Mike (as Joe) had practiced. Mike's singing, though, was edgy and explosive. Perfect for the song.

Soon, they started 'Stand Up and Shout', and this is when Bill knew that Mike had won the audience. The band reached the lyrics "stand up and shout", and the audience shouted it along with Mike. And at Mike's recorded off-script instruction to Angie, "You've got to shout!", much of the audience shouted *that* line. At the last verse, Mike didn't sing. He let the audience shout the phrase.

A few songs later, and they were into 'Ice Age'. Bill started to relax. Mike was competent, and he had a connection with the audience. Then Bill started to have fun. He looked across at Roger, and Roger smiled and nodded.

After 'Ice Age', Mike stopped the band. Addressing the audience, he began the introductions. "I'd like to introduce the members of the band. On drums, the irascible Ed. Brettington!" Ed laid down a simple beat for a few seconds. The crowd responded. "On bass, the oneiric Roger. Novak!" Roger played an interesting bass riff. "And on keys. The pedagogical Bill Myers!" Bill played a few chords and promised himself he would later look up 'pedagogical'. "And me, well, I've already been announced, but I am the esemplastic Mike Smith!" As the audience cheered, Bill decided he'd better look up that word, too, whatever it was. And the one for Roger.

Mike chilled the audience, and the band played 'Fort Wayne' and 'Isolation', both from the 'Xenon' album. They were mellow songs, both decent when positioned properly. The intent was to mellow the audience in preparation for 'Anesthesia'. As 'Isolation' tapered off, the spotlights fixed on Bill, and he kept playing on keys morphing into his solo. It was a fittingly thoughtful solo, easy to play, but with a winding exoskeleton, and then Bill flattened it out and drew it long and shaped it into the 'Anesthesia' intro.

During rehearsal, Mike (as Joe) had insisted that Bill play 'Anesthesia' solo. And tonight, as it came off his fingers, Bill understood why. The power of 'Anesthesia' wasn't in the music or in the singing. It was in the ideas. And with the music and the singing played down, the ideas hit with more impact. Bill finished the song and tied it up.

There was a long (2-second?) silence, then Mike shouted, "Bill Myers on keyboards!" There was some applause. Bill stood, and applause doubled. As the applause tapered, Mike said, "And now, Ed Brettington on xylophone! The spots shifted to Ed.

'Anesthesia' had brought the concert pace to its slowest and deepest point. As a release, Burrill had the band next play their "fun" songs and progress toward the harder rock songs.

To write the song 'Xylophone', Ed had bought one. He messed around with it and found that he liked playing it. And playing the xylophone for fun became the subject of the song. On the road, the song itself was odd, because while Ed was xylophoning, no one was playing the drums. Essentially, Ed played the drums on the xylophone.

Today, like in past performances, Ed put down a beat. Bill followed with some background tones. Roger had a simple, two-note bass rhythm. Mike made a point of watching Ed play. He said, "Good job, Ed. Keep it goin." Mike hit a chord. He hit another. He walked downstage to the mic stand and hit another chord. Ed focused on the xylophone rhythm. The chords weren't bad, Bill decided. They were definitely recognizable as chords. Mike sang. He had regained much better control than he had since the train-wreck of 'Tina'. His guitar-playing was adequate. He sang with a relaxed confidence. Ed focused. Playing the xylophone was fun, but playing it well required concentration. As the song concluded, Mike faded back until he stood beside Ed. At the last note, Mike shouted, "Ed Brettington!" Cheers. Ed gratefully sat back behind his drums.

Mike played the intro to 'Delta Kronecker' as he walked back toward the mic. He stopped by Roger. "Roger, you doin okay?" Mike asked.

Roger smiled and answered, "I'm doin okay, Mike."

Mike went back to the mic and played the song. At its end, Mike asked, "You may be thinking, 'So, X Band, what other songs do you have about quirky women?'"

The crowd cheered. Cries of 'Xylene!' sprang from the audience.

"But first," Mike told the audience, "But first, lemme introduce Denise Enders!"

Some cheers. Denise came onstage carrying a cordless mic. She stood beside Mike. The juxtaposition accentuated Denise's tall-ness, darkness and gorgeousness.

"Are you ready, Denise?" Mike asked.

Denise nodded.

"Or. Should I call you. Xylene." The audience laughed.

Mike hacked into the 'Xylene' intro. Roger backed him up with a bass line. Bill laughed. Mike was having fun, despite the pressure, despite the exposure, and despite the mistakes. Bill looked back at Ed. Ed saw Bill and smiled. And played the drums. Mike pretended to cozy up to Denise during his lines. And while Denise sang, she deliberately ignored Mike.

In the control room, Angie realized, "He's doing it. He's going to get through." But she knew that "getting through" was the lowest hurtle. Beside her, Sam and Patty ran their boards. Not with the terror of a rodeo-rider like the night before. It was all business. Sam jotted notes. He used his chair, and Patty used hers.

The song concluded, and Denise left the stage. The audience cheered for her. "Ain't she great?" Mike asked. "Swate Jasus."

Sam leaned forward. "That sounds familiar!" He listened to Mike talking to the audience. Sam pointed at Mike and turned to Angie. "I know! It's Joe, right? After the seizure! And *that's* why you're here!" He looked out at Mike and back at Angie. "I definitely need to talk to you after the show."

Next was 'Perihelion'. Angie knew there were a few songs that Mike struggled with, and this was one. It involved a complex duet with Bill. It had the complexity of a guitar solo, but it had to be synchronized with Bill. For the challenging guitar line, Mike stood like a statue, staring at his hands. He made minor mistakes and plunged on. Then he relaxed in rhythm as Bill played the melody on keyboards. 'Perihelion' had only a few lines of lyrics, and Mike sang them. And then he played as the duet approached. As he played, Mike walked over so he could see Bill's hands. The duet began.

It turned and flowed, and it rippled. Mike played riffs that Bill followed, then Mike picked them back up again. Bill saw that Mike was timing his playing from watching Bill's hands. Then it got challenging.

Mike stared at his hands, oblivious to all else. His right hand flew across the strings, fingers tapping down or bending strings in rapid succession. Meanwhile, his left hand picked with a blurring speed. Mike had each hand, and probably both of Bill's, in his peripheral vision. Concentration consumed him. Sweat ran down his forehead, dripping off his eyebrows unnoticed. Then Mike slowly looked up at Bill, his visual connection with his guitar severed. His hands carried on without him. And then Mike recognized Bill, and Mike smiled a broad, approving smile. Bill connected with Mike, and the two played in synch, urging each other on.

They concluded the duet, and Mike walked away, completing the song. "Give Bill Myers a hand!" Mike shouted, and the audience gave Bill Myers a standing ovation.

Ed saw what had happened. He locked eyes with Roger, and both nodded.

Mike kicked off the next song, 'Cincinnati Fan'. This was not a challenging song, but it ended with Ed's drum solo, if he chose to perform it. But Ed knew he should perform it, because they were all told to "stretch out" the show. They worked the song. Bill detected something new: Mike was adding stylistic improvisations. Probably no one noticed it but him. The song neared its conclusion.

Then Ed's solo loomed. The music stopped abruptly, and, in accordance with Burrill's plan, Ed kept going. Leaving the others behind, Ed charged forward, continuing the beat he'd been laying down.

Drummers keep the beat. It's dogmatic. The other band members depend on the drummer to keep them aligned and steady. But Ed never bought into that. What about the 'Perihelion' duet just now? What about the stylistic patterns Ed laid down in some of the songs? No one could follow a beat like that. One time, Ed overheard Mike (as Joe) say to Bill, "I'm following Ed, but it's messing me up." Bill instructed him, "Don't follow Ed. Try following Roger." So Ed knew that he did not carry the beat.

Ed knew that he relied on the others to pace him. And now the others were gone, and Ed was striking out alone. He sustained the rhythm. He felt the rhythm. He had planned to depart and hit a series of cymbals, but it didn't feel right. He altered the beat, not consciously, but the new beat sounded better. He replaced one of the toms with a ride cymbal. He took off and inserted a splash. Not so good. A crash sounded better.

Sweat ran down his face and back. It flew off the ringlets of his hair. Ed felt his body temperature climb to 120°, and his body felt fluid; thin. The sticks were lighter and faster. The air was easier to breathe.

Spotlights targeted the drum platform, deluging Ed with light and casting unfamiliar shadows. Beyond the sphere of illumination was nothing, and irrelevant, because it was outside of Ed's visual universe. And he couldn't hear anything but the thundering of his drums.

The beat changed again, and Ed kept up with it. He deviated, then returned. The transitions pleased him. He shifted between beats and added a third and rotated among them. He didn't think he could have done this, live. This was the border of new territory. Could he change from 4/4 to 3/4? Without deciding, he did it, and he adapted his beats to accommodate the change. Ed liked 3/4 time better, anyway.

Playing the drums, Ed walked a tightrope, and the band was his net. In a drum solo, the net was taken away. But Ed was no longer concerned about the absence of a net. He could fly.

Pure joy washed through Ed. Ed could be a drummer. He *was* a drummer. He had it mastered. Unanticipated tears flooded his eyes. Sweat issued from every pore.

And then a shadow fell over him. Mike was standing over him, leaning over his tom-toms. In an instant, Ed realized where he was. He had stolen the light. He had overindulged, and Mike was angry. Ed stopped, sticks in mid-stroke.

Mike pointed down at Ed. "ED!" he thundered so that the drum mics picked him up. "What we need now, is for YOU to do your JOB!! GET BACK TO WORK!"

Ed swelled with pride and confidence. His whole face smiled. "Yes, SIR!" he yelled, and he did his job. He flew, until he knew it was time to land.

He heard Mike yell, "Ed Brettington on drums!" And the applause replenished him.

The applause subsided, and Mike said, "This is the title track of our second album, 'Xenon'."

Angie was impressed with Ed's solo. She knew he had struggled with it, and it came out better than she expected. But now, Mike faced 'Xenon'. His nemesis. It was a test from beginning to end. Mike dove in, working the guitar. It reminded Angie of how he drove the manual transmission. He just did it. The band backed him up. Playing, Mike stepped back until he was between Roger and Bill. He faced Roger, and the two played together. He turned and faced Bill. And they played together. Bill had never felt such a connection with Mike. Then Roger and Bill came together, and Ed joined them. Mike, carried by his band, floated away. He paced around the stage, playing the most difficult music Joe could write. And he wrung it out. The song ended. Mike looked whipped.

Into his mic, Roger yelled, "Mike Smith on guitar!"

The crowd thundered approval. Mike looked up and smiled. X Band surrounded him. They bowed. They waved. The concert was over. They bowed again. They waved again and left the stage.

Off-stage, Bill listened. He'd heard crowds cheer, but not like this. He put a hand on Mike's shoulder and said, "Good job, Mike." And he meant it. Mike hugged him. "Thank you, Bill," he cried. Roger embraced the two of them, and Ed wrapped his eight-foot arms around all of them. They separated. Ed embraced Denise.

McCann was there. "Hold for your encore." Even McCann looked happy. Or relieved.

Mike faced Roger. He said, "I played the music."

Roger answered, "I could tell."

They caught their breath. They toweled off. McCann pointed to Mike. "You're up."

Mike nodded and went back onto the stage. A stage hand had left a stool by the mic. Cheers. He went to the microphone. The audience quieted. "I want to play for you," Mike announced, "the first song I learned to play on the guitar. It's called 'Twinkle Twinkle'." The audience roared approval. Mike perched on the stool. He picked the notes.

Roger, Ed and Bill came out and took their places. And then they created music together. It was a union of talents. They challenged each other. They frolicked with each other. They exhausted each other. They brought it around to what Mike called 'the intermission' and stopped.

Mike stood at the mic. He sang. Bill was astonished. An audience of three thousand stood, mesmerized, while Mike, in a thin, reedy, insubstantial voice sang.

> Twinkle twinkle little star,
> How I wonder what you are.
> Up above the world so high,
> Like a diamond in the sky,
> Twinkle, twinkle little star,
> How I wonder who you are.

The audience went crazy. Ed thumped on his bass drum, and the others came together. Mike sat back on the stool and returned to picking the notes until the end of the encore.

Chapter 25

Aftermath

Mike flew into the green room, in which Bill, Ed, Roger and Denise were cooling off. The costume girl was collecting their Xylene shirts to launder them for the next performance. Mike said, "McCann said you guys were in here."

"Yeah, where've you been?" Ed demanded.

"I got delayed," Mike explained. "Whew!" He peeled off his sopping mechanic shirt and handed it to the girl, who thanked him for giving her his dripping shirt. Bill noticed that Mike was indeed a little heavy. Yes, fifteen pounds off would be about right. The tour would take care of that.

The others were putting on their day-clothes, but Mike had just handed his to the girl. Denise handed him the Xylene shirt intended for Joe. It was big in every dimension except the waist.

Mike fell into a chair.

Angie, Sam and Patty came in the room.

Angie kissed Mike and sat beside him.

Mike exclaimed, "Sam and Janet Evening! How did it mix? Okay?"

Sam told him, "It's a good thing Patty and I are really good at what we do."

"That's why we hired you," Mike replied. "I mean, I'll bet that's why *they* hired you."

Sam said, "But, yeah, it mixed just fine. Good thing you know the show just as well as Joe Ecks would have." He stared at Mike and said, "Someday *real* soon, you're going to tell me what the heck happened here."

Mike drank from a water bottle. He said, "Yep, Sam. You and Janet deserve a thorough explanation."

Patty frowned at Mike. "Joe used to call me 'Janet', too."

Bill asked Mike, "So how did you like playing a concert?"

Mike said, "Man, you guys, this was the coolest thing ever! I was on a stage with X Band, playing guitar with them! Guys, we were so workin together, it was amazing! There is nothing else, not even *nothin*, like that, where we're workin together that closely and producin something so beautiful and so ephemeral! God, it was better than sex!"

The room stilled. Everyone looked at Mike, then at Angie.

Mike said, "Uh, from what I've heard, anyway."

Ed said, "Mike, are we going to have to send you to O'Reilly and Tsuzi for a lesson?"

"No!" blurted Angie. She diffidently explained, "There are some things *I* want to teach him."

Mike grinned and blushed.

Ed said, "The good news for you two is we get a day off, and then we're only going to Charlotte."

"Not true," Sam said. "The next show is tomorrow, and that's in Troy, New York. It's a late addition."

Several people groaned. Bill told Mike, "We'll introduce you to The Bus, our home away from home. You'll get to know it well."

Mike looked at Angie. "How far is Troy from Avon? Could Douglas drive there and pick you up?" Mike turned to Bill. "Can Angie take the bus to Troy with us?"

Alarmed, Angie declared, "Oh, no, Mike, I finally got the real you; I am *not* going to be apart from you for months! I'll be your roadie, uh, girl."

Mike smiled. "You'd live with us on the bus? Really?" He looked at Bill and Ed.

Bill grinned. "The bunks can fit two people, but it gets real cozy." He sighed, remembering. "Cassie toured with us for a while."

Mike asked Angie, "You'd do that? You'd really live like that? It's hardly a life for a lady of such class." He smiled again and added, "But I'd really like to be with you."

Angie smiled, too, but sadly. "Besides, I don't have a home to go home to."

Mike said, "Angie, I've got a surprise for you, but I'll tell you about it later."

Richard came in the green room. He looked typically dour. He glared at Mike suspiciously.

Ed shouted, "Well? Did we pass?"

Richard scowled at Ed. "The tour isn't cancelled, if that's what you mean."

"What did the scouts say? Did we get a contract?"

"No," Richard answered. "Most of the guys I talked to are hedging. They're planning to see your show in Charlotte. But a guy from Meadow Trail Records wants to talk to me tonight. He told me to bring a contract with Mike's signature on it as proof that he's in the band." He unfolded some papers and held them out to Mike with a ballpoint pen. "Initial each page and sign at the end."

Mike took the papers and looked at the front page. He flipped through the pages. "This is Joe's contract with 'Joe Ecks' crossed out, and 'Mike Smith' handwritten in."

"I didn't think to bring a blank contract for the tour," Richard grouched. "I should have planned ahead."

"I'm getting a double share like Joe did?"

"Just sign it," Bill said. "Richard just needs your signature. We'll argue about shares later."

Mike looked like he wanted to argue about shares now. Richard fidgeted. Mike signed.

Richard turned to Ed. "Did you announce that X Band is putting out a Christmas album?"

Ed searched his memory. "I guess so. Someone asked me if we were going to do other songs like 'Twinkle Twinkle'. I said, 'Wait until you hear our Christmas album!'"

Richard winced. "Ed, don't announce things like that unless... Just don't announce things like that."

As Ed answered, "Okay", Mike held out the contract to Richard. Richard gave Angie a curious look, took the contract and left.

Ed had a huge smile. "A guy wants to talk to Richard," he recapped.

Bill said, "Ed, what the hell? Now we have to do a Christmas album? What would we even call it?"

After a microsecond of thought, Ed replied, "'X Mas'". He smiled.

Bill looked at Roger and Mike.

Mike said, "That's so perfect, we may hafta do it. Assumin we get a contract."

"A guy wants to talk to Richard," Ed reminded Mike.

Sam told Mike, "I wouldn't worry. Looks like you're all set for the rest of your life."

"Thank you," Mike said, "but don't ever say that to me again, okay?"

Chapter 26

Blare's Concert Review

Blare's Concert Review, Collegiate Times, Friday, October 4th, 1985 (page 6)

Ex-Ecks X Band

September 29th, X Band kicked off their 'Xylene' tour by playing a largely-filled Roanoke Coliseum. The Roanoke Times dubbed it 'The Joe Show' and asserted, "Joe Ecks doesn't need to launch a solo career, because he already has, and his back-up band is X Band."

I've been following the progress of X Band since their debut album 'Xylophone'. There have been some changes as the band matured from a one-hit wonder to a supergroup. Shane Skinner left the band after 'Xylophone', and Bill Myers replaced him. More recently, Ecks struggled for an image make-over, but he demonstrated in Roanoke that he was the same old Ecks: A little too skilled, a little too polished, and a little too in-your-face.

So, poised for Ecks adulation, the crowd of 3105 at Burruss Hall was taken aback when chubby, short, buck-toothed Mike Smith loped to the microphone and struck the opening chords of 'Tina'. Who was this guy? What happened to Ecks?

Then we were treated to the expected X Band fare: 'Tina', 'Let's Move', and 'Contents Under Pressure'. 'Stand Up & Shout' and others got us boiling, and then they put us on simmer with 'Fort Wayne', 'Isolation', and 'Anesthesia'. The latter was performed exceptionally well with keyboardist Bill Myers taking lead vocals. After grappling with the concept of a soul, X Band put on some of their more playful tunes, such as 'Xylophone', 'Delta Kronecker', and 'Xylene'. They wrapped up with 'Xenon'. Their sole encore offering was 'Twinkle Twinkle' that rocked for over twenty minutes. The whole time X Band jammed behind him, Mike Smith sat on his stool and picked out 'Twinkle Twinkle'. It was a part, and a role, that Joe Ecks could never play.

You see, Smith is everything that Ecks is not. Engaging, for example. From the first notes of the concert, I found myself rooting for him as he fumbled his way through the night. And then I realized I wasn't watching a preformatted media entertainment event. I was watching a talented band play as a band. First, they all looked happy to be there and playing for us. Second, the show hadn't been professionally choreographed and practiced a hundred times. Like, for example, Brettington's drum solo. Here was a musician carried on his enthusiasm for the music, exploring it as it played from his hands. And Mike Smith stood over him, urging him on. An act? If this is an act, these guys act better than anyone in Hollywood.

No one at the concert saw what they expected to see, but they saw something better, if they recognized it. I don't know if Smith is going to stay with X Band, but I hope he does. And I look forward to the band's first album in their post-Ecks era.

Chapter 27

Postlude

October 1st, 1985, X Band played for a small audience at Rensselaer Polytechnic Institute, and the next day, they played for a larger audience in Charlotte, NC. A bidding war for their next three records was furious and exhilarating and finally awarded to Shepherd Music on January 13th, 1986. X Band's 'Xylene' tour ended abruptly after ten months when bassist Roger Novak could no longer play for health reasons. He succumbed to stomach cancer on December 15th, 1986, surrounded by friends and family and friends who considered themselves family. At his funeral, as a tribute, keyboardist Bill Myers played 'Anesthesia' for the last time.

April 4th, 1987, X Band began their European 'Xylene' tour that spanned ten weeks with bassist Jack "Carp" Carpenter, who later joined the band as a full member.

Subsequent albums were 'Xenotheology' (an instrumental), 'X Mas', and 'Xerxes'. The enduring success of 'X Mas' alone assured X Band's long-term survival, and as of 2025, X Band is still producing top 100 albums and playing to sell-out crowds.

Stuart Cress, in 1985, lost his job at Theremin Records, and his agent business (Cress & Associates) floundered. In 1986, he was convicted of bank fraud. In 1989, he was convicted of bank fraud again, and in 1995, he served four months in minimum security for insurance fraud. After paying his debt to society, he achieved some career success as a real estate agent in the Oakland, CA area until he lost his license for ethics violations.

Michael Rost and Theremin Records were sued by Metro Gnome for breach of contract and embezzlement and settled out of court. Michael left Theremin in 1986 and finished his career in 2008 as sales manager at an injection molding facility in Phoenix, AZ.

Sam Foley remained X Band's sound engineer for recording, mixing, and touring. He retired in 2021 and moved back to Seattle, where he repairs and collects vintage radios.

Patricia Clark worked alongside Sam for four years before landing a job with Sound View Recording Studio as a Senior Recording Engineer. Eight years later, she met and married Jovan Jefferson, a talented jazz saxophonist. Now widowed, she lives comfortably in eastern Long Island.

Bill and Cassandra Myers had a daughter, Susan Myers (b.1989). In 1992, they divorced. Bill recorded his solo album, 'Knock It Off' in 1994, and it achieved some critical success, but modest commercial success. In 1995, Bill Myers, amid some scandal, married Ellen J. Trudeau (17). Bill and Ellen had three children, Matthew (b. 1995), William (b. 1997) and Jeffrey (b. 1998). In 2020, Bill officially retired from X Band. He and his wife Ellen live in Sacramento, CA.

Edward Brettington never married. As of 2025, he still lives in Wallingford, Connecticut and has been sober 29 years. He never learned to play the drums "correctly".

Joe Ecks co-hosted, with Marilyn McCoo, the television show 'Solid Gold' 1986-1987. He became Joshua Eckstein in 1989 and received his bachelor's degree in business management from the University of Connecticut in 1994. He received his MBA in business administration from The Hartford Graduate Center in 1996. In 1998, Joshua purchased his first radio station, WDAQ ("98-Q") Danbury, Connecticut, and, as of 2025, he owns 38 stations, mostly on the east coast. In 2010, he married his long-time friend and business partner James Trainor.

Angela Brettington Ecks became Angela Eileen Brettington in 1987, and she became Angela Brettington Smith in 1989. In 1992, she gave birth to Michael Koop Smith, III, who later found a career in family law. In 1994, Angela gave birth to Edward Brettington Smith. Eddy took to the family business and became X Band's agent in 2015 when Richard Sheridan retired. In 2016, Angela authored 'The Inside

Story of X Band', which achieved an esoteric success. Years later, a brilliantly fictionalized version was released.

Michael Koop Smith, Jr. lost those fifteen pounds, and his teeth eventually were replaced with implants. In 1995, he was able to wear contact lenses, and in 2001, he underwent Lasik surgery so that he no longer needed vision correction. But he never stopped trying to push up his glasses. As of 2025, Mike and his wife live in a modest mansion in Durham, Connecticut. They are all set for the rest of their lives.

The End

Acknowledgements

I'd like to thank the many people who provided feedback that helped me shape Xylene into its finished form. To have provided feedback, though, one must first have endured listening to or reading some part of a rough draft. In no particular order, these people are: Ursule Molinaro and that creative writing class, Barbara Doczy, Eileen Pepe, Luke Maucione, Dr. Jen D'Angela, Carla Bock, Katherine Meikle, Jasper Harvey, Sienna Volpe, Maxwell C. Harvey, Sam Spencer, Sandi Wolford, Nan Harvey, and Robert "The Smart Guy" Hilton. And I'd also like to thank Larry Lindland who recounted many stories from his brother whose band, Crystal Pistol, landed a three-record contract (that then caused the band to self-destruct). And I will add that every one of these people contributed more to my book than they realize. Even if their advice was I should go into journalism.

About the Author

Born in 1960, Charles Harvey grew up in northern VA and then attended VA Tech at which he wore shoes to all his classes. Between bouts of unemployment, he has worked as a Manufacturing Engineer in CT. His hobbies include writing, processing firewood, and reading. Now a full-time writer/forklift driver, he lives in Durham, CT with his son Jasper. He is all set for the rest of his life.

If you liked 'Xylene' and want to see bonus content, check out www.xylenexband.com.

CPSIA information can be obtained
at www.ICGtesting.com
Printed in the USA
JSHW031913290622
27458JS00003B/10